CN00840532

LOVE APPLES

Melissa van Maasdyk

ISBN: 978-1-4834-5288-3 (sc)
ISBN: 978-1-4834-5287-6 (e)

Library of Congress Control Number: 2016908794

Cover illustration by Eloise Timmis

Lulu Publishing Services rev. date: 8/31/2016

For Glenn

Pomme [pom]: *nf* apple; (*de terre*) potato; (*d'arrosoir*) rose; (*de douche*) shower-head – **d'Adam** (*anatomie*) Adam's apple; – **d'amour** (*confiserie*) toffee apple; (*tomate*) love apple.
ORIGIN: old French term for tomato, thought to be an aphrodisiac, possibly Eve's real temptation in the Garden of Eden

Amuse-Bouche

CHAPTER 1

The Last Supper

'I want to experiment, but I can't remember if you like beetroot.' Kate had to shout into her phone to hear herself over the buzz of shoppers trawling Borough Market.

'You know I'm always a willing guinea pig when you're wearing the lab coat,' Daniel said. 'Anyway …' An industrial-strength meat slicer nearby let out a high-pitched wail and drowned out his last words.

'Sorry, I didn't get that.' Kate plugged her left ear with her index finger to hear him.

'It was probably a bit sordid for a Friday afternoon. When will you be here? I want to linger over our last supper.'

Kate laughed. 'Not long. It's too damn cold. I'll stick to essentials.'

'Yeah, right,' Daniel said sceptically, as Kate generally found it impossible to resist the multitude of edible treasures laid out on trestle tables here, and would inevitably buy more than she needed. Tonight, however, she too wanted to savour every last minute with her sexy significant other, so she would make a concerted effort not to go off-list.

'O ye of little faith,' she said. 'See you very soon; I can't wait.'

As she paid for the prime specimens of the purple root vegetable, she felt a twinge of guilt about having so easily dropped Daniel's favourite dish from the menu. Although she was in the habit of putting her job before anything and anyone, this was to be their last meal together for a while – and she had planned to surprise him with roast pigeon. When the beetroot had presented itself, however, her desire to try out a recently sampled dish for a future recipe column had proved greater than her desire to please Daniel. She would make it up to him in other ways, she decided, sweeping away her momentary misgivings with thoughts of the potentially career-changing trip that lay ahead. A frisson of excitement ran through her, and she pulled her coat around her to contain it as she re-entered the stream of shoppers weaving through the market's stalls.

True to her word, she resisted the lure of black olives gleaming in large barrels, jars of jewel-coloured relishes vying for attention with slabs of marbled country pâté, and a stall where a bearded man in an orange windcheater was doling out oysters with a dash of lemon and Tabasco. Just a couple of those oysters would be the perfect antidote to Kate's hunger pangs resulting from a missed lunch, but she continued resolutely on in the direction of her organic chicken supplier until a cloud of fragrant steam brought her to an involuntary halt. She inhaled the sweet chocolate aroma rising from a tray of just-out-the-oven brownies and considered buying one for the road, but her recollection of a recent dressing-room encounter with her reflection in a bathing suit propelled her on. A bathing suit! It was hard to imagine that she would soon be in an environment conducive to shedding the layers she was currently wearing – a grey silk jersey shift dress, knee-high boots, and a black coat – in favour of flesh-baring attire. It was even harder to believe that she would be doing this in the name of work. *Lifestyle di-rec-tor; directorrrrr; direct-or.* She rolled her new title around in her mouth, savouring its rich flavour, but stopped short of swallowing, all too aware that until her probationary period was over, the title wasn't truly hers. This upcoming trip, however, was her chance to prove that she was truly worthy.

A table piled with jars of tapenade caught her eye – one of Daniel's favourite things. She would buy some as a parting gift to him, she thought, and as some form of compensation for not getting the pigeon. Of course, he hadn't known about the pigeon, so he wouldn't feel short-changed, but she still couldn't shake off the feeling that she had been unnecessarily selfish, particularly given that Daniel had recently sampled a steamed sheep's head on her behalf in a Moroccan restaurant.

After Kate handed over a sum of money more befitting a jar of caviar, the woman behind the counter said, '*Merci.*' There was a heftier price tag attached to produce bought from a woman whose family grew the olives for her tapenade organically in just the right *terroir* – or a man who knew by name every cow that produced his thick clotted cream – but it was worth it to Kate, who had absorbed a passion for good food as if by osmosis in her mother's kitchen while growing up. That was when it had been all sugar and spice, of course, before things had turned sour and Kate had begun to fantasise about a very different life from one dedicated to hearth and home. It was ironic, she thought as she made her way down London Bridge Road, passing stores glowing yellow in the grey dusk light, how this foodie gene that she had once fled had finally been the ticket to her dream job. Stranger still was that, having once reviled her mother's thankless devotion to the domestic domain, Kate now used Annie Richmond's talents like a secret test kitchen, to the extent that she sometimes felt like a fraud accepting accolades for the recipes she presented on the page. The new role, however, entailed a broadening of scope and would allow her to make her own honest mark in virgin territory, which she craved. The question, of course, remained whether, without this crutch, she would fail. As she drove along the Thames to Daniel's apartment, she thought of the stumbling blocks she had already encountered while preparing for her first major assignment, and panic began to rise in her. What if she really was only as good as her mother's last recipe?

'I see you stuck to essentials,' Daniel said at the door, talking not so much to Kate as to a bunch of deep-purple tulips. He kissed her forehead, which was the only exposed bit of flesh, as he rescued the flowers from their precarious perch atop a large brown paper shopping bag.

'I did. Anything not specifically for dinner has been purchased to keep you sweet while I'm gone.' Kate followed him into the kitchen and deposited her bags on the counter that separated the kitchen from the living area. One bag slumped, and a wheel of dark yellow cheese rolled onto the floor.

'I don't think anything in these bags is going to compensate for your absence,' Daniel said, stooping to pick up the cheese.

'There's tapenade,' Kate said, pulling the jar out of the bag she was unpacking.

'Perhaps I'll survive then. … Beyos,' Daniel read off the cheese packet. 'Flinty-textured, tangy, and smooth.'

'Cheese tasting's the new wine tasting. Didn't you know? That's also for your private consumption, by the way. And this.' Kate pulled a bar of artisanal dark chocolate out of the bag – 85 per cent cocoa solids was too bitter for her liking, so Daniel would appreciate that this was purely for him.

'But, Madame Ambassador, you are spoiling me,' Daniel said in a confused foreign accent, affectionately running his fingers over the bridge of Kate's nose. He took delivery of the chocolate and then turned to his glass-fronted wine fridge. 'Red or white?' he asked. 'Or something more befitting the launch of a maiden voyage?' He reached inside and pulled out the type of bottle that never failed to excite Kate, one with a bulge at the top sheathed in foil. This particular bottle had a pink hue to it and an instantly recognisable garland of white flowers highlighting the name.

'Perrier-Jouët.' Kate swooned. 'Mm. I don't know; it might be tempting fate at this stage – you know, celebrating the birth before I've come to term.'

'You're not serious?'

'I think I am. … Yes, I am.'

'Really?' Daniel cocked an eyebrow and held the bottle up at a jaunty, come-hither angle.

'Let's save it for when I get back. Provided that I haven't screwed things up, of course. White would be good for now.'

'Crazy Kate.' Daniel put the Champagne back into the fridge. 'You're brilliant. The job is yours. And you deserve it.'

'I'm not; it isn't actually 100 per cent yet. And Amber's definitely not convinced I do deserve it. She's stated quite clearly that I'm on probation.'

Although prone to paranoia, Kate knew that in this case her trepidation was not unfounded, as the job had not so much fallen into her lap as been plucked from the Fates via some artful manoeuvring. Since her focus in the past had largely been on food writing and styling, she wasn't the ideal candidate for the job, which entailed editing an entire section encompassing food, décor, and lifestyle. But she wanted this job more than she had wanted anything in her life before. So she had made a pitch to *Be*'s editor with bells and whistles – elaborate storyboards and feature plans – that she hoped would drown out the quieter CVs provided by more qualified but less hungry contenders. Mission accomplished, she now had to live up to the hype she had created.

'I'm pretty sure that this trip is my ultimate test and that I'll be out on my ear if I don't pull it off,' she added.

'What makes you think you'll fail?' Daniel asked. 'You've planned the whole thing like a military operation.'

'Well, the troops aren't exactly happy.' Kate snipped off the stem of a tulip with a little more force than was required. 'Roberta found out today that the hotel I've arranged for us doesn't have a spa.'

'Ah, the lovely fashion editor?'

'Director.'

'Which effectively puts you on a par with her now, right?'

'Except she's not on trial, and the fashion team occupies a higher plain than do those of us dealing with the mere necessities of life like food.'

'You mean a plain where a spa is a standard? Like pay TV and a minibar?'

Kate laughed. 'Yes, precisely. Argh, I don't know how I'm going to survive eight whole days in that woman's company.'

'We clearly need to get some of this into you pronto,' Daniel said, pulling the cork out of a bottle of Pouilly-Fumé.

'I should have mentioned that the good stuff is wasted on me,' Kate said. 'Alcohol of any description would serve my needs just fine, but thank you.' She kissed Daniel's nose as she reached over his shoulder to get a vase from an open shelf. 'And sorry, I will stop ranting, but she's been on at me all day. I mean the hotel isn't fantastic. It's a little bit plastic and familyish, but we're not *Vogue*, who could get an entire five-star resort in exchange for a mere paragraph.'

Kate's first major task had been more difficult than anticipated. 'Find us a location for our summer special,' Amber had said. 'Something beachy, but with standout cultural elements that we can integrate into the resort-wear and food pages.' Apart from showcasing barely-there bikinis and other seasonal essentials, the destination would be a backdrop for warm-weather food, as well as décor and outdoor entertaining ideas. Kate's mouth had watered at the delicious possibilities. *No problem,* she thought.

'Accommodation also needs to be boutique or four- or five-star to cater to our reader profile,' Amber added, 'and our budget is more or less nil, which means this has to be a barter deal.'

'And I'm not keen on Asia,' Roberta said. 'It won't work with the new collections. I'm thinking colonial island style: Mustique, St Barts ...'

Big problem. Mustique and St Barts were quickly crossed off the list since it was peak season in the Caribbean and rooms at hotels on these high-end islands weren't going for a song of praise in a new, unfamiliar UK magazine. More rejections from other islands followed.

Kate had been surprised and disappointed to find the wings of her imagination clipped just as she had been poised to soar, leaving her scavenging like a seagull for what she could get. Even more distressing was the discovery, now that she was in the management sphere, of just how badly affected by the financial crisis *Be* was. She had been aware that the magazine was under financial pressures; seven months after the Lehman Brothers collapse in September of the previous year, many sectors were now feeling its snowball effects, but *Be* had appeared to be in excellent health. Although just under two years old, it had recently scooped Women's Lifestyle Magazine of the Year at the prestigious Ink Publishing Awards, where it was described as 'a delicious blend of style, substance, and savvy', 'a magazine with savoir faire and savoir vivre', and 'a beautifully packaged manual for modern living'. Added to this, its owners, Eric and Terry Lowell, had been lauded for making such a success of a new launch at a time when electronic media was encroaching on print.

Having made a small fortune churning out community newspapers bulging with classified-style advertisements, along with low-budget IT and DIY magazines, the small-town rough diamonds behind Lowell Media had decided two and a half years previously – some might say untimeously – to produce their first upmarket magazine. After identifying a gap for a women's glossy with a strong lifestyle focus, they had poached one of the hottest editors in the genre, Amber Love, to serve as the magazine's face, giving her carte blanche to hand-pick an editorial team to mould the body into shape. For Kate, being selected to take charge of the food pages of the highly anticipated title had been like finding Willy Wonka's golden ticket wrapped up with her favourite chocolate bar.

However, the financial crisis, coming so soon after *Be*'s launch, had hit the magazine where it hurt most, in advertising. Even Lowell Media's cash cows were being milked by cutbacks, while its fledgling thoroughbred was getting a real whipping, losing to more established titles such as *Marie Claire*, *Red*, *InStyle*, and *Living Etc.* when advertisers were forced to choose. And the Lowell brothers were getting nervous. It was make-or-break time, Amber had told Kate upon announcing her new role. Everything was riding on a bumper summer issue that would take ABCs to a healthier level and drive advertising sales up.

Kate had thus felt her failures in the Caribbean acutely and experienced sleepless nights before finally coming up trumps in the Indian Ocean, where Mauritius's Sunshine Hotel Group had agreed to accommodate the entire team in their four-star property Paradise Bay.

'Let's see if this is the right medicine for you.' Daniel inhaled the small taster of pale gold wine he had poured, and then tipped it into his mouth and sucked in air. As a wine broker, he did this out of habit, but it still made Kate smile. He had such a serious, earnest expression when tasting wine, like he was taking Communion rather than mentally assessing the wine's legs, nose, and body. Kate in turn considered his. He was still wearing his navy suit trousers from lunch, but his jacket and tie had been discarded and his pink cotton shirt, now untucked, hung loosely on his tall, slim frame. She found him particularly sexy when he was slightly dishevelled, and she suddenly felt aroused at the thought of having a whole evening ahead with him.

Having assessed the wine to be 'very drinkable', Daniel half-filled a second glass and handed it to Kate, who took a generous sip. 'Heavenly. I feel better already,' she said. 'Salvation in a glass of wine – does that make me an alcoholic?'

'Not in such mitigating circumstances. Are you going to take off your coat?'

'I have to get my bag out of the car – my hands were full.' Kate reached for her keys on the counter, but Daniel got to them first.

'But you're half undressed. And it's all the way past the corner store.'

'Relax. I need to pick up some milk anyway.'

'Well, at least have a nut for the road.' Kate dipped a hand into a brown paper bag and placed a smoked Spanish almond between his lips.

'Mm, you know how to whet a man's appetite,' Daniel said, his mouth curled in a delicious grin. 'I'll be as quick as I can.' He slipped his feet into a pair of loafers that he kept next to the door for making milk, bread, and newspaper runs. 'And I want this nut to forget about work for a bit, please.'

After watching the door close behind him, Kate took off her coat and finally sank into the sofa, stretching out along its length, her glass of wine poised to wash away the day's stresses. *Bliss. Or almost.* She propped a fluffy purple angora cushion behind her head and placed a red velvet one on her tummy to support her glass. These were two of a collection of mismatched cushions strewn on the couch that Kate had added to soften Daniel's flat in the course of the year and a half they had been together. When they had met, the second-floor warehouse conversion overlooking the Thames had been stylishly minimalist and defiantly bachelor, something one might see in *Wallpaper* magazine. There was the blue leather corner sofa she was sitting on pushed against the exposed-brick wall, the angular glass dining table on trestles surrounded by red Verner Panton chairs that looked like upside-down question marks, a large flat-screen TV, and a foosball table. 'Defiant' wasn't far off the mark, she had later learnt; he had bought the flat and furniture shortly after his ex-wife had walked away from their marriage, taking with her their Blackheath house, two golden retrievers, and Daniel's squash partner. He said he missed the dogs most, but he hadn't played squash since that time – and it was obvious he had been deeply hurt.

The only things he had hung onto had been his CD collection (largely from the 1980s, which was an inexplicable passion for a man in his mid thirties, Kate thought, so there was unlikely to have been a tussle) and the colourful pop-art-influenced collage above the sofa by a London-based Moroccan artist. Kate had taken this as her cue for the swirly Pucci-style rug that she had rolled out under the coffee table to add a bit more warmth to the space, aided by the junk-shop chandelier hovering above it that she and Daniel had found together on a stroll through the Columbia Road Flower Market.

She pressed play on the Bang & Olufsen CD player, which hung like a painting on the wall beside the sofa, and braced herself for Madness or Spandau Ballet, but the player generously regurgitated innocuous lounge music. She closed her eyes and sighed contentedly. Having once thrived on mingling with an eclectic bunch of media types in hot new bars on weekends, she now enjoyed nothing more than her and Daniel's Friday night ritual, shunning all social engagements to cook and eat together – their own special form of foreplay. And tonight would be the last for a while, she reminded herself, so she should relax and enjoy it. Anyway, there was nothing more she could do now. The boxes of bikinis and floaty frocks for the fashion shoot were packed and on their way, along with accessories for the food shoot, while the human contingent was all set to depart the next day, whether or not the destination held any appeal for certain prickly passengers.

The tablecloth didn't arrive, a voice announced somewhere in the corridors of her mind. Kate opened her eyes. *The tablecloth. Damn.* Laidback Living was meant to have delivered it earlier that week, since it had still been en route from India when they had delivered their other items. However, in the midst of squabbles with a certain fashion director, Kate had failed to notice the tablecloth's absence. *What else? Oh no, oh God, the napkins and vases were also in that shipment.* Part of *Be*'s promise to readers was that they could source everything that appeared in its pages to recreate a look or an entertaining idea at home, and all of these items – the beautiful block-printed tablecloth, in particular – were key to setting the tone for Kate's food shoot. She looked at her watch. The head office would be closed, but she had her marketing contact's mobile number, she recalled, and got up to retrieve her phone from her coat pocket. When there was no answer, her heart and mind began to race. She would have to arrange for Laidback Living to send the items on, she decided as she paced up and down in the kitchen. It was a stupid oversight, but the situation was salvageable, unless there was something else she had forgotten. *Maybe Roberta's right and I'm not a big-picture person,* she thought.

She sat back down on the sofa and took a large glug of wine to calm herself, but she found it impossible to relax now. She should start cooking, she decided. Cooking always soothed her – something about the order of it and the fact that as long as she followed a recipe or obeyed the basic cooking principles that were part of her DNA, a dish generally worked out. Even if it didn't, except in the case of soufflés (Kate had had some bad luck with soufflés), she had picked up all sorts of tricks to remedy things from her mother. Béarnaise sauce curdled? Add a little ice water, a teaspoon at a time. Dish too salty? Balance things out with a teaspoon each of cider vinegar and sugar. Mayonnaise separated? Break an egg into a new bowl and whisk in the broken mayonnaise little by little. It was a pity that her mother had no such remedies for a marriage turned sour or, for that matter, an editorial assignment showing signs of going the way of so many soufflés.

Kate pulled herself off the sofa and, as she returned to the kitchen, decided to make her chilli-chocolate almond cakes for dessert, since just the smell of chocolate melting had an uplifting effect. *Bikini-ready body be damned – desperate measures are called for.*

She was chopping butter into cubes when Daniel got back.

'You've started,' he said as he came up behind her and put his hands firmly on her hips, drawing her in close. 'So it's going to take more than a glass of wine to sort you out?'

Kate turned in his grip and wrapped her arms around him. 'Thank you for doing that.' She tipped back her head to receive the kiss he leant in to give. 'And I'm sure you'll find a way.' She felt her body begin to relax in response to his warmth.

'So what's my portfolio?' Daniel asked as he filled up her glass.

Kate pointed the knife at a neat pile of onions, garlic, and ginger on the counter.

'Ah, the fun stuff.'

And so the mating dance began, with Kate leading and Daniel keeping in step, anticipating her every move and need. As Kate stirred chocolate, butter, and honey over a pot of boiling water, Daniel chopped onion, crushed garlic, and grated ginger, all of which she fried in peanut oil with ground cumin, enveloping the kitchen in an earthy, spicy cloud. Daniel chopped coriander stalks and shaved palm sugar, which Kate stirred into the mixture before adding a dollop to the pockets she had cut into chicken breasts, along with slices of creamy white cheese. Then she browned the breasts in butter and olive oil while Daniel stroked beetroots across a mandolin, producing matchsticks that Kate glazed with butter, orange juice, and marmalade.

Finally, as the chicken breasts reached readiness in the oven and Daniel set the table, Kate folded frothy egg whites into the melted chocolate, along with flour, sugar, and spices, before spooning the mixture into ramekins and putting them in the lower oven.

'Camera-ready,' Daniel said as Kate placed their two plates on the table. He was quietly bemused by her obsession with presenting even TV dinners like her magazine spreads, but he was never overtly exasperated by this as previous boyfriends had sometimes been.

He filled two fresh glasses from a newly opened bottle of white wine and then sat down opposite her. This bottle had no label, marking it as one of the wines he had discovered on a recent buying trip. 'It's not Leflaive,' he said, 'but Roger loved it ... wants everything I can give him. He's going to make it his house white.'

'It doesn't taste like a cheapie,' Kate said after taking a sip without any preamble. 'So the lunch was a success?'

'It's taken the pressure off. He's still feeling the effects of Lehmans – everyone at Canary Wharf is – but he thinks he'll survive.' He cut a piece of chicken and pushed some beetroot onto his fork. The golden breast was beautifully offset by the deep-purple relish. *But what about the taste?* Kate's eyes followed the fork to his mouth, as anxious for a positive review as a participant in *MasterChef*. 'You can breathe,' he said. 'It's good; I like the smokiness of the chicken with the beetroot's sweetness. ... So what's it for?'

'September's "Season's Greetings,"' Kate said. Every month, her food pages included a collection of recipes starring a new seasonal arrival, which in September would be beetroot. This dish, a variation of one she had recently tried in a restaurant, would share the platform with beetroot hummus, beetroot risotto, and a chocolate and beetroot cake.

'But we were in April last time I checked; that's aeons away,' Daniel said.

'I wanted to try it out while the taste of the original was still fresh in my mind.' In truth, it could have waited. Daniel would have loved the pigeon – not just the taste but also the thought. She pushed aside the guilt and changed the subject. 'It really is fantastic that Roger's placed another big order. You must be relieved.'

'I'm just lucky that he liked this particular bottle so much, because he says he's had to cut back a lot.'

The oven timer buzzed, and Kate got up. 'It's crazy how fast it's all happened,' she said as she crossed the room, 'like a house of cards going down. You're lucky you got out.' Daniel had been made redundant from his position as a currency trader at a small investment bank a year before the Lehman Brothers crash, and rather than re-enter the market, he had decided to turn his hobby and passion into a full-time career as a wine broker, taking part of his pay-out in liquid assets from the bank's well-established wine cellar.

'Yes, except the banks have still been paying my bills,' Daniel said. 'I'm just farther down the food chain. I really must get my s-h-1-t together and start diversifying my client base, look at more budget options.'

'You'll be fine,' Kate said, taking the baking tray out of the oven. 'God knows we all need a drink more than ever in this climate, and everyone knows you've got a nose for sniffing out the best wines on the planet.'

'As long as you "nose,"' Daniel said.

'I "nose" better than anyone.' Kate laughed with an exaggerated snort. She pressed the top of one of the chocolate almond cakes. *Perfect. ... If only there was a fail-safe formula for perfection in other areas of my life,* she thought, feeling far less confident about her own chances of surviving the financial meltdown. What if she had bitten off more than she could chew and would now choke? Given the state of the publishing market, she wasn't sure she would find another job if her greed ended up costing her this one.

She returned to the table and, repressing her concerns, settled into the rhythm of their dinner. They were serenaded now by *Paris*, a CD that she had snuck into Daniel's collection for a bit of relief from 1980s and lounge music, which featured singers reviving the chanson style that she loved of Edith Piaf, Yves Montand, Jacques Brel and their ilk.

'*On me dit que nos vies ne valent pas grand-chose,*' sang Carla Bruni. '*Elles passent en an instant comme fanent les roses. Pourtant quelqu'un m'a dit que tu m'aimes encore. Serais-ce possible alors?*' Next, someone described her heart as dancing a samba, and Tryo sang about the exquisite pain of being in love – of being hugged till one choked, kissing and biting simultaneously, bleeding for each other. The variety of feelings expressed in the different songs was an endorsement, Kate thought, of Leo Tolstoy's observation that if it is true that there are as many minds as there are heads, then there are as many kinds of love as there are hearts. She wasn't sure where her version fitted in, but she envied the intensity expressed by some, not possessing the courage herself to let go and live love to the full. Even now.

The CD ended, giving way to the sound of the river slapping against the building's brick wall two storeys down. Kate's eyes travelled across the water to the source of the waves: a long white dinner cruiser gliding by, the muffled strains of its live band adding to the river's melody. When she looked back at Daniel, she found he was looking not so much at her as into her.

'I'm going to miss you,' he said. 'I wish my trip wasn't dovetailing with yours to make the absence even longer.'

'I'll miss you too,' Kate said, slightly surprised that it wasn't so much a flippant response as a heartfelt one.

'I've been thinking,' Daniel said. Kate didn't like sentences that began with those words, since, in her experience, they were seldom followed by something like 'I'm going to get a haircut.'

'I know we said we wouldn't rush things, but …' Kate took a generous sip of wine and then swallowed it with an audible gulp. She coughed – some wine had gone down the wrong way. Daniel laughed. 'Don't look so nervous. I'm not about to go down on one knee. Although the idea does have a certain appeal.'

'It does?' Kate asked nervously.

'I think what we have is pretty good,' he said, continuing to look at her so intently that she felt a little piece of her melt just below the ribcage.

'It is,' Kate said, tempted to add that this was probably because it hadn't been diced, minced, and liquidised by the mighty marriage machine. Neither of them had to look very far for proof of the institution's power to pulverise love, and she thought it a miracle that anyone still bought into it. Her primary dreams, therefore, did not involve walking down the aisle, except the kind that ran down the middle of an aeroplane bound for an exotic destination, in order to cement her relationship with a beautiful career.

'I really could imagine it, you know.' Daniel laughed as Kate took another hefty swig of wine. 'But lest you choke again, I should add that, much as I fancy the idea of totally possessing the gorgeous Kate Richmond, I'm simply proposing, in the loosest sense of the word, that she move in with me.'

Kate exhaled. 'I think you might get bored with a Kate if she were around all the time. Like that,' she said, pointing at the foosball table, which Daniel had recently talked about selling.

'I think a Kate is slightly different. For one thing, she has knockout pins ensuring superior playability and a whole lot of extra features that could take years to figure out.'

'I'm not convinced,' Kate said. 'Let's not forget the MP3 player; I can't remember when I last saw that.' Everything had more appeal when it was shiny and new or still on a shelf in a shop window. Kate had recently exchanged a large portion of her salary for a pair of stilettos that gave her blisters, and she now found herself drawn to the same shop in search of an alternative pair. So for her, being on the shelf, as a couple of her mother's contemporaries considered her at the age of thirty-one, had only positive connotations.

'You're impossible.' Daniel shook his head. 'Will you at least think about it while you're lying on the beach?' He got up and picked up their plates. 'But I think it would be great. Think about all the extra time we'd get to spend together in between all the running around we're both doing.'

She watched him walk through to the kitchen, where he rinsed the plates and put them in the dishwasher. He was a tidy, organised yang to her messy yin. When she cooked, she cared only for what happened on the plate, with no concern for the havoc wreaked backstage, whereas he cleaned as he cooked – and as she cooked – which made them an excellent dinner-party team. They did work, Kate thought as she carried the not-quite-empty bottle of wine through to the kitchen. More than that, she could think of nowhere she would rather be right now and no one she would rather be with. She did love Daniel. But love was so hard to define and difficult to capture. It expanded and contracted at will and could change state from rock solid to fluid in an instant, which meant it could easily slip through careless fingers and disappear through cracks in the floorboards. Not that she felt unsafe in Daniel's hands; her fidgety fingers were stilled in his strong grasp. But it was easy to throw herself into the trapeze act of love when there was a safety net to catch her, in the form of the flat she shared with her best friend, Chloe.

'You know I adore you,' she said, 'but do you think you're ready for that? Living with me? With anyone?' She found the cork on the counter and secured it in the neck of the bottle.

'Don't try to turn things around,' Daniel said. 'There is life after divorce, you know. But I'm not the problem here, am I?' He turned from the sink, where he had put the pans in soapy water to soak. His sleeves were rolled up, and his hazelnut-brown hair, which was longer than he liked but just right for Kate's tastes, flopped forward slightly. 'Anyway, I don't want to waste time debating this on our last night together for a while.' He walked over to Kate and encircled her with his arms as she ran a knife around the edge of a chocolate almond cake to loosen it from its ramekin. Then he slipped his hand into her dress and under her bra, which sent a crackling signal down her body, causing her to catch her breath and to crush the soft, warm cake in her hand. She put a piece in his mouth and kissed the crumbs off his chin with a little bite.

'Tasty; I like the kick,' he said.

'I threw in some chilli powder. I thought it would work well with the ginger ice cream I made last week.'

'I'd far rather nibble on something else,' Daniel said, lifting her long honey-blonde ponytail and nuzzling her neck. Kate inhaled the faint scent of his aftershave and some lingering cigar smoke from the restaurant on his collar, and then she let a moan slip from her throat as he lifted the hem of her dress and brushed his hand over her panties.

'You're such a tease,' she said, although she loved this particular part of these evenings when he got her body tingling and anticipation hung in the air.

She placed the cakes in two shallow white bowls, added a scoop of ice cream and a sprig of spearmint to each, and then settled at the kitchen island beside Daniel, her stool swivelled towards his, their knees touching. The warm, spicy chocolate cake was beautifully offset by the cool ginger ice cream, but, when Daniel placed a hand on her shoulder and began to tease her neck with a finger, any pleasure derived from the dessert was eclipsed by a rising surge of warmth from below. *What would be so bad about making this permanent?* she wondered. *Wouldn't it be nice to feel grounded finally, in a space in which I feel happy, both physically and metaphysically?* The idea was certainly appealing … except … except that there was such a fine line between *grounded* and *stuck*. She would think about it when this trip was out of the way, she decided. First she needed to secure her new role, and right now there were more pressing things to focus on.

As she licked the last remnants of ice cream off her spoon, Daniel moved his hand from her shoulder across her breasts, and slid it seductively between her thighs, massaging the flesh as he worked his way up her leg.

'Mm. Please, sir, can I have some more?' Kate said when his hand reached the top of her thigh, and her spoon clattered into her bowl.

First Course

CHAPTER 2

Island Dish

Kate stretched, enjoying the touch of the cool linen sheets on her sun-kissed skin. Someone was taking a shower; she could hear the hiss of running water nearby. 'Oh, hell,' she groaned. She could now add 'thin walls' to Roberta's long list of complaints.

As expected, Paradise Bay had fallen well below the fashion director's deluxe standards. She could not shoot on their beach, she had said minutes after arriving, littered as it was with plastic chairs, sunbeds, slides, and pedal boats. 'The only thing plastic is good for is paying with.'

'*Pas de problème,*' the hotel's PR manager had said. The *Be* team could use the more exclusive beaches of Paradise Bay's wealthier siblings, and a fact-finding excursion had proved that these were indeed more natural beauties. Roberta had even managed a few superlatives upon viewing a tiny fried egg of an island, reached by boat from one of the hotels, with a yolk of fir trees and a wavy rim of white sand peppered with wooden sunloungers.

Kate peered through the murky morning light at the radio alarm clock on her bedside table. Its illuminated red numbers glowed 8.00, which meant the bikini special would finally be under way – well on its way, she thought with a sigh of relief. Roberta and the crew would have been down the coast for a couple of hours by now. She stretched again, and then pulled herself out of bed and padded across the room to indulge in her new through-the-looking-glass world of flamingo-pink cabanas set on a manicured lawn, steps away from white sand and a shimmering sea.

'Nooooooo.' A grey veil – God's own shower – lay across the picture-postcard view that had welcomed her the day before. She instinctively looked at the phone, expecting Roberta's witchy powers to divine this moment of her discovering the shoot-averse conditions. It didn't stir, but it would, she knew, so she decided to flee before it started shrieking at her. She hurriedly pulled on a pair of taupe shorts; selected a pink vest featuring a line drawing of Buddha, in the hope of adopting his sense of calm; drew her hair into a ponytail; and then stepped through the glass sliding door onto the wet lawn.

Once on the beach, she settled into a rhythmic jog, staying close to the lacy edge of the sea where the sand was firm. The rain felt soothing somehow. It was warm and soft – so different from cold, hard English rain. Not that this would be any comfort to Roberta, the mere thought of whom made Kate feel less soothed.

I can't be blamed for the weather, she told herself.

Perhaps not entirely, an inner voice answered, *but you knew that it was the low season, which usually entails less-than-optimum conditions. You probably shouldn't have leapt at the first offer.*

Kate quickened her pace to shake off the accusatory thoughts, but they caught up to remind her that there was also the case of the forgotten items for her shoot. She had been unable to get hold of her contact at Laidback Living over the weekend, but now that it was Monday, she would be able to phone the office later in the day. She would have to convince them that given their own culpability in the matter, they should courier the items at their own expense – because it was imperative to Kate that word of this screw-up wouldn't get back to Amber.

Forced to turn back when a giant's handful of black boulders tumbled into the sea in front of her, Kate saw that she was no longer alone on the beach. Three men were wiping down plastic sunbeds in the distance, and another carried cushions across the beach from a thatched open-sided hut. The rain had been diminishing gradually as Kate ran, and milky sunshine now leaked through cracks in the clouds that hung above the sea. Beyond the reef, a wooden fishing boat slowly cut through the glass-like water, its crew of four men and their fishing rods silhouetted against the sky. Kate stopped to observe the tranquil scene, watching the men silently doing their job – work motivated by the need to eat, she thought, as opposed to feeding people fantasies that would make them hungry for more of what they didn't need and often couldn't afford. She suddenly felt less stressed about her missing luggage and the shoot-averse weather. *First World problems,* she told herself, continuing her run with a lighter step as she lapped up her exotic surroundings.

'The sun'll come out tomorrow …' she sang to herself, channelling her inner Annie, as she turned her gaze to a row of elegant white houses strung out along the beach on her left. 'Bet your bottom dollar that tomorrow, there'll be sun.' A man on the balcony of one of the houses, dressed in a white towelling robe, raised his coffee cup to her. She smiled back at him. *What joy it must be to start every day like that,* she thought. Wondering if there was a woman in a matching robe, she was imagining herself in the woman's place, sipping a coffee beside this tanned stranger, when she felt something sharp hit her ankle. Seconds later, she landed face first in the sand, a piece of driftwood and her lack of mindfulness having claimed her gazelle-like poise.

'Shit,' she said, spitting out sand as she instinctively looked back at the man. Having disappeared from the balcony, he emerged seconds later on his sloping front lawn and began to walk towards her. 'Shit, shit, shit. Can you not put a single foot right on this trip?' she muttered to herself as the stranger approached. Humiliated, she brushed herself down and shouted, 'All in one piece,' before taking off with a lopsided gait.

This is no time to be daydreaming, she told herself. *And anyway, what are you doing imagining yourself living with a complete stranger when you can't even contemplate moving in with a man you know and love?*

As she made her way back to the hotel, she thought about Daniel's suggestion to move in with him. *It's not such a big leap, really,* she told herself. *I'm spending every weekend with him anyway these days.* Still, she felt anxiety begin to rise in her at the thought of it.

Don't I love Daniel enough? she wondered as she opened the door to her room. *Is that why his offer is so hard to consider? Or are my commitment issues just tripping me up again?*

Deep in thought, she walked through her room to the bathroom, turned both taps on full, and emptied the green liquid contents of a small plastic bottle into the bath. She was dabbing the gash on her ankle when the phone's ringing sliced through the warm sanctuary of steam.

'Kate? I need you in reception now.'

'Roberta.'

'I can't work like this.'

'I'm sorry about the weather. I … um …' *What are you going to do, give the rain a good talking-to?*

Roberta interrupted her thoughts. 'The rain's only part of it; these people have no idea.'

'Who?' Kate sat down on the bed.

'They have no sense of time. We might have got something done if they'd actually arrived when we'd asked them to.'

'Okaaaay.' Kate exercised her powers of interpretation. 'So the driver was late?'

'An *hour* late. A *crucial* hour late.'

'I'm sorry … um … well, the sun's out now.' Kate put a sunny smile in her voice.

'Thanks for pointing that out,' Roberta said in a tone that suggested she meant to say, *Thanks for pointing out the bleeding obvious.* 'But by the time we've packed up the van and driven over there, the sun will already be too intense.' Kate heard a splash and glanced through the bathroom door to see a snowy mountain of bubbles cascading over the edge of the bath.

'Shit. Hang on a minute, Roberta.' She dropped the receiver on the bed and ran through to the bathroom, tripping on the ridge that separated carpet from tiles. 'Ow. Bloody hell.' Hopping on one foot, she turned the taps off. Then she threw a fluffy towel on the floor to soak up the flood.

'Sorry,' she said after she had reluctantly picked up the receiver again, clutching her throbbing big toe. The positive energy generated by her run was leaking out of her like the blood that had begun to seep from the wound on her ankle, but still she tried. 'You can shoot later this afternoon, right?'

'Yes, but the light … the whole mood will be totally different.' Roberta sighed heavily. 'You really don't get it, do you? Anyway, it's not just about the driver. I can't work in this environment. It's totally at odds with my aesthetic integrity.'

Whatever aesthetic integrity is, Kate wondered.

'Do you know, there was an aerobics class going on in the lobby when we got back this morning,' Roberta continued. 'In the *lobby*. And I detest these tacky sea motifs everywhere.'

Kate rolled her eyes as she lay back and listened with half an ear to Roberta's litany of complaints about everything from the size of her so-called suite to the lack of à la carte options at breakfast.

'Anyway, I've arranged to meet that PR woman … Sandrine,' Roberta said.

'Solange,' Kate corrected her. Except for supermodels and A-list actresses, Roberta never remembered people's names.

'… in the lobby in ten minutes' time. And I need you there. I've thought of a simple way to get around this.'

'I'll be as quick as I can,' Kate said. 'I was about to get into the bath. So what exactly are you suggesting, just so we're on the same page?' Except when it came to Roberta's wardrobe of classically cut clothes in neutral tones and natural fabrics, simplicity wasn't her forte – and, if understated, her designer garments generally came with an inflated price tag. Kate thus felt uneasy about what Roberta had in mind.

'It's nice for some,' Roberta said. Then the phone went dead, leaving Kate to ponder what her so-called solution might be. Anxious to find out as soon as possible, she ditched the bath for a quick shower before rushing over to the main hotel building.

She spotted Roberta and Solange on the other side of the lobby. They were sitting on a cane sofa upholstered in pistachio fabric splashed with pink palm fronds, and even from this distance, Kate could see that Solange was displaying symptoms of Roberta's venomous bite: writhing uncomfortably and wringing her hands. When she reached the pair, Solange looked up at her as one might at someone who carried the antidote to a life-threatening affliction.

''Ello, Kate. I am sorry to 'ear zere are problems wis ze driver,' she said in her heavy French-Mauritian accent. 'It is très embarrassing for us. 'Owever, we will do everysing to make sure you are completely satisfied from now on.'

'But not to the extent of moving us to the White Sands,' Roberta said, pursing her collagen-enhanced lips, which were the only fat thing about her. Reportedly in her mid forties, *Be*'s fashion director was the kind of woman who would be beautiful at any age. Apart from her willowy frame, she had pronounced cheekbones, green almond-shaped eyes, and translucent skin. So, even scowling and slumped in her chair, as she was now, her arms folded over a long black and white kaftan, she was attracting repeat glances from passers-by.

Although this was the first Kate had heard of a proposed transfer, she made an effort to assume an expression of consensus as she sat down, deciding it best to present a united front. 'So that's really not an option?' she asked.

'I understand ze problem, and I wish I could 'elp you, but ze White Sands 'otel is completely full,' Solange said. 'Would you like somesing to drink?' She waved at someone over Kate's shoulder.

'That's not really good enough,' Roberta said. 'It would be fine if we could shoot at Paradise Bay, but we can't. And it's inconvenient and time-consuming having to cart everything down the coast.' Her top leg bounced up and down, a black leather flip-flop accessorised with mother-of-pearl buttons making a slapping sound with every movement.

An idea fluttered into Kate's mind like a rainbow-winged butterfly on a grey day. 'Would it be possible to give us just one room at the White Sands that we could use for wardrobe?' she asked Solange. 'That way, at least we wouldn't have to lug everything over there.' She realised as she spoke that this idea would put Tamsyn and Kirsten at the White Sands, leaving Roberta stranded here at Paradise Bay, which wasn't going to work.

'Well, zat might be possible, *oui,*' Solange said, smiling and nodding enthusiastically. *Perhaps the antidote would work,* her eyes said.

A waiter wearing a shirt that matched the sofa's upholstery approached. 'What would you like?' Solange asked Kate. 'Roberta, anozer one?' She nodded towards the bottle of Pellegrino on the table.

'Let me be frank,' Roberta said.

Ha, Frank is Roberta's middle name, Kate thought.

'Paradise Bay doesn't work for us on any level. If we were a family magazine, maybe, and even then, it's just not what we're about – and being here is putting the entire shoot in jeopardy.'

'I'll have a cappuccino, please,' Kate said to the waiter, who turned to Roberta and waited expectantly. With a subtle movement of her head,

Solange drew his attention to the empty Pellegrino bottle. The glimmer of hope that had lit up her eyes moments before was now gone.

'What about the Roche d'Or?' Roberta asked.

Solange choked on her tea, probably because the Roche d'Or was the group's most exclusive property and twice the price of Paradise Bay. Roberta was thus asking for a transfer from the ridiculous to the sublime. 'I'm afraid at ze Roche d'Or, we never give ze rooms away,' Solange said. 'But … er … if you could pay 70 per cent of ze room rate … per'aps …'

'That would be difficult,' Kate said, 'but we could offer you more pages – maybe an advertorial in a future issue.'

'I think I should point out that you're not exactly giving away the rooms,' Roberta said. 'You're getting excellent exposure in an award-winning magazine in exchange, and as far as I'm concerned you're not fulfilling your part of the bargain.' Kate felt a mixture of embarrassment and awe at Roberta's gall.

'If it was up to me, I would,' Solange said. 'I see ze problem. But we 'ave strict policies on zis.'

'Funnily enough, so do I,' Roberta said, 'and I cannot work in these conditions. So what exactly would 70 per cent amount to?' She turned to Kate. 'I think it's time for a chat to the home office.'

Certain that the home office would not inject any more cash into the shoot, Kate asked Solange if she would investigate whether the rules could be bent a little. Solange promised to do her best, and, when Kate's cappuccino arrived, she clicked across the lobby in her kitten heels on a mission to look into the matter – and clearly attempting to distance herself from Roberta as quickly as possible.

'You know Simon's not going to pump more money into this shoot,' Kate said as soon as Solange was out of earshot. In an attempt to curb costs, the Lowell brothers had recently transferred overall financial control from *Be*'s managing editor to the financial director of Lowell Media, whose accolades included saving a supermarket chain from certain ruin through brilliant cost-cutting measures. He had several solutions for *Be*, the majority of which Amber had called 'short-sighted at best and brand suicide at worst'. It was only thanks to Amber's daily battles – helped, it was rumoured, by a few clauses in her employment contract – that the magazine still boasted a glowing complexion.

'There's the emergency fund,' Roberta said.

'I'm not sure this counts as an emergency,' Kate said. 'What if there's a real emergency?'

'Are you always this negative?'

Roberta inhaled deeply in preparation for a sigh, and her dress tightened over her chest, revealing that she wasn't wearing a bra. Kate envied her pert breasts and long, angular body, which meant that she looked good in anything, whereas Kate had to choose what she wore more carefully. Not that she was fat. She doggedly fought deposits on her hips and thighs with regular runs, and was thankful for her long, naturally slim legs. But her D-cup breasts supplemented by the occupational hazards of her job – recipe testing, restaurant reviews, product launches – meant that she was never at any risk of being called skinny. The term *curvy* was sometimes applied, which she hated. And, despite the fact that her olive complexion inherited from her half-Greek mother, combined with her father's fair hair and grey-green eyes, made her attractive, she was intimidated by small-boned classic beauties like Roberta. She realised, however, that she was going to have to learn to stand her ground if she wanted to make a success of her new role.

'I think the word is *realistic* rather than *negative*, Roberta,' she said. 'It was hard enough getting this deal.'

'Well, I'll speak to Amber if you won't.' Roberta sighed and shook her head in irritation. Her shaggy asymmetrical bob swung across her face, causing a brunette strand of hair to get caught in a mascaraed lash, which came out as she pulled off the hair. 'Ugh, today is really not my day.'

* * *

Eight hours and countless phone calls later, Kate locked her door and stepped onto the torch-lit path that meandered through tall, slim casuarina trees from the Royal Villas to the main hotel. Finally settled at a table on the shore of the lake-sized pool, she ordered a Campari and soda, and then leant back to take in her surroundings.

A few children lingered in the shallow end of the pool, which was lit up and cast eerie green shadows, while on the other side a game of volleyball was under way on a floodlit section of beach. Paradise Bay was very resorty and family-oriented; Roberta did have a point, Kate thought. But despite the numerous manmade pleasures foisted upon it – two swimming pools, six tennis courts, mini golf, giant chess, boats and beach toys of every description – the island's irrepressible God-given beauty pushed its way through everywhere. Magenta bougainvillea dripped from the pergola above her; the thick night air bristled with the hum of cicadas; and the scent of frangipanis hung in a light breeze, which prickled her bare shoulders and lifted the hem of her turquoise dress to caress her legs.

It felt good to have traded heavy, wintery clothes for this light wisp of a dress that had always felt too perky in London media circles, where black was never back because it had never gone away. Roberta would almost certainly disapprove of this fashion-backward shade, Kate thought, much as she would of her hint of a suntan (Roberta guarded her own skin from the sun's ageing rays with long-sleeved clothes, high-SPF creams, and a collection of Chinese parasols), but Roberta was no longer in close enough proximity to cast a critical eye over Kate. The fashion director and her entourage were now ensconced at the luxurious White Sands Hotel, where rooms had been made available by upgrading a few guests to the even more luxurious Roche d'Or after some intense negotiating on Kate's part.

Although she still thought the move unnecessary, Kate needed every aspect of this assignment to shine in order to pass the test, so she had pitched an idea borrowed from a hotel at which she had worked as a student. If repeat guests at the White Sands Hotel were offered a complimentary upgrade as a kind of loyalty reward, she had suggested, this would potentially encourage more visits in the future. Solange had put the idea to her superiors, and they had bought it. The magazine would still have to pay a supplement, but it was lower than that at the Roche d'Or. And Amber had agreed: 'Whatever it takes to get the job done – within reason. Simon won't be happy, but I'll deal with him. It really is essential that this issue is a knockout.' She had sounded stressed and irritated, seemingly in agreement with Roberta that Paradise Bay had been a bad idea from the start. Kate was relieved that at least she would be able to keep the Laidback Living saga under wraps since her contact had promised to dispatch the delayed Indian shipment, as soon as it had been cleared by customs, the following day.

Her drink arrived, and she reached into her bag for the treat she felt she deserved after the day's trials and tribulations. After lighting up, she closed her eyes and relished the mind massage that smoking always provided. However, the cigarette's relaxing effects were soon tainted by pangs of guilt, first for polluting the clean air and second for breaking her New Year's resolution to finally give up smoking, not only for health reasons but also because Daniel didn't smoke – although, ironically, cigarettes had brought them together in the first place.

Before their first encounter in the flesh, Kate had met Daniel virtually in the pages of *Grape Expectations* wine magazine. His witty, irreverent column had appealed to her, and she had loved how, even though he clearly knew his stuff, he didn't take it or himself too seriously. The small portrait accompanying his column – intelligent blue eyes framed in small black-rimmed glasses, wry smile, floppy brown hair – had added to the attraction and made her wonder what was beneath the surface. So when she had received an invitation to a food and wine pairing dinner where he would be the guest speaker, it had gone directly to the top of her 'Definitely yes' pile.

The evening had, however, got off to a bad start. She had been monopolised by a notorious wine bore and, while this clinging vine had stammered on about his vinicultural interests, had only been able to watch her own interest chat to other guests across the room and later to describe the wine chosen to match each dish.

When waiters had begun to circulate with cheese, Kate had finally given up all hope of talking to Daniel. She held up a hand to halt the descent of a plate in front of her – a calorific indulgence too far – but nodded at a waiter hovering with a bottle of golden wine to fill a fresh glass, 'All the way to the top, please.'

'Whereas a macho Cabernet gets on well with a voluptuous Camembert,' Daniel was saying, 'you don't want to come on too strong where a shy goat's cheese is concerned. This discretely flirtatious Muscat with peach and apricot flavours is thus the perfect match for the chèvre de Rhone.' Following his cue, the vine bore dipped his nose into his glass, closed his eyes, and inhaled. Taking advantage of his moment of rapture, Kate grabbed her bag and glass, gave Daniel a last longing glance, and slipped through a set of French doors into a cobbled courtyard, where a concrete cherub pouring water from an urn offered concealment. But no sooner had she perched on the edge of the fountain and lit up than she heard the crunch of shoes on gravel. She looked up, expecting to see the ruddy face of her latest, 'grapest' fan, but instead she found herself staring at Bacchus himself.

'It's you,' she said stupidly, as though she had just spotted Father Christmas emerging from the fireplace. She stubbed out her cigarette and dropped it on the ground, realising too late that she now looked like a pseudo wine appreciator with no concern for the environment.

'I hope you didn't waste that on my account,' Daniel said. 'Do you mind?' He nodded towards the spot next to her on the fountain's edge. 'I needed a breather. It's hard work in there, though I guess you've done your share tonight, having Stan as a dinner companion.'

Well, that has to be a good sign, Kate thought; he had noticed whom she was sitting next to. She wondered if it was too much to hope that he had seen her leave the room and then followed her. She would later learn that he had.

'Please,' he said, picking up her box of cigarettes and handing it to her, 'don't stop on my account. I'd join you if a whiff of lingering smoke wasn't in danger of closing a chequebook in there.'

Kate laughed. 'If you're sure you don't mind?' She removed another cigarette from the box. 'I'm Kate, by the way.'

'I know. I've had you for dinner.' Daniel smiled suggestively.

Kate looked at him quizzically.

'I've tried one of your recipes.'

'You read *Be*?' Kate asked in a tone better suited to an expression like 'What a cute puppy.'

'A client sent me your recipe for salmon with Pinot Noir butter because he knows it's one of my favourite cultivars. I've always enjoyed it with salmon, but I'd never thought of marrying the two on a plate.'

'You cook?' she asked, trying to lose the puppy-dog tone without complete success. *Throw in a subordinate clause or two the next time you speak, you jabbering idiot.*

'I do, but it's generally a bit more random than that, and I've never produced anything quite so sublime. Maybe you can give me some lessons?'

This delicious proposition had led to an informal, wine-fuelled cooking class in Daniel's flat, followed by far more tasty experimentation on later dates, when student had become lover. The subsequent days, nights, and months had sewn together so seamlessly that it had come as a surprise to Kate when he cooked salmon in Pinot Noir butter for their dinner one night, pointing out that it was exactly a year since the night they had met.

Even more surprising was that, in all that time, there had been no warning shots to send her fleeing the cosy nest of coupledom and hightailing it back to her natural habitat: the single life, where, like a bird in the treetops, she felt light, free, and safe. Triggered by her father's first affair when she was still young, this reaction to any sign that love was on dangerous ground had developed, with time and repetition (subsequent infidelities on her father's part added to a few of her own painful run-ins with love), into a Pavlovian-style reflex that never failed to kick in at some point in a relationship. But Daniel had given her no reason to take flight. Their relationship was an expansive sanctuary; his apartment, a downy, comfortable nest.

So why does the thought of moving in with him still send a wave of panic through me? Kate wondered as she lit a second cigarette. She wouldn't be putting all her eggs in his nest, since she would still have a couple deposited in *Be.* And they weren't talking marriage, although he had hinted at it, she recalled. Still, was marriage really so impossible to contemplate, even with Daniel? *Maybe not … well, yes, actually, it is,* came the answer from within. She had seen that piece of paper used by couples as a contract to take each other for granted too often, breeding a sense of ownership and ultimately contempt in some, and a feeling of being trapped in others. It was far better to be in a relationship where the cage door was open.

Which would, in fact, be the case if you simply moved in with Daniel, an exasperated inner voice said.

Still the hesitation.

So you're just going to hop from nest to nest eternally and wind up an exhausted, lonely old bird without even Be *or a facsimile to keep you warm eventually? Is that what you want?*

No … I don't know.

God, you're irritating.

Perhaps she needed to return to Dr Cook's couch and continue to work through those events that had created the reflex in the first place.

'Ms Richmond?' Kate looked up at a set of perfect white teeth.

'Mr Dubois?' He didn't look like a Mr Dubois.

'Fai. Monsieur Dubois sends his apologies.'

'Kate.' She extended her hand, which felt clammy and warm in his cool grasp.

The hotel's manager had fallen ill, his substitute told her as they crossed a manicured lawn from which shadowy, red-bloomed flame trees erupted, lit from below. They then stepped onto a deck set on stilts over the sea, where a woman in a long dress sat at a piano singing in French, and hurricane lamps flickered on tables. Everything here was subtler and more discreet than elsewhere in the resort. Kate was relieved to have found at least one area that she could exude about in her coverage of Paradise Bay without having to embroider the truth.

'You'd better look at this,' Fai said, passing Kate the wine list once they were seated. 'There's not much need for wine expertise as a children's activities coordinator.' It was a considerably lower rank than hotel manager, Kate noted. She wondered if this dinner date downgrade had anything to do with Roberta's tantrums – not that the alternative was in any way unattractive, she thought, running her eyes over Fai's face and physique.

He was a fourth-generation Chinese Mauritian, Fai told Kate as the buttery Chardonnay moved conversation on to personal history. 'My great-grandfather came here from China to work in the sugar cane fields. He was from a very poor family, so it was a decision inspired by a better life here. It was tough at first, I believe, but he worked hard and saved almost everything he earned until he could afford to buy a trading store in Port Louis.'

'And now?' Kate asked.

'It's still in the family. My father and brother run it.'

The family business wasn't for Fai, however. He had studied marketing in the hope that it might open doors to a career beyond the island, but he had been waylaid at Paradise Bay. 'Most people end up in tourism these days,' he said. 'It's taken over from sugar as one of our biggest earners, along with textiles. You might have heard that the industry is in trouble because of falling sugar prices worldwide, so a lot of jobs are under threat. How do you like that?' He nodded at Kate's starter, which had been delivered as they talked and which Kate had absent-mindedly started on while absorbed in his fluid storytelling.

'Mm, very nice,' she said, now fully registering the delicately braised parchment-like palm hearts, which were tossed with spring onions, lemon juice, and olive oil to delicious, zesty effect. 'But I can't help feeling sad that an entire palm had to be cut down in its prime for this pleasure.'

'I'm sure it would be happy to know it had given its heart to a beautiful travel writer from London.' Fai smiled, a flash of white in the flickering lamplight, and Kate felt a flickering sensation inside her in response to the compliment. 'It must be an interesting job.'

'It is,' Kate said, 'although, to be honest, this is my first official travel assignment; my real forte is food writing.' She gave him a neat précis of her career history, telling him that her original goal had been to become a serious journalist but that her dormant foodie genes had risen up and conquered her.

Fai leant back in his chair and elaborately considered her form. 'You don't look like you eat a lot,' he said.

'Thank you,' she said, feeling a misplaced rush of warmth through her body as his eyes caressed the curve of her breasts.

'It sounds like a very good life, to live in London and do what you do. You're lucky,' he said.

'Living in paradise must have a few merits,' Kate said. She looked out at the calm sea, which had absorbed the night and was a swathe of black taffeta shimmering in the moonlight; she almost felt she could grab it and wrap herself in it. 'This is a dream world.'

'Living in a dream can feel claustrophobic,' Fai said. 'I need to get off the island but it's difficult with this global financial crisis, you know.'

'You'd really leave this beautiful place?' Kate asked.

'It's too small,' Fai said.

'It's quite big as islands go.' Kate found it interesting that even people living in paradise were looking for paradise elsewhere.

'It is, but it feels smaller, partly because we only represent around 3 per cent of the population, and there's not a lot of intercultural mixing.'

'The majority's Indian, right?' Kate asked.

'Yes, mostly descendants of labourers brought out to work on the sugar cane plantations after slavery was abolished. The Creoles make up the second largest percentage, and the Franco-Mauritians are an even smaller minority than us, but they still own most of the country's wealth and seem happy to live in a very separate world.'

Be that as it may, Kate found that Mauritius's disparate components got along very well on the palate when palm hearts gave way to prawn rougaille, which Fai told her was a fusion of Chinese, Indian and French ingredients.

'Remind me what's in this sauce.'

'Ginger, chilli, curry leaves, thyme, garlic, *pommes d'amour* …'

'A bit of him, a bit of me and a bit of her.' Their waiter gestured towards the singer as he filled up their glasses.

Kate laughed and then turned back to Fai. 'Pommes d'amour? Tomatoes? You actually call them love apples?'

'It's stuck from the time when the French were in power,' Fai said. 'They believed that tomatoes had aphrodisiacal powers.'

'I know. They're on my list of aphrodisiacs; I just haven't heard them referred to as love apples in everyday conversation.'

'You have a list?' Fai raised his eyebrows.

'Strictly for business purposes,' Kate said with an exaggerated air of professionalism. 'I put together a menu of aphrodisiacs for our Valentine's issue.'

'As I said, you have an interesting job.' Fai smiled as he undressed one of the prawns on his seafood platter, adding its pink suit to a pile in front of him. Watching him deftly perform the task caused another strange sensation inside Kate. 'So what do you think?' Fai asked. 'Do pommes d'amour live up to their name?' His eyes followed Kate's, and she felt her cheeks heat up as she averted her gaze, hoping her expression hadn't revealed the alternative task to which she had imagined his hands applied.

'Honestly, I've never had tomatoes down as a particularly romantic food,' Kate said. 'I had no idea they'd ever been regarded as aphrodisiacs until they came up in my research. I also learnt that, far from being romantic, they were actually thought to be poisonous when they landed in England from South America in the sixteenth century.'

'Poisonous? Why?'

'Apparently, when the Greeks classified tomatoes, they put them in the mandrake or nightshade family, which includes belladonna, so it was assumed they were deadly too. They were therefore originally only grown for decoration. Their Latin name translates as "wolf peach", which is kind of as far from love apples as you can get.' Kate caught herself rambling and paused. 'Sorry, I'm probably boring you with all this trivia.'

'Don't be. It's interesting. So what made the French decide tomatoes were worthy of the name "love apples" rather than "wolf peaches"?'

'It's quite blurry,' Kate said, 'but ironically it also seems to stem from their classification as part of the mandrake family, with particular reference to mandrake's mention in the Bible. Genesis talks about Leah and Rachel using the mandrake's roots as a love potion, and the Hebrew word translates roughly as "love apples". It's typical of the French to latch onto the romantic aspect, whereas we hung onto the old "wolf peach" until the eighteenth century. You might be aware of the British reputation for erring towards the negative.'

Fai laughed. 'You've done your research.'

'I'm a little obsessive once I get my teeth into something.' Kate bit into a prawn as if to demonstrate her point. The firm, white flesh was complemented but not overpowered by the sauce's blend of tomato, spices, and chilli, while the grainy coconut chutney added sweetness along with another dash of heat that hit the palate like an afterthought. 'This really is delicious.'

'We call it Mauritius on a plate,' Fai said.

And, thought Kate, you could call Fai Mauritius on legs, with his skin the colour of golden sand, his hair reminiscent of the island's volcanic rock, eyes like coffee beans, and teeth as white as sun-bleached coral. *Enough of that,* her conscience scolded. Perhaps it was the setting that was giving her romantic ideas about this man, she thought, from which she must desist. Even thinking them felt like a betrayal of Daniel. She redirected her attention to the dish on the table.

'I wonder if your chef would share the recipe for this?' she asked. 'Though I can't imagine it tasting the same with the tomatoes I can get back home. So often they taste of nothing at all, but these are really intense and so red. I personally think it's the colour wherein lies the myth of love. In fact, if my research proved anything, it's that food's seductive power generally has more to do with what it looks like and suggests than with any chemical components.'

This had been disappointing news to Kate, who sometimes wished there were a magical potion, like the flower nectar struck by Cupid's arrow in *A Midsummer Night's Dream*, which would make her fall so deliriously in love that all her questions disappeared.

'Figs are another case in point,' she added. 'Most of their aphrodisiacal cred comes from the fact that, when open, they're believed to look like a … um … well, like a vagina.' *Did I really just use the word* vagina *in polite conversation? Move over Eve Ensler.*

'So you're saying that nothing on your list has special powers?' Fai looked disappointed. Perhaps he was also looking for a magic formula for love.

'I don't think there's anything foolproof,' Kate said, 'but certain foods could be said to enhance … um, things in that area.' She laughed. 'This isn't the type of thing I usually discuss with people I've just met.'

'It makes a nice change from child-friendly sunscreen,' Fai said. 'Humour me.'

Kate told him that the zinc in oysters and caviar was an important factor in the production of testosterone, which was responsible for enhancing both men's and, to a lesser extent, women's libidos, as was the trace mineral boron, contained in honey and beetroot. *So maybe beetroot wasn't such a bad substitute for pigeon after all,* she thought as her mind drifted back to her last supper with Daniel and the inspired lovemaking that had followed. But Spanish fly, which was actually made from a crushed beetle, she told Fai, was the most potent of all aphrodisiacs, proven to produce an erection by causing gastrointestinal irritation and increasing blood flow to the sexual organs. 'It's potentially fatal, though,' she added, 'so probably not something you want to feed to someone you truly love.'

Fai laughed. 'You're funny. I probably shouldn't tell you that you weren't a popular choice for dinner tonight. We thought you'd all be the same.'

'You mean your manager is suffering from an allergic reaction to prima donnas?' Kate said. Throwing around barbed comments about one's colleagues wasn't very professional, but this was beginning to feel a lot less like a business dinner and more like a first date. *Which it isn't,* she emphatically reminded herself.

'Dessert or coffee?' Their waiter hovered with menus.

'Just bring the *addition*,' Fai said.

His abrupt response hit Kate like the stray bit of driftwood that had knocked her off her feet that morning.

'Sorry, that probably sounded rude,' Fai added, perhaps noting her ill-concealed disappointment. 'I'm really not good at this, am I?' He laughed apologetically. 'Of course, you must have dessert if you'd like, but I thought you should experience some real Mauritian flavour – and this isn't the place for it.' *He's definitely not going for the hard sell,* Kate thought, relieved.

The rest of the night passed in a happy blur, with Kate and Fai drinking rum cocktails in a thatched bar on a public beach. Kate didn't arrive back at her room until 2 a.m., feeling as if the bar's three-man band had caught a ride home in her head. She took a bottle of Evian out of the minibar, lit up a cigarette, and stepped onto her verandah, where she lay back on a sunlounger and gazed up at a moon that hung like a spotlight in the sky. Fai, the moon, the alcohol – whatever it was, she liked that warm sensation she felt in her belly as she dozed beneath the velvet sky.

CHAPTER 3

Sugar and Spice

When the taxi swerved to miss a chicken, Kate felt like her stomach had been left behind at the side of the road.

'Are you all right?' Tristan asked. 'You look pale.' Kate might have asked him the same thing. The photographer was pressed against the car's door, one white-knuckled hand gripping the handle and the other clutching his camera equipment as though his life depended upon it. It probably did, since Roberta would tear him apart with her perfectly manicured talons if this frivolous travel shoot jeopardised the serious business of fashion. Having 'lent' Tristan to Kate for a couple of hours while the light was at its harshest, she wanted him returned in perfect working order as soon as the light softened again, in the late afternoon.

'I'm fine,' Kate lied. In truth, her head felt like a cocktail shaker in which her brain was being muddled with the rum still in her system from her night out with Fai. However, she didn't want news of her binge to filter back to Roberta, and inevitably to Amber. It had been irresponsible of her to get drunk the night before a shoot, especially one with so much riding on it. The upgrade had already put Amber's hackles up and, with the Laidback Living items still at large, Kate couldn't afford to make any more mistakes if she wanted to hang onto this job.

Just as her stomach recovered, the car swung violently again to avoid a bus that was hurtling towards them. This had evidently had to skirt a truck that was stopped in the middle of the road, its driver leaning out of his window and chatting to a woman in a bright pink sari. Tristan's audible intake of breath matched Kate's own as they narrowly avoided a collision, following which they let out a collective sigh.

A middle-aged Indian man with thick, wavy black hair, Sanjay, their driver, looked over his shoulder and smiled. 'In Mauritius, we are a little bit confused,' he said, thankfully returning his attention to the road ahead. 'You see, when the French were in power, we were having to drive on the right. Then the British were taking over and we were driving on the left.' He glanced at his passengers in the rear-view mirror. 'And now that we are independent, we are just driving in the middle of the road.' His deep, throaty laugh matched the hoarse rumble of his car's engine and drowned out the laughter from the back.

Sanjay slowed the car as they entered a village that they had passed through while scouting for locations. 'This is Trou d'Eau Douce,' he said. 'Nice place. Shall I be stopping?'

'Please,' Kate said, desperate to be on solid ground.

'Definitely,' Tristan said. 'Oh my God, I know I said it before, but the paintwork on those houses is phe-*nom*-e-nal.'

The whole scene was a photographer's dream, Kate thought as she took in the shacks painted in contrasting pastel shades of blue, green, pink, and yellow with their peeling shutters and bright floral curtains, a group of Afro-Creole children playing with a ball in the shade of a large leafy tree beside them.

They pulled up in front of a small white building with a corrugated iron roof and a large metal Coca-Cola sign attached to the wall.

'"Trou d'Eau Douce" means "hole of sweet water,"' Sanjay said, yanking up the handbrake. 'Its name is coming from a freshwater pool from an underground stream down there.' He pointed towards a narrow road that snaked past the wooden huts, leading to the sea.

A woman's head and shoulders were now framed in one of the houses' windows, her chin propped up on an arm that rested on the windowsill. She was watching them. *A nice picture,* Kate thought. 'How do people feel about being photographed?' she asked, clambering out of the car. 'Is it culturally acceptable?'

'It's usually fine,' Sanjay said, 'but ask first. Mauritians are friendly, but we are not liking it when tourists are treating us like animals in the London Zoo.' This occasioned another burst of laughter.

Tristan slung his camera bag over his shoulder. 'Let's start with the pool; I didn't see it last time,' he said.

'I'll be in here,' Sanjay said, pointing to the white building against which a handwritten sign was propped, promising curry, dholl puri, cooldrinks and beer. 'Call me if you're needing any help.'

Tristan tapped his pocket, acknowledging that Sanjay's number was present and correct, and then set off down the tree-lined road before Kate could ask him to wait. She hurriedly picked up a much-needed bottle of water and then stumbled after him, glugging it down and wishing that she had thought to pack some Rescue Remedy.

'Talking about animals in the zoo, I feel like I've just escaped from one,' Tristan said when she caught up with him. 'Roberta's becoming more rabid by the minute.'

'I thought she'd be happy now that she's ensconced in luxury,' Kate said.

'Puh-lease. That woman will always find something to bitch about,' Tristan said.

'Ain't that the truth,' Kate said. As long as there were fat people in the world, food contained calories, eternal youth remained elusive, and life was anything short of five-star, Roberta would have a bad word to say about something.

'But she's outdoing herself now,' Tristan added. 'I think the Botox has gone to the brain.' Kate was surprised by this display of anti-Roberta-ism, since Tristan was usually gossiping *with* the fashion director rather than about her. He could always be relied on to laugh at her jibes or compliment her on yet another '*fab*-u-lous' outfit, which was probably just a necessary survival tool for a freelance photographer dealing with a fashion director whose ego was twice her body weight.

'So what's Roberta on about now?' she asked. 'She can't have a problem with the White Sands, surely?'

'No, now it's all about Tatyana's acne,' Tristan said. 'I wouldn't mind calling that home.' He came to an abrupt halt in front of a colonial-style villa with bougainvillea cascading over its wall, and Kate, still in her hung-over daze, walked straight into him. The house reminded her of those she had run past the day before, which brought to mind the man with the cup of coffee. As Tristan took several shots, she pictured the stranger enjoying a pre-lunch pastis while gazing out to sea now, and imagined herself joining him in a glass of the anise-flavoured drink. She gave herself a virtual slap on the wrist. What was it about this island that was giving her these romantic notions all of a sudden? Perhaps there was something in those pommes d'amour after all, she thought as they continued on their way.

'Her skin is pretty bad,' she said, picking up from where she had left off before the impromptu stop. Kate had seen Tatyana in magazines, but the model she had met at the airport only looked vaguely related to the cover girl with wheat-blonde hair, creamy skin, and eyes like transparent turquoise mosaic pieces. This version had hair that was greasy and stringy, skin that was blotchy, and even Kate thought she was verging on being too skinny. 'Is she ill?'

'Sick? Depressed? Drugs? God knows. All I know is she was freaking amazing when I worked with her a few months ago, and I really pushed for her as a result. So now, when Roberta's not bitching about Tatyana, she's bitching about my bad judgment.'

That explains his defection, Kate thought.

Once the slope flattened out, they saw the pool ahead, its emerald waters contrasting with the turquoise sea. 'Awesome,' Tristan said.

'Well, we'll always have Photoshop,' Kate said.

'Yes, but you know Amber's feelings on overdoing it. Anyway, Roberta sent Tatyana for a major overhaul in the spa today, so let's see.'

Another expense, Kate thought.

Tristan set his bag on the ground and squatted down, training his camera on the pool. 'But whatever happens,' he said, 'it looks like we'll have to use April for the cover now. And she's totally pissed because she was set on blonde. So here ends my beautiful relationship with *Be.* Wish me luck as you wave me on my way back to Cape Town.'

'You'll be fine,' Kate said. 'Amber's crazy about your stuff.'

'Yeah, maybe, but those two are as tight as a pair of tinned sardines.' He turned his camera in the direction of three Creole women who were doing their laundry, rubbing an array of clothes against the rocks.

'Whoa,' Kate said, 'I'd better ask if they're happy to be photographed.' She walked over to the women, who nodded enthusiastically in response to her rusty French and, after adjusting their colourful headscarves, put on dazzling smiles for the camera.

'Won't you tell them to pretend I'm not here?' Tristan said. 'I'd rather they didn't look like abnormally happy housewives in a Third World washing-detergent commercial.'

Kate rolled her eyes, not even remotely motivated to attempt making that request. Eventually the women returned to their chatter and Tristan came through with some beautiful, colourful natural shots.

'Roberta does seem to have some kind of weird hold on Amber,' Kate said as they walked back up to the main road. Trailing them at a slight distance now were three barefoot Creole children, who were attracted, Kate imagined, as much by the camera as by Tristan's loud pink and purple camouflage T-shirt and spiky, dyed-so-black-it-looked-blue hair. 'I mean, Amber's meticulous about everything except for when it comes to Roberta. No one else would get away with some of the stuff she turns in.'

'Well, you know their history …'

'What history?'

'You don't know?' Tristan stopped and raised his sunglasses, screwing up his eyes in disbelief. 'I guess you wouldn't,' he conceded, thus confirming Kate's suspicion that for all her efforts to get up to speed with *Be*'s fashionistas, she still hadn't graduated to cool.

'Don't know what?' Hot gossip was always sweeter when it was cooked up in the kitchen of revenge. Kate could sniff it on the breeze.

'That they were an item,' Tristan said.

'What? You mean à la Ellen DeGeneres and Portia de Rossi?' Now it was Kate's turn to freeze in her tracks.

Tristan nodded. 'You could say that.'

'Fuck,' Kate said. The reason for Roberta's immunity suddenly became crystal clear, and she realised that if she valued her job she probably shouldn't alienate her any more than she already had.

'Language!' Tristan gave a sideways glance at a skinny young girl dressed in a dusty lace party dress, who, like a sparrow with its eye on a precariously placed crumb, had inched closer.

'*Tu envie prend nous photo?*' she asked in lilting French Creole, hopping from one leg to the other and twisting a glossy black curl of hair around one forefinger. Kate translated for Tristan, who nodded as he squatted down, beckoning the girl and her friends to come closer.

'But they're not an item anymore, right?' Kate crouched down next to Tristan. 'I mean, Roberta's been married, what, four … five times, and Amber …' Come to think of it, she had never seen Amber attached to a man, either in the flesh or in the press, and she was an attractive, intelligent woman. *Aha!* she thought. Punchlines did sometimes take her just a little while longer to get.

'No, I think their relationship's been purely platonic for a while, but it was apparently full on. You know they go way back?'

'I didn't,' Kate said.

'They did some modelling together in New York in the eighties, which is how they met. Even did some adult-magazine stuff, apparently.' Tristan beckoned the children to approach and then showed them the images on his camera's digital read-out. This elicited whoops of joy and turned him into the Pied Piper, attracting a swelling band of followers as he and Kate walked along the main street, stopping to capture Tristan's beloved shacks, a tailor at work on a pedal-operated sewing machine, and a group of old men playing *boccibal* in a shady square. Here, the throng fell silent and, for a while, the only sounds were the intermittent clink of the small silver balls when they collided, accompanied by French expletives. The scene could have been transposed from the village square in Vence, where Kate and Daniel had watched men play *boules* one bank-holiday weekend. She was sure he would translate well to the island life, and a part of her wished he were here right now to share in this vision.

'This place is like Disney's Epcot Center,' Tristan said. 'You've got France, the Caribbean, and India, all in a row.' He nodded at the old men, the shacks, and a weathered Hindu shrine draped in a garland of marigolds, in turn.

Not forgetting China, Kate thought. 'We'd better get on if you want to make it back before curfew,' she said, although she was more concerned about missing their next engagement in Port Louis.

'You have no idea how much I don't want to go back there,' Tristan said as they walked back to Sanjay's car.

'Mm, I don't envy you,' Kate said distractedly, still dwelling on Tristan's earlier revelation. 'I just find it really hard to believe that she ... Roberta, I mean ... she devours men.' Kate thought of their first dinner at Paradise Bay, when Roberta had stripped the male model Marius down to his thong with her eyes, and she had probably later removed that too – with her teeth.

'You *could* say she has the best of both worlds,' Tristan said. 'I dated girls until I discovered true compatibility with my psychoanalyst in my twenties. And I still wouldn't say no to Kylie. It's about being open.'

'Maybe,' Kate said, 'but for some of us, I think things are pretty much predetermined in that area.' Following the demise of one love affair, Kate had almost considered embarking on a relationship with someone who was guaranteed to know the location of the clitoris. But a few kisses had convinced her that girlfriends could only ever be sugar in her coffee or honey in her tea, whereas men were tonic to her gin and Champagne to her cassis; they alone had the power to make her hormones fizz.

Tristan and Kate found Sanjay sitting at one of the tiny curry bar's four tables, opposite a wiry Indian man with near-black skin and snow-white candyfloss hair. The old man stood up as they approached. 'Sit, sit,' he said, picking up two empty beer bottles from the table.

'Will you be drinking something before we go?' Sanjay asked. 'This is being our most famous of beers.' He held up the bottle he was drinking from – 'Phoenix', the label read, and Kate wondered what hazards this might conjure on the journey ahead. Although tempted, she quelled the impulse to opt for hair of the dog and ordered a more sensible Coca-Cola instead. Tristan ordered the same, and the old man disappeared through a swinging door, reappearing minutes later in a cloud of fragrant steam, almost buckling under the weight of a large wooden tray.

In addition to two bottles of Coke, the tray held three plates, each bearing a yellow-coloured pancake topped with a tomato-based sauce.

'Dholl puris,' the old man announced as he placed a plate in front of each of them with a flourish. Kate's stomach protested vehemently and begged her to decline, but the glint of pride and excitement in the old man's eyes compelled her to accept graciously. Under his watchful gaze, following Sanjay's lead, she folded two sides of the warm pancake inwards, rolled once, and then picked it up with both hands and gingerly bit into it. She waited for complaints from within, but they didn't come. Instead, applause met the exquisite symphony of flavours and textures that filled her mouth as the light and flaky pancake gave way to a comfortingly mild bean curry, offset to perfection by crunchy pickles and a hint of sweet-and-sour chutney.

'What's the secret of these pancakes?' she asked after savouring the last mouthful. 'They're so light. I haven't tasted anything quite like them.' In answer, their host beckoned her to follow him into the kitchen, where a diminutive Indian woman in an emerald green sari was standing at a rusty old stove, frying pancakes in two large pans.

He pointed to a bowl on the kitchen counter.

'Aha, split peas?' Kate said, bending down over the bowl of yellow peas soaking in water. 'What else goes into them?'

She pulled out her notebook and began jotting down the recipe related by the woman, until an anxious Tristan dragged her out of the kitchen, still frantically writing lest she forget the recipe. *Roll the dough into a small ball,* she noted, *then make an indent in the top with your thumb. Fill this with ground yellow split peas and cumin* – she put an asterisk next to this, since it was apparently the secret to the pancakes' flakiness – *and then close the hole and roll out to form a thin, round pancake.*

As they stepped onto the street, Tristan looked up at the sky and groaned. 'I sure as hell don't like the look of that.' In the distance, a thick bank of clouds was slowly rolling towards them like an incoming tide.

'You have been hearing the cyclone warning?' Sanjay asked nonchalantly. Kate waited for the hoarse laugh to follow, but this was no tourist joke.

'What?' Tristan said.

'Cyclone?' Kate said.

'The hotel hasn't been telling you?' Sanjay asked. He opened the back door for them, nodding knowingly. 'Sometimes they're waiting till they are sure it's going to come and to learn how bad it will be. They are knowing that the holidaymakers are getting angry. You would not be believing how many guests are asking for a refund because the weather is not like it is in the brochure.' Now the laugh came, but it was in no way comforting.

'You're sure?' Kate asked, rooted to the spot. 'It's official?'

'When?' Tristan asked.

'You never can be telling for sure.' Sanjay shrugged. 'It can be going slower, faster, changing direction any time.'

So life as I know it isn't over just yet, Kate thought.

'But on the TV today, they were saying that it will most definitely be arriving tomorrow,' Sanjay added.

Kate wondered who 'they' were and if their assessment could be trusted. 'Why is this happening to me?' she asked the tranquil blue heavens directly above her. Not in her worst nightmares had things turned out quite so disastrously.

'What should we do?' she asked Sanjay in a panic. 'Should we go back to the hotel now and warn everyone? Is it safe to be on the coast? Do we need to evacuate?' She felt hysteria rising in her.

'There is no need to be evacuating; don't be worrying,' Sanjay said, 'because it is most definitely only in the number one or two category.' This meant nothing to Kate. 'No one will be dying,' Sanjay explained. 'It will just be something of an inconvenience.'

'Just shoot me now, please,' Tristan said, and Kate's self-pity turned to empathy because she certainly wouldn't want to be anywhere near Roberta when she found out about the cyclone.

They left the village in silence. Even Sanjay seemed infected with the sombre mood. He now drove at a pace more befitting a funeral procession than a stock car track, giving his full attention to the road ahead, although every now and then his eyes flicked to the rear-view mirror to check on his passengers.

Kate was relieved when they turned inland and lost sight of those grey doomsday totems, and even more so when they arrived at the Port Louis market, where, as arranged amid tipsy goodnights, Fai was waiting for them.

He kissed Kate on both cheeks and then stretched out an elegant, long-fingered hand to Tristan. 'Fai Li.'

'He's got fantastic cheekbones,' Tristan whispered into Kate's ear as they followed Fai into the market. 'Any chance he's in my camp? My gaydar's always a bit out with Asians.'

'I don't think there's anything camp about him,' Kate said, feeling more gratified by this innate knowledge than she should. Out of his Paradise Bay uniform, wearing jeans and a grey T-shirt, Fai looked older, she thought, and more self-assured.

They became pieces in an ever-turning kaleidoscope of shoppers, traders, and exotic goods changing hands: woven grass baskets and table mats in orange, turquoise, fuchsia, and lime green; hand-carved miniature wooden boats; embroidered tablecloths; and saris waving in the breeze.

'You have to bargain,' Fai said, as Kate prepared to hand over the asked price for a yellow sari intricately embroidered in gold. 'Halve the price and go from there.' His mouth was so close to her ear that she could feel his warm breath, like a caress, on her neck.

When clothes and fabrics gave way to fruit and vegetables, Kate thought how much Daniel would love this place. He had a knack for wandering through fresh markets and picking out ingredients at random, later transforming them into original dishes at home. She, on the other hand, went to market armed with a plan and a list, and envied his ability to follow his instincts, not only when it came to shopping and cooking but also when it came to life in general. He balanced her, she thought; apart from their delicious sexual chemistry, she was so much more relaxed and playful when hanging out with him. However, when Fai touched her arm, the electric-oven fan that he turned on inside her made her wonder whether there wasn't a whole new level of chemistry to explore here – in a league with molecular gastronomy.

'Pommes d'amour,' he said with a knowing smile, pointing to pyramids of deep red, plum-sized tomatoes.

'Ah,' Kate said, turning to him and raising her eyebrows suggestively as she put her hand on the warm place where his breath had again touched her neck. Tristan looked from Fai to Kate, narrowing his eyes suspiciously, but the beeping of his phone distracted him.

'Roberta,' he said, reading the new text on his phone's screen. 'She's just emerged from a flotation tank and has found out about the cyclone. So I'm afraid I'm going to have to call it a day.'

'Damn,' Kate said. 'So it's happening?' Distracted by Fai and shielded from stormy skies by the covered market, she had almost forgotten about the impending cyclone. 'I'd better come back with you. There must be something I should be doing about this.' She felt a mixture of regret and relief at the thought of leaving Fai.

'What are you going to do?' Tristan asked. 'You heard Sanjay. It's probably more important to get in Chinatown before the storm. Since

I, however, won't be able to make it, Fai, would you do the honours in my last shot, over there?' He pointed to a trestle table piled high with knobbly ginger, chillies, and herbs. 'He definitely works out,' he said to Kate discreetly from behind his camera while Fai chatted to the vendor in an effort to act natural, as instructed.

'Mm-hm,' Kate agreed, having already noted how the sleeves of Fai's T-shirt tightened over the tops of his toned and tanned arms.

Fai rejoined them and Tristan prepared to leave. 'Do me a favour and add a little "God save the Queen" to your prayers tonight, Kate,' he said, before adding in a whisper, 'And don't do anything I would.' He glanced suggestively in Fai's direction.

No, she wouldn't, Kate resolved. She decided to apply herself instead to ticking off the spices on her list, starting with the vanilla beckoning with fragrant fingers from a nearby table.

'It's expensive,' Fai said as the stallholder scooped vanilla beans into a brown paper bag, and Kate once again noted the heady sensation his proximity evoked.

'It's a lot cheaper than it is back home,' she said, instructing her senses to behave, 'and it's worth it.' The vanilla's warm, intoxicating scent matched him, she thought. She could imagine that if she inhaled him as she might the orchid that had borne the vanilla pod, then this would be what he smelled like. *Enough. You're incorrigible.* She wasn't going to let herself get into that kind of predicament. 'It's warm in here,' she said.

'I know what will cool you down.' Apparently oblivious to the effect he was having on Kate, Fai strolled to a neighbouring stall and exchanged a few coins for two cups of bright pink liquid that seemed better suited to a twelve-year-old. On closer inspection, the liquid appeared to have black ants floating on its surface. Kate wrinkled up her nose.

'Basil seeds,' Fai explained. 'It also contains agar, a kind of seaweed, which thickens it to make it like a milkshake.' The promise of these natural ingredients was encouraging, and a tentative sip revealed that the ice-cold liquid was sweet but not overly so, while the seeds were encased in slippery, jelly-like balls that created a strangely pleasant sensation in her mouth. Kate was reminded of the fantasy candies in Enid Blyton's *Magic Faraway Tree*, and as she and Fai left the market, she felt herself slipping into a similarly dreamy and magical world.

This feeling was compounded by the exotic sights, sounds, and smells of Chinatown, which was an authentic world of incense-fragranced pagodas, street-side grocers selling unfamiliar ingredients, wind chimes tinkling in shop doorways, and old men in traditional dress playing mah-jong, the clunk of their tiles joining the hum of shoppers. Then there was the intoxicating presence of Fai at her side.

Without Tristan tagging along, Kate suddenly felt like she was on a date. Not even the sight of clouds gathering above them as the afternoon progressed, or of shop owners putting up hurricane shutters, could dull the sense of fluttery anticipation she felt. This swelled to a powerful surge of warmth through her body when Fai placed his hand on the small of her back to usher her into a restaurant, and Kate began to wonder if she shouldn't just throw caution to the intensifying wind. But then Fai achieved what the rain clouds had failed to do.

'So do you have a boyfriend in London?' he asked once they were settled at a paper-clothed table, fragrant steam rising from large bowls of fish broth in which dumplings bobbed.

'Boyfriend.' The word had been circling in the air around them like a fly, but Kate had been keeping it away with regular mental swats that were making her dizzy. Now it settled at the table, tainting the meal.

What is wrong with you? an inner voice scolded. *How can you be comparing Daniel to a fly when, in fact, he's exactly whom you would have asked your fairy godmother to conjure if you had one: your first Prince Charming with happily-ever-after potential?*

If he's so perfect, why can't you even contemplate hopping in the carriage and going to the ball then? asked another, more lusty voice.

Well, we all know it's not about him; it's the horse-and-carriage that I have issues with, Kate answered.

She didn't dispute that love and marriage went together like the proverbial horse and carriage; she just didn't think that this was necessarily a good thing, since inevitably the horse got tired of pulling that heavy old carriage or else its occupant began to take the horse for granted. It was only a matter of time.

Okay, glass slippers and church aisles aside, what about the fact that you couldn't even commit to moving in with Daniel? the lusty voice shot back. *Don't you think that's alerting you to something you're feeling deep down?*

Well, actually, I've been giving it some thought, and I do think that I probably really could live with Daniel.

'Probably really could'? Do you hear yourself?

No, really, I just have a couple more issues to iron out, and then I'll be there. I do want to be with Daniel. I love him. Even as she thought about him, a warm feeling swelled in her chest and solidified.

And this? You know you want to explore it. What happened to your adventurous spirit?

If Kate wasn't sure what *this* was, she was suddenly very sure that she shouldn't allow it to jeopardise what she had with Daniel. Her inner conflict about relationships always rose up to test her, but this time she wasn't going to let it win. *No, siree!* She shook her head.

'No?' Fai asked, misinterpreting her headshake.

'Sorry? Boyfriend? Yes, yes, I do,' she said, nodding emphatically.

'He's lucky,' Fai said.

'I'm not so sure about that.' Kate laughed nervously.

CHAPTER 4

Out to Lunch

Kate watched a corrugated iron roof being ripped from a house like a Post-it note by giant invisible fingers. Wind speeds were in the region of 140 kilometres per hour, the reporter on the TV screen said, which was demonstrated now by fuzzy footage of a petrol pump being plucked from its bed of cement like a carrot from well-turned soil.

She turned away from the TV and wandered over to the glass sliding doors, which were still being pelted with rain. Beyond them, the casuarina trees that had been standing tall when she had arrived at Paradise Bay were bent over sideways, their feathery tresses seemingly contorted by a giant turbo-powered hairdryer, while the same sea that had cradled her in its gentle embrace had shattered into sharp white shards.

'This is not your fault, okay?' Daniel had said when he had finally got through to Kate on the hotel's landline, all Internet and mobile phone connections having been down since the cyclone hit the day before. 'Do not beat yourself up about it. It's also not the end of the world.'

His words had been like aloe juice applied to a jellyfish sting, momentarily soothing the painful sensation left by a call from Roberta, who laid the blame firmly at Kate's door. 'I knew Mauritius was a bad idea,' she had shrieked down the line.

And Kate *did* feel responsible because she had known there was a chance of tropical cyclones in the Indian Ocean at this time of year, but since it was the very tail end of the season, she had decided to take a calculated risk. In hindsight, she should have searched elsewhere in the Caribbean, where hurricane season only kicked off in June and the weather was currently 'bloody marvellous', Roberta had pointed out.

There was a raging muddy river on the TV now, which, on closer inspection, Kate saw was actually a road. She wondered again if Sanjay would be able to ferry her to the White Sands hotel, as arranged. Since the barter deal required her to review all three hotels in the Sunshine Group, she would be spending the next two nights at the White Sands before moving on to the Roche d'Or, but she was particularly anxious to get there in time for a conference call, wherein she, Amber, Simon and Roberta would discuss contingency plans. She wanted to have Roberta where she could see her during these discussions.

'No problem,' Sanjay had said dismissively over a crackly line. 'This is nothing.' And true to his word, only twenty minutes later than the allotted time, he was in the lobby, bedraggled, windswept, and wearing his signature smile.

'I've never seen rain like this,' Kate said as Sanjay's car waded along the main road, its wheels submerged in water. 'And I live in London, where rain comes from.' She watched a steel drum drift past, a couple of chickens perched perilously on top, probably wishing they were ducks. 'Are you sure your car's up to this?'

'This is nothing,' Sanjay said for the second time that day. 'You are being enormously lucky that it is not hitting the island directly, like it was five years ago. Cyclone Hadagada ... that was bad.' His head bobbed from side to side like a metronome.

'I can't imagine anything being much worse than this,' Kate said. She was feeling anything but lucky right now.

'People were dying, 80,000 were losing their homes, 250 million rupees worth of damage. We were having half our house washed away.'

'I'm sorry to hear that,' Kate said. 'What about this time? Is your home all right?'

Sanjay waved a hand dismissively. 'We're having some small *flooding*, but luckily my wife has always been insisting that we are keeping the plastic covering on all the chairs, so we are not having too much damage.' A customary chuckle followed, and Kate thought that if he could laugh this off, then so should she. Having her castle in the sky eroded was nothing compared to real homes being washed away. Still, she couldn't help but mourn a little the death of her plans for a sizzling summer shoot and, very likely, the imminent demise of her career.

Perhaps noticing the frown flickering across her forehead, Sanjay added, 'But I am of course understanding that the tourists are not being very happy when they're paying so much money for paradise, especially those who are here on their honeymoon.'

In a way, this trip was meant to have been a honeymoon, Kate thought, because her relationship with *Be* was the only one to which she had ever truly committed, and she had hoped that this assignment would solder the bond with her new role. If, for Marilyn Monroe, diamonds could be relied upon to 'pay the rental' when beauty had faded and lovers had run off, Kate's career was her rock – because, 'square-cut or pear-shaped', she figured it wouldn't lose its shape as quickly as her mother had done after giving birth to three children in quick succession, with the result being that her husband had gone in search of a shapelier model. *Well, so much for that theory.*

Kate was jolted out of her descent into despair when the car shuddered violently and slowed down. Sanjay pumped the accelerator and turned the key several times. The car coughed, spluttered, and then died.

Kate looked at him in dismay as, unmoving, he stared at the dashboard.

'Battery,' he said. 'What to do? I'd better be getting it to the side of the road, and then I'll call my wife's cousin's father-in-law, who is something of a mechanic.' He moved the gear into neutral and then wrestled the door open. As it yielded, the sound of the downpour reached a crescendo, like applause at the end of a virtuoso performance, and rain swept in before Sanjay's bulky frame blocked its course. He leant all his weight against the door frame, holding the door open with one arm and turning the steering wheel with the other. The car barely moved.

Kate looked down at her three-quarter-length, dry-clean-only, bronze cargo pants and hesitated. She then looked at Sanjay, who, cheeks puffed out and wheezing, looked at risk of suffering a similar fate to his car's, which was enough to propel her out into the rain. Unable to hold the door open against the deluge, she moved to the back of the car and put all her weight against the bumper. Solid sheets of rain pummelled her back and shoulders as if she were standing under a gushing waterfall. Muddy water splashed up, instantly turning her bronze trousers to brown. But rather than being upset, she suddenly felt an overwhelming sense of release. As the car slowly inched forward, she started to laugh, quietly at first and then madly, allowing her laughter to gurgle up and merge with the roar of the rain.

* * *

Two hours later, Kate walked into the White Sands' lobby, looking like she had swum ashore from a shipwreck. Drenched and windswept, with her trousers now puckered and her vest stretched shamelessly across her chest, she turned heads as she squelched through the airy, Moorish-domed space, leaving a trail of mud on the white marble tiles.

As she stepped up to the reception desk, the man behind it blinked exaggeratedly.

'Kate Richmond,' she said, pushing a damp strand of hair out of her eyes. Having laboriously straightened her honey-blonde waves in preparation for her reunion with the fashion team, she realised that her hair was now pasted to her cheeks like tangled seaweed. 'I'm with *Be*,' she added, eliciting an 'Oh' that seemed to say, *That is even more distasteful than your appearance.* Roberta had obviously been spreading her good cheer here too. Kate glanced down at her feet, where a puddle was forming, and a giggle escaped as she imagined what she must look like to the designer-clad couple beside her. They averted their stares when Kate looked their way, but she didn't care. Having been paralysed by fear and panic, she found that her mini adventure, culminating with a tractor ride, had released something inside her.

'I have a message for you,' the man at reception said, handing her a notecard. She recognised Roberta's looping letters.

> *I presume you've been held up by this weather. I couldn't wait, so I had the call without you. We're going through to lunch at the Coral Terrace now. Meet us there. Or give me a call if you're later than two o'clock and I'll tell you what we've decided.*
>
> *—RV*

Not liking the tone of finality in the last sentence, Kate felt a tightening of whatever had been released in her core. She hurried upstairs to her room, where she showered quickly and, after pulling on a pair of jeans with a sparkly Juicy Couture T-shirt, and sliding her feet into her flood-proof Havaianas flip-flops, made her way to the restaurant.

A sanctuary of cool minimalism, the Coral Terrace was awash with marooned sun worshippers. The sombre mood was only marginally brightened by a banquette along the back wall scattered with vibrant orange-pink silk cushions, glass vases dripping orchids, and an imposing chandelier that was an oversized facsimile of an unbleached piece of reddish coral hanging above. She found the team seated at a table along a bank of windows, currently protected by hurricane shutters, against which the suicidal rain threw itself noisily.

'So they finally let you out of Disney World,' Roberta said from behind a pair of large Jackie O sunglasses, which she had teamed with a cream turban to movie-star effect.

'Hello', 'Hi', 'Hi', 'Hiya, Kate,' the others chimed in a flat baritone as she sat down in the only empty chair at the table, which was, not surprisingly, next to Roberta.

'Lovely day, huh?' Tristan said.

'It's a whole lot brighter for your shirt,' Kate said. A Hawaiian classic featuring surfers riding waves interspersed with large purple flowers, it was like an oasis in the desert of neutrals worn by the rest of the team.

'I'm sorry I missed the call, Roberta; our car broke down and my mobile's still not working. How did it go?'

'As well as I've learnt to expect on this disastrous expedition,' Roberta said.

A waiter handed Kate a menu. Momentarily distracted, she glanced around the table and noted that everyone had eaten, apart from Tristan, who was finishing off a banana split, and Tatyana, who was pushing lettuce leaves around her plate with a fork. The model's face was still slightly puffy, but her skin looked a lot better now, and with her hair scraped back into a brown floral bandanna, she almost looked like cover-girl material. Next to her, Marius was downing an espresso, while Roberta; her assistant, Kirsten; the make-up artist, Tamsyn; and April were all sipping herbal tea.

Kate craved a glass of Sauvignon Blanc, but there was no alcohol in sight amid these glum faces, so she ordered a Pellegrino. Ravenous after the morning's exertions, she also ordered a smoked marlin salad, which she pounced on the minute it arrived.

'I don't know how you can eat that,' April said, flicking her auburn ponytail streaked with gold. In glowing good health, the second model boasted a slightly tanned face with a sprinkling of freckles, and a Lauren Hutton gap in her teeth.

Kate had only just managed to navigate a morsel of paper-thin heaven into her mouth and was savouring the fish's smoky flavour. 'Sorry?' She wondered if, unbeknown to her, marlin contained large stores of fat.

'They're such beautiful, courageous fish. Have you seen the way they fight for their lives?' April said.

'I'm, like, soooo with you on that,' Marius said. 'It's, like, soooo cruel. And the bad karma that must get into your body when something has struggled and suffered so much!' Kate watched the male model in the contingent turn his blue eyes on April, evidently seeing her in a whole new light. As he held her in his gaze, Kate took advantage of the moment to sneak another mouthful.

'I can't believe you'd be sitting there eating that if you'd ever watched marlin fishing.' April's eyes were back on Kate, forcing her to swallow quickly without chewing. 'Not after seeing the pain in their eyes.' The model narrowed her own emerald green eyes accusingly at Kate, who was tempted to say that those creases could turn to crow's feet, which someone whose face really was her fortune could ill afford.

'It's probably hypocritical,' she tried, 'but I prefer not to think of the actual living fish while I'm eating it. When it's on my plate, sliced or diced, I simply see it as delicious, nourishing food. And, you know, like it or not, marlin are just part of the food chain. They don't think twice about eating tuna and mackerel.' But April's words had now given life to the tasty morsels on Kate's plate, which became less appetising as she recalled TV footage of marlin skimming through the water at the end of a line behind a boat, thrashing about to save their lives. Kate always felt sorry for the desperate, graceful fish, and contempt for the men – it was almost always men – who wrestled with their fishing rods, salivating at the prospect of the kill. She sometimes wondered if God had implanted a predatory gene in men's make-up to ensure that they would always be able to bring home the bacon – or the marlin – and, since the thrill of the hunt extended beyond fish and game, to perpetuate the human race, whereas women were programmed to blindly take the bait time and again.

'I suppose you'd eat dolphin too?' April said.

'I wouldn't, actually; I have a policy of not eating anything with a higher IQ than certain people I know.' Now unable to eat her marlin salad, Kate discovered that hunger was making her nasty.

'I'm, like, a total vegan,' Marius said, running tanned hands through his polished mahogany hair.

'Me too,' April said so smugly that Kate had to retaliate.

'You probably don't read much,' she said, 'but there's a book called *The Secret Life of Plants* that claims flora feel pain too. And in India there's a religious sect that disallows the eating of root vegetables because of the millions of creatures massacred during harvesting. Snack on *that* next time you snack on a carrot stick.'

Tristan was watching Kate, slack-jawed, but April's attention span didn't currently extend beyond Marius, so Kate dropped the topic.

'I hate to break up the Greenpeace convention,' Roberta said, 'but right now we have more important things to save than a marlin.' If she had caught the lusty look that passed between the two 'model' environmentalists, her outsized dark glasses made it impossible to tell. 'Kate, God knows if this weather will ever improve, so it's time for contingency plans. And since you weren't here for the call, we've made a few without you.'

'Did you tell Simon that the airline's agreed to change our flights at no extra cost if we extend?' Kate asked. 'And that the hotel will give us extra days on the current basis?'

'I did, but it's immaterial,' Roberta said, 'because he's not prepared to pay any additional fees for this lot.' She glared at April and Marius in turn.

'So he won't let us extend at all?' Kate asked, horrified. 'But that's crazy. ... It's so short-sighted.'

'You don't have to tell me that, but it's his final word. In fact, he's not prepared to plough another penny into this trip.'

Didn't I predict that this would be the case, not so long ago? Kate wanted to say.

'And by the way, that includes paying the supplement for the upgrade. He says forget about it.'

'But Amber gave it the green light; we agreed to it.'

'*I* didn't agree to anything,' Roberta said, leaning back in her chair with her arms crossed. 'Anyway, as I've said before, they should never have put us in that hellhole in the first place.'

'Roberta, are you out to lunch? You know as well as I do that we're obligated to pay. They could sue us.'

'Let them try. Really, look at this mess. They should be compensating *us*. I'm not sure how we're going to put out a magazine at all, let alone a bumper summer issue.'

'You can't blame them for a cyclone,' Kate said. Then, realising that she was getting nowhere, she changed tack. 'And it's not over yet. The weather report said it's going to start clearing tomorrow, so we should have a couple of good days to work with.' She nodded at the hovering waiter to remove her unfinished salad.

'Depending on your definition of good,' Roberta said. 'Have you thought about what the beaches are going to look like after all this rain and wind? And that village where we were going to shoot resort wear? I imagine it's a total shambles. Accept it: this whole trip is a washout!'

'We do have quite a lot in the bag already,' Tristan said. 'We've made a big dent in bikinis, and Beach Accessories is more or less a wrap.'

'I think less,' said Roberta. 'And what about the cover? We don't have anything that vaguely fits the fashion-in-motion brief.' To reflect *Be*'s lifestyle-oriented approach, the covers showed women in action rather than in static poses – doing yoga for the spring 'detox' edition, sipping Pimm's on a riverbank to tie in with 'the season', or partying in a spangled dress for New Year.

Roberta sighed heavily. 'It's lovely that you two are looking on the bright side, but do you hear that?' She cocked her head towards the violently rattling hurricane shutters, which sounded like they were under machine-gun fire.

Kate began to think that perhaps *she* rather than Roberta was out to lunch for believing this was salvageable. But, given everything that was riding on the issue and the pressures that the magazine was under, she couldn't just let it go. 'It's make or break time,' Amber had said, and come hell or high water – quite literally in this case – Kate had to make it work. She closed her eyes, and the sound of the rain drumming on the shutters filled her head. This brought to mind the rain pounding her back earlier that day, and running in rivulets down her face and arms, the power and beauty of it. Ideas suddenly began to flow.

'You know, maybe we're approaching this in the wrong way,' she said, opening her eyes. 'We're thinking of how we're going to get around the cyclone, but maybe it's a question of working with it instead. On the way over here, I was thinking that there's something very beautiful about seeing nature in the raw; there's an honesty and integrity to it. We could harness that to give Fashion a real, edgy feel. Pristine dreamscapes are such a cliché anyway.' Roberta opened her mouth to say something, but Kate didn't let her speak. 'I also have an idea that could work for resort wear. You're right about Trou d'Eau Douce; it's a mess. But Port Louis market would work brilliantly; it's colourful and vibrant, and will suit that whole 1960s hippy chic thing you've got going. A lot of it is also covered, so even if the weather persists we could shoot there.'

'It's a good idea,' Tristan said. 'It might even be better than the village – and you know how much I loved those chic shacks, so that's worth something.'

God bless the Queen.

'Covered, you say?' Roberta said. 'If any of the so-called covered markets I've visited are anything to go by, then I imagine its excuse for a roof will be leaking like a sieve. But whatever we come up with, the fact remains that we've lost days and still have a major time issue. This means a few things have to go, and Amber has decided that one of the easiest things to lose is the food section.' The pronouncement popped out of Roberta's mouth as lightly as a bubble, and hit Kate like a bullet.

'What?' she said. 'You can't be serious.'

'If I had my way, your décor shoot would be going the same way. But Amber wants to hang onto that since we can't magic up a colonial beach house in London. The food, on the other hand, can be shot in studio or some garden with island props.'

'But that's not our style,' Kate said, 'and Amber's always maintained that food's as important to the mix as fashion; we're about living, not just looking good, remember? I can't believe she agreed to this.' One of the ways that *Be* had set out to distinguish itself from other women's magazines was to couple inspiration with lifestyle-enhancing tools. In keeping with this aim, Kate's pages didn't just serve up a collection of recipes but presented food in interesting social settings, with tips on entertaining, table settings, and which wines to serve. Last summer, there had been a finger lunch on a yacht in Devon, and for New Year she had featured one of London's celebrated chefs throwing a black-and-white cocktail party, at which the plates had adhered to the dress code too, from fried halloumi wrapped in squid-ink-dyed pasta to miniature dark and white chocolate mousses. But this was going to be her pièce de résistance: a seafood barbecue served up in a private cove to members of the fashion team masquerading as people who actually ate. She couldn't bear to let it go, not only because she wanted to see her vision roll out, but also because she truly believed that losing it would let the magazine down.

She looked around the table for support but realised that she had no allies here. Tamsyn was filing her nails into an advanced state of perfection; Tatyana was snapping toothpicks; Kirsten and April were engaged in a whispered conversation; and Marius sat with a vacant look on his flawless face. Tristan simply shrugged defeat when Kate caught his eye.

Roberta got up. 'Feel free to discuss this with Amber yourself,' she said. 'I, for one, have an appointment with a charming masseur called St Jean who offers room service.' She looked at Marius in a way that left no doubt that she had caught the stolen glances. She then glided out of the room like an expensive motor launch, leaving Kate like a becalmed yacht in her wake.

'I'm sorry, Kate,' Tristan said, 'but you know my position – caught between the devil and the deep blue sea.'

'Or the deep grey sea,' Kate said, slumping at the table. 'I understand, but this is just so disappointing.'

'At least you don't have to work with her 24/7,' Kirsten said. 'I think we all need a stiff drink. A few G&Ts will get lost on the expense form among all the massages she's having.'

'God, I hope she isn't expensing them,' Kate said. 'And I'm sorry to have to remind you that alcohol is also for our own accounts.'

'Well, the sauna doesn't cost a thing, if anyone would like to come and sweat out some of this bad karma.' April gave Marius a suggestive look.

'I go to my rrrom,' Tatyana said. She stood up to reveal a tiny pair of white shorts and endless legs that made Kate feel a little less sorry for her. 'I need to make coll to London. I veel see you all laterrr.'

Kate too had a very important 'coll' to make to London, so, excusing herself, she hurried back to her room, where she lit up a cigarette and took a few deep drags before dialling Amber's mobile number.

Amber picked up immediately. 'Kate. I thought you'd call.' Her tone indicated that this was an unwelcome inevitability. 'I imagine you're upset about Food, but it really is the only solution.'

'It just seems like such a bad idea,' Kate said. 'We've been getting such good feedback on the section – our last market research showed that over 35 per cent of readers buy the magazine specifically for the sections on food and lifestyle. A UK shoot will ruin the whole balance.'

'Balance is a luxury right now,' Amber snapped. 'I just hope to goodness that we can get something – anything – on the page. I'm beyond furious that Simon won't give us the extra days, which is shooting ourselves in the foot, frankly. But it is what it is, which means we have to work smartly, and Roberta says she needs everything she's got for Fashion. I *would* like to try for Décor too, if the weather allows, although Roberta's not hopeful. Is there any sign of an improvement on the horizon?'

Kate shared the forecast that things would start clearing on the following day. She also told Amber about her idea to shoot Fashion at Port Louis market, for which Amber commended her. Detecting a softening in her tone, Kate decided to put in one last plea for the food shoot: 'Could we not possibly keep things open and squeeze it in at the end if there's time?'

Amber wasn't budging. 'Look, I agree that it's a pity to compromise,' she said, 'but the fact is that most of our advertising is riding on the fashion pages, so it's imperative that those shine, and I don't want to rattle Roberta any more than she is. Please work with me on this, Kate, and let Food go. It's far more important for you to keep things under control and watch the expenses. Oh, on that subject, did Roberta mention that we can't pay for the upgrade? Simon's adamant. Could you make that your focus and let me know where we are?'

The call ended abruptly when Amber's 12.30 appointment arrived. Kate put down the phone, feeling drained and despondent. *If you can't beat them, join them,* she thought, opening the minibar fridge and reaching for the gin. Everything else was on the rocks, so she might as well be too.

After downing two gin and tonics in quick succession, she drifted off to sleep, later to be wakened by the phone next to her bed.

'Yes?' she said groggily. The room was now dark. *What time is it?*

'Hi. You sound different.' *Fai.* 'I've been thinking about you and wanted to see if you were all right. This weather must be making things difficult.'

Kate told him that *difficult* was an understatement. She then found herself regurgitating the afternoon's events, finishing off with the demise of her food shoot. She suddenly felt tearful and wished it were Daniel on the other end of the line.

'Would it help if you could find another photographer to do the shoot?' Fai asked. 'I know someone.'

'Oh,' Kate said. It hadn't occurred to her to look for an alternative photographer on the island. 'It might,' she said, 'but I don't think we could afford it; we're already stretched.'

'He would probably do it for free,' Fai said. 'He's an old friend, and I know he's desperate for international exposure.'

Desperate was not a strong selling point. 'That's kind, but I don't think my editor would go for that,' Kate said. 'She's ... tricky.'

'He's good. His family owns the oldest photo studio in Chinatown. Why don't you at least talk to him?' Fai said. 'Have a look at his work and then decide. You've got nothing to lose.'

'True,' Kate said. 'Maybe it's worth a try.' *A drowning woman has to clutch at even the most fragile twig stretched out to her, after all.*

'I'm also calling to find out if you'd like to go out for a drink in Grand Baie tomorrow,' Fai said.

'I would love to,' Kate said without hesitation. It had been a day on choppy seas, and Fai was an inviting harbour. She needed the mooring.

Main Course

CHAPTER 5

Bananas Flambé

As Kate and Fai approached Grand Baie, the sugar cane on either side of the road gave way to shadowy eucalyptus trees, glistening with moisture from the departed storm. Their branches reached out to each other over the road so that the moon cast eerie shadows on the tarmac ahead of them.

'Thanks for putting me in touch with Serge.' Kate had to shout over the Creole music blaring out of Fai's car speakers.

Fai turned down the volume. 'Do you like his work?' He glanced at her and then returned his gaze to the road, giving Kate the opportunity to look at his finely drawn silhouette traced in silvery moonlight. He had a dark freckle just above his lip, she noticed, wondering again if it had been wise to accept this invitation.

'I think it's excellent,' she said honestly.

Having been told by Serge over the phone that he specialised in weddings and tourist brochures, she had anticipated a portfolio of mediocre, clichéd fare when she opened his website, but instead she had scrolled through real flavour. Admittedly, there had been few images with a culinary bent, but Kate had a gut feel that he was the real deal, and so had arranged to meet him at his studio the next day.

'Serge appreciates the opportunity,' Fai said.

'I hope we can do it then,' Kate said, 'but my editor still hasn't given me the go-ahead.' In truth, Amber had said no to the shoot before it was out of the starting gate. She couldn't imagine that a local photographer – a *free* one at that – would be up to the magazine's standards. And anyway, they didn't have time to waste on this. Kate should stop thinking about it, she said, and make sure that everything else was on track, particularly the finances. End of discussion.

But Amber hadn't seen Serge's portfolio, so Kate had decided to make one last-ditch attempt to convince her. She was now working on a persuasive email to accompany a link to his website. Surely when Amber saw the portfolio, she too would realise that it was worth taking their chances.

Her resolve had only been compounded while watching the resort-wear shoot in Port Louis market unfold that afternoon. She and Tristan had gone ahead of the crew to scout the market for the driest and most attractive spots, and then she had stood back and watched her vision unfold just as she had known it would. The market had been in a state of disarray, with puddles everywhere and buckets of water catching drips from gaping holes in the roof, but this had just served to offset the bright and beautiful fashion. It had also brought some fun and energy to the images.

In one memorable shot, April, surrounded by colourful saris, leapt over a puddle, giggling as she held up the hem of her maxi dress, trailed by Marius balancing a large watermelon on one shoulder. And in Kate's favourite, April and Tatyana, dressed in hot pants with stilettos, sheltered from the drizzle at a bus stop, flanked by local shoppers with boxes of fruit and vegetables. Shoots had always been one of Kate's favourite parts of the job. She loved watching ideas and tactile elements translate into pictures; how, working with a photographer and her own well-honed intuition, she could create a story that would titillate her readers. While not directing this shoot, she had almost salivated at the thought of how the island elements would translate on the food pages too. It was a sensual feeling, bordering on sexual.

'It could change his life to have something in an international magazine,' Fai said. 'He's applied for magazines in South Africa, but they all tell him that he needs editorial experience.'

'God, I hope he understands that nothing's guaranteed,' Kate said. Up until now, she had only been thinking about saving her shoot, but suddenly she realised that she was knitting other people's hopes into her technicolour dream coat, perhaps only to be unravelled ultimately. 'I don't think I was totally clear on the phone.' *You know you weren't totally clear on the phone.* 'I was just so impressed by his photos. And when I get excited about something, I can get carried away and speak really fast, so even my good friends don't understand a word I'm saying.'

'Sorry, I didn't get that.'

'I'm just really worried …' The moon illuminated the glimmer of a smile on Fai's face and his eyes gleamed as they darted across to catch hers. 'Oh.' Kate realised he was teasing her. *Lighten up.*

'Don't worry, he knows it's not definite,' Fai said.

'I hope you're right,' Kate said, 'because, as I said, my editor's difficult, so there's a very good chance that I've got his hopes up for nothing. Part of me says I should have let it go right at the beginning, but there's a little voice inside my head that says, "Why settle for acceptable when it could be sensational?"' Kate sometimes wished she could go with the flow more – it would be far less stressful – but the compulsive fear that drove her obsession with career made going with the flow impossible. She felt that if she made one slip-up on her quest for success, or let her standards drop, she would tumble down a rabbit hole and find herself barefoot and pregnant in a kitchen in Cornwall. Of course, disobeying Amber's orders might turn out to put her on the ultimate wrong footing, so she must tread carefully.

'I don't think you should apologise for being strong-willed,' Fai said. 'There's a Chinese proverb that goes, "Great souls have wills; feeble ones, only wishes."'

'I like that. I wonder if I could get it on a fridge magnet.' Kate was always on the lookout for inspiring quotes. She collected them in her head, in journals, and on her silver Smeg fridge at home, which was littered with magnets with sayings like *Life is not about finding yourself. It's about creating yourself*; *Luck happens when preparation meets opportunity*; and *Why should I get married? I didn't do anything wrong.* 'Seriously, though, thank you for making my pig-headedness seem noble,' she added, thinking that if Fai could read her mind, he would know that she had a few wishes too.

They were quiet for a while and the music took over, the twangy guitar and drumbeat drifting on the exotic night air, filling Kate's head with a sense of abandon. The beat was in sync with the accelerated rhythm of her heart, and the passionate French lyrics seemed to be taking on a physical presence inside her like a hallucinogen.

'J'entends des tam-tams dans la nuit. Dans ma tête souffle un vent de folie; irresistible tentation, qui me devore. J'en perds la raison. Inavouable obsession …'

It did indeed feel that a wild wind was taking over her being and that, whatever her mind said, her body might follow this 'irresistible temptation' wherever it led.

'*Voila le diable dans la maison. Voila le diable dans la maison*' ('The devil in the house, the devil in the house'). The chorus reminded Kate of her shadowy depths and inner demons. She pitied Daniel right now for his commitment to her, considering this wave she was surfing.

'I like this music,' she said, partly to break its hypnotic effects. 'It's so passionate and alive. It has real soul.'

'It does,' Fai said. 'You can feel it.'

Kate wondered if he was feeling it to quite the same extent that she was.

'There's a saying here,' Fai continued, 'that the Indian culture is the island's head because the Indians are in government; the French culture, its mouth because French is the language most widely spoken; English, its limbs because British laws govern business; and Creole, its soul.'

'And the Chinese culture?' Kate asked.

'You could say that we feed and clothe the island because we have the monopoly on retail,' Fai said. 'That one's all mine, by the way.'

Kate laughed. 'Is this music all local?'

'It's a mix of Creole songs from around the world – that last song's by a French band originally from the West Indies called La Compagnie Creole – but they all have their roots in the slave culture, so they often share themes of love, loss, and longing.'

Longing. Now there was a theme Kate could relate to, and even more so when Fai's hand brushed her leg as he retrieved a CD from the glove compartment, setting every fibre in her being vibrating, just like those twangy guitar strings.

* * *

The club took Kate back to her teenage Saturday nights, when a DJ and a glitter ball transformed the drab community hall into a dance and make-out zone. Outside, three young women in short skirts leant against a car talking and smoking, and close by a young man sat side-saddle on a motorbike with a girl spliced between his legs, their lips glued together. On closer inspection, Kate determined that they all looked closer in age to her youthful community-hall compatriots than to her thirty-one-year-old self. Glancing at Fai, she was reminded that he too was certainly a few years younger than her, and she suddenly felt foolish for playing childish games. Once again, she tried to banish the fluttery feeling invading her solar plexus.

It was smoky inside, crowded, and very low-key. There was a bar on one side, and plastic chairs and tables, all occupied, around a dance floor. After briefly scanning the room, Fai spotted a couple he knew, and Kate followed him to their table, feeling at once relieved and disappointed that they wouldn't be alone. Fai introduced Ajit, who was a dive instructor at Paradise Bay, and his girlfriend, Pria. Then he crossed over to the bar, returning with two pale cocktails. As Kate watched him approach, cool in jeans and a black mandarin-collar shirt, the feeling she had suppressed returned unbidden and stayed with her, full of nervous energy as they drank the intoxicating mixture of white rum, green lemons, and cane syrup over crushed ice, then took their chances on the dance floor.

The music was clearly pitched to please everyone a little – and probably no one a lot – ranging from 1990s numbers to recent hits and misses in French and English. When 'I Want to Know What Love Is' belted out, it brought Daniel into the space, as Foreigner was one of his favourite bands. Although this version of the 1980s hit was by Mariah Carey, Kate felt Daniel's presence and was reminded that she and he were a desirable duet on so many levels. She was momentarily glad that Fai was apparently treating the information about the boyfriend in London with the respect it deserved, but at the same time she was all too aware that if he did make a move, she would go wherever he led.

After they had danced for a while, Fai mimed a drinking motion with his hand, and when Kate nodded, he returned to the bar to get another round of cocktails, while she rejoined Ajit and Pria. Watching him from the other side of the room, she saw a tall and lithe woman with short dark hair approach him and kiss him on both cheeks. She looked like she knew him intimately, touching him as she talked and leaning in close, her lips brushing his ear. *The music is loud, but not that loud*, Kate thought, and that unbidden feeling inside wanted to march across the room and tell the woman to take a hike.

Fai is not your boyfriend, her conscience scolded. *That would be Daniel back in London, where you live and where your future lies. Think of all you've got, all you stand to lose. You know that people who play with fire get burnt.*

Kate was well aware of this fact but jealousy had just handed her a box of matches and when, back at the table, Fai reached for her hand, he wordlessly presented a very strong case indeed for playing with fire. It could have such delicious results, after all, her inner defence argued. *If further evidence be needed, consider the case of the misdirected flame that set a pan of crêpes, Grand Marnier, and orange juice alight in a Monte Carlo restaurant in 1865, giving birth to crêpes Suzette and making a hero of the waiter, Marcel Charpentier, who had made the miraculous mistake.*

This mistake had been the inspiration for Escoffier's famous cherries jubilee, Kate knew, which were flamed in brandy and kirsch; not forgetting Brennan's bananas Foster, which had been a favourite treat for Kate when she was growing up. She remembered how she and her sisters would watch in anticipation as her mother fried bananas with butter, brown sugar, and cinnamon, and then doused them in rum before finally setting them alight to thrilling effect. But the anticipation she had felt back then was nothing compared to what she felt as she and Fai left the club.

Kate had learnt that the flame applied to the alcohol in a flambé changed the chemistry of the fruit, intensifying its flavour, and as her feelings simmered below the surface, she thought how delectable these would be if Fai put a flame to them.

Just consider what a shame it would be if Charpentier had never made that mistake, a wanton voice inside urged. *Sometimes mistakes aren't mistakes, or – what was that quotation on the fridge magnet? Your best teacher is your last mistake.*

Fai unlocked the passenger door of his car, but instead of opening it he turned around and leant against it, putting his hands around Kate's waist. 'I really like you, Kate,' he said. *Like* sounded so harmless compared to what she was feeling. Then his hands moved up to her neck. 'Are you okay with this?' he asked. *Okay?* Kate nodded, not trusting herself to speak. Her mouth and throat were dry, which meant she would sound like the frog rather than the princess.

In order for a flambé to succeed, the alcohol needs to be heated, but not overheated to the point of evaporation, and Kate's feelings were clearly at that optimum point, because when Fai finally kissed her, the flame took immediately and heat licked through her whole body.

The two remained standing together against the car for a while, Kate savouring every delicious moment, until Fai pulled away and asked, 'Would you like a nightcap? At my place?' And with thoughts of something far more satisfying than a cocktail playing on Kate's mind, they drove south below a sky turning from black to navy.

As they finally passed through the familiar gates of Paradise Bay, Kate could barely breathe, and as she followed Fai up a concrete staircase in a nondescript building at the back of the property, she hardly noticed the steps beneath her feet, propelled by the thought of his skin against hers.

They entered a small studio flat dimly lit by an outside light that spilled through the open balcony door. Fai flicked a switch, which set a ceiling fan whirring into motion, leaving the room in semi-darkness. He then turned around and kissed her, causing her legs to buckle slightly under her. Past the point of resistance, Kate stepped back until her calves pressed against the double bed that almost filled the room, and there was nowhere to go but down. She sat on the edge of the mattress and unbuckled Fai's belt while he ran his fingers through her hair, pulling it with a gentle tug as she savoured him in her mouth. Then, hungry for more, she pulled his jeans down and he pulled her halter top over her head before tenderly pushing her back onto the bed, where he removed her bra and brought his cool lips to her breast, filling his mouth with it. Allowing her conveniently buckle-free wedges to drop to the floor, Kate ripped his shirt off, popping buttons everywhere, and ran her hands over his body, which was as smooth as a sea-worn pebble. Then she sank her hands into his hair, as black as volcanic rock but soft as silk, while he adeptly unbuttoned her white jeans and finally coaxed her lacy thong to the floor. She moaned as he felt her wetness. Arching her back, she held his lean, naked body between her thighs, inviting him to enter her; and at last, he was inside, his body lapping hers. She felt like she was swimming in warm, tropical waters, being carried out to sea on a strong current. She didn't care if she ever found her way back to shore.

CHAPTER 6

Breakfast and Epiphanies

The phone woke Kate, and Fai's voice poured down the line into her like strong, hot espresso, perking up all her senses. This was the wake-up call she had requested, he said. He hoped she had slept well.

Kate replaced the handset and stretched, letting the memories of the night before wash over her like a warm tide. Her body throbbed as her mobile phone beeped, announcing a text, and she lazily reached out for it.

'Hi, beautiful. Hope meeting with photographer went well & all set. Off to do cellar assessment, so will call later. Love you.' Daniel surfed into her consciousness on a wave of guilt. Not sure how to explain the date with Fai, Kate had lied to Daniel the previous afternoon, telling him that she was meeting the photographer that night – and indicating ill intentions from the start. Now, she clamped the palm of her hand on her forehead as if, like a plunger, it could extract the remorse from her brain along with everything that had got her into this situation in the first place.

Why now, after almost two years of such blissful unity, of finally believing that you have it in you to do this, to be in – and enjoy being in – a committed relationship?

Because, the answer swiftly came, *once sex with Fai was on the table, resisting him would not have been so much like resisting a particularly delicious dish as preventing one's salivary glands from responding to the smell and vision of it – as unavoidable as a natural reflex.*

So it was just lust then? It felt like more; she had resisted men before, but with Fai it was different. Where did lust end and love begin, and where did Daniel fit into this? Kate really wanted to believe that Daniel was the Adam to her Eve, which meant that Fai was perhaps the quintessentially irresistible juicy apple or pomme d'amour to challenge her. Well, she hadn't just taken a bite; she had made puree.

A light knock on the door interrupted her thoughts, followed by a muffled 'Room service,' reminding her that she had ticked a few boxes on the in-room breakfast menu. Glad for the diversion, she emerged from the luxury white linen sheets and wrapped a white cotton robe around her body to greet the waiter at the door.

'Would you like it here or outside?' he asked, brandishing a huge wooden tray.

'Outside,' she said, leading him across the room, enjoying the cool tiles underfoot, and opening the double doors onto a partly cloudy, breezy day. Once the waiter had laid the table, Kate sank into the amply cushioned armchair and watched him pour steaming coffee from a small, heavy silver pot into a white china cup, leaving her to add milk, which she was pleased to find was hot. Taking a sip of the rich, reviving drink, she leant back and took in her altered surroundings. Like smudged make-up, puffy eyes, and blotchy skin after a heavy night out, there were signs of the cyclone everywhere, despite the hotel's best efforts to cleanse and tweeze away its effects. Near the shoreline, a group of men were at work with rakes and spades, removing the tangled seaweed, reeds, and driftwood that littered the beach, but there wasn't a lot they could do about the murky water, which remained choppy beyond the reef. As she nibbled on slices of papaya and artfully carved pineapple, Kate wondered how the shoot was going and if Roberta was working with the cyclone aftermath rather than around it. She had her doubts, but she hoped that the absence of telephone calls was a sign that things were at least not intolerable.

This is certainly not intolerable, she thought as she folded back a starched white napkin and removed a pain au chocolat from the pastry basket. It was warm and soft, the chocolate inside neither liquid nor solid. It dissolved in her mouth in minutes. 'Yummy,' she said out loud as she reached for the second one, savouring it as her mind drifted to Fai and her dilemma about seeing him again tonight. Throbbing with desire at the mere thought of him, her body cheered the motion, while her mind shouted from the sidelines that it wasn't a good idea. *It definitely isn't if I value my relationship with Daniel,* she thought, *which I do.* She noncommittally sprinkled the remains of her second pain au chocolat onto the ground for two fat waiting sparrows. 'If only you were bluebirds,' she said, wishing she were somewhere over the rainbow in a place where she could indulge her fantasies with no repercussions back home.

Her mobile phone rang and brought her back to earth.

'Save me,' the voice on the other end said.

'Kirsten?'

'I'm either going to kill her or myself,' the fashion assistant whispered.

'What's she done now?'

'*She's* done nothing – *I'm* the one bringing the whole swimsuit shoot crashing down because I've forgotten the star bikini. She absolutely did not tell me to bring it, but she's adamant. I get the feeling there's some very desirable freebie at stake.' Alarm bells went off in Kate's head as Kirsten's comment reminded her that there had been no further word from Laidback Living about her own forgotten items, which had been grounded in London as a result of the cyclone. Her contact in marketing had promised to chase them up but hadn't come back to her.

'So what are you up to right now?' Kirsten asked.

'You don't want to know,' Kate said. *What are you doing indulging in sexual escapades and leisurely breakfasts when there are pressing matters to attend to?* she asked herself. *Do you actually want to have a job to go back to?*

'Well, do you mind if I join you for a bit? Roberta's called in a diving team to clear away some of the debris in the lagoon, so we've been given a couple of hours to play.'

'A diving team? You're not serious?' Kirsten didn't reply. 'Oh God, you are. Ka-ching; that woman has serious budgeting issues. I mean, really, it's admirable that she regards her work as a higher art form, but she's not Michelangelo, for Christ's sake.' Kate immediately felt a stab of guilt for saying the *C* word; her Catholic mother would have put hot mustard on her tongue by now.

'Well, you'll be glad to know that she has kind of been working your windswept feel,' Kirsten said. 'Driftwood is a strong presence; the water, though, just looks dirty and ugly. So can I pop over? I thought maybe we could get in a bit of sunbathing.'

Kate looked at her watch. She would prefer to get on with chasing the missing items and preparing for her move to the Roche d'Or hotel, but there was a note of desperation in Kirsten's voice. And they *had* just gained an extra day as a result of the airline moving their flight due to backlog, she reasoned. 'Sure,' she said. 'I have a couple of hours before my appointment with …' She stopped herself in the nick of time. She was in fact meeting with Fai's photographer friend, Serge (for real, this time), but she thought it best to keep her plans from Kirsten until she had Amber's approval. She really shouldn't have let it go this far. *What if Amber says no?*

The minute Kirsten hung up, Kate called Laidback Living, only to be told by an early bird in marketing that, due to some confusion, the package would leave that night, which would, Kate told her, be too late.

Note to self: Never use Laidback Living again, she vowed, slipping a yellow sequinned kaftan dress from Port Louis market over her black halter one-piece. She wondered what to do next. *Perhaps this Laidback Living debacle is a sign that I should finally let the shoot drop,* she thought.

Kirsten's arrival put a halt to her ponderings. 'Wow, someone's been living it up,' she said as she stepped onto the terrace and took in the breakfast spread. 'Not that I have any hard feelings like you-know-who. At least someone's having a nice time here.' She helped herself to a croissant from the pastry basket. 'Do you mind? I really shouldn't, but I've piled on so many pounds since giving up smoking that it's not going to make any difference. I wish cigarettes weren't suddenly so bad for you.'

'Well, at least your starting point was a size zero, so you still look amazing,' Kate said as she spread a towel on one of the two teak sunbeds on the beach in front of her terrace.

'I wish,' Kirsten said. 'Roberta says I'm the first fat fashion assistant she's ever had.' She dropped her bag on the sunbed next to Kate's and pulled her lace baby-doll dress over her head to reveal a body that was still enviably svelte for the extra pounds, clad in a chocolate brown bikini top with a gold ring at the bust and teeny low-rise bottoms.

'It's all relative,' Kate said, feeling suddenly less svelte and regretting the second pain au chocolat. 'You spend too much time around skeletal models.' She ditched her SPF 20 sunscreen and began to slather on SPF

8 oil, in the hope of benefiting from a pound-shedding tan sooner rather than later.

'Actually, a skeletal model is coming to the rescue at the moment,' Kirsten said, lying back on her lounger. 'Roberta's using up all her toxic energy ranting about Tatyana, so there's none left for me. Part of me is relieved, but I also feel sorry for Tatyana.'

'Tristan told me. Why's she such a mess?'

'Boyfriend trouble, apparently.'

'*Pardon, mesdemoiselles.*' Like a genie, a waiter had appeared in front of them, proffering a large tray piled high with miniature fruit kebabs: green and orange melon balls on one; a pineapple wedge, a black grape, and a cube of mango on a second; and slices of papaya, banana, and a strawberry on a third. *Tristan would create a beautiful image of this,* Kate thought.

'Boyfriend trouble?' she asked, helping herself to a kebab as she watched Kirsten line up four on her stomach.

'Well, fiancé trouble. She's engaged to that guy who owns About Face, the cosmetic company – totally loaded and hot, but a complete psychopath. Apparently ever since they got engaged, he's become totally possessive and even violent. There's a thin line on her neck that Tamsyn has to cover up because he tried to strangle her after catching her flirting with someone at a club. April told us. She says he's known for being all charm one minute and then turning. Apparently he beat up a previous girlfriend so badly that she was hospitalised, but he threw money at the situation and it went away. So Tatyana's been on this huge binge of uppers and downers and who knows what.'

'And she doesn't leave him because ...?'

'She loves him.'

'She thinks that's love?' Even by Kate's low standards, she knew that *that* didn't fit the criteria.

'She's only nineteen.'

'I forget how young some of them are,' Kate said, as if being ten years older had made her any wiser to that notion.

'I think she's also kind of banking on him as her ticket to stay in London,' Kirsten said. 'You know she's from Belarus, so she's only on a temporary work visa, and Roberta's not helping matters. Along with muttering that she'll be having words with the agency, she keeps saying, "Thank God for Photoshop."'

Of course, *Be* readers would never know about the puffiness or thin red line, Kate thought, thanks to a few adjustments administered by the art director. Yes, the magazine industry's virtual plastic surgery could be a godsend at times like this, but the images of unattainable perfection it created could also be dangerous. She sometimes thought that, in order to protect readers, magazines should come with a health warning: 'Caution. Some of the models on these pages have been digitally improved. Do not try to achieve this level of perfection at home.' But then she wondered if readers wouldn't be just as outraged as the inhabitants of a small African town who, when first presented with cigarette boxes bearing the warning 'Cigarettes kill', demanded to have the old kind back.

People didn't want to know the ugly truth. For all the experiments by magazines to put daringly unretouched pictures of celebrities in their pages or to use 'normal'-sized models on their covers, they generally returned to the airbrushed version of reality. People wanted to believe that perfection was out there – achievable – and magazines took them there.

'I guess we're lucky we get to see what goes on backstage,' Kate said. 'Before *Be*, I used to think that being drop-dead gorgeous would be the key to eternal happiness.'

As the quintessential plump 'Plain Jane' schoolgirl with a pageboy haircut and braces, Kate had grown up obsessed with the popular girls and the notion that everything came so much more easily to beautiful people. Even later, she had often thought that with a few less insecurities to trip her up – less pronounced feminine curves, smaller breasts, thicker hair – life would be that much better. However, working in magazines, she had discovered that beautiful people also suffered indignities. Castings, for one thing, were like a cattle market – 'too fat'; 'big mouth'; 'yellow teeth'; 'bad hair'; 'sallow skin'; 'too fair'; 'too dark'. They reminded her of the very first time she had stepped behind one of life's many facades and learnt to her disappointment that appearances could be deceiving.

She was eight, and her mother had taken her and her sisters to see the circus in Truro. By the end of the show, Kate had been convinced that the circus was where her future lay – riding elephants, flying through the air on the trapeze, and jumping out of boxes at the wave of a magician's wand, dressed from head to toe in sequins. However, all the sequins in the world couldn't have made up for what was revealed to her when her younger sister begged to go behind the big top to see the 'lines and elly pants' again.

First up, the lions were bony and mangy, and looked miserable in their cramped quarters. Then there were the elephants attached by chains to iron pegs hammered into the ground, their eyes watery and mournful. But most shocking of all was the sight of a woman sitting smoking on the steps of a caravan. Kate recognised her immediately as the magician's assistant because her pretty pink sequinned dress with the feathers around the neck was visible where her faded grey dressing gown had fallen open. But in the daylight, the dazzling woman whom Kate had wanted to emulate was as worn as that dressing gown and even older than Kate's mother. What's more, her caravan wasn't anything like the ones Kate had seen in books – the round kind painted in bright colours with pretty wooden shutters. Instead, it was a muddy white trailer with dirty curtains and washing hanging outside. All it was, she could see, even at that young age, was illusion and disillusion.

Her plans to join the circus summarily shelved, Kate had conjured up other glorious ways to escape the boredom of life in the small, smelly fishing village. Movie stardom was an option. But it was all mere daydreams until, when she was thirteen, escape became an urgent need.

Kate still recalled that day as if it were yesterday, when she had come home from school to find the house changed. The hall was in darkness because the living room curtains hadn't been opened, and none of the usual sounds emanated from the kitchen: the radio hadn't been turned to *Four o'clock Classics*, and there wasn't the chatter of her sisters doing their homework at the kitchen table. Most telling that something wasn't quite right, though, was the smell. There was none. And her mother's house always smelt of something: fresh-out-the-oven cakes or biscuits for tea or a fete; the dense nutty bread that she baked to make sandwiches for her daughters' school lunches; jams and preserves made with berries from the garden; or the beginnings of an experimental dinner.

Finding the kitchen empty, the plates from breakfast still on the table, and a pot of congealed oatmeal on the stove, Kate had gone upstairs to find her parents' bedroom door closed. As she opened it carefully, she heard a whimper and, in the semi-darkness, made out the grey shape of her mother curled up in a ball on the unmade bed. 'Your father's gone away, honey,' she said, and Kate thought that her father must be dead, since this was how her mother had explained dead budgies, guinea pigs, and hamsters in the past – 'Snowy has gone away, honey.'

Over the next weeks, homemade biscuits and bread were replaced with bought versions while the girls' evening meals were seasoned with salty tears and bitter accusations over the telephone. Kate had started to think that life would never be normal again. But then one day her father was back, and it was almost as if he had never left. The rift had left a scar, however, which was sometimes barely visible and at other times pronounced, like the hair-thin crack in her mother's white porcelain fruit bowl that became a red gash when the juice from strawberries or raspberries seeped into it. 'Where were you? I'm not blind.' 'If it wasn't for the children, I'd be out that door ...'

In the end, Kate's father had been the one to leave permanently, but only much later, long after Kate had thrown out her mother's recipe book for life and written her own, omitting sacrifice and including independence, glamour, and excitement as key ingredients, with men only as spicy seasoning. An international career in journalism, she finally decided, would be her ticket to a life as far removed from her mother's as possible.

'Hellooooo ... anyone home?' Kate heard Kirsten say.

'Sorry, I think I dozed off there.'

'I'm going for a swim. Want to join me?'

If murky, the water was a perfect temperature – similar, Kate imagined, to that of the amniotic fluid in the womb. *No wonder babies come out screaming; they're saying, 'Put me back.'* The two of them swam out to the reef, from where, treading water, they looked at the crescent of sand sprinkled with umbrellas sheltering pairs of honeymooners on parallel sunbeds. For some of them, Kate was sure, this would be the last time that their hopes and dreams would be as perfectly aligned as those sunbeds. Still, at least they had got this far.

'It's tragic being in a romantic place like this alone,' Kirsten said. 'By the time Mark and I can afford this kind of luxury, we'll need Zimmer frames to get to the beach. Not that you have anything to complain about.' She looked at Kate with a suggestive smile.

'What do you mean?' Kate asked.

'Let's just say that someone was spotted kissing a tall, dark stranger this morning.'

'This morning? Where?'

'In the road behind the villas, according to April. Tristan wanted to know if he had fantastic cheekbones.'

'What was April doing wandering around at the crack of dawn?' *Damn!* Kate had been so careful to avoid bumping into anyone. She had left the group at the dinner table surrounded by chamomile and peppermint teas, and when Fai had dropped her off this morning, she had been sure that the only witness to their illicit liaison was a stone Buddha.

'She was taking the circuitous route back to her room,' Kirsten said.

'From?'

'Marius's.'

'Oh. So Roberta …?'

'Has moved on to St Jean the masseur, apparently. I don't think Marius was ever a serious contender anyway; she only toys with models enough to make sure she knows they think she's hot, but she says she's more into people with substance these days. Her last boyfriend was this big-deal yogi.'

'You'd never know,' Kate said, 'but at least I'm not the only one sleeping on the job.'

Kirsten laughed. 'So who is he?'

On one hand, Kate was reluctant to reveal the previous night's antics to Kirsten, who still hovered somewhere between colleague and friend. On the other hand, she was relieved to be able to take the lid off the internal pressure cooker of thoughts and feelings that were steaming up her mind, and release some of the evening's intense aroma and flavour.

'Nothing like a holiday fling,' Kirsten said. 'Short and intense, no strings attached.'

Of course, Kate thought, *Fai wasn't a meal.* He was a side dish that could just as easily be left off the menu. People had holiday flings all the time and then left them behind. In her serially single days before Daniel, she had had her fair share. Her mind flitted back to the close call with Paolo in Tuscany, when she had spent an idyllic few days exploring farmers' markets, hillside villages, and olive groves by day and flirting with the villa's waiter by night, first between courses and later between the sheets. She had left amid impassioned declarations of love, and that had been the end of that. Or so she had thought, until she had received a badly written and poorly thought-out letter from him – all hearts and kisses – with a proposition about bringing the family egg business to the United Kingdom. Kate had shut down their correspondence forthwith, convinced that the relationship had as much chance of success as the bottle of cherry liqueur she had brought back from the trip, which had tasted like nectar on the terrace of a quaint village bar, and like sweet, viscous cough syrup back home.

Even though she felt she had established something deeper and surprisingly real with Fai in a very short time, it was just a fling, Kate realised, and, if prolonged, the repercussions would be so much worse than bad eggs and cough mixture. She thought of Daniel at home, weaving plans to move in together, and she suddenly missed him terribly, all the more now that she had placed under threat their daily conversations and texts, intimate dates *à deux*, dinner parties *à dix*, and lazy weekends with no plans and no need for them because everything she wanted was right there beside her.

'But I, um, you know, I'm seeing someone at home,' Kate said, 'so, um, if you wouldn't mind ...' Trust was such an important issue for Daniel.

'Oops. Is it serious?' Kirsten asked. 'The London thing?'

'Yes,' Kate said. 'It is. Does everyone know about this? Roberta?' Kate didn't want Roberta to have further ammunition she could use against her, because if she could, she would.

'I don't know. She generally doesn't join our conversations,' Kirsten said, 'and the Botox means you never know what she's thinking.'

Weighed down now by guilt and regret, with self-castigating thoughts nibbling at her conscience like piranhas, Kate suddenly felt tired of bobbing in the water, so she and Kirsten swam back to shore.

As they lay back on their loungers, another waiter approached, this one armed with a white cloth and a pump dispenser, and offered to clean their glasses. Intent on making use of all the little extras, Kirsten enthusiastically handed hers over, but Kate declined; she was suddenly seeing things quite clearly enough, thank you very much.

'So do you think you'll see him again? Your mystery man?' Kirsten asked.

'No, no, I won't,' Kate said. 'Definitely not. Nothing to write home about.' One infidelity could be swept under the carpet like a bit of dust, but if they started piling up, someone might trip over them.

CHAPTER 7

Playing with Fire

The Roche d'Or's executive chef, Philippe Besson, pushed fresh dill into the cavity of a large fish that was already stuffed with lemongrass, basil, parsley, onion and slices of lemon. 'You should let the herbs stick out a bit,' he said. 'It prevents the fish from drying out while it's cooking.'

'Okay, thanks,' Kate said, making a note beside the recipe for linefish with salsa verde in the sheaf of recipes attached to her clipboard.

She had had to curb the creative enthusiasm of the young Creole chef with Michelin stars in his eyes, but they had finally come up with a selection of barbecue dishes that would be tasty and exotic yet simple enough for readers to make back home. Philippe was currently preparing these at a table set on the sand in a secluded cove.

Looking up from the recipe, Kate saw that he was reaching for foil to cover the fish. She put up her hand to stop him.

'Could we get a close-up before you put it aside?' she asked. 'Serge?' She looked behind her at the photographer, who had been shooting the scene from a distance. Now he came forward to kneel in the sand beside the table, training his camera on the fish.

'Sorry, hang on,' Kate said. She rearranged a couple of fronds of parsley with tweezers before trimming the dill with nail scissors to give it some attractive layering. 'Fine,' she said, standing back. It had taken Amber's pulling of a couple of shoots for Kate to realise that food, like its flesh-and-blood counterparts in fashion, required a fair amount of primping and priming in order to be glossy-magazine-worthy. Cadavers were happily far less emotional, though, and there was no risk of their turning up with bad hair and acne.

'I had no idea there was so much involved in food shoots,' Serge said, inadvertently reminding Kate of his lack of experience in this particular genre. His scruffy schoolboy looks topped off with thick, black-rimmed spectacles didn't fill her with confidence either.

'But you're okay with it?' she asked, trying to disguise the panic in her voice.

'Yes, sure. I always shoot the food at weddings. People think it's weird, but it's the only chance I get.'

'You've also shot quite a bit for travel brochures, right?' Kate had seen the proof, but she desperately needed confirmation now.

'Yes, but they're a luxury; weddings are the bread and butter.'

Art happens. No hovel is safe from it; no prince can depend on it; the vastest intelligence cannot bring it about. This quote by Whistler had become something of a mantra during Kate's first months at *Be* when, feeling out of her depth and intimidated by her sophisticated colleagues, she had used it to quell many a panic attack. Now she reached for it again. She reminded herself of the beautiful pictures she had seen in Serge's portfolio, which had convinced her that he had an eye and natural talent that could not be taught. The fact that the bulk of his work consisted of shots of happy couples was, therefore, immaterial – art was art, and she had to trust that Serge was the artist she believed him to be.

The real problem was that, even if art *was* happening, she hadn't got around to telling Amber that it might be.

Kate had started writing an email to Amber several times, making a stronger case for using Serge with every new edition, but none, to her mind, had been quite strong enough to elicit a definite yes, and so all had remained unsent. As she headed to her meeting with Philippe the previous day, she had promised herself that she would definitely address the matter upon returning to her room. However, she hadn't bargained on Philippe's palpable excitement, the sublimity of the location, or the perfect placement of the custom-made table. Finally, when he had handed her the file of neatly typed recipes, it became clear to her that things had already gone too far. She would have to go with her gut, embrace the big picture, and pray that Amber would also come to see that this had been too good a photo opportunity to miss.

'What's the worst that can happen, huh?' Kate threw her hands up to the cloudless sky in mock challenge.

Whereas more experienced photographers would have captured the food from every possible angle in order to ensure that one shot was perfect, Serge stood up after taking precisely three.

'Art happens,' Kate repeated to herself. *'No hovel is safe from it; no prince can depend on it; the vastest intelligence cannot bring it about.'*

Philippe handed the platter to a waiter and then turned to Kate. 'This only needs around fifteen minutes, so I'll put it on when everyone's already seated at the table.'

The 'everyone' he referred to were the human props Kate had hurriedly found to replace the fashion team – and they were all now officially late, she noted, glancing down at her watch. She looked across the beach towards the gap between large boulders that provided access to this private cove from the hotel, but the only sign of life was a waiter hurrying towards them with an armful of anthuriums. He joined others who were putting the finishing touches to the table, which was bathed in the soft late-afternoon light.

Set on handwoven rugs close to the sea, the low table was surrounded by square floor cushions in jewel colours, matched by large round paper lanterns that hung from several coconut palms like brightly coloured fantasy fruits in purple, pink, turquoise, and green. Adding yet more colour were quirky recycled-glass table lanterns and kitsch wine glasses with coloured stems shaped like pineapples, along with Kate's makeshift substitutes for the missing Laidback Living items. She had replaced the forgotten tablecloth with a fuchsia sari from Port Louis market and would include the names of good fabric shops in Brick Lane in the stockists' list; an assortment of glass cooldrink bottles stood in as vases, from which single anthuriums sprouted, and she had simply used paper napkins instead of linen ones (it was a barbecue, after all). She wondered why she had lost so much sleep over this.

A thrill ran through her as she pictured people seated at the table and all the elements of the shoot coming together like the ingredients in a perfectly balanced dish. In the back of her mind, however, the fear remained that, given the unknown quantity that was Serge, the dish could still go horribly wrong, much like fugu fish prepared by a novice chef.

Kate remembered being told by a leading Japanese chef she had once interviewed that just one fugu fish contained enough of the poison tetrodotoxin to kill thirty people. Its preparation, therefore, involved a meticulously executed multistep process to remove most of the tetrodotoxin stored in the organs, leaving just enough to cause a tingling sensation and a subtle numbing of the lips that were part of the dish's appeal. Kate had learnt that years of training were required to achieve this delicate balance without killing anyone, and as she watched Serge absent-mindedly fiddling with his camera like a photography student with a new toy, she wondered if this concoction too wasn't in danger of causing sudden death, in this case to her career. She closed her eyes, took a deep breath, and hit play on the mantra in her head.

''Ello, Kate. 'Ow is everysing?' Kate spun around to see one ingredient that was in no danger of letting the dish down. Solange would make a very attractive garnish indeed, she thought, dressed in three-quarter jeans and a diaphanous top featuring pastel swirls, her copious brown curls cascading over her shoulders.

'Zis is my 'usband, Pascal,' Solange said. With a hand clutching a pair of silver flip-flops, she gestured towards a slim, bespectacled man, who looked less inspiring but acceptable in jeans and a green Ralph Lauren shirt.

'Ooh la la, it looks good.' Solange leant over the table, where Philippe was now chopping papaya with quick, evenly spaced thrusts. A pushover for expert knife skills, Kate watched the blade coming down again and again, its effect slightly hypnotic, until it suddenly slipped and the trance was broken. Blood spurted from Philippe's left hand. But the chef appeared not to have noticed as he stared over Kate's right shoulder. She turned around to track his gaze, and her eyes alighted on Finola, human prop number three, walking towards them with her husband, Thomas.

Kate had spotted the glossy blond couple at breakfast that morning. After peering at them surreptitiously over the top of her newspaper for a while – observing their natural good looks, stylish attire, and relaxed air – she had decided they would be perfect for the shoot. So, made brave by desperation, she had approached them with her bartering deal of a fun foodie night out in exchange for their presence as walk-in extras on her renegade food shoot.

'*Merde,*' Philippe said, finally looking down at his hand. A significant amount of blood had seeped into the orange fruit and subsequently into a wad of paper napkins, which immediately turned red as Kate turned white, believing this could mark the end of her precarious mission.

'What can I do? Where can I get help?' she asked.

'Don't worry, I will be fine,' Philippe said. He shouted something over his shoulder in Creole, which conjured a man bearing a red box, from which he proceeded to pull bandages and dressings. As his left hand was attended to, Philippe waved his right hand at the barman farther along the beach, this time conjuring a silver tray loaded with bright pink watermelon Martinis. His magic skills extended beyond the kitchen.

'You look fabulous,' Kate said to Finola as everyone helped themselves to Martinis. 'You both do.' Thomas was wearing three-quarter khaki cotton drawstring pants and a short-sleeved white shirt with flowers stitched roughly on it. But Finola stole the show in a white tube top hugging breasts that would have rivalled Marie Antoinette's as the perfect mythological mould for the Champagne coupe, teamed with an Indian-cotton skirt featuring horizontal panels in varying shades of pink and a chunky resin necklace that toned with the Martini. The most experienced stylist couldn't have contrived her whole look better.

Amber would definitely approve, Kate thought as she watched Finola help herself to a drink. *Hell, Roberta would probably approve.* And so, evidently, did Serge, who had his camera trained on Finola and, for the first time in the course of the shoot, was clicking continuously.

'Would you mind moving down towards the water?' he asked the group. 'Over there?' He pointed at the water's edge. Having something animate to engage with now, he was clearly in his milieu. Kate was happy to let him take the initiative, as she returned her attention to Philippe, who had reassigned the chopping of the papaya to a sous chef and was arranging oysters on a platter. The food was now well protected from the wound on his bulging thumb by a protective plastic sheath that looked disturbingly like a yellow glow-in-the-dark condom Kate had once encountered.

After slipping a chicory leaf under each of the oysters and dispatching a waiter to serve them, Philippe turned his attention to the lobsters. Kate watched him deftly cut away the membrane on the underside of a tail and then bend the crustacean backwards to crack the shell. 'This prevents them from curling while cooking,' he explained. 'They won't take long, so if you want to shoot them on the fire, we should get Serge up here before I start.'

Kate looked down the beach and saw that Finola was now standing in the water, running a hand through her hair as a wooden fishing boat slid across the frame behind her and Serge continued to shoot as if in a trance. Reluctant to break the spell, she finally called him back to the barbecue, where she was relieved to find that the effects of his new-found muse were still in evidence. He was suddenly on a roll, zooming in as Philippe placed the lobsters on the barbecue's grid and again when he turned them with the tongs. The fire hissed as moisture hit the coals and a pungent, salty smell rose from them. The whole scene was hypnotic, and Kate began to relax.

'It's important to cook them with the shell down first,' Philippe said. 'About seven to ten minutes that way, then flesh-down for no more than two. This prevents them from drying out. But you probably knew that.'

'I didn't, actually,' Kate said. 'We don't have much scope for barbecuing back home; I think there were only two weekends last summer when it didn't rain, so any tips are most welcome.'

Apart from the British weather's limitations, barbecues had never been part of Kate's mother's repertoire, so Kate wouldn't be able to get much guidance from her. This was unusual, since she never signed anything off without first checking some detail at the very least and often using recipes concocted by her mother in their entirety. There was something of *Cyrano de Bergerac* about it, Kate often thought. Whereas in Edmond Rostand's 1897 play, the dashing guardsman Christian captivated Roxanne with his good looks and charisma, it was the poetry of the big-nosed and unwieldy Cyrano, recited by Christian as his own that truly won her heart. Similarly, Kate's readers were captivated by the beauty, poise, and va-va-voom of her dishes on the page, but it was her mother's deep, real, and true understanding of food and flavour combinations that ensured flop-proof recipe after flop-proof recipe and kept those readers true.

Right now, it was va-va-voom time, so Kate ushered everyone to the table, where they settled on the floor cushions while lanterns were lit and the pineapple-stemmed glasses were filled with white wine. The sky was now tinged with pink and Kate was finally satisfied. The scene was set. *Art happens. Surely all the components to win Amber over are here,* she thought as she watched Philippe warm two flat loaves of yellow turmeric bread on the fire before plating up a lobster with a mound of papaya salsa.

'Could you hold the plate in front of you?' Kate asked him, after placing a knob of coriander butter on top of the lobster. Philippe was wearing a sandy brown apron over jeans teamed with a salmon-pink cotton shirt, sleeves rolled up, to achieve the relaxed look Kate had requested. She could see that this moment had the makings of a beautiful image. 'Yes nice,' she said, 'but would you mind just moving your injured thumb under the plate? Perfect.'

And so the parade of fashion plates commenced. Each one posed for a close-up and then strutted onto the table, where Serge snapped the diners enjoying the food before returning to the barbecue to capture Philippe charring thick, juicy octopus tentacles, whipping up a vibrant salsa verde, and grilling the fish to golden-brown perfection. Finally the vanilla bavarois brought the show to a close: a beautiful white volcano with passion-fruit lava running down its side into a sea of tropical fruit.

'This is delicious,' Thomas said.

'Mm ... yes, it is rather sublime, isn't it?' Kate said, scooping her finger through the last of her lava and sucking it clean. The colour had now drained from the sky and, with Serge's lights packed away, the table was lit only by lanterns, which brought a relaxed lull to the evening.

'The whole meal 'as been *superbe*,' Solange said, dipping her spoon into an ample second helping of the dessert. 'You are very lucky, Kate. I would kill for your job.'

'I am,' Kate said. She looked around her at the setting and her glamorous company. *This is it. This is the dream.* She wanted to pinch herself to make sure it was real.

'I don't know how you manage to stay so slim, though,' Finola said. She was drinking chamomile tea, having refused the dessert because she had a promotional shoot coming up for the launch of her debut album. 'I think I'd be the size of a house in your place – it gets harder and harder to keep the weight off. In fact, my deepest regret about producing my first CD at forty is the fact that it would have been so much easier to look the part in my twenties. How do you keep in such great shape with all this temptation around?'

'Believe me, my weight goes up and down like Tower Bridge,' Kate said. 'Food reviews especially are an occupational hazard. But to keep full-blown obesity at bay, I run.' Although she had relinquished herself to her foodie heritage, she was determined not to give in to its potentially ill effects. And the battle she waged on the treadmill, on the street, and recently on the beaches wasn't just about weight control. It was a deeply personal one that extended to the trenches of her mind. Perhaps her father wouldn't have strayed if her mother had not let herself become a plump Cornish hen whose eggs were past their sell-by date, compared to the long-limbed flamingo for whom her father had finally flown the coop, whose eggs were, it emerged, fresh and fertile. A baby was already well on the way when he had hopped from their family nest straight into hers.

'So what made you become a food writer?' Philippe asked. He had joined them at the table after serving dessert. 'Is it something you always wanted to be?'

'No,' Kate said. 'I had absolutely no intention of working with food; quite the opposite actually.' She told them how her culinary heritage had pursued her from her mother's kitchen in Cornwall via Paris to London, despite her best efforts to outrun it. She kept things light, leaving out her real motivation for needing to flee as far from her mother's domain as possible.

Step 1: *Transform yourself into a worldly sophisticate.* Taking her cue from Audrey Hepburn in *Sabrina*, Kate had taken a gap year after school and, with savings from a waitressing job, headed to Paris in the hope that the glamour of the city would rub off on her and that afterwards, like the simple chauffeur's daughter, she would return home transformed. Only, unlike Sabrina, she wouldn't be returning with Cordon Bleu skills, but with polished French to give her a head start in international journalism.

Things had certainly started out well. Her job as an au pair allowed her to study French while the children were at school, and at night she learnt how to smoke and throw back strong French espresso and cheap Beaujolais at pavement cafés. She got a French haircut and a chic wardrobe and was well on track for a very different life from her mother's until the De Villeneuves' chef fell ill on the night of a dinner party and she volunteered to help out. This won her a regular spot in the kitchen on the chef's days off for extra pay, and when the De Villeneuves headed to St Tropez for their summer vacation, they asked Kate to work as the villa's chef. Despite herself, Kate had relished cooking with the area's abundant produce – fresh seafood, sweet olive oils, sun-ripened vegetables, aromatic Mediterranean herbs, cheeses – and, against a backdrop suited to holiday romance, she had started a love affair with food all over again.

Step 2: *Embark on a journalism degree.* Literature had always been Kate's form of escapism as a child, which meant she had excelled in English at school. With her French skills honed too, she fancied the idea of becoming some kind of foreign correspondent who bravely jetted between danger zones, her name attached to the headline news. But her political and business writing skills never quite matched up to the pieces she wrote on food and fashion, and her lecturers told her that this was the direction she should head in.

Step 3: *Find an exciting job on a leading newspaper or glossy magazine.* Easier said than done. Kate had languished at a couple of community newspapers in Truro before finally getting into the subediting department of a second-grade London homes magazine, where her culinary skills had shone through once more. Finally writing and editing the food section, she had produced a feature on an alternative Christmas lunch entitled 'Cool Yule' that had caught Amber's eye and launched Kate into the glossy world.

'So you could say I'm here despite my best efforts rather than because of them,' Kate said.

'Sometimes, I think destiny has a better idea of what's good for us than we do ourselves,' Finola said. 'I was convinced that everything would happen for me in London. I really fought to stay there, but it was only when I went with the flow and headed back home to Australia that things fell into place.'

She told them that she had moved to London, hoping to make it on the West End, but that endless auditioning had only got her a couple of bit parts in musicals, so she had settled for a full-time job as a music teacher by day, playing the piano and singing in clubs and bars several nights a week. Eventually composing some of her own music, she had produced a demo and garnered some interest, but the big break had never come. Finally, when the club she was working at closed down in the same week that the heating in her flat blew up, and her mother announced that she was going in for a hip replacement, she had realised that the universe was telling her to go home. 'I was nervous because I felt I'd failed, but amazingly, within weeks, I was spotted doing a gig in a real dive in Sydney, and here I am. I also met Thomas.' She smiled across the table at her fiancé.

'So what kind of music do you sing?' Kate asked.

'A mixture of things: jazz, pop, ballads ...'

'I would love to 'ear you,' Solange said. 'Can you not sing somesing for us now?'

'Well, I'm not at my best ...'

'Go on, babe, sing for our supper,' Thomas said.

'Okay, but understand that I'm doing it without music and I've drunk a bit.' Finola got up unsteadily and stepped away from the table. 'I'd like to dedicate this song to Philippe and Kate for the delicious meal they've prepared for us tonight,' she said. 'It's called "Recipe for Love."'

The song had a catchy rhythm and was delivered in a voice that was as warm, rich, and spicy as bourbon.

'Cherry lips and a sweet sugar kiss,' the chorus went.

'A bit of chilli and a cool lemon twist. You're my chocolat, my baby chocolat. My chocolat, my baby chocolat.'

Swaying bodies and tapping fingers turned to applause and hollers, creating an impromptu ending to a perfectly orchestrated evening.

'Brilliant,' Kate said. 'You'll have to let us know when the CD's out. I could probably get something on the music page.' She was full of Martini and good cheer, feeling invincible even though there was still no guarantee that this piece would be in the magazine or that she would still have a job when the CD was released.

Finola handed her card to everyone, saying they should email her their addresses so she could send them each a copy of the CD. Then, hand in hand, she and Thomas made their way back across the beach. As Kate watched them melt into the darkness, she suddenly missed Daniel with a dull ache under the empire line of her maxi dress. If only there *were* a recipe for love, she thought. If only it were a simple blending of cherry lips and a sweet sugar kiss, a bit of chilli and a cool lemon twist.

A mobile phone rang in the shadows, from which Serge emerged. 'My lift will be here in five minutes,' he said. 'I'll make a selection and drop off a USB at the hotel tomorrow. I hope you think it went well.'

'It was brilliant,' Kate said. 'If you wouldn't mind, Serge, could you please let me have all of the images unedited as well, just in case we need more?' In truth, she wasn't sure that his editing skills would be up to standard, so she wanted the option to get them done at home.

'We should also be going,' Pascal said, getting up and pulling Solange up after him.

'Kate, it really was *fantastique*,' Solange said, 'and I 'ave decided zat I really must 'elp you. So I 'ave been sinking about it and zere is one ozer possibility.' Earlier that day, Kate had phoned Solange yet again to find out if there had been any change of heart regarding the fee for the upgrade, as well as to enquire about a possible discount on the yacht that Roberta had chartered for the cover shoot. Solange now told Kate that she was going to try to set up a meeting for her with the Sunshine Group's all-powerful chairman and CEO, a self-professed foodie who also happened to be the owner of the yacht.

Delighted that things seemed to be taking a turn for the better, Kate plonked herself down on a cushion opposite Philippe, who was smoking a cigarette as he looked out to sea. He offered her one, and she took it.

'I think it went really well,' she said.

'You do?' He looked anxious. 'It's the first time I've done something like this for an international magazine, so I wasn't sure.'

'Really, you were superb,' Kate said, 'distracted self-mutilation aside.'

He laughed. 'Yes, sometimes I take the knife for granted.'

Kate glanced at Serge, who was bent over his equipment in the shadows of the casuarina trees, and wondered if he had captured Philippe's brilliance adequately. The images she had seen on his camera had looked good, great even, but it was impossible to tell if they would transfer as well to print. What if he hadn't pulled it off and Amber threw the pictures out? How indeed was she going to broach the subject with Amber?

Kate was pondering these questions, gazing absent-mindedly into the casuarinas, when one of the trees transformed into the tall, graceful silhouette of a man: Fai. He stopped and said something to Serge. Then he looked up and started walking towards the table.

'Hi,' Fai said, looking down at Kate. 'How was it?'

'Good … brilliant.' Kate hastily got up, avoiding his eyes lest they ask her something she couldn't refuse. She had made up her mind not to see him again, but her head was still at odds with her heart.

'Serge asked me to pick him up,' Fai said, clearly registering her discomfort. 'His brother's doing a wedding down the road, so I'm going to drop him off there – they share a car.' Kate wasn't listening to his words; she was watching his lips move, remembering them on her own lips and breasts and legs. *Perhaps looking into his eyes would be a safer bet.*

Philippe got up. 'I'll think about my last meal and give you something tomorrow,' he said.

'Last meal?' Kate looked up at him blankly, unable to process what he was saying as a result of the crackly interference caused by Fai's presence. 'Oh, of course, thank you,' she said, finally registering that she had asked Philippe for a description of what he would choose for his last meal, which was something she asked all contributing chefs to provide.

'Let me know if any of the recipes aren't clear,' Philippe called back over his shoulder from the shadows. He then left Kate to deal with her own shadows once more.

'I'm sorry I had to cancel on you last night,' she said.

'Don't worry about it,' Fai said.

'I am … I did really want to see you again, but …' *You did what you had to do, and it was the right thing to do,* her conscience murmured, barely audible over her palpitating heartbeat and the rush of blood in her head. As if responding to a powerful magnetic force, she reached for his hand. *How could something that feels this good be bad?* 'It's a pity you have to go now. I'd love to spend some more time with you,' she said. She felt like a ventriloquist's doll, the words emerging from her mouth without her putting them there.

'I would too,' Fai said. He put his hand on her neck, which was suddenly on fire. Then he leant down and kissed her, precipitating a glorious internal eruption of sensations that incinerated any remaining doubts. 'I could drop Serge off and come back, if it's not too late for you,' he said.

Looking into his dark, liquid eyes, Kate felt sure she could swim to the bottom of them and discover the meaning of life.

'That would be perfect,' she said.

CHAPTER 8

Cold As Ice

You gather that Mauritius was created first, and then heaven, and that heaven was copied after Mauritius.

Mark Twain

The sea looked like a solid sheet of Murano glass in various shades of blue, cut only by a speedboat pulling a skier around the lagoon. The sound of its engine reached Kate across the water like the lazy hum of a bumblebee, while inside her whole being hummed with unadulterated contentment. Yes, it was the kind of day that would have inspired those words from Mark Twain, she thought, and he hadn't even had a night with Fai.

Adding to her contentment was the fact that her first décor shoot had gone well that morning. The colonial beach house had had a cool urban vibe, featuring white painted wooden floors strewn with a mix of contemporary and ethnic pieces and splashes of Hindu iconography. On top of this, the leggy homeowner, who had graced a number of the shots, had applied the same impeccable taste to her clothes as she had to her home. Little styling had thus been required, and it had been the fastest shoot in Kate's magazine history, sped along by a plague of calls from Roberta, telling Tristan and Kirsten to hurry up and get to the marina for the cover shoot. This was currently under way on a luxury yacht, so the summer special was almost a wrap. Kate had just one last issue to sort out, and the potential solution was sitting opposite her in the form of Jacques Renaud, the Sunshine Group's chairman and CEO.

'This sushi is wonderful,' she said before nimbly navigating an oyster wrapped in yellowfin tuna into her mouth with chopsticks.

'It's the best sushi on the island,' said Jacques. 'In fact, it's among the best in the world. We stole one of Tokyo's top sushi chefs.'

The CEO was treating Kate to the full PR song-and-dance routine. For the past forty five minutes, he had been belting out the merits of the hotels in the chain and dropping the names of celebrity guests like plates in a Greek restaurant. The charm offensive was not required, of course, because Kate had a song and dance of her own to perform. Unsure of how much Solange had told Jacques about her reason for meeting him, she was waiting for the right moment to broach the topic.

'*Et Amal? Connais-tu la chanteuse Amal?*' Jacques asked. Kate had told him that she spoke French, and so, although he had a perfect command of English, he had been peppering the conversation with French words – *part of the charm offensive, no doubt.*

Kate was only able to nod, as her mouth was occupied with a delectable lobster and black bean maki roll. Jacques had moved from the formal *vous* to the more familiar *tu*, she noted, a grammatical shift that suggested he had warmed to her and might be almost ready for her cost-saving suggestions.

'She has paid for a suite here for *toute l'année*,' Jacques continued, 'just so she can pop in *quand elle veut*, but she has only been here for two weeks in ten months.'

'It seems fitting that someone who sings like an angel should inhabit heaven on earth,' Kate said. Her words tasted sickly sweet, but she would swallow whatever it took to achieve her aim. Jacques was after a good write-up on his chain, and she needed a discount on a yacht.

'So you have enjoyed your stay with us?' Jacques asked.

'Absolutely,' Kate said. 'I'd also consider a year-round suite if I had a Grammy-winning singer's cash flow.' Although, right now, a small studio without a sea view had a whole lot more appeal. Kate was looking forward to a dinner cooked up by Fai that night and, even more, to everything that wasn't on the menu. Her mind flitted back to the evening before, when Fai had arrived in her room and their bodies had not so much come together as dissolved into each other, creating an intoxicating cocktail, the individual components of which were impossible to break down.

'Perhaps we can arrange something for you.' Jacques smiled. 'Solange tells me that you are giving our group excellent coverage. She said your shoot last night was *formidable*.' And there it was: the opening Kate had been looking for.

She drained the zesty Sauvignon Blanc from her glass, took a deep breath, and said, 'Actually, speaking of deals, there is something I'd like to discuss with you.'

'Yes,' Jacques said. 'Solange did mention this was not all for pleasure, although it has been. A real pleasure. Tell me.' He leant over to fill up her glass, and Kate noticed his gaze travelling appreciatively up a tanned leg that was exposed boldly to the thigh in her new yellow kaftan dress. While generally not one to rely on womanly wiles to achieve her aims, she made an exception this time, swinging her legs out and recrossing them to afford Jacques an even better look. Something about needing this to work to save her career had activated the predator in her. She decided it was time to go marlin hunting.

'Basically, as you probably know, because we moved from Paradise Bay, we're paying a supplement for our accommodation at the White Sands, which wasn't in our initial budget.' Kate explained the circumstances that had led to the move and then detailed some of the other unexpected expenses that had come up as a result of the cyclone, including the yacht, which Roberta had hired to sail to clearer waters. 'Anyway, to be honest, it's put us … it's put *me* in a difficult position,' she said, shamelessly playing the 'damsel in distress' card. 'So I'd like to propose some other exchange. Have you seen the magazine, by the way?'

'No,' he said. 'I don't have time for magazines, unless we are in them *bien sûr*. Then Solange sends me the clippings.'

A waiter removed the empty bottle from the ice bucket and held it up.

'*Encore?*' Jacques asked Kate, nodding at the bottle.

'*Non, merci.*' Kate had drunk most of the bottle herself while Jacques had stretched one glass of wine over the whole lunch, a trick she had seen mastered by a few people whose job it was to peddle pleasure. She waved away the dessert menu too but said yes to an espresso. Then she brazenly took a copy of *Be* out of her bag and put it in front of Jacques. 'You should read it; you might be pleasantly surprised by how much it has to interest a man of vision and taste like you. Of course our core readership is female, but we're talking about intelligent, independent women with disposable income to spend on luxuries like travel, so I truly do believe we're a good target market for you.'

'You care a lot about your magazine,' he said.

'I do,' Kate said. 'It's like a child to me, much as, I imagine, your hotels are to you. I really do have a sense of responsibility and love for it, which is why I'm so anxious to sort something out.' Here, she was speaking from the heart.

Jacques smiled indulgently. 'So what are you proposing?' He took a box of Gauloises out of the pocket of the light linen jacket hanging over his chair and held the box out to Kate.

'There are a number of things we can do for you.' Kate helped herself to a cigarette and then leant forward to allow Jacques to light it – so much the better to lure him in with ample cleavage. 'Advertorials in a couple of issues, a special reader offer, or a competition around your cookery classes, perhaps, which sound exciting.' Solange had told Kate that, as a foodie, Jacques was particularly enthusiastic about the hotel's newly introduced cooking school.

'Interesting,' Jacques said, looking not so much riveted as bemused.

Kate forged on nonetheless, adding a few more carefully rehearsed points before winding things up. 'Anyway, I don't want to waste any more of your time, but I thought you might like to have a look at this.' She handed over the media kit she had had emailed over by the sales manager, which detailed circulation figures, *Be*'s reader profile, and advertising page values.

'Being in your company could never be a waste of time,' Jacques said. He smiled flirtatiously, which produced creases around his hazel eyes. He was probably in his early fifties, Kate thought, although he was in good shape for his age, his physique and tan speaking of swims in the ocean and runs along the beach. Only his crow's feet and silver-streaked hair gave his age away.

'Well, I can tell you now that the yacht is yours,' Jacques said after casting a cursory glance over the documents, 'but I'll need to talk to some people and do a few sums before I can give you an answer on the rest. Solange said you're leaving tomorrow?'

'My flight's at ten in the morning,' Kate said.

'Well then, let me look at it this afternoon, and we will discuss it over dinner tonight,' he said. 'You have not tried our Belle Ile restaurant, I think?'

'No,' Kate said as calmly as possible, while her heart did somersaults. She already had a dinner date and it was Fai she wanted to see. 'But I know you're a busy man, and you've been more than generous with your time already.'

'It would be my pleasure,' Jacques said. 'And we can't let you leave without trying the best restaurant on the island. Nothing compares with the experience.' Kate could think of at least one thing that would compare with the experience. But she had hooked her big fish, and now she had to reel in the much-needed prize for *Be*. It could be a catch-and-release situation, she reasoned; she would close the deal over dinner and then join Fai afterwards. Food was, after all, immaterial in his presence.

'Shall we say 7.30 p.m. at the Champagne bar?' Jacques asked.

*   *   *

One Kir Royale and six courses later, each of the latter paired with a different wine, Kate tackled the last obstacle to her date with Fai in the form of roasted figs with thyme-infused goat's cheese ice cream and a pink peppercorn tuile.

'You were right,' she said to Jacques. 'This truly has been one of the best meals I've ever had.' She tipped back her glass and drained it. 'Mm, I do love Sauternes. I feel truly spoilt, thank you.'

'Have you ever tried Canadian ice wine?' Jacques asked.

'No, but I've always wanted to.'

'But that's terrible,' Jacques said, 'for someone like you not to have tried one of the best wines ever created.' *This from a Frenchman.* 'We must correct the situation *immediatement*.'

Damn. Wrong answer, Kate thought. 'I don't know,' she said. 'I've already had so much to drink.' *And I would far rather be drinking in Fai right now.*

'Just one glass?' Jacques said.

'I guess it would be a pity not to.'

'I have one of the best bottles the country has ever produced at my villa. It was given to me by Canada's foreign minister when he stayed with us, and it would be my honour to share it with you.' *No, no, no, no, no.*

'Oh, I see. Um … I'd love to,' Kate said, 'but I do have an early start tomorrow.' *Not that I plan on getting any sleep.*

'I live five minutes away,' Jacques said. 'Come for one glass. I'll have you back here in an hour.'

Kate hesitated. Jacques had agreed to the barter; she didn't need to do this. *But the ink hasn't actually dried yet, and you don't want to mess this up now by seeming to be rude,* a voice inside argued.

'Well, maybe just one glass,' she said, aware that Jacques probably had his own barter deal in mind, and that she would have to play things carefully if she wanted to keep him sweet and still have her date with Fai.

On the ten-minute drive along the coast in Jacques' Mercedes convertible, she began to realise that it would be more difficult to extricate herself from this situation than she had at first imagined. And as she leant on the balustrade of his sweeping balcony, looking down at the beach gleaming in the moonlight, she began to wonder if she would make her date with Fai at all. *Don't be a fool; you have to make it,* an inner voice said. *You know that's where you want to be. You only agreed to one glass; stick to your guns.*

'*Et voila.*' Jacques emerged through French doors carrying two small glasses of honey-coloured liquid. He looked like he had stepped out of the pages of *GQ* magazine in his white open-neck shirt and stone-coloured trousers, his tanned feet now bare. Kate felt like she was watching herself play herself in a soap opera – dissociated from the action and as anxious as a viewer to know how this would end.

'Mm, pure nectar,' she said after her first sip. She tasted honey and apricots followed by lemon meringue pie. 'It's sweet, but there's still enough acidity so it's not at all cloying.'

'Exactly,' Jacques said. 'You have a good understanding of wine.' This would have been Kate's cue to mention her wine broker boyfriend, but she didn't, because she was still trading on a subtle sexual promise, even if she had no intention of delivering on it.

'You don't see it a lot in London. I remember it being very expensive,' she said.

'That's because it takes more grapes to make this than any other wine, and there's a lot of risk involved.'

'What kind of risk?' Kate asked.

'First of all, the grapes must stay on the vines much longer,' Jacques explained, 'because they can only be picked when all the water in them has turned to ice, leaving *un très petit pourcentage* of concentrated juice. This means they are more at risk from predators like birds.'

Much as the longer you stay here, the more at risk you are of being plucked by Jacques, Kate told herself. *You must leave after this glass of wine.*

'Also, they must stay frozen throughout the picking process and then be pressed before they melt,' Jacques continued. 'So they generally pick them by hand in the middle of the night.'

'And they can't just freeze the grapes?' Kate asked.

'No. If the freezing is not totally natural, they can't call it ice wine.'

'It seems a lot of trouble to go to for something that's gone in seconds,' Kate said.

'I think the sweetest things in life always involve some sacrifice,' Jacques said.

What is the sweetest thing in your life? Kate asked herself. Until not so long ago, she had thought it was Daniel, yet she had betrayed him with Fai. And now she was here, purportedly to secure a barter deal, but was that all this was about? Jacques wasn't an unattractive man. She would love to hear what her psychologist, Dr Cook, would have to say about all this.

'It *is* one of the best things I've ever tasted,' Kate said. *My soul for a glass of wine.* Looking down at the beach as she sipped the sweet nectar, she recognised it for the first time as the one she had run along on her second morning in Mauritius. So much had happened since then. It was hard to believe it was only just over a week ago.

'I ran along this stretch of beach when I was at Paradise Bay,' she said. 'It was raining and deserted, and I felt so peaceful.'

'Ah, I thought I recognised you from somewhere,' Jacques said. 'I was here, having a coffee. I wondered who the crazy girl was out running when most tourists were still in bed.'

Kate recalled the man in the towelling robe. *Of course.* She should have known that the universe had a joke up its sleeve when she imagined herself on the balcony with him. She hadn't meant it quite like this. *Careful what you wish for.* Then, remembering her humiliating fall and flight, she felt her cheeks heat up.

'That was quite a fall,' Jacques said as if reading her mind. 'I was worried you'd hurt yourself, but then you were gone.'

'I'm sorry. I should have thanked you. It was kind of you to come to my aid, but it was nothing,' Kate turned her head to look at the beach. 'The view's beautiful.'

'That's what I was thinking,' Jacques said, leaning on the balustrade and looking at her. *Very smooth.*

He bent over and kissed her bare shoulder, which tingled, and then he moved to her neck. Kate knew she should move away, but she didn't. The alcohol in her system had dulled her senses, and she felt as though she was suspended above reality like the stars above her. She stared at the shimmering path cast by the moon on the sea, reaching all the way to the horizon like an undulating yellow brick road to the end of a dream. London and Daniel couldn't be farther away. *And Fai? What about Fai?* He was a holiday fling, and though she felt a pang of longing coupled with guilt for deserting him, didn't all holiday flings ultimately fade like dreams in the blazing fluorescent lights of one's everyday life, anyway? The only consequence she had to worry about involved safeguarding her career – *the sweetest thing after all?* And, for that, she needed Jacques.

Their glasses empty, Jacques disappeared inside to get the bottle. *Now,* a voice inside said. *This is your last chance.* And when Kate still didn't budge, the voice asked, *What's wrong with you? Are you really going to sell yourself out? Which makes you what?*

It made her Kate Richmond – a disaster zone when it came to affairs of the heart. It was inevitable that she would fuck things up, so it might as well be for a good cause, she told herself, although she knew that her reasoning was morally flawed and that she herself was flawed in all sorts of ways.

'I want to know what love is. I want you to show me,' she sang to the glittering night sky, transforming the Foreigner hit into a prayer. 'I want to feel what love is. I know you can show me.' Kate's tone was tortured by alcohol and anguish as she continued her lament. 'In my life there's been heartache and pain …'

She heard Jacques behind her, and seconds later she felt his fingers in her hair and his breath on her neck as his lips brushed her ear.

'You smell nice,' he said. 'Givenchy?' *Bingo.* He put his hand on her back as he filled her glass. 'You're cold.'

Yes, indeed. You're as cold as ice. You're willing to sacrifice our love, her inner voice now sang, picking up on the Foreigner theme. *You never take advice. Someday you'll pay the price, I know. You're digging for gold, yet throwing away a fortune in feelings …*

'Shall we go inside?' Jacques asked, and Kate let him take her hand and lead her to a low modular sofa in the living area.

'I don't think I should be doing this,' she mumbled as he manoeuvred her into a reclining position. But her words hit his chest and fell in pieces to the ground, where the fluffy flokati rug muffled their sound.

Jacques' hand cupped a breast over her slip dress as he leant down to kiss her and, although her body didn't shout 'yes', it didn't shout 'no' either. She felt coolly distant from her actions, as though watching that soap opera again, in which Jacques now, seemingly in one adept movement, lifted her dress, slipped off her panties, and parted her thighs. Then, after briefly and roughly rubbing his hand between her legs – more, it seemed, to prepare the way than to impart any pleasure – he entered her and moved on top of her like rhythmic waves crashing down on a beach, while she, like the sand, was compliant and yielding, until finally the tide subsided.

'Was it good for you?' Jacques asked, absent-mindedly circling one of her nipples with a finger.

Kate wanted to throw up. Her head was spinning and her body felt numb and used, but she mumbled, 'Yes,' which appeared to satisfy him. *Who is the hunter and who the hunted now?*

Jacques reached over her to retrieve a box of Gauloises and a gold lighter from the coffee table. 'Cigarette?' he asked, holding out the familiar blue box. She took one, and he lit it before lighting his own. 'What about something to drink?' he asked. 'Cognac? *Encore du vin*?'

'Something soft would be good,' she said. She had had more than enough of the hard stuff in every respect.

'I'll see what I've got. I'm not very good at stocking up when I'm on my own,' he said.

When he's on his own? When Jacques wasn't on his own, Kate imagined he would be spending time with the petite platinum blonde and the two teenage boys in the photographs on the bookshelf next to the TV. He hadn't mentioned a family, but in Kate's current dichotomous – make that 'trichotomous' – situation, who was she to question this omission?

As he walked across the room wearing nothing but his white shirt, she couldn't help observing that he was in good shape for a man his age, for a man of any age, although her body had no opinion on the matter. She felt like a blow-up doll, fast deflating after being of service.

She heard the sound of a fridge opening and ice being wrenched from an ice tray as she moved back into the upright position and picked up her black lace Agent Provocateur panties selected for Fai this evening.

Is infidelity hereditary? she wondered as her mind drifted back to that day ten or eleven years ago when she had realised that her father was up to his old tricks again.

She had been in the middle of exams at university and, having reached information overload, had taken the train into London with her friend Joanna, in search of some bling at the Selfridges sale for the end-of-year ball. And, of all the unlikely places, *that* was where she had seen him: her father, a man who hated shopping. He was in the women's coat section next to accessories, and Kate's first thought was that her mother must have dragged him there. It was strange, though, that her mother hadn't mentioned a trip to London, considering that this required an overnight stay at least and a fair amount of planning. Then her father moved slightly, and she saw that he was with a woman who wasn't her mother.

Perhaps this is a business trip and this woman is a medical rep? Kate thought, or hoped. But why then was his hand resting intimately in the small of her back? As she pondered this question, her father must have said something funny because the woman looked up at him and laughed, at which point he leant down to kiss her on the mouth, putting an end to any ambiguity.

What most bothered Kate was the type of woman this person was – not the cheap tart with whom she had imagined her father having an affair the last time. This one looked nice, her fair hair cut in a neat bob. She actually looked strangely like Kate's mother, but a younger, slimmer, more up-to-date model, like this season's coats, nipped in at the waist. When in her thirties, Kate's mother had also been slim and probably more attractive than this model, but now, stretched out of shape by three pregnancies, one miscarriage, and a 'mismarriage', she was clearly last season's offcast.

Unable to stomach watching her father with this woman for a moment longer, Kate raced outside, where she promptly threw up on Selfridges' grand doorstep, infuriating a woman wearing green suede pumps that got caught in the crossfire. Kate had never been able to look at green shoes again.

Is infidelity part of my DNA? Kate asked herself again as she stubbed out her cigarette in an ashtray on the coffee table. *An inescapable character flaw passed down from one generation to the next? Or, in trying not to become my mother, have I simply become my father instead?*

CHAPTER 9

Tea and Sympathy

Kate's head felt like the inside of a washing machine. It was one of those occasions when she had mistakenly thrown in a belt, and the buckle was clunking against the drum with each rotation. Now a piercing, ringing sound penetrated the spinning drum. She had to stop it. She reached out in the direction of its source, and her fingers found the edge of the side table. Finally, they landed on the telephone's receiver, which she brought very slowly to her ear.

'Good morning, this is your six o' clock wake-up call. Have a nice day.'

She let the receiver drop on the bed and groaned as consciousness began to enter the cloudy foam in her head, allowing her to make out individual pieces of dirty laundry rolling around. The detour to the villa, the wine, the sofa … Fai, she thought. She recalled his numerous texts and voice messages, a note of concern creeping into his tone by the third one, and then his final resigned goodbye. *Oh God.* Guilt was added to the load, making her feel even more nauseous. *What must he think?*

She should phone him and explain. *And what exactly are you going to say? 'Sorry I didn't make it last night. I was held up shagging your CEO, but don't worry, it was a mere business transaction, as passionless as an appointment with the dentist.' And Daniel?* She would think about him later. *One load of dirty laundry at a time.* But first she would take a shower, the only cleansing she could manage for now.

She emerged from the bathroom with a fluffy white towel wrapped around her throbbing head, feeling cleaner but no clearer on what she should say to Fai. Part of her wanted to simply dump the dirty laundry and run, but he didn't deserve that. She had to at least say goodbye, she thought as she gingerly picked up the receiver and punched his number into the keypad. It rang for a while, during which time her inner coward hoped she would get his answering machine.

'Hello, this is Fai Li.' She waited for the rest of the message to play out, now disappointed that she wouldn't get to speak to him after all.

'Hello?'

'Oh, right. Hi. It's me. Kate,' she spluttered.

'Ah, Kate.'

'I … I'm sorry I didn't make it last night … I …' *What? What possible excuse is there for my behaviour?*

'Don't worry about it,' he said. His tone said she should worry.

'I know I should have called you. I feel terrible. I don't know why …'

'It's fine. Forget about it. Really.'

'It's not, actually. It's just, I drank too much and I …' She was going to say, 'Passed out'. *So you're just going to pile lie upon lie now? What's wrong with you?* If under the influence of about six different wine cultivars, she had been completely aware of what she was doing; her morals and judgment were simply warped. 'I'm sorry, Fai. I truly did want to see you, but I just …' There was no logical explanation, beyond the fact that when it came to love, she, like the black widow spider, was programmed to weave a web of deceit and finally eat her mate.

There was a knock at the door.

'I'm coming,' Kate shouted. 'I really loved my time with you,' she said, as the knock became several knocks. 'Sorry, can I call you back?'

'Don't worry about it.'

'I'd like to …'

'Really, I'd rather you didn't.' His tone was cold, not like ice, which might melt, but like a heavy stone that had sunk to the bottom of the Arctic Ocean and could never be retrieved.

'But …'

'You don't need to explain anything,' Fai said. 'Look, to be honest, I spoke to a friend on reception and he told me that you left with Jacques and didn't get back till this morning. Anyway, we know what this is … was.

I should have realised. I just thought this was diff— ... It really doesn't matter. Goodbye, Kate.' The phone went dead.

Kate opened the door to find her personal butler, Sandeep, standing on the other side. 'I have a message from your colleague Kirsten,' he said. 'She urgently needs you to go to the White Sands hotel on the way to the airport. She says there's a problem with the account.' Kate's heart sank as she wondered if her bargaining prowess hadn't sealed the deal after all, making her not only a tart but also an incompetent one.

* * *

Many hours later in a different world, Kate passed a handful of notes and coins through the glass partition that separated the black cab's passenger section from the driver. 'Keep the change.'

'Thanks, love. Mind you don't get too wet out there. Sugar melts.' *Lucky then that a little water never bothered a toad,* Kate thought. She appreciated the sentiment nonetheless and was grateful for his much-needed warmth. *Cabbies are London's guardian angels,* she thought as she stepped out onto the pavement and reached back in for her luggage, at which precise moment the rain doubled in intensity, instantly soaking her through.

'Why don't you throw in some hail and lightning while you're about it?' she shouted up at the sky. 'We all know I deserve it.'

'All right back there, sweetheart?' the cabbie called out.

Once under the cover of the portico outside her building, she rummaged in her bag for the keys, finally stepping into the drab, musty-smelling common hallway littered with pamphlets for takeout curry and pizza. *Toto, I've a feeling we're not in paradise anymore.*

'Hi, Kate. Welcome back,' Chloe's voice issued from the living room as Kate finally crossed the threshold of the apartment and dropped her luggage in a heap just inside the front door, not sure how she had made it up the two flights of stairs and certainly unable to take the bags any further. 'Sorry, could you come in here? I can't move.' Kate dumped her soggy suede jacket on top of everything and then took a step in Chloe's direction, almost tripping over Mushroom.

'Mushy,' she said, leaning down and scooping up her Persian cat, named for his coat, which was the grey-brown tone of shiitake mushrooms.

She had started out calling him Shiitake but had realised her mistake the instant she had affectionately called him Shitty. 'How's my favourite man?' she asked, hugging him to her as he purred and vibrated like an old generator. 'Have you missed me?' *Probably not,* she thought, knowing that in her absence Chloe would have fed him more tasty things than cat food. If no longer true for the modern metrosexual male, the way to this cat's heart would always be through his stomach.

Clutching Mushy, Kate followed Chloe's voice into the living room, where she found her best friend and housemate on the couch, one foot up as she painted her toenails.

'Hi, Chlo,' she said. 'I didn't expect you to be here. What happened to yoga?'

'I cancelled. I wanted to see how you were and to give the flat a bit of a clean before you got here,' Chloe said.

'Uh-huh,' Kate said as she swept the room with a glance, taking in two red-wine-stained glasses on the mantelpiece, a couple of mugs on the mosaic-topped coffee table, and magazines strewn on the floor next to elements of Chloe's jewellery-making endeavours. Kate wasn't particularly tidy, but she was a minimalist activist on a par with John Pawson in comparison to Chloe. She bent down to kiss her friend, careful not to upset the nail polish. 'Midnight blue – très dramatic.'

Much like her flat, which featured jewel-coloured walls – ruby red in the living room – and pre-loved furniture invigorated with mosaic, Chloe's body was just another canvas for her artistic expression. Her strawberry blonde hair currently boasted blue streaks; she had an angel tattooed on her shoulder; and she was wearing a maroon vest with cotton drawstring trousers personally screen-printed with purple and orange flowers.

'You look fantastic, K,' Chloe said, 'although I guess you don't feel it. You must be shattered?'

'Thanks, and I am,' Kate said. She dropped into one of the armchairs, jarring Mushy, who jumped out of her arms. He crossed the room to rub himself against Chloe, who dived for the open nail polish bottle just before his tail swept the coffee table.

'You are one fickle feline,' Kate said as Mushy hopped onto the sofa next to Chloe. 'I bet you haven't opened a single tin of cat food while I've been away,' she said to Chloe.

'I hate the smell of that stuff,' Chloe said. 'And it's good for him to have a bit of variety.'

'At the expense of my carefully budgeted meal plan,' Kate said. But it was good to find her cat as fickle as ever, her friend's unsanitary habits unchanged, and things generally much as she had left them, especially when it seemed that a cyclone had ripped through her psyche, leaving her own interior décor in total disarray.

'So how did it go?' Chloe asked. 'Did you manage to get everything in despite the weather? What a nightmare.' She started painting a toe on her second foot. 'Sorry, I will give you my full attention in a minute, but if I don't finish now, I'll never get around to it – and it's very distracting looking at odd feet during yoga.'

'I think we've got the makings of a summer special,' Kate said, 'but it was exhausting. I feel like I was just putting out fires the whole time, and not very successfully. I'm glad it's over, actually.' She sighed deeply and pressed her eyebrows to release some of the tension behind them.

Chloe scrutinised her through her small, round, wire-rimmed glasses. 'Actually, you do look tired,' she said. 'Can I make you a cup of tea?'

'There are not words to describe how good that sounds, but let your toes dry first.'

'Normal or special needs? Something relaxing maybe?' Chloe compensated for a lack of interest in foodstuffs containing any nutritional value with a supply of herbal teas to solve every mental or physical ailment from a postnasal drip to PMT. Kate didn't think there was one for a cheating heart.

'I think I'll stick to PG Tips with milk and sugar, thanks,' Kate said, too tempted by the tea to protest any more. Chloe hobbled across the room with a red rubber toe divider still in place on her left foot, followed closely by Mushy. 'What have you been feeding my cat, just so I know what I'm up against?'

'The usual – tinned tuna, fish and chips, burgers,' Chloe said. Fast food was one of the basic food groups for Chloe, whose culinary skills didn't extend much farther than heating things up. Her body was nonetheless enviably sylphlike because, unlike Kate, she barely thought about food and sometimes forgot to eat altogether.

Kate heard Chloe's retro kettle whistle. A few minutes later, her friend returned bearing an oversized white mug of steaming milky tea and a plate topped with two slices of Battenberg cake. 'Welcome home,' she said, handing the cake to Kate with a flourish.

The pink and yellow checked sponge confection wrapped in marzipan was one of the few things that Kate and Chloe both loved equally and had loved since they were children. Although Kate's mother had sometimes baked Battenberg cake, Kate had always preferred the unnaturally bright and overly sweet kind available from the corner store that was served up at Chloe's house and that she was currently wolfing down. She was ravenous, she realised, and the comforting cake hit the spot. She also appreciated the gesture because, for her and Chloe, Battenberg wasn't merely cake; they had decided early on that it was symbolic of their friendship, the yellow squares representing fair-haired Kate, and the pink ones, strawberry-blonde Chloe.

Their contrasting hair colour aside, Kate and Chloe were as different as those yellow and pink squares in a number of other respects, from their tastes in clothing to their views on politics (Chloe was a pacifist), plastic surgery (Kate wasn't averse to the idea), and love (Chloe believed in The One). But seeing things differently, they had been able to help each other through some difficult times – they had both lost a father, although in very different ways –and their shared experiences were like the apricot jam that held the squares together, with their common roots in Cornwall being the marzipan that enfolded the cake.

'I almost forgot,' Chloe said, getting up. She left the room, and returned with a smoky blue glass ice bucket overflowing with dusty pink peonies. 'For you.' Chloe placed the bucket on the coffee table in front of Kate.

'Oh wow, they're beautiful.' Peonies were Kate's favourite flowers. 'You're a sweetheart.'

'K, I love you dearly, but flowers? They're from Daniel, idiot; the ice bucket too. He dropped them off before he left.'

There was a note tucked into the flowers.

> *Welcome back, beautiful. I missed you hugely. Sorry I'm not there, but you're in big trouble on Thursday. Love you. —D*
>
> *P.S. When you're done with the flowers, there's something to take their place in the fridge. And, yes, it is appropriate.*

'Pink Champagne,' Chloe said. Kate remembered the bottle she had passed up at their last supper, when it had seemed premature. Well, now it was 'postmature'.

'He's a prince,' Chloe added.

'I know,' *said the toad.*

'He felt bad that he couldn't be here to pick you up from the airport.'

Kate stared at the flowers and suddenly felt very sad. A dark tide of emotions began to gather deep down inside her. Building and pushing, it turned into a wave that moved up through her chest and into her throat before filling her head and prickling the backs of her eyes. Finally, tears began to flow.

'Shit, Kate, what's wrong?'

'I ...' Kate couldn't breathe. She sucked in air, gasped, and then let out a strangled sob.

'Everything's ...,' Kate said. 'I'm ... I've really fucked things up.'

'Don't be silly; I'm sure you did the best job possible in light of the cyclone,' Chloe said.

'It's not just the job,' Kate wailed. 'It's ... I'm a fuck-up.' *Literally.*

'You're tired,' Chloe said. 'You've had a lot to contend with.'

'I have,' Kate said, 'and you don't know the half of it. You have no idea what I've done. I've ...' Where should she begin? After gasping again for air, she wailed, 'I'm going to end up with a chimpanzee.'

'What?'

'A chimpanzee,' she repeated. 'Like Trista Holmes. And it's all I deserve.'

'I have no idea what you're talking about,' Chloe said with a baffled expression, since she wasn't familiar with the fifty-something former editor of *Dazzle* magazine who had spent her childbearing years in magazine never–never land, using men like vibrators, and who now shared her life with a pet chimpanzee. 'But before you go cuckoo on me, I do think you should have a long relaxing bath and then get a decent night's sleep. You don't have to go to work tomorrow, I hope.'

'You're kidding, right? Of course I do. I've got so much to catch up on, and there's ...' The prospect of unveiling her food shoot set off another emotional uprising. 'My career's probably over,' she said, before breaking into another wave of sobs.

'Breathe,' Chloe said. 'Deeply.' Kate breathed in and choked, and then coughed. 'Again. In for the count of four. Hold it.' Chloe paused. 'And out for the count of six. And in. Okay, keep that up while I run your bath. I'm also going to put a piece of clear quartz next to your bed, which I want you to hold over your solar plexus for about ten minutes, breathing deeply. I promise you, you'll feel a whole lot calmer. Just trust me on this and do it, okay?'

When Kate heard Chloe dragging her suitcase along the passage, she wanted to tell her not to worry, but she didn't have the energy; she felt like a washed-up, waterlogged bit of post-cyclone debris. A few minutes later, the soothing sound of running water reached her, and answering its call, she found the bathroom transformed into a sanctuary of flickering candlelight.

'You're an angel,' she shouted to Chloe as she immersed her body in the warm, patchouli-scented water. She thought how lucky she was to have such a stable and enduring friendship as theirs. *At least this is still intact.* But when a relationship came with a penis, everything seemed to change.

'You're projecting your mother's relationship with your father onto your own experiences with men,' Dr Cook had said. *Not exactly a Nobel Prize–winning prognosis.* 'While you fear rejection, you want to be loved, as you feel she was never loved. And you are caught in a cycle of seduction-or-nothing.' *Marginally more insightful.*

While Kate's serial singledom had not bothered her through her early twenties (it had, in fact, been a choice – get in, enjoy, and exit before things turn bad), she had begun to question whether a series of short, passionate love affairs could, after all, add up to a lifetime of happiness. So, on the advice of a friend, she had found herself on Dr Cook's couch.

Could she recall a relationship that hadn't been overshadowed by this fear of rejection, Dr Cook had asked, thus bringing Rupert Irving to the surface.

He had been in her English class at university and had also spent the previous year abroad, in his case as an exchange student in Chile, which had given them something in common. Although he was fanciable – he had dark hair, blue eyes, and a consistent, sexy amount of evening shadow – friendly coffee company and foreign-movie dates had been just fine for Kate until, one night at a party, things progressed to drunken bathroom sex and later to something with less hilarity and more intimacy. She had fallen deeply, unquestioningly, unconditionally in love for the first time in her life. Suddenly every love song made sense and every commonplace experience was like an exotic trip. Until the day that she caught Rupert staring longingly at a tall, slim girl with long dark hair and knew with sickening certainty that he wasn't quite as deeply, unquestioningly in love with her.

Jealousy had begun to gnaw at her stomach like a flesh-eating parasite, before moving on to her brain tissue, making her paranoid. She saw predators and danger signs everywhere. But there were moments of such beauty along the way that she forged on, hoping that the relationship wouldn't end badly, much as she had hoped when reading *Anna Karenina* that the heroine wouldn't be cast aside and then throw herself under a train, although it was already written.

It was shortly after her inevitable and devastating break-up with Rupert that Kate had run from the scene of her father's infidelity in Selfridges and returned to finish her exams, numbing her pain – and getting her cardio – by sleeping with any guy who looked at her. Later, when she had confronted her father, he had vowed never to do it again while she had agreed to say nothing of it to her mother. But in the end, he had left anyway because the baby was on the way.

If the combination of her own heartbreak, her father's serial infidelities, and her mother's declarations that men were all bastards had not inoculated her to love entirely, Kate had, from that moment, become extra vigilant at spotting the first signs that a relationship might cause pain, and eliminating it before it spread to the heart and any serious harm was done. No symptom was too small to ignore. If, for example, a boyfriend flirted with a waitress, Kate would wonder what he would do if she herself weren't around – ask for the waitress's number? Or if he mentioned anything that implied he thought she had put on weight, even something as mild as, 'You're really having another piece of cheesecake?' she would think, *What about when I've had a third baby? Is that when his eye will start wandering?* If there were issues when love was fresh and dewy, then what would happen when time started to turn its petals brown? No, it was safer to nip it in the proverbial bud. So began her cycle of seduction-or-nothing.

Then Kate had fallen deeply, madly in love for the second time in her life, this time with her job at *Be*, and suddenly there was neither the time nor the need for Dr Cook and her affirmations. Entering Kate's life when the love affair was in full bloom, Daniel had initially been like the third party in a ménage à trois. Kate had simply enjoyed the attention, the intrigue, the seduction, and the companionship without thinking about it too much. It was only when he had said those three little words and she had said them back that she realised they were heartfelt.

So why did I cheat with Fai? she asked herself as she lay in the bath. But even as she thought of him, a warm tide washed over her body, telling her that given another chance she would do it again.

And Jacques? That was going to take a lot more than tears and a soak in the tub to figure out. She could say she had taken one for the team, had simply lain back and thought of *Be*, but if she was honest with herself, then she had to admit that she had been thinking of no one more than herself, forsaking all others. *Maybe Dr Cook got it all wrong and my problem isn't a lack of self-love, but rather a surplus of it,* she thought.

In bed, after trying Chloe's quartz trick and failing to calm the kaleidoscope contemplation in her mind, Kate turned out the light on the musings of the protagonist in *The Transit of Venus*. Drifting off to sleep, she felt soft fur brushing her cheek and rich purring filling her ear.

'So you do still love me?' she murmured sleepily. 'At least I'll always have you.'

As Mushy assumed his usual position behind her back, Kate wondered if a cat as a life partner was really any different from a pet chimpanzee.

CHAPTER 10

Walking on Eggshells

Kate slid her access card through the electronic scanner and, since her hands were full, nudged the office's glass door open with her shoulder. Unusually for someone often introduced as 'the Late Kate', she had come in early (and very much alive – for now) to clear her desk and prepare for the battles that lay ahead. The office was thus in darkness and devoid of life apart from shafts of dancing light entering through the double-volume warehouse windows.

The nondescript space furnished with standard desks in departmental clusters generally disappointed magazine outsiders, who expected the office to be as glossy as *Be*'s pages. And it looked even more bland than usual at this hour, Kate thought, while walking past the fashion department's bare clothes rails. She stopped in the beauty department next door in order to deposit a brown paper bag on the beauty editor's desk. This contained a vile-tasting herbal tea from Port Louis market, which advertised itself as a cellulite-combating miracle, the quest for which was a type of holy grail for Jasmine. Moving aside an eyelash-perming kit and nose-lifting cream to make space for the bag, Kate thought that if she ever felt her vanity was shallow, she only had to take a peek in here. 'Here's hoping! —K,' she scribbled on a Post-it note, which she attached to the bag, before moving on to the features department.

She found her desk plastered with yellow Post-it notes bearing messages received in her absence, and scattered with packages in every shape and form. Although tempted to investigate their contents – particularly what looked like two cases of wine tucked under her desk – she simply removed a couple of packages from her chair so that she could sit down and address the most urgent item on her agenda: Operation Covert Photo Shoot.

She plugged Serge's USB into her computer and clicked on the folder entitled 'Selection'. Although, as requested, Serge had supplied all the images unedited as well, Kate found that his choices and touch-ups were good, and seen in the context of these grey London surrounds, they looked even more vibrant than they had in Mauritius. She could almost taste again the sweet white flesh of the lobster with the coriander butter melting into it, smell the herb-infused fish on its platter, hear again the hiss of the fire as moisture from the octopus hit the coals, and sense the air of camaraderie as everyone pulled together to create magic. She was so in awe of the images' beauty that, for a moment, she entertained the possibility that Amber would thank her for forging ahead with the shoot despite explicit instructions not to. Returning to the land of the lucid, she told herself that the chances of that happening were slimmer than Kate Moss in her 'rexy' heyday. *How am I even going to bring it up with Amber?* she wondered as she saved Serge's selection to a new USB. Perhaps caffeine would help.

One of the advantages of having an editor who survived largely on stimulants was that *Be* had a top-of-the-range Gaggia coffee maker along with a Baratza grinder and a constant supply of Amber's preferred free trade coffee beans, the only indulgence Simon had thus far overlooked. Back at her desk, Kate rested her elbows on her desk and wrapped her hands around the large, warm cup, grateful for this small mercy. Inhaling the coffee's rich aroma, she looked down at the damp street two storeys below, where a small queue was already forming at the hole-in-the-wall coffee outlet over the road. On these rare occasions when she made it in early, she was always surprised at how much life was in evidence at this ungodly hour.

'Hi. Nice holiday?'

Kate jumped. Hot coffee spilt onto her hand, scalding it. 'Ow. Shit.' She turned around to see *Be*'s chief subeditor standing behind her.

'Wow, Jugs, why so on edge?' Harry's nickname for Kate derived from the fact that she was one of the few *Be* staff members with breasts larger than sultana grapes. He thought the term hilarious. Kate did not, but she had long since given up asking him to refrain from using it.

'I didn't hear you. Could you make a little bit more noise if you're going to approach in the shadow of darkness?' Kate paused to suck her scalded hand. 'And it wasn't a holiday.'

'Whatever you say, but look at it through the eyes of a sad scrubber, stuck here cleaning your copy while you find inspiration in a drink with an umbrella in it. Nice tan, by the way.'

'Thanks.' Kate glanced down at a brown arm. Admittedly, it did form a stark contrast to Harry's translucent skin, which, teamed with his red-tinged, sleep-deprived eyes, white-blond hair, and wheaten brows, invited comparisons with *Alice in Wonderland*'s White Rabbit, particularly when he was rushing towards a very important deadline.

'It did have its moments,' she admitted, 'but, as you've no doubt heard, it wasn't exactly a long, cold Pina Colada either.'

'No, more like a Sex on the Beach, by the sound of things.' Harry smiled suggestively, putting Kate's triggers suddenly on high alert.

She narrowed her eyes questioningly at him. 'What do you mean by that, exactly?'

'Oh, I don't know; I just heard that it wasn't all work and no play for some happy campers.'

'Don't believe everything you hear,' Kate snapped. *Shit.*

'I hear Food had to go,' Harry said.

'Mm-hm,' she said without looking at him. She would have to keep the shoot to herself until she had revealed it to Amber.

'Amber says you've still got to decide on a location, so I've moved it to the back of the schedule,' Harry said. 'That means I'll need Travel and Décor sooner. I'll pop over the July flat plan and production schedule later.'

'No rest for the wicked,' Kate said.

'Definitely none at all for you then,' Harry said with a wink in his tone.

'What exactly are you insinuating, Harry?' Kate asked. 'Could you spit it out or give it up, because I'm really in no mood for guessing games?'

'Jeez, Jugs, take a chill pill and let me know when you're feeling its effects.'

Harry moved on in his brisk, White Rabbit way, leaving Kate to her edgy paranoia. *Who could have told him about my island affair?* she puzzled. Kirsten would have been in email contact with Harry regarding the schedule, but she was aware that it was a delicate situation. Kate didn't think she would have betrayed her trust. Roberta didn't concern herself with the love lives of the common people and certainly didn't engage in banter with minions such as Harry. Everyone else on the trip had been freelance. To take her mind off the matter, Kate began to sort through the contents of her in tray, arranging its contents into piles according to rank.

Top priority: Amber's comments on Kate's proposal for August's and September's food, travel, and décor stories; an invitation to appear on an obscure radio programme, for which she would need approval.

Definitely yes: An invitation to the launch of Sunrise Sausages' new packaging – not because of a burning desire to see what had replaced the sausages on sunloungers, but because Sunrise was an important advertiser and Simon had issued strict instructions that editorial was to be nice to advertisers right now; an invitation to an awards dinner sponsored by a washing machine company – printed on a box of washing powder, this was equally unexciting but essential to revenue; the launch of an alternative tea menu at the May Fair Bar, introducing the delectable likes of a peppermint tea Martini, served up with cupcakes at 4 p.m. daily – *one has to consider the needs of readers, too, after all.*

No: An invitation to the launch of a Cuban cigar lounge – although appealing and accompanied by a cigar and cigarette lighter bearing a picture of Che Guevara, it coincided with the washing powder awards dinner.

Perhaps: Invitations to interesting but non-essential events; press releases that may or may not translate into editorial …

Halfway down the pile, there was a black envelope tied with a purple ribbon, with a handwritten note paper-clipped to it.

Hi, Lovely,

This is a little thank you for putting me in touch with Daniel. He's been enormously helpful, and my client, De-Vine Beauty, adores him, which is very good for me. This was a freebie, so you don't have to be too grateful, but I do hope you both enjoy it. Look forward to hearing all about the trip.

Jas
xxx

Finding a voucher for a couples massage inside the envelope, Kate remembered that she had given Jasmine Daniel's number for a South African skincare company, which had been looking for a London-based wine expert for some reason. At the time, she had thought it wonderfully synchronous because Daniel had recently started to look at the South African wine market, but now she decided that synchronicity was overrated. She must get to the bottom of who was spreading the gossip.

The door banged closed. Kate turned to see Amber's assistant, Vanessa, enter dressed in her signature head-to-toe black. Not one to chat, Vanessa waved hello across the room, setting a chunky silver charm bracelet jingling as she marched directly to her desk. Five minutes later, Kate's landline rang.

'Are you in this afternoon?' Vanessa didn't have time for niceties.

'Yes, I'll be here all day,' Kate said.

'Amber wants to see you. Can you do two thirty?'

'That sounds fine.'

'And you need to get a full rundown of expenses to us and Lisa in accounts ASAP, by no later than eleven.' Vanessa didn't say 'A-S-A-P' but 'Asap', like it was a word.

Kate sighed. She had hoped to be able to put off filling out the expense form until the next day, as she knew she would need all her strength to do it. When she had received Kirsten's urgent message regarding the account in her hotel room the previous morning – was it really only a day ago? – she had presumed the worst: that Jacques had reneged on their barter deal. As it turned out, he had been a gentleman in that respect at least. But add in a diving team, minivans, reconstructive facials, and designer mineral water, among other expenses notched up by Roberta, and the bill had still been astronomical. After going through it rupee by rupee with the taxi waiting, Kate had been forced to accept it for fact and just sign off on it.

Now, as she pulled the wad of bills out of her bag, she realised that explaining the food shoot might be the least of her worries. And when Daniel's name popped up on her mobile phone's screen ten minutes later, she was reminded of that other whole can of worms that remained to be opened. She felt the space below her ribcage contract, trapping her heart like a small bird that began to flap wildly as she put her phone to her ear.

'Hi, Dan,' she said tentatively, doing her best to control the tremor in her voice.

'Sorry, did I wake you? I'm guessing you got in late last night.'

'Oh, I wish you had, but I'm already at work – so much to do. How are you?'

'You didn't call? I gave Chloe strict instructions.'

'I'm sorry. I was so exhausted, I just crashed the moment I got home.' She was becoming a veritable Mata Hari lately, with lies tripping off her tongue, but she couldn't blurt everything out now. *How on earth am I going to confess to him?* 'Thanks for the flowers. They're beautiful. And the ice bucket.'

'Don't thank me now; I'm looking forward to being thanked in kind.' It was strange to hear genuine warmth in his voice, knowing that she was so undeserving of it. 'Can you make it over after work tomorrow night, do you think? I'm flying into City Airport at six, and I don't think I'll last till Friday.'

'Of course,' she said. The bird had stopped flapping its wings.

'And I've been scouring the markets here to indulge you over the weekend. I wish you were with me. You'd love this old lock-keeper's house I'm staying in. I want to bring you here one day.'

'Mm, sounds lovely,' Kate said, thinking regretfully that she would almost certainly not be going to any lock-keeper's lodge in France.

'Oh, and by the way, Wapping has been declared a work-free zone for the entire weekend, just so you know,' Daniel added.

Kate laughed as the phone on her desk started ringing. 'Hang on a sec, sweets. It's Dave in art, and it's never a good idea to ignore him.'

'I'll let you go,' Daniel said. 'I'll ring you later. I love you.'

'Me too,' Kate said, feeling the sentence ambiguous enough to be true – *I love you too/I love me too.*

* * *

Separated from the rest of the space by a glass wall, Amber's office resembled a giant fish tank in which the editor could be observed going about her activities like a decorative tropical fish, stingray, or shark, depending on her attire and mood. Today, wearing a black dress with a full skirt, and a wide belt that accentuated her tiny waist, Amber resembled a feathery-finned Siamese fighting fish, Kate thought as she approached the office. Since this was a fish whose delicate beauty disguised a vicious capacity for stealth attacks, she felt even more nervous about the very solid grounds for aggression she was clutching in her sweaty palm.

Amber was standing behind her desk (a hybrid of Victorian dining table legs and a modern glass top) with one arm stretched out of the window, sprinkling cigarette ash onto the heads of unsuspecting pedestrians below.

'Close the door,' she said in an icy tone.

Kate did as she was told. Then she took a couple of steps and hovered halfway between door and desk, all the better to flee when the contents of the USB attracted a volley of verbal bullets.

'Sit,' Amber said.

Kate once again obeyed. She sensed a forbidding mood, and momentarily questioned why this might be, since she hadn't yet divulged the shoot. The reason became immediately apparent when she saw the telephone directory of expense forms sitting squarely in front of Amber's chair.

'I don't know where to begin,' Amber said.

Since Kate didn't know where to begin either, she mutely tracked the journey of Amber's cigarette back through the window, noticing that Amber's hand was shaking slightly as she brought the cigarette to her ruby lips. 'How on earth did the expenses get so out of control?' Amber didn't look at Kate as she asked the question. Instead, she focused on the plume of smoke rising into the air. Unprepared for this line of attack, Kate too simply watched the plume of smoke.

'I realise the cyclone threw things out,' Amber continued, 'but this is ridiculous.' She picked up the wad of expense forms with her free hand and slammed them back down on the desk.

'I'm sorry,' Kate said in a tinny voice. 'I know they're high – a lot higher than I expected, actually – but there were quite a few fires to put out.' *Don't apologise, idiot. The expenses, for one, are not your fault.*

'Well, you should have found more cost-effective ways to put them out, especially after I expressly asked you to keep on top of expenses,'

Amber said. She stubbed out her cigarette in an ashtray on the windowsill that was already brimful with lipstick-stained butts, and then sat down. Perching her vintage diamante-studded glasses on her nose, she began to riffle through the papers, affording Kate a view of the top of her head. Her thick red hair, pulled back into a chignon, looked unusually greasy, Kate noticed. 'A luxury camper van, diving services – what on earth were we doing paying for these?' Amber said, looking up. 'Do you understand the meaning of the word *barter*, Kate? It means the exchange of goods or services for other goods or services, not cash.' Kate was inclined to mention that she had in fact exchanged certain services for the upgrade. 'And oxygen facials?' Amber looked at Kate incredulously.

'You know that Tatyana was in pretty bad shape when she arrived,' Kate said, 'and Roberta thought that they would help.'

'Why wasn't I consulted?' Amber asked.

'I was under the impression that Roberta *had* spoken to you about it,' Kate said. 'She actually didn't pass a lot of that stuff by me.'

'And yet you blindly signed off on it all and paid,' Amber said. Now the penny dropped as to why Kate had been summoned to the White Sands en route to the airport. There had been no discrepancy with the account; Roberta had simply wanted to pass the buck and ensure that Kate's name rather than her own was attached to the expenses. Kate was horrified, not only by Roberta's slyness but also by her own naiveté.

'I presumed that since Roberta and I both have signing powers on the card, she was equally at liberty to make decisions regarding expenditure,' Kate tried. 'She certainly gave me that impression.'

'True, but she operates in the creative sphere,' Amber shot back, 'whereas you were in charge of logistics and should have maintained control. Perhaps if you hadn't been running around the island with some …'

Some what? Running around the island with some what? Shit, shit, shit.

'Well, maybe that's none of my business,' Amber continued, 'but this is.' She dramatically fanned the wad of papers as Kate opened and closed her mouth like a goldfish, left speechless by the fact that Roberta had not only made her accountable for the expenses but had also thrown in the tip-off about Fai. *So she clearly has heard about the affair.* Knowing now about Roberta's special relationship with Amber, however, Kate realised she had little chance of turning this back on her co-worker.

'I did manage to cancel out the upgrade, as well as the yacht,' Kate said. 'They would have added a couple of thousand pounds to the bill.'

'Yes, I do appreciate that,' Amber said, 'but we shouldn't have had to pay for the upgrade in the first place, since Paradise Bay was evidently well below par. You should have adopted a harder line in your negotiations right from the start.'

Thinking of Jacques' poker-hot desire, Kate could have argued that she had adopted a very hard line indeed. She was furious that for all her efforts to steer things back on course, she was being accused of gross negligence, while Roberta had made the hit and driven off scot-free.

Amber took off her glasses and massaged her temples. 'I'm not sure you begin to realise what a fine line we're treading at the moment,' she said. 'We're not only up against a publishing market experiencing its worst slump in history, but I'm also dealing with resistance from within. The Lowells can't seem to understand that the cost-cutting measures they've applied to their ghastly rags don't work for a glossy, which means I have to fight with Simon daily to maintain our editorial standards. If I have any hope of success in the long run, I need to be able to trust my editorial staff to do what they're mandated to.' She looked down at the expense forms. 'I need to think about how I'm going to deal with this, and you need to go away and think about whether this new role really is for you.'

The USB in Kate's hand now felt like a grenade that would blow up any vestiges of a job she still had, sending her tumbling down the rabbit hole to Wonder-if-I'll-Ever-Get-Another-Job Land fast and furiously. She was tempted to leave it right where it was. She could explain to Solange that the food photographs hadn't worked out. But how would she explain it to Serge, who had so many hopes riding on this? Or to Philippe?

'Sorry, Amber, there is one more thing before I go. I'd like you to have a look at this.' Kate extended the USB across the desk to Amber.

Amber looked at it without taking it. 'What is it?'

'Images,' Kate said. 'Food.'

'Food? Which story would that be?'

'They're from Mauritius.'

'Mauritius? But we cancelled that.'

'I, um … I managed to organise something after all – once the weather cleared.' When Amber still didn't take the USB, Kate put it down on the desk in front of her.

'What?' Amber looked at Kate with her mouth wide open. 'I thought we'd … I expressly said … Tristan didn't mention anything.'

'Tristan wasn't involved. I used a local photographer. I did mention him to you,' Kate said.

'Yes, I remember. I also remember telling you not to touch him. We can't afford …'

'He did it for free.' Kate interrupted the mounting tirade.

'I was going to say we can't afford to jeopardise our reputation by presenting anything but perfection in our pages right now. And I can't imagine that some photographer you picked up on the island is going to be up to our standards.'

'I think you might be surprised,' Kate said. 'I'm sorry, I just couldn't bear to throw away the opportunity, as the setting was so perfect. I'm sure if you'd been there, you would have felt the same way, so I thought it was worth a try.' Kate tried but failed to find the conviction she had had in Mauritius.

'*You* thought it was worth trying,' Amber repeated, 'when *I* expressly told you not to waste our time? This is exactly what I was talking about a minute ago.'

'I'm sorry. I do realise now that it was a mistake, but they are good. I really wouldn't ask you to consider them otherwise. Would you please just look at them before you make a decision?'

'I really don't see why I should.' Amber leant back and crossed her arms.

'You have to,' Kate said, surprising herself with her vehemence. 'It's done now, and I've involved other people. So for their sakes …'

'What other people, exactly?' Amber sat up straight.

'Well, the photographer and …' Kate swallowed. 'The PR manager and the chef at the Roche d'Or …'

'Who, I imagine, were all under the impression that you were acting on behalf of the magazine?' Amber spat. 'You do realise that this constitutes gross misconduct. I would fire you on the spot if I didn't have more important concerns at the moment. I really do suggest you leave my office now, for your own good.'

Kate looked down at the USB.

'Leave it,' Amber said. 'Since there may well be legal implications, I'd better find out what I'm dealing with.' She shook her head. 'Unbelievable.'

Kate had to hold back the tears as she crossed the room and went back to her desk. She held her tears again when she saw two missed calls from Daniel and a text asking how things had gone with Amber. Although there was no one she wanted to talk to more right now, she felt that to call him for reassurance would be like reusing a tissue she had already blown her nose on and tossed aside. She was relieved to remember that Chloe had promised she would be home for a proper catch-up over supper.

* * *

Kate was caramelising onions in butter and olive oil when Chloe got home from her yoga class. 'Smells good,' she said, entering the kitchen with Mushy wrapped around her legs like a pair of mohair leg warmers.

'I'm making that caramelised-onion, potato and spinach frittata you like,' Kate said.

'Oh,' Chloe said. Her expression said that she had no recollection of said frittata. 'Well, whatever it is, it'll be my first home-cooked meal in … how long have you been away?'

'A lifetime.'

'Is there anything I can do to help?' Chloe asked purely as a formality. After several mishaps – olive oil in a Thai curry, breadcrumbs mistaken for brown sugar, balsamic vinegar used instead of soy sauce – both had agreed that in respect of kitchen matters, Chloe should remain a bystander. 'Help yourself to some wine,' Kate said, nodding towards the fridge.

'Yippee, a well-stocked fridge again,' Chloe said on opening it.

'Like you'd notice if there was anything other than chocolate milk and squeezy cheese,' Kate said.

'It's comforting; it feels like home. And it's a relief from Luke's fridge – all beer and week-old pizza crusts. I'd forgotten how revolting a boys-only digs can be.' Chloe topped up Kate's glass, filled one of the glasses on the wooden kitchen table, and sat down. 'Nice mats,' she said. Kate had set the table using the fuchsia grass table mats she had bought at Port Louis market, which added just another splash of colour to the eclectic kitchen. Others were provided by lime-green cabinets, a multicoloured mosaic splashback, quote-bearing magnets on the silver Smeg fridge, and Kate's collection of coloured-glass Iittala ice cream bowls on an open shelf.

'They're from Mauritius,' Kate said. 'That too.' She pointed to a brown paper bag on the table. 'A present for you. So things have moved to the knowing-the-contents-of-the-fridge stage with your boy?'

Chloe had recently met Luke (twenty-six years old to her thirty-one) at Camden Market, where she had a weekend stall selling jewellery she made from tin cans – an outlet for the surplus of creativity remaining after spending her days designing cereal and tampon boxes for a packaging company. Luke, having taken pity on the waiflike girl selling what looked to him like bits of junk, had bought her a coffee a few weeks before. The following Saturday, he bought her a chocolate brownie, and a week later he had asked her on a date.

'He's sweet,' Chloe said as she opened the bag. Sweet wasn't good. Sweet meant he would do for now. Until Matt came back – if he came back. 'Oh, wow, I love it.' Chloe pulled the yellow and gold sari out of the bag. 'It'll be perfect for a wedding I've got coming up. Thank you. But from now on, this conversation is all about you, okay? How are you feeling? You look calmer.'

'No small thanks to this.' Kate held up her glass of crisp Sancerre. 'I've guzzled half a bottle in less than an hour, but Louis Pasteur claimed that there's more philosophy in a glass of wine than in all the books in the world, so I'm calling it a quest for clarity.'

'To clarity,' Chloe said, holding up her glass. 'So how were things today?' She broke off a piece of the skinny artisanal baguette that Kate had put on the table and dipped it into the small bowl of olive oil alongside it. 'Yum. I'd almost forgotten what real food tastes like. I bet things went better than expected.'

Kate realised that Chloe was still under the impression that the previous night's outburst had been all about the job. Since this had now indeed become a crying matter, she thought she wouldn't correct her just yet. 'I wouldn't say that,' she said. 'In fact, I'm really not sure I'm going to have a job at the end of the week.' She poked a cube of potato in a pot of boiling water and, finding it done, took the pot off the heat.

'Which is, of course, you just making a drama out of a crisis, right?' Chloe said.

'No. True story. Amber actually said she would have fired me today if she weren't so busy trying to keep the magazine afloat. She's under huge pressure from the financial director, and my allowing costs to go into the stratosphere on this trip isn't helping matters.'

'I'm sure you're exaggerating,' Chloe said.

'I wish I were, but we did go way over budget.' Kate tasted a piece of onion and, finding it sweet and soft, turned off the heat under the pan and mixed in the potato. *If only everything were as easy as caramelising onions,* she thought, wondering if she should have stuck to what she was good at: food. But she reminded herself that as far as the expenses were concerned, she really hadn't been at fault. She suddenly felt angry with Amber for laying the blame at her door and allowing Roberta to get off scot-free. 'Anyway,' she continued, 'the expenses aren't actually my sackable offence. There's something else that I probably ... well, definitely shouldn't have done.' There were a whole lot of things that Kate probably definitely shouldn't have done, *but one bad deed at a time*; she didn't want to give Chloe indigestion. So, as she pitted olives and washed spinach leaves, she told Chloe about the food shoot. 'It felt so right at the time, but when viewed from a distance, I can see that it was out of order. *I* would fire me if it was in my power.'

She cracked an egg, parted the two sides of the broken shell, and dispatched its contents into a glass bowl with a quick, sharp movement of one hand, simultaneously taking a generous sip of wine with the other.

'Now that's what I call multitasking,' Chloe said. 'You didn't even look at the egg.'

'Necessity's the mother of invention.'

'It was quite a bold move,' Chloe said.

'Not really; just a technique I saw in *Sabrina* and perfected in my teens.'

'No, K, the shoot, silly. I'm not sure I would have been so brave, but if you say the photos are good, then they're probably brilliant, which means Amber will love them and it will have been worth the risk. Happy ending. As they say, you can't have omelette without breaking eggs.'

'She's so angry at the moment, I'm not sure she'll give them more than a cursory glance.' Kate whisked the eggs and milk into a froth, along with her anxiety about letting Serge and Philippe down, not to mention Fai. He already had her pegged as morally challenged and would realise that she was in fact morally bankrupt when he discovered that the whole shoot had been a scam too.

'But that's not all.' Kate took a glug of wine. 'I slept with someone.'

'Oh,' Chloe said, clearly surprised that the conversation was taking this turn. '*Okay,*' she added, with an expectant upward lilt of the voice.

'Actually, I slept with two people,' Kate said. 'Not at the same time – *that* would have been multitasking.'

Chloe laughed. 'Sorry. Shit. Who?'

Where do I start? Kate wondered. 'Hang on a sec. Let me get this in the oven, and then I'll tell all.' She tossed the spinach and pitted black olives with the onion and potato in the pan, then poured the pale yellow froth over them, and crumbled goat's cheese on top. At last, as the frittata cooked through in the oven, releasing its rich aroma into the room, Kate released some of the more flavourful moments of the trip.

'So you're saying it was mind-blowing sex,' Chloe said.

'Unbelievable. I mean, with Daniel, sex is intimate and easy, and it just somehow flows, but this was just …' *How do I begin to describe it?* With Daniel, there had been chemistry from the start. Sexual tension simmered below the surface on their first date and then came to the boil, to delicious effect, on their third, but sex generally started somewhere – with a touch, a look, a conversation over a meal – in the mind, whereas with Fai it didn't start anywhere. 'It was just there,' Kate continued, 'like I was connected to its source somewhere so deep I wouldn't know where to begin to look for it.'

'Was that all it was, do you think? Great sex?' Chloe asked.

'I don't know. I don't think so. I even thought for a minute that I could chuck up everything and move to Mauritius just to live that feeling forever. And yet, when Daniel asked me to move in with him, I almost fainted, which is crazy, really, because things have been so good with us and I really do love him … well, I thought I did.'

'Daniel asked you to move in with him?' Chloe asked.

'Sorry. It was the night before I left. I would have told you, but there wasn't time, and now, well … fuck.'

Chloe looked pensive. 'It does sound like you had a really good connection with this guy,' she said, 'but if I can play devil's advocate here, maybe because you were on holiday, or sort of, you weren't thinking so much, so it was easier to let go and just be in the moment. But back here, with Daniel, or anyone really, you're always analysing the should-you-shouldn't-you stuff and looking out for issues that can trip things up.' She paused and took a thoughtful sip of wine. 'Do you think it's possible that Daniel's asking you to move in with him made you want to head for the hills, even subconsciously, and that's why you let loose in Mauritius? You say there was another guy?'

The timer buzzed, and Kate got up. 'Saved by the bell,' she said as she walked over to the oven. She put on the grill and moved the frittata to the top shelf. 'I need to watch this like a hawk or it will burn.'

'Okay, I'll let you get on with it while I reply to Luke's one hundred and one texts. But you're not off the hook.'

'He sounds smitten,' Kate said. 'Are you sure he isn't becoming more than just a friend with benefits?'

'I told you we're not going there,' Chloe said. 'You just get that frittata on the table, and then we'll continue the conversation. About *you*.'

Kate wondered if Chloe was right, that it had been easier to give herself over to the moment with Fai because she hadn't been in her real world. Her response to Daniel's proposal was certainly proof that she was still fearful of commitment, and she had felt an unusual sense of abandon on the island. *But was Fai simply a flight response?* Her mind wandered back to their last night together, when their lovemaking had been like a force of nature, her body and soul responding to his like the tide to the moon, following which they had talked until the dawn light crept into her room. No, it had been something more.

Still, whatever she may have thought in the heat of the moment, even if the relationship were still on the table, it had always been destined to end, because hadn't she always said she would never throw everything away to follow her heart as her mother had done and warned so often against: 'Believe me, girls, love is not enough'; 'Don't ever give up on your dreams for a man'; 'A career is what it's all about'; 'And if you must get married, make sure you have something solid to fall back on.'

Annie Christakos had, in fact, had a very promising career herself as an assistant fashion buyer for Debenhams in London when she met Kate's father, Alistair Richmond, at a party. The hosts, freshly returned from a weekend in Brussels, were misguidedly serving steak tartare made with cheap, standard-grade mince for supper, and Kate's father said to Annie that they should run for their lives because he, as a vet, knew the meat was dangerously high in bacteria and not even fit for a dog. So they escaped to a pub, where Annie had fallen instantly and madly in love with the tall handsome man with witty repartee.

A year later, balancing work and married life, Annie was as happy as she had ever been. Then Kate's paternal grandfather had suffered a stroke and Kate's father was called to a small town in Cornwall to take over his father's veterinary practice. This meant the end of Annie's career in fashion, but, still in the bloom of love, she was happy to move to the country to start a family. Eight years later, however, stuck at home with three daughters under the age of six, and a husband who was often absent on house calls – or barn, stable, and pigsty calls – she began to feel bored, isolated, and depressed. Until a conversation with Annie's father marked another turning point. In response to his daughter's tearfully lamenting the lack of purpose in her life and her missed career, he said, 'Well, love, how about working with what you've got? Make your home your brilliant career.'

That was when Annie had really started experimenting in the kitchen. She began to grow her own fruits and vegetables, which went into homemade jams and relishes. She made pies with the lightest pastry, gourmet meals à la Julia Child, Elizabeth David, and the *Time-Life Foods of the World* cookbooks, and birthday cakes so fantastical that Kate's classmates talked about them for weeks after her parties. It *was* a brilliant career, but one devoted entirely to her home and family, making first her husband's infidelities and finally her total abandonment by him all the more devastating.

Kate took the frittata out of the oven and set it aside while she made a salad dressing. As she whisked together Dijon mustard, olive oil, vinegar, honey, and chives, she wondered how she would explain Jacques to Chloe. If her father's extramarital affairs of the heart had been bad, perhaps trampling and manipulating love to achieve personal goals was even worse. It sickened her to think that she had become the kind of person who used sex to get ahead.

'Yum,' Chloe said as Kate placed a large wedge of golden-brown frittata and a mound of salad in front of her before topping up their glasses. 'Okay, so the other guy?' she asked, as Kate sat down.

Kate took a large sip of wine and then dished up the final course in her sexual saga.

'So while there might have been a frisson of attraction, what it really boiled down to was sealing the deal,' Kate said finally, 'which is mercenary, especially considering the amazing connection I had with Fai. What is wrong with me?'

'You do have a habit of sabotaging relationships, K,' Chloe said, mopping up her salad dressing with some bread. 'This has all been delicious by the way.'

'Programmed to screw up relationships,' Kate said. 'If only I could get reprogrammed.'

'You can, actually,' Chloe said. 'There's this thing called holographic re-patterning that I tried a little while ago. It's based on the theory that we're all operating according to subconscious patterns created through experiences. These turn into frequencies through repetition, which makes us keep doing the same thing over and over. But you can actually retune yourself with crystals, chanting, music, and stuff.'

Chloe had always had a leaning towards the esoteric side of things, but ever since her so-called soulmate, Matt, had jilted her days before their wedding, she had become a walking, talking New Age encyclopaedia, having sought answers and comfort from anyone from psychics to shamans. Kate had always found these types of therapies self-indulgent, preferring to live by the motto borrowed from George Bernard Shaw: *Life isn't about finding yourself; it's about creating yourself.* However, given the mess she was in, she had to consider that fridge-magnet psychology wasn't the most solid instruction on life.

'Maybe this re-patterning thing is worth a try,' she said. Chloe had certainly moved from devastation to relative contentment in the year since Matt had gone to find himself in the Great Barrier Reef, so something was working. 'In the meantime, what am I going to say to Daniel? How am I going to tell him?'

'Just take things as they come when you see him,' Chloe said.

'You mean, rather than taking them as I come?' Kate asked.

CHAPTER 11

Puttanesca

Kate was relieved when she received a call from Vanessa saying that Amber wanted to see her immediately. She had been waiting for Amber's verdict on the shoot all day and, whatever it was, she wanted the wait to be over. When she looked in the direction of Amber's office, however, her heart froze, as she registered that the venetian blinds spanning the breadth of the glass wall were closed. This usually meant one of two things: Amber was hiring someone or she was firing someone, and since the former wasn't a possibility, the latter looked highly likely.

With her heart racing, and sweat dampening her blouse, Kate entered Amber's office, where her panic immediately doubled upon spotting the remnants of a melted mozzarella and tomato Panini on the desk. This was a very bad sign indeed, since her editor only consumed anything containing wheat, dairy, or carbs when she was angry and needed to take it out on someone, starting with herself – a mild form of self-harm.

Amber looked up from her computer as Kate sat down. 'Kate, to say that I'm unhappy with you is an understatement,' she said. 'I've been thinking a lot about what you did over the last twenty-four hours; in fact, I've been able to think of little else, and, no matter how I look at it, your actions were completely out of line. Do you understand that putting the magazine's reputation at stake, as you did, is totally unacceptable behaviour?'

'I do,' Kate said, 'and I *am* sorry.'

'Incontrovertible grounds for dismissal?' Amber gave Kate a steely stare.

Kate gulped. She had allowed herself to hope that the quality of the images would win Amber over, but this wasn't looking good.

'My blood boils when I think about it. I'm still inclined to ignore the photos outright on principle, apart from which I don't have time for this. But since you've involved other people ...' Amber returned her gaze to her screen. Kate could just make out the thumbnail images of her shoot reflected in stereo in her vintage glasses. She watched each one enlarge to full size as Amber clicked on it. She had assumed when summoned that the verdict had been reached, but it appeared that the jury was still out. She found herself holding her breath as each image appeared, hoping Amber would exclaim at its beauty. But she was disappointed each time.

Amber must have gone through all of them when she finally broke the silence. 'A Mauritian photographer, you say?'

'Yes,' Kate said. 'Chinese-Mauritian. His family has one of the oldest studios on the island.' There was no need for Amber to know that the studio itself probably hadn't changed since it was founded early in the former century, down to its painted backdrop of pagoda and willow tree for family portraits. Amber would have run screaming from the building.

'Well, he certainly has a knack for food,' Amber said. 'These are surprisingly good, though it irks me to say it.' Usually not satisfied with anything less than 'excellent', Kate found that Amber's 'good' sounded like 'cum laude' today. She released the breath she had been holding and relaxed a little into the chair. 'Who is this woman?' Amber asked, peering at the screen again.

Kate had little doubt, but she walked around to the other side of the desk to look over Amber's shoulder.

'Her name's Finola,' she said. 'She's Australian.'

'But *who* is she? A model, actress? And where did you find her?'

'She's a singer,' Kate said. 'She was staying at the Roche d'Or.' She thought back to how she had approached Finola over breakfast as though under some island spell.

'She's magnificent. Her skin … did Tamsyn do her make-up?'

Kate wanted to say it was a skin-brightening technique commonly known as afterglow, but she wasn't on stable ground yet, so she said, 'No,' allowing Amber to hold the floor.

'This is exactly what I was after for the cover,' Amber said. *The cover?* 'It just oozes "Summertime and the living is easy," whereas Roberta's shoot on the yacht says, "Summertime and the living is rather dull and lacklustre." Everyone seems so subdued, almost miserable.'

That would be because they were. The cover?

'Roberta wouldn't like it, of course, but we just haven't got the luxury to indulge egos at the moment. Has Dave got these images?'

'Not yet,' Kate said. 'You're the only person I've shown them to.'

'Well, go ahead and give them to him. I also want him to integrate a couple into the teaser on the website and in the media kit. Advertising's not looking nearly as good as I'd hoped, but perhaps these will help.' Amber paused. 'But don't mention the cover yet; we'll need to tread carefully there.'

As Kate got up to leave, Amber added, 'You're lucky the images are good, Kate, but don't make a habit of this. I mean it.'

Despite Amber's threatening tone, Kate floated out of her office, feeling all the joy of a criminal on death row after being granted a reprieve. Just then, a swish of a glossy black ponytail caught her eye, which effected a detour to the beauty department.

'Hi, lovely. What do you think?' Jasmine held her hand up, dangling a cosmetic bottle at the end of a shoelace. 'It's a cunning styling technique I've devised for next month's lead story, "Beauty on a Shoestring."'

'Clever,' Kate said.

'Or desperate,' Jasmine said. 'My budget's been slashed, which is fine for this particular theme, but things are going to start looking ugly if we continue like this. And you know how much I don't like ugly. Anyway, you, for one, are looking fabulous, except …' She narrowed her eyes accusingly. 'I don't think that tan came out of a bottle.'

'No, it didn't,' Kate said, relieved that a bit of illicit sunbathing was her only transparent sin.

'Well, you need to rehydrate *tout de suite*,' Jasmine said. 'I'm going to give you a multivitamin masque, which you should apply at least twice this week.' Upon discovering that Kate had reached her twenty-ninth birthday without ever using eye cream, Jasmine had become her self-appointed fairy beauty therapist. As a result, Kate did feel glossier than she had two years previously, although she suspected she would always be several plucks and peels behind the average *Be* girl. 'Ooh, and before I forget, thanks for the cellulite tea.'

'It's a pleasure,' Kate said. 'Fingers crossed. And sorry, thank *you* for the voucher, but please remind me what a wine broker has to do with beauty.'

'This South African company I'm using for an anti-ageing story is launching a new skincare range of products made from grapevines,' Jasmine said. 'They already have totally brilliant serums containing grape extracts, but now they've had a breakthrough with a polyphenol from the vine, which has even stronger antioxidant properties and stimulates the production of collagen; revolutionary stuff.'

'I'm still not sure where Daniel comes in?' Kate said.

'They want to do some sort of tie-in with South African wines at the launch event. And FYI, Daniel has been a-*ma*-zing – they totally love him. He got them an excellent deal on a venue, and when they heard he wrote a wine column, they asked if he'd give a talk. Actually, I might be a little in love with him myself because I'm sure he has everything to do with the fact that they've just booked six months' worth of advertising. Not sure why that's suddenly part of my gig, but he's got Simon off my back. Advertising coups aside, though, what a great guy. Definitely a keeper.'

A bit too late for that advice, Kate thought, wondering what Jasmine would think about her dalliances in Mauritius. Would news indeed eventually reach her via the office gossip, whoever he or she was?

Jasmine's phone rang. 'Sorry, sweetie, I've got to take this, but I want to hear all about Mauritius. Let's have a drink next week. And give that divine man of yours a huge hug for me.'

A few hours later, Kate stood outside the 'divine man's' door, feeling all the anticipation and trepidation of a participant on *Blind Date* when the screen was about to move back and reveal the mystery date she had picked from three candidates on the basis of his witty repartee. Kate wondered if Daniel would prove to be a less than perfect match when compared to Contestant Number 1 – 'Our Fai', as Cilla Black would say – if definitely not to Contestant Number 2, 'Our Jacques'. And what would he see in her face? Guilt? Regret? She prepared to form her features into a smile, whatever she felt.

As it happened, when the door opened, there was no effort required, because it wasn't a stranger on the other side. It was Daniel, wearing a familiar long-sleeved blue T-shirt and jeans hanging loosely on his lanky frame. With his reading glasses perched on top of his head, he looked slightly weary, but gorgeous and loveable.

'Look at *you*,' he said, holding Kate at a slight distance as though admiring something shiny, beautiful, and flawless, which she was decidedly not. He ran his hands through her hair, kissed her forehead, her eyelids and then her nose before tipping her face back and kissing her on the mouth.

'Mm, I missed this,' he said. 'I missed you.' He leant in to kiss her again and Kate didn't feel compelled to pull back and start explaining. She let go and melted into the long, deep kiss, detecting a slightly new flavour, her guilt and a hint of regret offsetting its sweetness, much like the bitter lime in a mojito.

Daniel pulled away and looked at her again, almost surprising her with the depth of love in his gaze. When she came clean, she thought, and the dust from her travels was washed away to reveal the cracks, that expression would go down the drain with the relationship.

Happily, she was spared the need to start washing up right away, as Daniel suggested they go out for a drink and a bite. He wanted to hold his haul of French cheeses, saucisson, pâté, olives, and other deli buys for their traditional Friday feast the next night. So, relieved, she left her dirty doings alongside an unwashed glass and a crumb-scattered plate in the sink, aware that the Fairy liquid would have to be availed of at some stage.

It was chilly outside, so Kate was glad of Daniel's arm around her as they walked along the cobbled street to their local pub, catching glimpses of the silvery Thames through narrow strips between the warehouse conversions that lined it. After her raging inner debate all the way over here, she was surprised to feel so at ease. She felt like she had slipped back into a pair of her favourite shoes, ones that were both sexy and comfortable, and that made her feel taller and more confident, without pinching anything.

Although not one of the area's famous old pubs once frequented by Dickens, Turner, and Whistler, the Captain Kidd shared those pubs' cosy olde worlde charm without drawing hordes of tourists. It had dark flagstones on the floor, low wooden beams, benches upholstered in brown leather, and lead-glass windows that didn't let in very much light. For all the pub's Dickensian flavour, though, in place of bawdy sailors, dockers, and market traders of the common and garden variety, its clientele included doctors, lawyers, and traders of the stocks and currencies variety, who, like Daniel, had latterly colonised Wapping for its proximity to London's financial centre.

Pete greeted the couple by name from behind the bar, and Kate thought, as she always did, that it was nice to have a place where the barman knew her name. He was probably in his mid fifties, with greying brown hair, permanent grey stubble, and a stomach that wobbled like blancmange when he laughed, prising open the buttons on his shirt when a joke was particularly good.

'So wha'll i' be?' he asked. 'A pig's an' a Calvin'?' He looked at Kate with the special smile that signified he was testing her.

'Calvin?' Kate asked.

'Klein,' Pete said.

'Wine?' Kate said.

'Goo' girl.' Pete had taken it upon himself to teach Kate rhyming slang, which was the equivalent of a foreign language to one born so far west of East London's Bow Bells, the proximity to which qualified one as a true Cockney. Kate had been familiar with some common rhyming slang such as the use of 'dog and bone' for phone, 'trouble and strife' for wife, and 'Adam and Eve' for believe, but Pete had taught her a host of new expressions. He had also told her that if she wanted to do it properly, then it wasn't good enough simply to reel off the whole rhyming expression; she had to leave off the final word that rhymed with the one being referred to. So she should call a phone a 'dog' rather than a 'dog and bone'; and a beer, a 'pig's' rather than a 'pig's ear'.

Kate glanced at the selection of wines chalked up on the blackboard behind the bar and, feeling chilly after the walk, opted for the 'warm and peppery' Australian Cabernet Sauvignon–Zinfandel blend.

She smiled hello to a couple of the men huddled around the bar, whom she knew by face because they were generally seated exactly where they were now, as if superglued to the bar stools. They were distinguishable as members of the area's diminishing 'native' inhabitants by their tired corduroy trousers, sweaters, and T-shirts, which hugged ample thighs, tummies, and torsos built on fry-ups and lager, contrasting with the more gym-toned and sushi-fed bodies of the booth members. One of the men at the bar greeted Daniel.

'So is this the trouble then?' he asked, nodding at Kate with an appreciative look.

'No, just the horse and cart … the horse,' Kate corrected, thinking how appropriate the term for 'girlfriend' had suddenly become, rhyming as it did with 'tart'. Her eyes alighted on two people leaving one of the pub's prime spots, an alcove overlooking the river, so she excused herself to secure it, leaving Daniel to bring the drinks.

'You batted off the trouble and strife pretty smartly,' Daniel said as he placed Kate's glass of wine in front of her.

'It's hardly alluring,' Kate said. 'And what was the other one? "Carving knife."'

'You do know that the whole point of rhyming slang was to outfox the authorities,' Daniel said, 'which wouldn't work if the meaning was clear. So no one could arrest me for saying, "You're looking so peasy, I'd like to take you up the apples for a Melvyn immediately."'

'When you'd actually be saying?'

'You're looking so hot, Peas and Pot, that I'd like to take you up the …'

'Stairs,' Kate filled in.

'For a shag, aka Melvyn Bragg.'

'Why, thank you kindly, sir,' Kate said in her best Eliza Doolittle accent. 'When did you get so good at Cockney rhyming?'

'I learn it from a book,' Daniel said in his best impression of Manuel from *Fawlty Towers*. 'But you *are* looking especially hot.'

'Thanks,' Kate said.

'You also look a lot less stressed than you sounded on the phone. Did Amber speak to you about your shoot?' Kate had spoken to Daniel before his flight, when she had not yet been summoned to Amber's office and had been certain that her career was over.

'Yes,' Kate said. 'Finally.'

'And let me guess, she loved them?'

'*Love* might be too strong a word,' Kate said, 'but she did like them enough to say she wants to use one on the cover.' She felt her cheeks glow with pride.

'The cover? Isn't that a bit of a coup? That's brilliant. You're a lunatic, but a very talented one.' Daniel held up his glass. 'Here's to your first cover, lunatic.' They clinked glasses and Kate felt awful again that he was being so nice to her when she had betrayed him so royally. It began to sink in exactly what she had done and what she stood to lose as a result.

'Now that the crisis has been averted, can you tell me about some of the good bits?' Daniel said. Kate realised that most of her conversations over the phone from Mauritius had consisted of her tabling the latest disaster and Daniel talking her down from the ledge. So now she told him about the good bits while necessarily avoiding some of the best ones, manipulating the facts as if writing a piece of fiction so that it began to feel more and more like she might be telling a story set in a mythical land, whereas this was real and it felt good. *What have I done?*

'It's criminal that you were there alone.' Daniel reached across the table and took her hand. 'I realised in France just how much I enjoy exploring new places with you; it's not the same when you're not there.' He looked at her with a gaze so penetrating that she had to look down at her glass for fear that her eyes would offer a peep show into her dark and devious soul. She was relieved when he got up to get another round of drinks from the bar.

She rubbed one of the steamed-up windowpanes with her sleeve and rested her forehead on the cool glass, looking for answers in the Thames's dark water flowing below. Something scraped against the window right in front of her face, and she pulled back from the glass with a jolt. It was the noose that dangled from a wooden beam jutting out above the window, she saw. This was a macabre tribute to the pub's namesake, Captain William Kidd, a privateer-turned-pirate who had seized an Armenian ship in the Indian Ocean off Madagascar, for which he had been hanged in 1701 within spitting distance of where Kate was sitting.

Now, Kate thought, *it's my turn to pay the price for my misdeeds in the Indian Ocean.* It was an interesting geographical coincidence. She looked at Daniel standing at the bar and felt a metaphorical noose tighten uncomfortably around her throat, just as she realised that she emphatically did not want this relationship to end.

Well, you should have thought about that before embarking on your shenanigans, shouldn't you? a cold and official inner voice said.

But it was out of my control, Your Honour, a mutiny of the body against good sense.

Captain Kidd, she recalled, had also claimed innocence, on the basis that his crew had seized his ship. She reminded herself that she, however, had not yet been accused of anything, and for the first time she wondered if indeed she had to confess.

Daniel returned and gave her a quizzical look. 'That's a funny expression,' he said. 'Penny for your thoughts?'

'I hear you're diversifying into beauty,' Kate said. *Could our relationship survive such a dark secret?* she wondered. *Or would it end up poisoning it in the long run, anyway?*

Daniel laughed. 'So Jasmine's told you?'

'She says you're quite a hit with De-Vine Beauty.' *Honesty is the best policy, of course, but if I tell him, he'll definitely leave me.*

'That's good, because I think it might be a useful connection. It's not my usual audience, though, and I do wonder if it really is such a good idea. Won't they be bored out of their minds?'

Then again, even if I don't tell him, there's the risk of his hearing about Fai from someone else now that our working lives are bizarrely intersecting.

'Kate?'

'Oh, sorry. Um, bored? What do they want you to do exactly?'

'They've left it quite open, but I'm thinking a short talk combined with a quick wine tasting. I'll probably need your help getting the tone right.'

'Well, make sure to have plenty of spittoons available, because the beauty tribe doesn't swallow *anything* containing calories,' Kate said. 'And definitely go big on wine's antioxidant properties – they love everything to do with anti-ageing. They also might be less inclined to reach for the Pellegrino if you tell them it's healthier to drink wine with a meal than water because it doesn't dilute the digestive enzymes. Ooh, and there's that research that's just come out proving that red wine actually slows down the growth of fat cells and stops new ones from forming. Apparently the trick is to drink a couple of glasses before you go to bed.'

Daniel laughed. 'There should be a restraining order preventing you from coming within a ten-mile radius of any AA meeting.'

Kate wondered if there would soon be a restraining order preventing her from coming within a ten-mile radius of Daniel. As they left the pub, arm in arm, head-to-shoulder, she thought again that she couldn't bear for this to be the case.

They crossed the road to Il Bordello, where they squeezed into a table at the back of the packed restaurant. Their regular waiter, Luigi, welcomed them with menus.

'Puttanesca?' Daniel asked over the top of his menu.

'Of course. It's all a whore should eat,' Kate said with a guilty laugh, deflecting what seemed to be a spotlight on her infidelities. She never, in fact, ordered anything else here. She loved the robust combination of tomatoes, anchovies, garlic, capers, olives, and chilli, named 'whore's pasta', she had read, because, like a lady of the night, it was quick, cheap, and easy, with a whiff of anchovies about it. Suddenly it seemed most appropriate that this should be her favourite dish. Daniel, however, remained oblivious to the fact. It occurred to Kate again how much of a love story played out in the mind and that, if written down, there would always be at least two versions. As Nietzsche said, 'There are no facts, only interpretations.' Of course there was also that shared chemistry, difficult to put into words, that brought the different stories together, and when Daniel placed his hand on Kate's knee at the end of the meal, she felt desire begin to rise in her like a sweet soufflé.

'Are you sure you don't want a coffee at least?' he asked as Kate waved away the dessert menu. 'Because sleep's not high on my agenda.'

'Nor mine,' Kate said, deciding that there would be no confessions that night. 'But I thought I'd make a little nightcap at home with some spiced rum I brought back for you from Mauritius. It's called Pink Pigeon.'

'Have I told you lately that I love you?' Daniel said.

They walked to the corner store, where Kate picked up the extra ingredients she needed for rum flips. Once back in Daniel's kitchen, she shook the rum up with egg yolks, cream, and sugar, and then, bathed in the atmospheric yellow glow cast by the wine fridge, the two of them sat at the kitchen counter and dipped biscotti into the creamy cocktail, exchanging rum-flavoured kisses in between sips and nibbles until Kate's soufflé of desire was almost risen to perfection.

Clearly hungry to get his fill, Daniel animatedly swivelled her stool towards him, dipped his finger in the cream, wiped it over her lips, and, placing his hands on either side of her head, pulled her into him to kiss her so intensely that the kiss's effects reached all the way to her groin. She simultaneously popped his button-fly jeans open, slipped her hand into the slit in his boxer shorts, and felt him grow in response as he moaned. His hands then moved firmly down her body to her waist, and he lifted her onto the counter, where he eased her back and pulled off her panties. Then, pushing up her skirt with one hand, his tongue slowly began to work its way up her leg.

When he reached the top of Kate's thigh, a feeling like warm caramel flowed over her body and she arched her back, gasping with pleasure as his tongue flicked her clitoris and then sank deep into her. She buried her hands in his hair and pressed down to precipitate the climax that seemed imminent, her whole body vibrating with pleasure. It was only when she heard the whirring sound and felt a tug on the opposite end of her body from where Daniel was that she realised the vibration was not the result of what he was doing with his tongue, but from the waste-disposal unit, which had sprung into action upon contact with her ponytail. She yanked her hair free and sat up with a jolt, as the two of them laughed at the fact that this was the one area they just could not get right in the kitchen. Kate simultaneously cursed the fact that she was to be cheated of the promised bliss. But the soufflé was so well on its way that nothing flopped. Daniel simply pulled her off the counter and, with her legs wrapped around him, carried her upstairs, where he poured her onto the bed and brought them both to a heated climax.

I don't want this to end, Kate thought, as she lay comfortably in the crook of Daniel's arm, sated and happy after their lovemaking had subsided. She listened to Daniel's easy breathing and inhaled his scent of musk, black pepper, and dark chocolate, while bittersweet thoughts played on her mind. *This is where I belong, where I want to stay – but is that even a possibility?* she wondered. Could they really continue as if nothing had changed? *You can't have your soufflé and eat it, can you?*

CHAPTER 12

Sour Grapes

Kate felt her before she saw her. The air around her chair went cold, and a chill ran through her. She looked up to see Roberta glaring at her.

'I just happened to be in the art department, and what do you think I saw on Dave's screen?' Roberta said.

'Um?' Kate said, knowing full well what would have conjured that malevolent look. She had been anticipating and bolstering herself for this confrontation for days. When there was none, she had decided that either Roberta was taking the news a lot better than expected or Amber had decided against using the picture of Finola on the cover.

'Oh, please, don't play the innocent with me,' Roberta said. 'You know exactly what I'm talking about.' Her arms were crossed over a grey cap-sleeved asymmetric jersey dress that skimmed her body to below the knee. With one leg slightly bent, she looked like a model asked to strike a fierce, no-nonsense pose.

'I'm guessing you mean the cover?' Kate said. 'Honestly, Roberta, I had no intention of hijacking it.' *Hijacking* was the wrong choice of word, she realised too late, implying as it did a criminal act.

'Oh really? And I suppose the whole little undercover food shoot just *happened* too? You know we spent the better part of a day on the cover, and it's not like we had an abundance of time, thanks to cyclones and God knows what else.'

'I really didn't mean to ...'

'Who is that woman, anyway?'

'A singer,' Kate said. 'From Australia.'

'Clearly D-grade,' Roberta said. 'I don't know what's happening to this place. We used to have standards, but now we've got singers no one's ever heard of playing at being models, and food editors playing at being fashion stylists. Well, if you ... if Amber thinks that I'm going to stand back and let this happen, then she's got another think coming.' She sighed deeply, shaking her head. 'You're quite an operator, aren't you, Kate? Well, be careful, because you've chosen the wrong person to take on.' Still licking her wounds from their previous skirmishes, Kate didn't take the threat lightly.

'Sorry to interrupt, ladies, but we have an issue to get out and we're running *pret*-ty late. Amber's on the warpath.' Lately, Kate had been inclined to run in the opposite direction when Harry approached, since he was generally after lagging copy, but his appearance now was a godsend.

'Who's *we*, Pale Face?' Roberta snapped. '*My* pages were done a week ago, but if Amber wants a fight, it's her lucky day.' With that, she spun around and strutted off in the direction of the editor's office, her skinny-heeled black ankle boots providing a curt punctuation point.

'Don't forget the cover meeting at eleven o' clock,' Harry said to Roberta's back. Turning to Kate, he said, 'Heart of gold, that woman.'

He put the pile of proofs he was carrying in front of her. 'Food and Décor,' he said. 'Amber's approved design and heads, and I need you to sign them off before you do anything else.' He looked at Kate's screen and saw that she was working on the Word version of the travel piece. 'And I want that on the server the minute you're done with these,' he added. 'Dave's been chasing me for it, and he's already started working on the layout with dummy copy. I've given him "Meet Me in Port Louis" as a working title.'

'I'm not sure that anyone other than geriatrics will get the play on "Meet Me in St Louis,"' Kate said, 'which I'm presuming it is.' She, for her part, did get it, having been brought up on the romantic old movies her mother loved. 'But it does have a nice ring to it.'

'Well, it works with your opener, and if you can't come up with anything better in the next five minutes, you'll have to live with it, because, let me remind you: You. Are. On. Borrowed. Time.'

'You know what, Harry, I love it,' Kate said, beaming generously at him.

He rolled his eyes. 'Okay, typos and factual errors only on those, please.' He nodded at the proofs in front of Kate and started to leave.

Kate held up a hand to stop him. 'Before you go, Harry, a quick question on a totally different subject. As a matter of interest, was it Roberta who suggested I might have been involved in some kind of … um … island fling?'

Harry looked at her blankly.

'In Mauritius,' Kate added.

'Oh, that,' he said in a tone suggesting that it was ancient history of absolutely no current interest. 'Tristan sent me a picture of a Chinese guy in a market and said something about being gutted that you'd got in there first. I'm not sure why he thought I needed to know this.' Kate suspected that this was just another of Tristan's subtle ploys to coax Harry out of the closet. Convinced that Harry was too uptight to be straight, Tristan had confided in Kate that he had a secret crush on the subeditor, believing him to be a dead ringer for Paul Bettany. However, to date, Harry remained oblivious to Tristan's campaign. He thus moved off with a baffled expression on his face.

Relieved to hear that her affair was yesterday's news, Kate turned her attention to the proofs in front of her. She always got a thrill out of seeing her words married to images on the page, and her food story made for a particularly happy union. It featured a beautiful opening spread with the barbecue in the foreground and cocktail-toting human props silhouetted against an orange-pink sky under the header 'Fire & Spice', followed by a colourful patchwork of recipes and images. After working through the feature, feeling a little smug about her courageous coup, Kate turned her attention to Décor. This was also high on visual impact and low on text, so she promptly dispatched both to Harry. Then she returned to the travel story on her screen.

This had taken far longer to write than usual because, for one thing, rather than making it a straight travel piece, Kate had had to ensure that the Sunshine Group got sufficient sunny exposure. For another, Fai kept popping up between the lines, taking Kate away from the page and on several internal excursions.

'Meet Me in Port Louis,' she added at the top of the piece, finding that it did tie in well with her opening paragraph. *Good call, Harry,* she thought as she began to read.

> I'm in a car headed for the capital of Mauritius, winding at high speed along a narrow coastal road. On my left, through a filter of feathery casuarina trees, I catch glimpses of white sand etched with turquoise sea, and on my right, a wall of tall sugar cane sways in the breeze, its burnt-caramel smell drifting in through the open windows. So far so paradisiacal, except that, directly ahead, there's a bus that's about to speed straight into us. After adeptly swerving out of impact's way, our taxi driver explains that when the French were in power, people drove on the right-hand side of the road, and then when the British took over, people reverted to driving on the left; but now that Mauritius is independent, people just drive in the middle.
>
> His throaty laugh tells me that this is an old joke, but it is true to say that, near-death experiences aside, the Indian Ocean island's delicious cocktail of cultural influences makes a stay here so much more than a mere beach getaway.
>
> Although known to Arab traders in the tenth century and discovered by the Portuguese in 1505, the island wasn't settled until the Dutch arrived in 1598 and named it in honour of Prince Maurits of Nassa, introducing …

Realising that she had dropped the *u* in *Nassau,* Kate corrected the error before continuing to skim through the piece, conscious of the fact that she was racing against the clock. Still, she couldn't help pausing at, 'The multitude of small red tomatoes draw me in to sample their succulent flesh,' which evoked the strong memory of Fai's breath on her neck in Port Louis market as he whispered 'pommes d'amour' in her ear. She forced herself on, but, after speeding through the wine-pairing meal at the

Roche d'Or – which conjured memories of the less pleasant pairing with Jacques – she came to an involuntary standstill again when she read over her description of the hotel room and felt Fai's silken skin against hers in the large hand-carved wooden bed.

Memories of Fai still had the power to evoke a physical response. Kate couldn't deny that there had been a strong connection. But with no further contact (her emails remaining unanswered), she thought of him less and less, while her desire for Daniel had intensified since her return, perhaps distilled by the threat under which she had placed their relationship. Sometimes she wondered if she should be honest with him, before deciding that the risk of losing him was too great. She hoped the guilt would eventually subside.

'Coming to the cover meeting?' Louise asked, getting up from her desk, which was beside Kate's.

'I'll be there in a minute,' Kate said, cross with herself for daydreaming. 'Harry will crucify me if I don't get this onto the server immediately.'

She reluctantly pressed Save, thereby relinquishing the story, and then hurried over to the art department, wondering if Roberta's meeting with Amber had elicited a change of heart. She felt ambivalent about the possible outcome. While her ego liked the idea of owning the cover story, her inner coward preferred the idea of a world in which Roberta was not Personal Enemy Number One.

She was met by three cover options pinned to the board above Dave's desk, all of which featured Finola. The only variations were the way in which the picture had been cropped and the use of different colour options for the masthead – white, blue, and watermelon pink. Kate couldn't even look at Roberta; the cost, she knew, would be high.

Members of the team representing a cross section of departments were gathered in the area, standing up or perching on desks, while Amber, wearing chic black cigarette trousers and a vintage blue silk Chinese jacket, was leaning over Dave's shoulder to look at his computer screen. She glanced over her shoulder and, satisfied that most of the team was present, straightened up. 'So what do we all think?' she asked.

There was a chorus of appreciative sounds from everyone except Roberta, whose lips remained pursed, her eyes narrowed on Amber. *She must be very angry indeed,* Kate thought since frowning was in strict contravention of Roberta's rule to avoid crow's-feet-forming expressions.

'She's a stunning girl,' Jasmine said. 'Her skin's incandescent. Nice work, Roberta.'

'Oh, don't congratulate me. Congratulate our foodie-turned-fashion editor,' Roberta said, with a smirk directed at Kate.

'What?' Jasmine looked confused.

'Haven't you heard? *Be*'s taking a reality approach to our cover shoots these days,' Roberta said.

If Amber heard the exchange, she chose to ignore it, steering the discussion from colour choices to coverlines, the most prominent of which was splashed across the bottom of the page: 'Summer Loving: Beach beauty to barbecues, island-style interiors to itsy-bitsy bikinis, plus tips on getting the body to wear them.'

'Sorry, Amber, I'm going to have to leave now,' Jasmine said after several additions and deletions had been made. 'We've got this De-Vine Beauty launch, which is on the other side of town.'

'Why people think that east London is an appropriate place for a launch, God knows,' Roberta muttered. 'It's going to take us a day to get there.'

Us? Roberta said 'us'? Kate's senses were suddenly on high alert.

'That's fine,' Amber said to Jasmine. 'Actually, I think we're pretty much done here. But before you go, I'd like to congratulate you all on a job well done. We've had some challenges recently, but everyone's pulled together and I think this is our best issue yet. It could mark a real turning point. Thank you, thank you, thank you. So unless anyone has anything to add ...'

When no one volunteered anything further, Amber leant over Dave's shoulder again. *Meeting over. Class dismissed.*

'I'll meet you in reception,' Roberta said to Jasmine before turning to Kate. 'I hear your boyfriend's the guest speaker; I'm looking forward to meeting him.'

'Why is Roberta going to the launch?' Kate asked Jasmine, hoping that she had only imagined the note of malice in Roberta's comment.

'She's taking Amber's place,' Jasmine said.

'But she's got nothing to do with beauty.' Kate tried to keep her tone from a shriek.

'She's going for the goody bag. Apparently they're giving away the entire range of product full size, and she heard that Charlize Theron swears by the anti-ageing moisturiser.'

'Shit,' Kate said.

'What's wrong?' Jasmine asked.

'I ...' Kate didn't want Roberta anywhere near Daniel with the dirty bomb she had at her disposal and the incentive to use it. 'I told Daniel I'd try to be there for moral support, but I've suddenly got so much on my plate.' It was only partly a lie because she *had* planned to go, but she had decided two days ago that her workload wouldn't allow it.

'Why don't you pop over for an hour or so?' Jasmine said. 'You have to eat at some point, and it's only a couple of stops on the Jubilee line. Roberta exaggerates. Then again, I don't think she does the Tube.'

'Do you think there will still be a place for me if I come a bit later?' Kate asked. 'I've got a phone interview with this Korean chef at twelve thirty, who's been impossible to pin down, but ...' *Nothing else matters, considering the stakes.*

'Definitely. Roberta's not the only one who thinks the word *Wapping* is a synonym for *ghetto*,' Jasmine said, 'and there are always no-shows. Just slip in when you can.'

* * *

You're panicking unnecessarily, Kate told herself as she sat tapping her foot on the Tube, which was stalled somewhere between London Bridge and Canada Water. *Even if Roberta does meet Daniel, what's she going to say?* They weren't in the playground where children told tales, ganged up on one another, and called others cruel names at the tops of their voices – 'Smelly Kat', for example, which had been applied when Kate's mother sent her to school with garlic sandwiches as a natural remedy for flu.

Kate was so lost in thought that she almost missed her change for the East London line, but she managed to squeeze through the doors. She finally emerged into the daylight at Wapping Station, and set off at a leisurely pace towards Wapping Food, but the walk she was accustomed to doing from Daniel's flat on weekends seemed a lot longer in high heels ill-matched to the cobblestones, amid mounting anxiety about Roberta's ammo. It was crazy that she was even in this situation, she thought, quickening her pace. *What are the odds of a wine broker having any reason to fraternise with members of the beauty and fashion industry in a professional capacity?* She looked up at the sky woefully.

When the face-brick façade of the former power station loomed into view, she practically broke into a run, finally bursting through the power station's double doors with all the zeal of a bomb squad on a bust, ready to wrestle the vicious-tongue-wielding perpetrator to the ground. She was met with nothing more sinister than a collection of groomed women and a scattering of men seated at tables around the room, all shimmering slightly in the light that was streaming in through skylights high above them. She scanned the vast industrial space, spotting her prime suspect at the far end of the room in deep conversation with the editor of *Glam* magazine, while Daniel was seated at a safe distance in the middle of the room. He had his back to Kate, but when Jasmine, sitting opposite him, waved, he turned around and started to get up. Kate shook her head and pointed at a table where she saw a spare seat beside another familiar face.

'It's Kate with the gorgeous skin,' Patricia Zee said as Kate sat down. *Glam*'s beauty editor, whom Kate had met through Jasmine, categorised everyone according to a standout feature. In Kate's case, it was her olive skin; in Jasmine's, her glossy black hair; in Kirsten's, her perfect butt. Said to be in her late-fifties, the beauty doyenne herself was notable for her chiselled cheekbones and incredibly youthful appearance, rumoured to be at least partly the result of plastic surgery. For some reason, though, she hadn't made any such rejuvenating efforts with her hair colour, which was natural silver albeit cut in a mod style: shaved at the back, graduating to a short, blunt bob in front.

'Kate writes about food for *Be*,' Patricia announced to the three other women at the table: a familiar-looking, reed-thin brunette and two blondes with Brazilian Blowout–straight hair, barely distinguishable from each other in black jackets with white shirts.

'A food writer? So you do this type of thing all the time?' the brunette said with raised eyebrows. 'I'd be a raging bulimic in your place.' Kate now recognised her as Susan Saunders, the author of a weekend column called

Calorie Crush that she enjoyed. Susan was eating her meal with chopsticks, she noticed, which was an interesting choice of implements for baked butternut and spinach penne.

'Chopsticks are the latest thing in dieting,' Susan said, alerting Kate to the fact that she had been staring too openly. 'You can only take in small amounts of food at a time, so you eat more slowly – and there's more time for enzymes to mix with food in your mouth. You should give it a go.'

'I highly recommend the venison, darling,' Patricia said as a waiter handed Kate the menu. 'It's lean, organic, and hormone-free, and this Pinotage that accompanies it is stunning.' She took a large glug to prove her point, swiftly followed by another. This was unusual behaviour for someone whom Kate had never seen drink anything other than mineral water.

'Red wine also zaps cholesterol and fat,' one of the blondes added, seemingly insinuating that Kate had excess fat in need of zapping. But ignoring recommendations and insinuations, she opted for the appealing roasted hake with creamed chermoula, mussels, and chickpeas, served with a glass of Snow Mountain Chardonnay, which Daniel had told her was the best of the bunch.

'It's a pity they don't have rosé on the menu,' one of the blondes said. 'The speaker earlier said it's very good for intestinal sluggishness.'

'Was he any good?' Kate asked, not sure how well a talk on food and wine pairing would be received by a circle for whom eating and drinking was a necessity at best, a liability at worst, and seldom a pure joy.

'Fabulous,' Patricia said. 'I've always found wine types quite stuffy, but he was a hoot and very informative. It's a pity you missed him.'

'He's actually my boyfriend,' Kate said.

'Really?' Patricia said. 'Aren't you lucky.' As they worked through their mains, she quizzed Kate about everything from how she had met Daniel to their marriage plans. Kate told her that she didn't believe in marriage but that they would be moving in together the following month. Every now and then she glanced over at Roberta, who remained engrossed in conversation and hadn't so much as looked at Daniel. So by the time the table was cleared and small glasses were placed in front of them, she was feeling calmer.

'Ooh, your man's back,' Patricia said, nodding towards Daniel, who was suddenly standing beside the steel-topped bar that separated the open-plan kitchen from the dining space. 'He's such a dish.'

He is *looking dishy,* Kate thought, taking him in objectively in his slim-cut navy suit with a purple and white checked shirt, and feeling a warm glow of pride and love inside.

'To finish, as promised, I'm going to take you through a quick tasting of the dessert wine,' Daniel said as waiters began to circulate with bottles. Kate and Patricia nodded eagerly when the waiter offered to fill their glasses, while their three lunch dates shook their heads. The blondes covered their glasses with their hands to make sure there was no mistake.

'I see hands waving away the wine,' Daniel said. 'But let me remind you that there are spittoons on every table and that it's every woman's prerogative not to swallow.'

'I think wine tasting's just become the new sex,' Patricia said. Susan Saunders shrugged her shoulders and nodded okay to the waiter, but the blondes resolutely shielded their glasses from the calorific beverage.

'If you need any more encouragement, Vin de Constance is, in fact, rated as one of the top forty-four wines in the world today,' Daniel said, 'and in the eighteenth and nineteenth centuries, its fans included Louis XVI, Jane Austen, Charles Dickens, and Napoleon Bonaparte. All that said, right now I'd like you to assess it at face value as you might someone who catches your fancy in a bar.' He held up his glass of deep golden liquid and tilted it slightly. 'So, starting with its appearance, it has an appealing deep amber-gold shimmer, which is testimony to its longer stay on the vines and access to plenty of sunshine, a bit like Shane over here, who's lived in Cape Town all his life.' He nodded at a good-looking tanned blond man at his table. 'All things considered, it's definitely worth a hello.'

Daniel swirled, tipped, and then righted his glass, watching the wine run down its sides in thick streaks. 'If legs are your thing, these should definitely do it for you,' he said, 'as they're seriously strong and robust, comparable perhaps to Russell Crowe's in *Gladiator*.' He smiled directly at Kate as he said this, since she had made this comparison before. She felt a frisson of pleasure run through her as their eyes connected across the room.

'You can tell he fancies the pants off you,' Patricia whispered gleefully. Kate smiled. Then, feeling the hairs on the back of her neck bristle, she swivelled her head to discover that Roberta too had noticed the glance and was looking at her with a smirk on her face. She held Kate's gaze for a moment and then, with a smug nod, turned her eyes back to Daniel. Kate's heart began to race.

'This is a very good indicator that the wine will be sweet and intense and therefore worth sniffing out a bit more,' Daniel said, 'which brings us to the nose.' He buried his own nose in his glass and inhaled, coming up to declare that the wine's delicious top notes of nectarine and quince, with floral undertones and a hint of sandalwood, meant it definitely merited a first kiss. 'In fact, the French writer Baudelaire said in his novel *Les Fleurs du Mal* that only the lips of a lover surpassed Vin de Constance in heavenly sweetness.'

'I've always thought these wine people were a bit ridiculous,' Susan Saunders said after swooshing and spitting, following Daniel's cue, 'but he does make sense of it all.'

'Finally, taking into consideration its delicious maple-syrup palate, I think it's fair to say that this wine is worth getting into bed with,' Daniel said. 'Also worth noting is its long finish, because, much like a lover, the true test of a wine is how long it stays with you after you've drunk it; the longer the better, of course.'

Beware the cheap one that runs off with an activities coordinator or a company CEO at the first sign of commitment, Kate thought. She automatically glanced at Roberta, who was looking at Daniel pensively with her arms crossed. *What is brewing in that evil mind of hers?*

'What did I say about shex?' Patricia whispered, beginning to slur her words.

As waiters served the mini desserts, Daniel noted that wine should always be sweeter than the food it accompanied while also connecting or contrasting with some of its key components. 'This wine works well with the lemon tart,' he said, 'because of their shared fruity top notes and the contrasting bitterness of the lemon, while the vanilla in the cheesecake connects with the wine's hint of sandalwood.'

He sat down to applause, and the tanned South African replaced him at the microphone to announce what everyone had been waiting for, that the goody bags were ready for collection. The two blondes sprinted to the door as Kate glanced in Roberta's direction, hoping that she, too, would move speedily in the direction of ageing's newest antidote. But she was still in deep conversation.

'Why should the wine be shweeter than the dessert?' Patricia asked after polishing off her cheesecake and draining a second glass.

'Because a dry wine would make the dessert seem too sweet and leave the wine tasting bland,' Kate said. 'So one of the biggest mistakes people make is serving good Champagne with cake at celebrations since the Champagne ends up tasting like dishwater.'

'I can shee why you're together,' Patricia said.

And so could Kate, now more than ever. Apart from their complementary trades, Daniel's sweeter, mellower character balanced her neurotic, sharper temperament much like the Vin de Constance complemented the lemon tart. The combination of their molecular flavours created delicious chemistry, both on a mental and a physical level, and she felt better for the pairing: lighter, happier, complete.

'Do you love him?' Patricia asked. 'Doeszh he put you first?'

Kate nodded.

'Well, letsh me tell you something, Kate. Thatsh what countsh at the end of the day. Not all thish.' Patricia made a sweeping gesture with her free arm. 'Take it from someone who'zh been around the block.'

Kate decided that, in order to protect 'thatsh', she should extricate Daniel from the new fans buzzing around him and precipitate his departure, but her plan was foiled by Jasmine.

'You made it,' she said. 'Wasn't Daniel great? I don't think anyone's had so much fun at a beauty launch.'

'Shit down,' Patricia said, getting up and swaying slightly. 'I'm jusht going to pop to the loo, and then I musht go.'

'I'm really sorry, Patricia,' Jasmine said. 'They're out of their minds.' She kissed her on both cheeks and gave her a hug. 'Let's get together soon.'

'Did she tell you?' Jasmine asked, sitting down in Patricia's place.

'What?' Kate asked.

'That she's been given the heave-ho?' Jasmine said.

'What? She's been ...?' Kate mimicked the motion of a knife slitting her throat. 'No, she didn't. Oh dear.' *That explains it.*

'Yes, put out to pasture. Rumour has it they've already hired Zara Thompson, who's about twelve years old. She can barely write, but she's totally connected and has a huge Twitter following. Poor Patricia. It's so humiliating. And it just goes to show, you can never get too cosy.'

'Speaking of cosy, have you seen Roberta?' Kate asked, nodding towards Roberta's table. 'She's been schmoozing Rebecca Todd all lunch.'

'It wouldn't surprise me if she's trying to worm her way in there,' Jasmine said. 'She's furious with Amber. She told me on the way over here that she's definitely not planning on hanging around.' Jasmine glanced at Kate uncertainly for a minute. 'She's not too ecstatic with you either.'

'What did she say?' Kate's heart skipped a beat.

'Just that she thinks you're a dark horse, and some stuff that I didn't really get about Mauritius.' She gave Kate another delving look before adding, 'It's probably just sour grapes, but I would be careful of her; she can be vicious.'

'Hi, beautiful. I thought you weren't going to make it.' Daniel kissed Kate. 'How do you think it went?'

'Youwerebrilliantshallwego?' Kate said without taking a breath.

'You were,' Jasmine said. 'My husband once dragged me to a wine tasting and I found it terribly dull, but you weren't at all.'

'Thanks, I think.' Daniel laughed and then turned to Kate. 'Sorry, hon, I've offered to buy the De-Vine guys a drink at the Prospect.'

Having planned to return to the office for a couple of hours, Kate changed her agenda in an instant. 'Why don't we go ahead and grab a table on the terrace. You know how quickly it fills up.' But her last-ditch attempt to get Daniel out of harm's way was too late. Roberta was already descending on them.

'Hello, Kate. And hello again,' she said to Daniel almost flirtatiously. 'That was enlightening. You've picked up quite a few fans in our little circle today.' She turned to Kate. 'You've kept Daniel very quiet. So did the two of you meet fairly recently?'

'Not very,' Kate said.

'It's getting close to two years,' Daniel said.

'Oh, *really*,' Roberta said with feigned surprise. 'Two *years*? So you were tucked away here while we were in Mauritius? No doubt Kate told you *all* about the fun and games we had.'

'Yes,' Daniel said. 'It doesn't sound like a picnic.'

'Not for most of us, but Kate's a real trouper; she didn't let things stop her getting out there and soaking up the local atmosphere.'

'That's Kate,' Daniel said. 'Never say die. Once she's got her mind set on something, she just can't let go.'

'Oh, don't I know it. And she grabs things by the balls, doesn't she?' Roberta said with a smirk. 'She was out there day and night trying out *all* the local specialities. She's quite a fan of Chinese, isn't she?'

Kate decided that in Jean Paul Sartre's version of hell, i.e. living in eternity with people who represented everything you hated, Roberta was all the company she would need.

'Really?' Daniel asked. He gave Kate a questioning look, as she generally avoided Chinese food, preferring less greasy Thai and Vietnamese when it came to Asian cuisine.

'Couldn't get enough of it,' Roberta said.

Kate gave Jasmine a pleading look and subtly gestured towards the door with her head.

'We should head back now if we want to miss the traffic, Roberta,' Jasmine said.

'You're right. Look at the time. It was nice to meet you, Daniel, and I hope we'll have more time to chat at Loredana Manzella's house next weekend. I believe you've agreed to host a private tasting. I can fill you in on all the bits that Kate missed.'

So that's her approach, Kate thought. *Slow and painful torture to the death.*

* * *

After a few drinks at the Prospect of Whitby, Daniel and Kate walked languidly back to Daniel's flat in the late afternoon. Kate's progress along the pavement mirrored that of a lone seagull weaving in the air above them until Daniel pulled her to him. 'Come here, you swallower, you.'

'You wish,' Kate managed, although she was really in no mood to joke.

'Seriously,' Daniel said. 'I have a new appreciation for your, shall we say, *relaxed* approach to drinking. It was like coaxing children to swallow medicine back there. I think the health benefits saved the day.'

'Yes, one of my lunch companions was very excited to hear that rosé is good for intestinal sluggishness,' Kate said, feeling her own intestine tying itself into ever tighter knots as she considered Roberta's thinly veiled threat. Of course, Roberta might just be tormenting Kate and may have no intention of taking it any further, but Kate couldn't bear it if Daniel heard the news from her. Although her heart broke at the thought of losing him, she realised that she couldn't tolerate the deceit any longer.

Back in the flat, Daniel unwittingly opened the channels for a confession. 'I see what you mean about Roberta,' he said. 'She's quite a piece of work.' He was standing at the kitchen island making a brie and cranberry jelly sandwich while Kate was curled up on the sofa with a mint tea, too nauseous to eat. 'And you're right; she really is hung up about you getting to do all the fun stuff in Mauritius.' He walked over from the kitchen and sat down on the couch next to her. He had taken off his suit and shoes and was wearing his shirt with boxer shorts and socks, looking particularly adorable. 'She genuinely seems to think you were just partying, which wasn't the case as I recall.'

Kate blew on her mint tea.

'And what was all that about Chinese food?' he asked. 'The last time I checked, you weren't particularly fond of it.'

'The version over there is Cantonese,' Kate said, 'so a lot is steamed and boiled rather than fried – and it felt a lot healthier.' Although this wasn't a lie, she was skirting the truth yet again. *Enough.* She sat up and looked at Daniel, feeling faint and dizzy all of a sudden.

'Are you okay?' he asked. 'You look pale. Can I get you a glass of water? I was surprised you drank that beer.'

'It's not the beer.' Kate took a deep breath. 'There's something I need to tell you. Something happened while I was in Mauritius. … God, there's no easy way to say this, but I met someone and …' She couldn't finish the sentence.

'What?' Daniel put the plate with his half-finished sandwich on the coffee table.

'I met someone and, well … I … I'm so sorry.'

'What? Who did you meet? What are you saying exactly, Kate?'

'I slept with someone, Dan; that's what I'm trying to say.' Kate didn't think she needed to mention that she had, in fact, slept with a couple of someones, since Jacques had no relevance here and would only double Daniel's hurt.

'Fuck.' *Yes.*

'I'm so, so sorry. It was a *huge* mistake. A holiday fling.'

'Shit,' Daniel said.

'I know I shouldn't have done it, but I was confused and swept away and ... Okay, there's no excuse, but I so don't want us to end.'

Daniel's eyes turned instantaneously from blue to grey as the colour drained from his face. Kate now felt bile rising up in her throat as she realised what was happening, that this was really the beginning of the end of her and Daniel.

'Shit. Fuck.' Daniel looked as if he had a gun at his temple; his body was rigid. 'So that's what Roberta was on about. Does everyone know except me?' he said. 'Wow, I feel like *such* an idiot.'

Tears were filling Kate's throat and choking her, so she was capable only of shaking her head. Daniel snapped out of shock mode and began to pace up and down. She had never seen him so angry. If she hated Roberta for pushing her here, she hated herself more for causing this distress.

'I don't get it,' he said, stopping for a moment and looking at her with disbelief in his eyes. 'I thought everything was so good. We were just talking about moving in together. I thought it was a sign that you were finally committed to us, but ... Why would you do this? Why now?'

'I'm so sorry, Dan, it's just ...'

'It's just what, Kate? It's just that you care so little for me that you'd risk everything we have on a casual fling and then wait weeks to tell me? Why tell me at all?' He shook his head. 'I don't know ... maybe it was never that good for you.'

'It was ... is. I'm sorry I didn't tell you. It's just taken these few weeks to figure it all out, and I'm still not sure I have. But I love you ... *so much.* I do, really.' Kate felt herself getting slightly hysterical.

'I don't think you know what love is,' Daniel said, 'or that you have any idea how much I love you. You know, I think about you constantly. I worried about you so much when the cyclone hit Mauritius, and all the time you were ...' He froze for a moment and then turned slowly to face her again. 'Please tell me you're not only telling me now because of what Roberta said.' Kate couldn't look at him. 'Oh God, you are.' Now tears spilled from his eyes. He rubbed them away. 'Anyone else you've fucked in the last eighteen months that you haven't told me about?' Kate was glad he didn't pause long enough for her to consider mentioning Jacques; she knew that would be as good as pulling the trigger. 'Just tell me what it was. Who was it?' he asked. 'Actually, I'd rather not know that either. Just tell me if it meant anything?'

If Kate had any hope of salvaging this, she knew she should say no to the last question without a moment's hesitation, but she couldn't do it because, if Jacques had meant nothing, Fai *had* felt like more than a casual fling. Plus, she found no more energy or motivation to lie.

Her hesitation and perhaps the look on her face was enough for Daniel.

'Bloody hell, Kate. And I thought this was it.'

'Maybe you're right; maybe I am so screwed up about love that I really don't know what it is, but I love you as much as I know how,' Kate said. Tears began to run in rivers down her cheeks.

'Not enough,' Daniel said and, without looking at her, he got up and walked upstairs.

Kate heard the shower running, turned to full, which was Daniel's way of clearing his head when he was stressed or frustrated. She wasn't sure what to do or what he wanted her to do. *Get out of his sight, most likely.* So she just sat on the couch, letting her tea get cold and her body go numb as tears and snot streamed down her face. The dull ache continued to seep through her whole body until it was impossible for her to move.

Eventually the sound of running water stopped and Daniel came down in his navy towelling robe. His hair wet and ruffled, his face still pale, he looked more attractive than he had ever looked to her.

'I'm going to call you a minicab.' He was cold and calm, resigned. She had preferred it when he was angry. He picked up the phone and dialled. 'Could you get it to London Bridge?' Kate croaked. 'My car's at work.'

'You can't drive,' Daniel said. 'Get it in the morning.'

Kate's sobbing doubled in intensity as she thought that, even hating her as he must right now, Daniel was thinking of her well-being. Every sailboat needs an anchor in turbulent seas, and Daniel, Kate realised, was that person who made her feel safe when life got rough.

Daniel turned on the television and stared at the news blankly as Kate did the same. There was so much she wanted to say, but she felt empty and incapable of speaking. When his phone rang, signalling the arrival of her taxi, she silently picked herself up off the sofa, grabbed her bag, and made her way to the door. She turned to say goodbye, but Daniel was right behind her. He slipped on his loafers, joined her in the lift, and opened the minicab's door. Then he stood with his hands in his dressing-gown pockets and watched her drive away as she looked back at him through a veil of tears and trauma. Her anchor had been ripped out and she was drifting into the vast, inhospitable ocean – alone and desolate.

Just Desserts?

CHAPTER 13

Sweet Revenge

The arrival of a new issue of *Be* was usually like the highly charged occasion of childbirth. But when Kate looked down at the pile of July issues on her desk, she didn't have an unbridled urge to take the bundle of joy into her arms. *This is your first cover,* she told herself, trying to elicit a positive reaction. Still not a flutter. She was emotionally exhausted, she decided, so wrung out by the tears and trauma over her break-up with Daniel that she had nothing left to give this baby she had wanted so badly. Perhaps a coffee would perk her up, she thought and, like a postnatally depressed mother, she crossed the empty office to the kitchen, leaving her newborn unattended on her desk.

She returned with a steaming cappuccino, which she sipped while gazing down at her first ever cover. Still not moved, she cut the umbilical string binding the magazines together, and picked up the top issue. It was heavy, definitely a healthy baby. She held it away from her, trying to see the cover image as objectively as a potential buyer in a newsagent might. Did it have that X factor required to attract the sales they so desperately needed?

Kate knew that answering the question of what made a magazine cover sell, much debated among editors, art directors, and industry commentators, had proved as difficult to reduce to a science as what constituted sex appeal. All agreed that if coverlines were important, then the image, and specifically the person in the image, was key. But even Jennifer Aniston and Sarah Jessica Parker could let things down if striking the wrong pose. While lacking celebrity cachet, Finola certainly hit the mark on that score, looking straight at the camera, as was said to establish an important connection with the browser. Added to this, she was dressed in popular pink and her hair was a consumer-winning tawny blonde. But was all this enough to draw attention away from the other beauties beckoning from the news stand like the ladies of the night lining certain streets in Amsterdam? Kate's gut said yes. She found herself smiling for the first time in days as she began to flick through the magazine, feeling a bond begin to form.

Since she had viewed the laid-out version of her travel story through an emotional post-break-up haze, she turned to that first. Only now could she appreciate the majestic beauty of the opener: a double-page spread of the road to Port Louis, with towering sugar cane on either side and a woman in a purple sari and matching parasol walking away from the camera, towards the dramatic black mountains in the distance. The head, 'Meet Me in Port Louis', stretched across the pristine blue sky in wispy white letters, followed by Harry's apt standfirst: 'Undulating sugar cane, white sand beaches, markets filled with exotic delights, and hedonistic hideaways to enfold you at night … the moment you set foot in Mauritius, the seduction begins.'

There was no hint of the dark clouds that had been rolling in behind the camera at that stage and, in the copy too, the cyclone had diminished to a mere squall, since the Sunshine Group had requested as much. It occurred to Kate again how much of what one saw in a magazine was an edited version of reality, an ideal world in which imperfections and unhappiness were just out of the frame or hiding in plain sight, as in the case of Tatyana. Thanks to Photoshop and some good styling, the troubled model looked in glowing health as she perused saris and pineapples in Port Louis market, sprawled on the beach, and draped herself over pieces of driftwood.

'Hi, Jugs.'

Kate jumped and turned around. 'I wish you wouldn't always do that, Harry. How do you manage to sneak up without making a sound every time?'

'Trainers,' Harry said. 'That's why they call them sneakers in the United States.'

'Ha ha.'

'I'm serious. The name comes from the word *sneak* because their rubber soles meant they were the first shoes that didn't make a noise. So what do you think of our editor's dark secret?'

'What dark secret?' Kate asked.

'What do you mean, "What dark secret?" You can't *not* have seen the pictures.'

'I have no idea what you're talking about, Harry.'

Harry looked at Kate incredulously. 'What planet have you been on?'

'You know I took a few days off.' After seeing the magazine to print, Kate had taken a long weekend to get herself together and, so she had hoped, to talk things through with Daniel. However, he had refused to see or talk to her, and so she had abandoned her phone, logged out of her life, and buried herself in box sets.

'As far as I know, you didn't go to Mars,' Harry said. 'And Twitter's probably available there by now.' He looked over his shoulder and then turned back with a glint in his eye. 'Okay, move over and pay attention. I'm going to have to be quick.'

He pulled Louise's chair across to Kate's desk and, with a few clicks, brought up an image on her screen that was suitable for neither the time nor the place. She felt like she was being offered a dirty Martini before breakfast.

'Why are we looking at porn at 8 a.m. on a Monday morning?'

'Recognise anyone?' Harry asked.

'No, why would I?' Kate looked more closely. 'Fuck me.'

'I'm sure she would if you asked her nicely,' Harry said.

'It's really her?' Kate asked.

'Our editor in chief, in the flesh, in every sense of the word,' Harry said. 'More than a few years ago, clearly, and at least two cup sizes larger. She would have given you a serious run for your money.'

'You're not kidding?' Amber's breasts were at least a DD or an E, which, combined with her long legs and very narrow waist, made her look like a redheaded Barbie in the buff.

The image on the screen was a PDF of a magazine spread that cleared up any doubts about whether Amber was a natural redhead. She was seated on the counter of an American-style diner, her stiletto-clad feet resting on two adjacent red leatherette bar stools. Holding a tall glass filled with layers of fruit and ice cream, she was suggestively licking a spoon.

'Okay, so I've dubbed that one "Knickerless Bocker Glory,"' Harry said, 'and, moving on, here we have "Cream Tease."' He pulled up a second image, in which Amber was lying back on a red banquette, straddled by a blonde wearing nothing but a red and white checked apron, who was squeezing whipped cream from a pump dispenser onto Amber's breasts. Kate found it difficult to reconcile the cool, steely Amber she knew with the hot-blooded seductress on her computer screen.

After Harry had clicked through several more images in which burger flippers and sugar shakers were put to imaginative use, Kate asked, 'Where did they come from?'

'I'm not sure, but they were suddenly all over the Internet on Thursday afternoon. Someone said they'd heard she did porn when she was living in the States in the 1980s. Who would have thought, eh?'

Kate recalled Tristan's newsflash in Mauritius about Amber's and Roberta's adult-modelling days. There was no sign of Roberta in any of these images, she noted. 'How did Amber react?' she asked as the door banged shut. Both their heads darted in its direction to be met by Vanessa, who was glaring at them from across the room. Although too far away to see what was on Kate's screen, she appeared to know exactly what they were up to.

'Are you and Vanessa always the first ones in?' Kate asked.

'Pretty much. I'm like the head butler, and she's the housekeeper; the magazine can only grind into action once we're at our posts.'

'You're such an unsung hero, Harry.'

'Indeed,' he said emphatically. 'I'm so glad you see that finally.' He gave her a Hollywood smile.

'So, how did Amber react?' Kate asked again.

'She disappeared on Thursday and didn't come in at all on Friday.' Harry brought Kate's email back up on her screen. 'I hope she makes an appearance today, though, because we need her decision on a few things. It will be interesting to see what happens.'

As people began to trickle in, it became clear that the images were on everyone's minds, lips, and mobile phones. Tweeting filled the air, and volume levels were on a par with the dawn chorus in a tropical rainforest by the time Amber walked in, at which point the place became as quiet as a forest before a storm. Wearing her faux leopard trench coat with 1930s-style black suede stilettos and a large pair of dark glasses, she clearly wasn't opting for an antidotal I-am-pure-and-virginal look, which was just like Amber, Kate thought. She closed the door behind her, and seconds later the blinds spanning the glass wall shot down. The twittering started up again, this time at a lower volume, stopping momentarily when Amber's door opened to admit Vanessa, who was bearing a large McDonald's bag: 'A triple cheeseburger, a double portion of fries, and a chocolate milkshake,' Lavinia at reception announced. Things were very bad indeed.

At 12 noon, a message from Vanessa addressed to the whole office appeared in Kate's inbox: 'The July post-mortem scheduled for 2 p.m. has been postponed until 4.30 p.m.'

At 2 p.m., the reason for this postponement arrived in the form of Eric Lowell. The older of the two brothers, he was wearing a dark tailored suit and sporting a head of thick blond hair in place of the grey and thinning crop Kate remembered from the last sighting. *Implants?* Kate thought he looked slightly ridiculous, except that his professionally whitened teeth were at least now in better company. Simon followed close on his heels, buckling under an armful of files. Fifteen minutes later, Terry Lowell strode in, looking like he had been called from a polo match, wearing jeans and a pale blue shirt with a cream jersey knotted around his neck. The friendlier of the two, he usually engaged with staff like Prince Charles on walkabout, but today he didn't even give a royal wave.

After Terry entered, voices were raised. Half an hour later, all three men erupted from the office and hurried out without a backward glance. Kate half expected Amber's heavy antique crystal ashtray to come flying out after them.

'It doesn't sound like that went too well,' Kirsten said. 'Do you think they could have fired her?'

'Surely not,' Kate said. She was sitting at Kirsten's desk, discussing August's food shoot, which would once again be dovetailing with a fashion story. 'Amber *is* the magazine. Without her ...'

'Some of that stuff was quite heavy,' Kirsten said, 'and you know how puritanical those two are. Did you see the movie?'

There was a movie? Kate wondered if there hadn't been a loosening of values in Eric Lowell's case; his hair implants seemed to support a rumoured affair with a blonde half his age in sales. But it was true that, despite the Lowells' recent inclusion on a list of London's wealthiest, their small-town roots remained a strong influence. The only time that they interfered with editorial was when things got too risqué.

'Does anyone have any idea where the pictures came from?' Kate asked, although she had her own strong suspicions.

'Whoever it was has covered their tracks very well,' Kirsten said, 'but ...' She glanced around and then lowered her voice. 'Amber and Roberta did this kind of stuff together way back, so it's funny that no pictures of Roberta have surfaced. And you know that she and Amber had a huge falling-out over the cover. I don't think they're even talking at the moment.'

Kirsten was distracted by a new message in her inbox. 'Okay, it looks like all will be revealed soon. The 4.30's now been moved to 5.00, and apparently there's going to be an important announcement. Everyone has to be there. I'd better call Roberta; she never checks her email and she hasn't been in all day. In fact, she's barely been in over the last week.

'You really think she's behind this?' Kate asked. 'Isn't that a bit extreme? I mean, I know she's vindictive, but sinking Amber's career over a cover?' She was suddenly filled with trepidation. If Roberta had indeed meted out this punishment to Amber, what else might she have in store for Kate? She had already destroyed her relationship with Daniel, so all that was left was her job.

'I've never seen her so furious about anything,' Kirsten said as she helped herself to some goji berries from a packet on her desk. She offered the packet to Kate, who declined; she had barely been able to eat since the break-up ten days before, and the news of Roberta's latest vengeful attack was making her stomach churn.

'I hope you know I had no intention of stealing the cover,' Kate said. 'It was all about the food.'

'You could have told me.' Kirsten scowled. 'It would have been nice to be prepared for the nuclear fallout. Don't be too sorry, though, because yours knocks the socks off our options on the yacht.' She looked down at the magazine on her desk. 'Nice.'

'Thanks,' Kate said, although the devastating results of her misdeeds behind the camera made it impossible for her to revel in this victory. She realised that she would trade the cover in a heartbeat to have Daniel back. 'Was your shoot really that bad?'

'Worse than bad. April was sulking, Marius and Tristan hadn't slept a wink, and Tatyana was even more out of it than usual, which I now know was because ... Oh my God, I haven't told you; she OD'd.'

'What? Who?'

'Tatyana. She took an overdose of sleeping pills just after we got back. Tristan told me a couple of days ago.'

'She committed suicide?'

'Well, tried. A friend found her in time, and they pumped her stomach, or whatever they do, but she was in hospital for a couple of days and she's a mess. She actually tried in Mauritius. Thank God she didn't pull it off there; can you just imagine!'

'Whoa! This is a lot to digest,' Kate said. 'In Mauritius? When?'

Kirsten told Kate that the night before the cover shoot, Tatyana had left the table to take a call and had not returned. Kirsten said that she knew now from Tristan that Marius had gone to check on her later and, when she didn't answer his knocks, convinced someone from housekeeping to let him into her room. He had found her in tears, downing pills with the entire contents of the minibar. Although Tatyana had begged him not to tell anyone, Marius had called Tristan for a second opinion on whether or not to call a doctor – and they had both kept a vigil for the rest of the night.

'Apparently her fiancé had called in a jealous rage,' Kirsten said. 'He'd gone into her email and found out about a lunch she'd had with an ex that she hadn't mentioned to him. So he told her that it was well and truly over, that he'd changed the locks, and given everything she owned to Oxfam.'

'Charitable guy.' Kate grimaced. 'Sounds like he and Roberta were separated at birth.'

'Funny you should say that, because it was Roberta who sent Tatyana over the edge the second time. Her agency told her they were cancelling her contract because Roberta had apparently laid it on *thick*.'

'But surely that's not a reason. ... She could find another agency, couldn't she?'

'Not in the state she's in. Word gets around fast. And she's totally broke because she's been sending all her money home. So she's back to square one. She was actually working in a lap-dancing club when she was spotted a couple of years ago.'

'Where's she now?' Kate asked.

'She's staying with Marius. He's such a sweetie; he's got her on a vegan diet and he's trying to help her extend her visa.'

Tatyana's story was like *Cinderella* without the fairy-tale ending, Kate thought. She had transformed her life and won her prince, but the glass slipper had shattered, Prince Charming had proved less than charming, and the wicked stepmother had won the day. *Life sure is no a fairy tale.*

'That woman is evil,' Kate said.

'She is,' Kirsten said, 'which reminds me, I'd better tell her about the meeting, and then I need to get onto sourcing wellies and brollies for Wednesday. You'd better get on with your sourcing too.'

The theme for Kate's feature was sophisticated picnic fare that might accompany a concert at Hampstead Heath, outdoor theatre at Regents Park, or an opera at Glyndebourne, the last of which was where the shoot was taking place. Dovetailing with this, Kirsten would be shooting evening dresses suited to a night at Glyndebourne. Rain had, however, been forecast for the day of the shoot, so they were teaming the evening dresses with wellington boots for the picnic segment, which they had relocated from the lawn to a stone pavilion. Kate thus had to source a tablecloth, a folding table, and folding chairs to replace the picnic blankets she had planned for the lawn.

Job done, she made her way to the third-floor boardroom for the revelatory meeting. When she entered the room, all eyes turned towards her and conversations were halted, resuming in hushed tones when it was established that she was a mere stagehand rather than the star of the show – until the door opened again.

This time, it was Vanessa who strode in. Dressed in a short black leather pinafore dress, a white shirt, and thigh boots, she looked like a dominatrix, Kate thought, especially trailed as she was by three 'submissives' from Pret, who were bearing cardboard trays laden with paper cups.

'Skinny lattes, Americanos, and cappuccinos,' Vanessa said, pointing to the first tray. 'Soy skinny lattes, Americanos, and cappuccinos.' She pointed at the second tray. 'And both soy and normal teas.' She made a twirling movement with her hand to indicate that the servers should circle the table.

As everyone helped themselves to the orders they had placed earlier, Vanessa removed two square boxes from the large purple Konditor & Cook paper bag she was carrying and placed them on each end of the table.

'Amber's running a bit late, so go ahead,' she said.

In accordance with *Be* tradition, the boxes contained petits fours custom-decorated in honour of the summer issue. Consisting of light-as-air lemon sponge cake with apricot jam, wrapped in marzipan and fondant icing, these were irresistible to even the calorie-counters, so it was to everyone's oohing and ahing, and deliberations over whether to have the sunglasses or the superyacht, that Amber quietly made her entrance. She had seated herself in the chair reserved for her at the head of the table before anyone noticed her presence.

'Is that everyone?' she asked as people sat back in their seats, replacing their expressions of sugar-fuelled delight with savoury ones. This was when Kate noticed that Roberta was still absent.

'Thank you for making this meeting,' Amber said. 'I'm sorry that we had to chop and change things around a bit, but I think everyone's well aware by now of the reasons for this.' Her eyes were red and her face blanched. 'While this meeting's agenda has changed, I would like to start by saying that the July issue is superb and you should all be very proud of yourselves. In fact, I can honestly say, hand on heart, that I think it's the best issue we've produced.' Amber placed her hand on her heart as she said this.

Kate looked down at the magazine, which she had brought along by force of habit even though they wouldn't be dissecting it as per the original agenda.

'It's also the biggest issue we've produced since last September,' Amber said, 'which is the result of great symbiosis between editorial and advertising. James, I must congratulate your team on a really excellent job.' Amber looked at the head of advertising. 'You're well over target, which is particularly commendable in this tough market. Everyone's done their bit, and I think I can say with every confidence that when we go on sale in a few days time, this issue is going to walk off the shelves. All of this makes what I have to tell you today that much more difficult.' She paused to pour herself a glass of water. Kate noticed that her hand was shaking as she took a sip.

'We're all adults here,' she continued, 'and there's really no point in my beating around the bush.'

Interesting choice of words, Kate thought. *So to get to the clitoris of the matter …*

'I think everyone will have seen the images that have been circulating for the last couple of days which relate to my past work in adult magazines.' There was a low murmur of acknowledgement. 'These are from my past – another lifetime, really – and have nothing to do with where I am now, and certainly nothing to do with *Be*. However, someone has seen fit to dig them up, and unfortunately certain parties in management have taken issue. They have also taken action – extreme action, I'm afraid.'

So Kirsten's right, Kate thought; *Amber's been fired.* She glanced at Kirsten, who gave her a look that said, *What did I tell you?*

'I've tried to convince them to reconsider, but their minds are made up.' Amber took a sip of water, closed her eyes, and swayed slightly. Kate thought she was about to faint, but then she opened her eyes and, gripping the table, said, 'There's no easy way to say this, so I'm just going to put it plainly with my deepest apologies. The Lowell brothers have taken the decision to close *Be*.'

Jasmine choked, causing a piece of petit four bearing the bottom half of a polka-dot bikini to shoot out of her mouth and land in Vanessa's Americano. Vanessa, however, didn't seem to notice. She continued to sip on her coffee, a stunned look on her face. While Amber's dismissal had probably been a foregone conclusion for most people, clearly no one had guessed that the whole magazine would be fired.

Jasmine eventually broke the silence. 'But that's a ridiculous reason to shut down a magazine. We were living in the twenty-first century last time I checked.'

'Yes, but the Lowell brothers are still living in the Dark Ages,' Amber said with some of her old fire. Small red points appeared in her cheeks. 'I really am terribly sorry. It is grossly unjust that all of you should have to suffer for my actions. I offered to step down, of course, but I'm afraid they're using it as an excuse. They've never truly understood the machinations of a glossy, and this economic meltdown has put enormous pressure on the whole company. In truth, they might have done this sooner if not for a number of stipulations in my contract, which they've been able to wrangle their way out of on the basis of my misconduct. Once again, I do humbly apologise for my part in this.'

'I presume we'll still put August to bed?' Louise said.

'I'm afraid not,' Amber said, her face aptly demonstrating the popular song lyrics 'turned a whiter shade of pale'.

'But that's madness,' Amanda from advertising said. 'Surely it's going to cost more not to put the magazine out? Just that bound-in watch supplement is pretty big. Are they really going to throw all that revenue away? It doesn't make sense.'

'I agree,' Amber said, 'but the Lowells are convinced that as soon as news of our closure gets out, people will start to pull ads.'

'How long are they giving us to wrap everything up?' someone else asked. Suddenly feeling dizzy, Kate didn't notice who it was.

'They want everyone out of the office by 5 p.m. on Friday.' Amber sighed. 'Look, I know this is a lot to take in. I suggest no one tries to do anything today. Go home and sleep on it. We'll tackle things in the morning.'

'They're giving us four days?' Jasmine said incredulously. 'That's insane.' There was an explosion of questions and comments around the table, but white noise filled Kate's ears as it began to sink in that the one thing she thought she could rely on if she played her cards right had collapsed. Added to this, seeing her own fear reflected in the ashen faces around the table, she suddenly had an overwhelming sense of guilt. Had she not enraged Roberta by forging ahead with her shoot, they probably wouldn't be in this situation at all. There was now no doubt in her mind as to who was behind the leak.

CHAPTER 14

Home to Roast

They were on the home stretch now, meandering along the Roseland Peninsula's narrow lanes with Chloe at the wheel of her VW Golf, Luke sitting beside her, and Kate in the back feeling like a loose and wobbly third wheel.

It was a week since *Be*'s final closure and almost a month since Kate's break-up with Daniel, during which time she had sat slumped on the sofa watching mindless television, unable to eat, while weeping into her Sauvignon Blanc. Chloe had thus decided that it was time for some home cooking and fresh sea air in St Mawes.

The familiar scent of cut grass and wild flowers wafted in through the car's open windows. This mingled with a hint of salt in the air, telling them that the sea was close by, although it was currently hidden from view by towering hazel hedges on either side of the lane, which made this part of the journey feel like navigating a maze. An ambling caravan up ahead, too wide to pass, was currently slowing down their progress, and a long line of traffic snaked behind them.

'There's always one, isn't there?' Chloe said. 'They lurk in the hedges and spring out to torment us like evil trolls the minute we can smell home. You'd better call your mum and tell her we're running late, K. There's sure to be something fabulous in the oven that's going to be ruined if you don't warn her.' She turned to Luke. 'I should warn you now that you're in no such luck. I'm just grateful if my mother has remembered to get bread and milk.'

'Said the pot,' Kate added as she fished her mobile out of her bag. 'I'm afraid the apple doesn't fall far from the tree, Luke, but while you might go hungry, you won't be bored; Felicity is highly entertaining.' It was a turn-up for the relationship books that Chloe had invited Luke home to meet her mother while, conversely, Kate would be returning home solo for the first time in a while. She felt a pang as she recalled her last visit with Daniel, when she had snuck down the passage to his room – her mother didn't believe in premarital bed sharing – and there had been much illicit fun before she had snuck back at daybreak.

'Well, I like the apple a lot, so a whole tree sounds grand,' Luke said. The drive had been Kate's first chance to talk to him at any length, and she discovered that she liked him. He exuded classic Irish wit and charm and was ruggedly good-looking with a twinkle in his green eyes. He had also distracted her from her inner turmoil with some hilarious compositions on his ukulele, which now shared the back seat with her.

'You won't be saying that if she serves up her infamous watery fish curry for lunch,' Chloe said. 'She learnt to make it during her bohemian days in Goa in the 1960s, and she still hasn't perfected it. But it's her special-occasion dish, so chances are …'

'I'm sure it can't be that bad,' Luke said.

'It is,' Kate and Chloe said in unison, and they both laughed.

On the domestic front, Felicity Chance was the antithesis of Kate's mother. In fact, when Chloe and Kate were children, at those times when illustrations for a book Felicity was working on were due, she sometimes forgot to feed them altogether, leaving them to fend for themselves. This had meant heating up bright pink hot-dog sausages in the microwave, baking piles of crinkly oven chips, slathering Nutella on hunks of white bread, and creating inventive concoctions such as melted marshmallows and Milo on toast. Kate had loved the free rein, which was in stark contrast to the more rigid meal routine at home. For her part, Chloe had enjoyed coming to Kate's house for lively home-cooked meals around the table with Kate's sisters and parents because she had only had a whole family until she was four, when her father had died in a car accident. This was a tragically unfitting end for an adventurer who had served as an officer in the Royal Marines, scaled Mount Everest, and circumnavigated the globe in several yacht races before winning Felicity's heart in the Azores. But Felicity kept his memory alive for her daughter with tales in which he was in a league with Odysseus or Horatio Nelson, Ernest Shackleton or Edmund Hillary, and Prince Charming to the end. Although widowed in her mid thirties, Felicity had never remarried because she said that John Chance had been the one and only love of her life, perhaps explaining why Chloe still believed so strongly in soulmates.

As Kate's own experiences had started to colour her views on romance, however, she had begun to wonder if Chloe's father would still be the hero he was in Felicity's tales if he hadn't become something of a romantic martyr. Perhaps the only perfect relationship was one that was frozen in time when still in its prime, like Damien Hirst's pure white *Dream Foal* with a unicorn's horn, preserved for perpetuity in a solution of resin, silicone, and formaldehyde. Felicity's embalmed version of love was certainly a lot more attractive than the tableau that Kate's parents' marriage had become, or indeed Kate's own relationship history, which currently looked more like Tracy Emin's *My Bed* installation, strewn with empty booze bottles, cigarette butts, condoms, stained sheets, and dirty knickers. She yearned for Daniel's freshly laundered thousand-thread-count cotton sheets, but she had made her bed and now she had to lie in it – alone. And for eternity, it seemed, as Daniel had made it very clear on their last encounter that he never wanted to see her again.

The day after the announcement of *Be*'s closure, Kate, hanging on by a thread, had left work and found herself driving to Daniel's flat like a homing pigeon. Although he had asked her not to call him again, she needed to see him and hoped that he might warm up if he saw her. But on opening the door, he had looked at her and shaken his head. 'You just don't understand, do you? You have no idea how much you hurt me, knowing that I've been through all this before. I'm begging you, could you please, *please*, let me get on with my life?' And when she had said she felt guilty and wished he could forgive her, adding that she missed him more than she thought possible, he had said, 'It's always about you, isn't it, Kate? About *your* crisis, *your* guilt. Well, I'm asking you just this once to think of my needs for a change. I'm tired. I'm dealing with a lot at work too, and I'd really appreciate it if you'd leave me alone to deal with this.' She hadn't told him about *Be*'s impending closure because he had hit a nerve. He was right, she thought as she drove home, barely able to see the road through her tears: she loved selfishly. No wonder he hated her; she hated herself.

'Thank the Pope,' Chloe said as the caravan turned into a side road. At last, they crested the rise at the back of the village, and the smell of the sea engulfed them as they plunged down the steep road towards the stone harbour before taking a sharp left turn into Kate's mother's driveway to be met with the welcome crunch of gravel.

As Kate took her bags out of the boot, her mother emerged from the house. Chloe got out to kiss her hello and to introduce Luke, who was at the ready to carry Kate's bags inside.

'He seems nice,' Kate's mother said as they waved Luke and Chloe off. 'It's good to see Chloe happy again, and wonderful to see you, my darling.' She gave Kate a hug, enveloping her in a cloud of her signature Chanel N° 5 perfume. 'You've got too thin,' she said when they drew apart. 'Skin and bones; let's go and remedy that.'

Too thin? Really? Kate wondered as she took her bags upstairs, experiencing her first moment of joy in weeks. Although her mother's 'thin' meant that she could probably still afford to lose a couple of pounds, a 'too thin' might actually mean that she looked slim. This was an Aladdin's Cave moment for one whose weight never fell off but had to be given a forceful shove.

Kate's room was now hers in name only. Literally. 'Kate' was written on a plaque on the door, while her sisters' names, 'Jenna' and 'Megan', were attached to the two doors on the other side of the passage. This was their mother's nod to the rooms' original inhabitants now that they were rented out to paying guests, while the door at the end of the passage, formerly the marital chamber, was labelled 'Lucy' after the family's golden retriever because, Annie said, it was true to say that the marriage had gone to the dogs.

The home's conversion to a B&B also meant that Kate's bedroom now came with a few extra perks, such as a tea tray with a kettle, a coffee maker, and a biscuit tin. She didn't need to lift the lid of the tin to know that it would contain her favourite cranberry and white chocolate oatmeal cookies. There was also a cabinet with a TV and a DVD player, and a comfortable feather bed clothed in a quilted blue bedspread sprinkled with blousy pink roses. At the bottom of this was a pile of fluffy pink towels, matched, on the bedside table, by a vase of roses wafting their sweet scent.

On the downside, Kate had had to pack all her personal possessions away in the attic, which meant that coming home no longer entailed a trip down memory lane via favourite books, photo albums, and her snow globe collection. But there was one thing that remained unchanged: the view. Kate stood in front of the large sash window and looked down across three rows of grey slate roofs to the small fishing harbour, where day trippers were lining up to board the ferry for Falmouth. Beyond the quay, a wooden fishing boat was drifting to shore shadowed by a cloud of seagulls, and several yachts with billowing white sails criss-crossed the bay. Kate's gaze breezed past them to the opposite shore, where sheep grazed lazily in the lush, green fields, and St Anthony's Lighthouse evoked happy childhood memories of playing at being the protagonists in Enid Blyton's *Five Go to Demon's Rock*, which was set in a lighthouse just like this one.

Perched above the sea to the left of the estuary, the Idle Rocks Hotel now drew her eye, conjuring less pleasant memories. Kate saw once more the paper lanterns strung out along the hotel's stone terrace, and the distant silhouettes of people who had gathered to celebrate her father's new beginning as a husband and soon-to-be father, while downstairs her mother's life seemed to be ending. Kate had refused to attend the ceremony and had instead come home for the weekend laden with delicious pâtés, cheeses, wines, and chocolates with which to distract her mother. But, unable to stomach any of it, Annie Richmond had watched the kitchen clock tick inexorably towards the hour of the wedding. At the stroke of 4 p.m., she had raised her glass, audibly exhaled, and said, 'So much for my brilliant career.'

'Kate, stop looking out of the window and come down,' her mother now shouted from the bottom of the stairs.

'How did you know I was looking out of the window?' Kate asked as she entered the kitchen, where her mother was pouring port into a roasting pan.

'Because that's what you're generally doing when you're upstairs and things go quiet,' her mother said through a cloud of steam. 'I remember when you were a little girl, I wouldn't hear a thing from you for hours and

I'd come upstairs to find you staring out of the window – if you weren't buried in a book. You were always such a dreamer.'

Kate was glad to see that her mother had set the wooden table in the kitchen rather than in the formal dining room. While the latter offered sea views through large bay windows, it lacked the kitchen's cosseting warmth and atmosphere. Still the soul of the house, this had doubled in size during the B&B renovations thanks to an extension, which was sympathetic to both her mother's needs and the Victorian style of the home. The addition of a spiral staircase leading up to a new bedroom gave Kate's mother the privacy of her own self-contained wing, and this downstairs space had all the luxuries she required. It included a small sitting area furnished with an antique desk, on top of which her computer sat, and a velvet sofa, where Annie spent hours propped against silk cushions perusing piles of recipe books and gourmet magazines from the floor-to-ceiling bookshelves that had long ago run out of space. Here, a faded Turkish kilim picked up the butter-yellow walls and blue kitchen cabinets while cosying up the patchwork of reclaimed Victorian floor tiles. The rug was a favourite spot for the family's aging golden retriever, Lucy, who thumped her tail loudly when she saw Kate and joyfully accepted pats, emitting the high-pitched squeal reserved for family members.

'I thought I'd do lamb because I know you never do a roast yourself,' Kate's mother said, 'and for starters, chilled pea soup with my first peas from the garden this season.' She placed two shallow white bowls on the table.

'It looks beautiful, Mum,' Kate said, sitting down. The vibrant green soup was decorated with a dollop of sour cream, a curl of lemon zest, a couple of pea tendrils, and a sprinkling of pansies.

'Thank you,' her mother said. 'Croutons?' She placed a bowl of perfectly crispy golden cubes of bread in front of Kate before pouring ice-cold Riesling into two small wine glasses.

'*You're* looking pretty good too,' Kate said. Annie's long, thick, salt-and-pepper hair was twirled up in a loose bun, and her olive skin, still remarkably line-free, glowed from the warmth in the kitchen. She wore a loose-fitting pink and white checked cotton shirt over three-quarter jeans, which flattered her fairly ample frame, but these days, rather than cursing her extra pounds, she was what the French described best as *bien dans sa peau*, a simple acceptance Kate had yet to adopt herself.

'So, my poor darling, what a thing to happen,' Annie said, sitting down at the table. 'I imagine it's been a tremendously difficult time. You must feel drained.'

'I am,' Kate said, slumping over her bowl. 'It's been crazy and kind of surreal, but it's good to be home – and mm mm mm, this is delicious.'

'It must have been such a shock, poor pet.'

'It still hasn't totally sunk in, to be honest,' Kate said.

Kate had arrived at the office the day after Amber's announcement, half expecting to find that it had all been some terrible mistake, but the contents of a large white envelope on her desk left no room for doubt. The next four days passed in a whirl as she made returns, cancelled shoots, copied files, mailed out the July issue, and informed all her contacts of *Be*'s closure. She had been surprised and touched by the outpouring of love for the magazine. But if most people were sad to hear the news, few were shocked. In a world in which financial giants were crumbling, it was hardly surprising that a boutique magazine should fold.

In the office that week, there had been a strange atmosphere of despair and hysteria mixed with camaraderie and sentimentality. Kate had done her bit to boost morale with gourmet crisps, biscuits, nuts, chocolates, and wine from her freebie food stash, while Jasmine had doled out beauty products, and Kirsten had hosted a one-pound fashion sale, with proceeds going to the BSPCA. Harry, having no copy to chase or clean up, had brought in his decks and surprised everyone with his deejaying skills. But on the last day, the atmosphere had changed dramatically when Simon swept in with a posse of henchmen to strip everyone of their access cards and ensure that all company property remained in situ, checking the staff members' bags and boxes before frogmarching them out of the building at 5 p.m. on the dot.

'The papers certainly had a field day,' Kate's mother added. 'It seems your editor has a lot to answer for. Who would have thought?' Before the magazine's closure had even been made official, the first feature appeared under the headline To Be or Not to Be, followed over the next few days by headlines like Be Gone and Be All and End All. Some media only mentioned the photographs of Amber in passing, while the smuttier weekend papers made a meal of them.

'I don't think she's really to blame,' Kate said. 'Those pictures were from years ago. There's actually someone else who has far more to answer for.' As her mother cleared their soup plates, insisting that Kate not move, Kate filled her in on Roberta's alleged part in *Be*'s demise.

'But why would anyone do such a thing?' Annie pressed.

'Well, if the truth be told, I had something to do with it too,' Kate said. Although her mother had checked the recipes, Kate hadn't mentioned the cover, because she had wanted to surprise her, and then she had forgotten to tell her amid all the madness. Now she revealed all.

'But you weren't to know that Amber would do that, were you?' Annie said as she placed a large white oval serving dish on the table, topped with a beautifully brown rolled loin of lamb. 'And I'm not surprised she did; it's a magnificent cover – you *are* clever. Oh, it's so sad it's over.' It occurred to Kate that her mother had also lost a job of sorts, as she had always relished her part in the magazine despite the lack of any real credit, which was just another thing for Kate to feel guilty about now. 'But I'm sure you've mulled over it more than enough by now,' Annie added. 'I hope this isn't overdone.' She sliced into the roast and the aromas of garlic and rosemary intensified. Kate found her appetite had returned.

'I'm sure it will be out of this world,' Kate said. There was never anything standard about Annie Richmond's food, even in the case of a roast, which on this occasion came stuffed with juniper berries, walnuts, and raisins, complemented by a port jus in which Kate detected a hint of anchovy. There were also crispy roast potatoes with fluffy centres, the sweetest glazed baby carrots, and tender French beans tossed with walnut oil.

'So I guess all of these are home-grown?' Kate looked through the glass-paned double French doors at her mother's vegetable garden, which stretched all the way up the sloping back garden. Once upon a time just a jumble of plants, it was now neatly divided into mulchy beds separated by gravel paths, the more fragile produce growing in the greenhouse standing on the left, and several pear and apple trees planted at the back. The trees were currently in flower, while the rest of the garden was a sea of greens ranging from the palest of lettuces to dark spinach leaves, with bursts of colour provided by raspberries, baby tomatoes, and yellow marrows peeping through the foliage. 'Ooh, you've got courgette flowers,' she added. 'Could we do something with those this weekend?'

'Yes, of course. I've booked the Tresanton for lunch tomorrow, but we could have them for supper.'

'Remember we talked about doing a flower-themed menu for *Be*?' Kate said wistfully. 'Now I've missed my chance.'

'It would have been lovely,' Annie said, 'but you'll have another opportunity.'

'I don't know,' Kate said. 'It's a pretty tough market.' Over the past week, she had scanned the job sections of the papers and had found nothing at all to fit her profile.

'Don't be silly; you've done so well. And you know how the saying goes: the cream always rises to the top.' Annie raised her glass of Merlot. 'Here's to a wonderful new job for you.'

'Thanks, Mum. Let's hope you're right. It costs money to breathe in London, so I can't afford to be out of work for long.'

'Why don't you come and stay here for a while? I would so love to have you,' Annie said.

'I couldn't do that; it's your busiest season,' Kate said. Her mother had had to transfer a houseful of guests to another B&B to accommodate this impromptu visit. 'And anyway, I need to be in London in case anything comes up.'

'Well, what about just coming for the first week of next month then? Sebastian has a conference in Brazil, so Megan and the girls are coming to stay and I've blocked it off. Do think about it; Megan would be thrilled.'

Kate's older sister – married, to an ophthalmologist, with two children – lived in Bath, and Kate hadn't seen her for several months, so the idea appealed except for one thing.

'She'll probably want to spend a lot of her time with *him*, though, won't she?' Kate was referring to her father, who had become the equivalent of *Harry Potter*'s He-Who-Must-Not-Be-Named ever since the day of his second marriage when, feeling her mother's pain so acutely that it might have been her own, Kate had built a Berlin wall where the marital divide was, planting herself firmly on the maternal side. Megan had, however, stayed close to her father, and her children got along with his second batch like siblings. Kate had always thought of this as fraternising with the enemy, but suddenly walls were crumbling and she realised she missed him. Love was a battleground, and given her recent tactics in the field, who was she to judge? Her mother had found peace, so perhaps it was time to call a truce. However, still bleeding out like a wounded soldier from her heartbreak, she decided to save reconciliation with her father for a future visit. She steered the conversation instead to her younger sister, Jenna – a lawyer living the *Sex and the City* lifestyle in New York – as they prolonged their indulgence with cardamom-flavoured panna cotta and rhubarb compote.

'Mm. Rhubarb's another thing that I never seem to cook myself,' Kate said. 'When I have yours, though, I always wonder why not. I love the rose water in the syrup, by the way.' She paused and allowed the subtle flavours to fill her mouth. 'It works so well with the cardamom. I want the recipe and the secret to making your panna cotta so perfectly wobbly. Actually, can I have all of today's recipes, please?'

'You were the only daughter who liked rhubarb,' Annie said. 'I would have given up on it if you didn't love it so much. And I'm thankful you did because my rhubarb and ginger preserve is a bestseller at True Brit – that and my tomato and caramelised-onion chutney. You must remind me to give you a couple of jars to take back.' Kate's mother had a secondary business supplying jams, preserves, and chutneys to local delis, which had become so successful that she now had labels, designed by Chloe, professionally printed. She had also recently had enquiries from some London delis.

'I wish I could have brought you some of the tomatoes from Mauritius,' Kate said. 'They're the deepest red, and they taste like no tomatoes I've ever had – earthy and sweet,' *just like Fai,* she could have added. 'They actually call them *pommes d'amour* over there – love apples – because the French thought they had aphrodisiacal powers. Come to think of it, I should have brought some back for myself. I could use some of their magic now that I've messed up my love life. *Yet* again.'

'I am truly sorry about Daniel, honey, but you'll get over him,' Annie said.

'I miss him. I miss him so much,' Kate said.

'Of course you do now, but these things take time. There are plenty of other fish in the sea; you'll see.'

'Hmm, I'm not sure I will, Mum. I really think Daniel might have been it, a real shot at a decent relationship with staying power finally, and I totally messed it up.'

'Oh, Kate, you surely can't blame yourself for this; it wasn't your fault. I know you won't like what I'm going to say, but I did worry, you know. I think you're probably lucky it ended sooner rather than later.'

'What do you mean by that?' Kate asked. She had always thought that her mother had a genuine fondness for Daniel, partly because he took a real interest in kitchen matters.

'I'm sorry, darling, but sometimes you don't see clearly when you're crazy about someone. I think he's charming and generous to a fault, but perhaps … perhaps he was a bit too charming. He reminded me of your father in that way. I always worried that you'd get hurt. And, well, now …' Given the volume of tears Kate had shed over the phone, and the omission of any real facts, it was understandable that her mother presumed that Daniel was the miscreant. Nonetheless, it irked Kate that she so readily jumped to this conclusion.

'But you've always liked Daniel. You never mentioned any reservations … ever. And he does love me; well, he did.'

'Of course he did, honey; I'm not saying he didn't. I'm simply saying that love never stopped a man from straying.'

Although aware that this was a simple projection of her mother's own experience, which made her always fearful that her daughters wouldn't be quite enough for the men they loved, Kate felt her temples throb and her nostrils flare. She was not going to help her mother bury this relationship along with her own self-worth.

'Actually, if you must know, Mum, Daniel's not the one with the wandering eye,' she spat. '*I* am. I slept with someone in Mauritius. Actually, I slept with *two* people.'

'Oh … well … Kate, honey … I …' Her mother was flawed.

'So Daniel's done nothing; in fact, he's the most wonderful, loving, and loyal guy I've ever met, whereas I'm …' *clearly my father's daughter.* She almost said the latter out loud, but she stopped herself. 'It's me who's fucked everything up.' Her mother hated it when she used the word *fuck*, but Kate was too livid to care. Somewhere deep down, she blamed her mother for where she was right now. She could see her own tendency to sabotage meaningful relationships as Annie's need to vicariously live, through her daughters, an independent life free of heartbreak. This lack of commitment, however, now threatened to break Kate's heart with loneliness.

'It's only because I care about your future happiness,' Annie said, visibly shaken. 'I've only ever wanted what's best for you girls.'

'Mum, I'm thirty-one. The future is kind of here, and it's looking bleak. Sure, Dad screwed up, but that doesn't mean every other man on the planet is destined to do the same. And at least you've got a whole lot more than the affections of a cat to keep you warm at night: you've got me, Jenna, Megan, and her girls, who adore you, although I know you've sometimes wished us away. I remember when we were young ...'

'Don't you dare suggest that I didn't care about you girls; everything I've done has been for you.' Annie began to cry.

'I'm sorry,' Kate said. 'I'm just really upset and fuck ... er ... messed up right now.' It was true that Annie had been a model mother in almost every respect. She had provided love and optimum nutrition, doled out remedies, soothing foods, and sympathy when her children were sick, bought and cared for a menagerie of pets, been on hand for help with homework and to take them to piano or guitar or horse riding or sailing lessons, provided a shoulder to cry on. ... Still, if not intentionally, she had certainly contributed to her daughter's emotional chaos, and Kate wasn't ready to forgive or comfort her just yet.

'I need some fresh air,' Kate said, getting up. 'I think I'll take Lucy for a walk. Thank you for a lovely lunch. And please don't clear up. I'll do it when I get back.'

She took Lucy's lead off the hook at the back of the kitchen door and, after attaching it to her collar, left, banging the door shut behind her. At the top of the driveway, she stopped to take in a deep breath, followed by another. The violence of her reaction had taken her by surprise. *Mum probably didn't deserve it,* she thought as she set off down the steep hill with Lucy trotting by her side, but she was still seething.

She turned right at the harbour and walked along the narrow main road through the village, passing the old teddy bear and fudge shops that had been there since her childhood, which were now joined by several more fashionable boutiques and cafés. She stopped in front of True Brit, a new deli featuring blond wood shelves stocked with boutique ciders, mustards, pork pies, artisanal cheeses, and jams. And there in the window, looking right at home among Britain's best, were her mother's preserves.

A couple emerged from the shop carrying a large True Brit bag. They were fortyish and ritzy, and Kate caught posh accents as they passed, probably marking them as guests of the chic Hotel Tresanton, which had played a large part in updating her humble hometown. It was an interesting twist of fate, Kate thought, that after her mother's lamenting her move from London for most of her married life, London was now coming to her and, capitalising on this, Annie had turned her role as homemaker into a successful career. Kate was reminded of a line from the poem 'Desiderata': 'Keep interested in your career, however humble; it is a real possession in the changing fortunes of time.'

The line stayed with her as she continued along the road, walking past the Tresanton, clinging to its hillside, passing the castle, and moving on to the footpath to St Just. *Perhaps I too should finally take heed of its message and truly embrace my foodie talents,* she thought. She had felt not only most confident on the food shoot in Mauritius, but also happiest. Of course, true calling or not, given the state of the market, she might have to embrace her inner grocery bagger instead.

There were a number of people on the path, which followed the rugged coastline, lapped by the khaki green estuary on one side and with cow-speckled fields sloping up on the other side. Kate felt lonely seeing most people in pairs, remembering the last time she had walked this way with Daniel. He loved exploring the area's history, and she recalled now that he had told her then that the famous twentieth-century courtesan and double agent Mata Hari had been arrested on a steamer in nearby Falmouth, little knowing that he had his own Mata Hari by his side.

Kate stopped in front of a stile and waited for a couple coming in the opposite direction to climb over it, preparing to give them her reserved-for-strangers nod.

'Kate? Kate Richmond?' the woman said as she alighted in front of her.

'Yes?' Kate said, looking at her blankly.

'Sorry, I guess it has been a while. Sophie Turnbull,' the woman said, introducing herself.

'Sophie, of course. I'm so sorry,' Kate said, trying to reconcile the spotty, plump teenager with wiry hair at school with the stunning, leggy, silken-haired brunette dressed in skinny jeans before her. 'It's been ages. How on earth are you?'

'Don't worry, it's easier for me because I've seen you in your magazines.' Sophie turned to the man beside her. 'Kate's the one who did that "Cool Yule" feature,' she said, before turning back to Kate. 'We loved that; it was so clever – and a nice change from turkey. This is my husband, Toby, by the way. And Ben.' Kate now noticed that Toby had a rucksack-like contraption on his back bearing a blond-headed boy.

'Nice to meet you.' Kate reached out her hand to Toby. 'And you.' She smiled at the ruddy-faced boy. 'He's gorgeous,' she said to Sophie. 'So what are you doing these days?'

Sophie told her that she was a primary school teacher and that Toby was a green architect and 'something of a self-professed eco-fascist. I always aimed to get to London, but then I met Toby, so here we are. Of course, I'm very happy.' She hugged Toby as if to reassure him. 'But I have to admit to being just a little bit jealous of the life you must lead. It sounds so glamorous.'

Kate, in turn, felt more than a little stab of jealousy. 'Well, you know I've been with *Be* for the last couple of years,' she said. 'You might have read about it in the papers?'

'Oh yes, of course.' Sophie's eyes widened. 'Gosh. I didn't put two and two together. Your editor's the one …'

Kate provided some of the juicier details of the magazine's demise, and Sophie thanked her for sharing such glamorous gossip with her 'country bumpkin friend' before walking off arm in arm with Toby, leaving Kate feeling like an outsider to their family club of love and marriage. Another line from 'Desiderata' came to mind as she continued along the path: 'Neither be cynical about love for in the face of all aridity and disenchantment, it is perennial as the grass.' Suddenly it made sense to her. Although love would probably never be enough in and of itself, it was perhaps more important and potentially more enduring than anything else in the world. She realised with shocking clarity that ultimately she wanted what Sophie had.

Really? Marriage? Despite all its flaws, its tendency to malfunction, and its dodgy guarantee of happily ever after? Are you sure? Why?

Perhaps she was less fearful of the concept now that she had learnt that there was such a thing as too much freedom for a human being, who was a domestic animal at heart, not suited to living alone in the wild. Or maybe, simply put in the words of Winnie the Pooh, it was just that life was 'so much more friendly with two'.

Kate sat down on a rock in the graveyard and drank in the beauty of the fourteenth-century stone church in its tranquil waterside setting, understanding, perhaps for the first time, why this 'backwater' she had once fled was such a magnet for tourists and weekenders. She even found herself envious of her mother, who had finally found her place in the world right here. She was reminded of her observation in Mauritius that even people living in paradise thought paradise was elsewhere. *Is it only when paradise is lost that one can appreciate it?* she wondered, longing for Daniel.

* * *

Kate got home amid a sudden downpour and was drenched by the time she reached the front door. She let herself in, and then ran upstairs, shouting towards the kitchen that she was going to have a bath.

Later, dressed in a fluffy pink towelling robe, she entered the kitchen to find her mother sitting at her computer. Annie looked up and smiled at Kate warily. 'Nice walk? I hope you haven't caught a chill from the rain.'

'It was invigorating. What are you up to?'

'I'm typing up those recipes for you. What's this?' she asked as Kate handed her the large brown paper bag she was carrying.

'A peace offering,' Kate said. 'I'm sorry.'

'I'm sorry too, honey. I was out of line. I really do just want you to be happy. I've often wished children came with instructions. You think it will get easier, but it doesn't. If anything, it gets harder to keep you safe.' She got up and moved to the sofa.

'It's just a couple of things from Mauritius,' Kate said. She sat down beside Annie and watched her pull out the vanilla pods and saffron, the bottle of rum, and finally a white embroidered Indian cotton shirt.'

'How pretty,' her mother said, holding up the shirt, 'and how special to have vanilla beans fresh from their source! I think I'll try out a tip I saw in a *Martha Stewart Living* magazine on how to create vanilla extract using vodka.'

'Mm, sounds like my kind of extraction technique,' Kate said, happy to be back in neutral food territory. 'What do you do?' she asked, intent on staying there.

'You split a pod lengthwise and then put it in a jar, cover it with vodka, and leave it for around six weeks; by then, it should have turned into a delicious vanilla essence. They say it's just the thing for French toast.' Annie picked up the bottle of rum. 'How do they take their rum in Mauritius?'

'Neat on ice or in various cocktails; I had a delicious one with green lemons, cane syrup, and soda.' Kate's mind drifted back to the night when Fai had introduced her to that particular cocktail and later put a flame to the rum in her veins, creating a delicious internal flambé. 'Another thing you could use it for is bananas Foster. God, I used to love that.'

'I don't think I've made that since you girls were little,' Annie said.

'Well, how about a revisit? Bananas Foster for supper?' Kate suddenly felt nostalgic.

'It's not really a supper dish, is it? I personally need something a little bit more substantial than that.'

'Pleeeeease,' Kate begged as she had when she was a child. 'What about French toast à la bananas Foster for something a bit more suppery? Daniel had it for brunch in a brasserie recently, where it was served with yummy crème fraiche infused with orange zest. Come on, how about it?'

'Well, I do have bananas and crème fraiche,' Annie said, 'but I haven't bought that banana liqueur in years.'

'We can live without the liqueur.'

'If it's really what you want ...'

'Yay!' Kate jumped up and did a little jig. 'I love you, Mum,' she said. She leant down to hug her mother.

They moved through to the guest lounge to watch television, and when they were feeling peckish again, they returned to the kitchen.

Kate soaked thick slices of Portuguese bread in a vanilla-flavoured custard and then mixed together crème fraiche with orange zest, while watching her mother heat butter, sugar, and cinnamon in a pan to caramelise the banana halves. Finally, as Kate fried the bread, Annie added rum to her pan and lit it to produce the dancing blue flame that had excited Kate as a child.

Savouring the dish's intoxicating mix of vanilla, cinnamon and rum brought Fai to mind – his scent, his warmth, his exotic flavour – and Kate thought that, in a parallel universe over the rainbow, he might have been

The One and that he would always be a part of her. Like the flame in the flambé, their affair had burnt out quickly, but not before the rum had changed the chemistry of the fruit to make it sweeter and more pliant. Her encounter with him, she saw now, had catalysed a re-patterning similar to the therapy prescribed by Chloe. She was sorry she had hurt him, though, and wondered if she could find a way to let him know that their time together had meant something to her.

* * *

That night, Kate had a dream in which she entered a darkened room with candles lit all around and a group of men singing a familiar song a cappella. As her eyes grew accustomed to the dim light, she saw a woman reclining on a sofa and watching the men as she smoked an opium pipe. On closer inspection, Kate saw that the woman was her mother, who called to her and invited her to sit on the couch beside her. She passed Kate the pipe. 'Here, try this,' she said. 'It takes away the heartache and pain.' Kate took the pipe, but before taking a puff she handed it back and said, 'I don't need it. I don't want to run away anymore; I'd rather risk the pain.'

CHAPTER 15

Noble Rot

Kate opened her eyes, and the realisation hit her with a sickening thud, as it had every morning since departing *Be*, that she had absolutely nothing to get out of bed for. She rolled onto her back and stared up at the expanse of white ceiling above her, feeling like she was looking at a mirror image of her life. Empty.

Noticing that she was awake, Mushy moved onto Kate's stomach and began to knead the duvet over her chest. Kate rubbed his head between his ears, and he purred contentedly. 'What are we going to do, Mushy? If I don't get a job soon, I won't be able to feed you and we'll be homeless.' *Correction: Mushy knows how to fend for himself and will simply switch allegiance and find his way back to Chloe's flat, leaving me all alone in my cardboard box.* It was frightening, she thought, the fine line between a glamorous salaried life and homelessness. Mushy placed a conciliatory paw on her cheek.

Kate had been aware that the market was bad, but it was proving even worse than envisaged. *Be* wasn't the only magazine to close down lately, and those publications still in operation were cutting back on staff. More people were therefore now fighting for fewer jobs – one newspaper supplement had let her down lightly by telling her that they had had over five hundred applications for the particular position she was after. To make matters worse, given her complicity in *Be*'s downfall, she felt the weight of everyone else's job search on her shoulders too, and no one seemed to be faring any better than she was.

Chloe's phone rang in her room next door. It was after nine o'clock, so Kate thought that her housemate must have forgotten her phone in her usual chaotic dash to work. When she heard Chloe's muffled voice answer the call, however, she realised that it was Saturday. Saturdays were good because they were not generally allocated to purposeful activity; Kate, therefore, felt marginally better about the absence of any. The downside of weekends, however, was that she couldn't help feeling like she was getting in the way of Chloe and Luke, who were now spending every weekend together. Life was like Noah's Ark, she thought: most commonly and harmoniously lived in pairs. Hearing running water and their muffled voices down the passage, she decided to kill two birds with one stone by both giving them their space and her body some exercise for the first time in weeks.

It was a crisp, sunny morning, she discovered, as she stepped onto the pavement outside the flat. The road was already filling up with pedestrians heading from Chalk Farm Tube to Regent's Park Road to make the most of it, so she made her way to Primrose Hill along some of the quieter surrounding roads. Finally leaning into the hill, she rued her days on the couch as her glutes felt the burn and she wheezed from the cigarettes she'd snuck. But once on the towpath along the canal on the other side, she settled into an easy stride. Although her loss of appetite, coupled with the absence of press lunches and recipe experimentation, meant that there was no need to burn off excess calories, it was good to breathe in the fresh air, feel the dappled sunlight on her skin, and hear the hypnotic thud, thud, thud of her feet on the path. As she looped back on the other side of the canal, she began to feel something she hadn't experienced for a while: optimism. *Endorphins are definitely not overrated,* she thought as she headed to the newsagent, allowing herself to hope that today was the day that the *Guardian*'s classifieds section had a job for her.

On entering the store, Kate was met by Finola smiling at her from the other side of the room, and she dutifully walked over to pay her respects. It was three days until the end of the month, when the magazine would be taken off the shelves for the last time, so she gazed at the cover girl as at someone in a coma whose life-support system was due to be turned off imminently.

A man joined her in front of the stand and Kate instinctively picked up the magazine, which was a form of subliminal suggestion designed to entice whoever was standing beside her to do the same. It was unusual for a man to pick up *Be*, so she felt a real sense of achievement when he did, and an even greater one when he continued to the till with the magazine in hand. Of course, this wouldn't serve as a kiss of life for *Be*, but it was a worthy farewell kiss all the same. Kate smiled as she moved on to the newspaper section, where her eyes alighted on the front page of *Gossip Gazette*, and her mouth dropped open.

'Wow,' she said aloud, causing the man at the checkout to turn around. This was not the first picture of Amber in a state of undress to have appeared in the press since *Be*'s closure, but unlike previous images, it appeared to be recent and was more tasteful than many of the others. In it, Amber was sitting on a grey horse, dressed in nothing but a pair of black lace panties, boots, and a riding hat, her toned body, in profile, looking as strong, athletic, and powerful as the stallion's.

Kate returned home with an armful of newspapers, all with images of Amber in their pages. She found Chloe sitting at the kitchen table in her blue checked men's pyjamas and working on her jewellery. Mushy was lying on his back next to the window, blissfully lapping up the first rays of sunshine that had flooded the place in weeks.

'Has Luke left?' Kate asked as she put her newspapers on the table beside a pile of empty cold-drink cans destined for transformation into earrings, bracelets, and pendants.

'He's just popped to Tesco to get stuff for a picnic,' Chloe said. 'We can't allow this sunshine to go uncelebrated.'

'I got you both some pains au chocolat and croissants,' Kate said. 'Those are cool.' She looked down at a pair of earrings made from strips of a Bitter Lemon can twisted into spirals.

'Thanks. I'm topping up the stock for the stall tomorrow before heading to the park. You should come.'

'I'd love to,' Kate said, 'but I have some stuff I need to do.' She dropped the bag of pastries on the kitchen counter and then began to take mugs and plates out of the cupboard.

'Surely you can spare a couple of hours,' Chloe said. 'Luke's housemates are coming. Maybe a date with a boy toy is just what you need.'

Kate had no interest in a 'boy toy' because, unbeknown to Chloe, she *had* been 'seeing someone'. In fact, she had a date the following night. Since she couldn't bear *not* to see Daniel and he couldn't bear *to* see her, she had devised a way to please them both. Donning her 'fat' jeans, which now hung loosely on her frame, along with a peak cap and a man's hoodie as a disguise, she had, on several occasions since her banishment, positioned herself outside Daniel's building, concealed by a wheelie bin, to catch glimpses of him.

She made these visits randomly, when the longing to see him grew too great, but she never missed a Sunday when a sighting was guaranteed, since Daniel ritually stayed in to do his accounts with a pizza, which he picked up from Il Bordello over the road. Just seeing him elicited such an outpouring of love and longing that it was all she could do not to reveal herself and beg him to take her back, but he had made his wishes clear. If she truly loved him, then she knew she had to respect those wishes. Unable to bear seeing him look so forlorn, however, she had finally resorted to the second best thing to a hug that she knew.

Arriving earlier than Daniel's scheduled pizza run on the previous two Sundays, Kate had stopped at Il Bordello and asked Luigi to give Daniel a dessert 'on the house', for which she had paid. There had been tiramisu on the first occasion (because the word *tiramisu*, she knew, was Italian for 'pick-me-up') and profiteroles on the next. Now, given the warm weather this weekend, she was thinking of cassata ice cream for the following day. These were small gestures, she knew, but food had always been dispensed to bring comfort while she was growing up and so it had become her way of showing love and offering solace too. 'Comfort me with apples: for I am sick of love' was a favourite biblical verse.

'Earth to Kate,' Chloe said.

Kate realised that she had stopped what she was doing and was staring dreamily into space, recalling the glimmer of a smile that had played on Daniel's lips upon exiting Il Bordello with his profiteroles. This was in stark contrast to his glum expression on entering, and so she had read it as a response to her culinary hug.

'You need to get out, or you'll forget how to interact with other human beings and start growing moss,' Chloe added.

'I will, I will, I promise,' Kate said, returning her attention to lining a small zinc bucket with a linen napkin, 'but I really do need to prepare for an interview on Monday.'

'Is it for that TV website?'

'No, I didn't get that.' Kate relived another acute stab of disappointment. 'It's just holiday cover for a chefs' trade magazine.' Judging the pastries to be still warm enough, she put them in the bucket and then placed the bucket on the table.

'It's early days. The TV people are probably still wading through applications,' Chloe said.

'No, it's definite. Got the rejection letter.'

The job had been the first to excite Kate. Apart from her lack of website experience, it fit her profile in almost every respect. Applicants had been asked to provide recipes for a summer menu, and she had given it her all, deciding on the picnic she had planned for *Be*'s August issue, which had never seen the inside of a picnic basket. There was chilled white gazpacho, a roasted butternut, sage, and pancetta quiche, cold rare fillet of roast beef with red onion marmalade, an oven-dried tomato salad, home-made lemonade, and, to complete the feast, a white chocolate and strawberry tart. In addition to supplying the recipes, she had enthusiastically prepared and photographed a couple of the dishes on a picnic blanket in the park: the soup served from a retro blue floral enamel flask; a slice of quiche placed on a pretty pastel melamine plate; the onion marmalade in an old-fashioned sweet jar. Finally, she had hand-delivered the recipes and images in a basket, together with a copy of *Be*'s July issue and a freshly baked tart, 'because the proof is in the pudding', she had written cheekily in her cover letter.

Given the extra effort she had put in, the form letter she had received less than a week after submitting the application had removed her will to get out of bed and sapped her energy to trawl the papers for jobs. It was only her diminishing bank balance that kept her mildly motivated.

Kate switched on the kettle and put a small saucepan of milk on the stove. 'Coffee?'

'Tea, please, if you're offering. Sorry, K, but I'm sure something else will …' Chloe stopped mid sentence. 'Gawd, I see Amber's back.' She was looking at the front page of *Gossip Gazette.*

'Yes. I haven't looked at it properly yet. Something about a new job with Newday Media.'

'Yes,' Chloe said. She read further and then added, 'On a porn magazine.'

'Porn?' Kate said, so shocked that she took her eyes off the milk. 'Are you sure?'

'Mm-hm,' Chloe said. 'She's going to be editor in chief of a brand-new adult title by Newday.'

'Really?' Kate turned back to the pot just in time to catch the milk before it overboiled. 'I didn't think they did that type of magazine.'

'It's their first, apparently,' Chloe said, continuing to read with her face centimetres away from the text, since she wasn't wearing her reading glasses. 'Amber comes across quite well. She almost manages to make it sound noble. Listen to this: "Asked about the risk involved in launching a magazine in a market that has seen a number of casualties in recent months, Love said, 'I've heard sex described as "the poor man's opera," so it might be the best time ever to bring out a magazine of this nature.'"'

Kate laughed. 'That sounds like Amber.' She handed Chloe a large cup of milky tea and then extracted the *Gossip Gazette* from her housemate as she sat down with her coffee.

Under the headline BACK IN THE SADDLE AGAIN, the standfirst confirmed that everything Chloe said was true: 'Former editor of *Be* magazine, Amber Love, is set to take the reins of a new title at Newday Media, marking a return to adult magazines.'

> It was announced yesterday that the former editor of Be magazine, Amber Love, has been appointed as editorial director of a new division of Newday Media, which is set to introduce adult magazines to the prestigious stable. This represents a radical departure for the multimedia group, which counts glossy magazines *Glam* and *Body Work* among its long list of titles. The group also recently acquired a television arm heavy on sport and lifestyle

> shows, but, so far, has not delved into the underbelly of adult media.
>
> For the forty-six-year-old editor and award-winning journalist, however, it is a return to an area with which she is familiar.

The article regurgitated some of the details of Amber's background in adult modelling that had already been covered ad nauseam in the press, and then it went on to give an overview of Newday's plans for the magazine, which the company's commercial director said would be the first upmarket publication in the genre 'with a partner app and strong retail element'. He said that in light of the sex industry's becoming increasingly mainstream, Newday had considered launching an adult magazine for some time, but the decision had finally been made when they were able to secure Amber as the editor: 'Amber Love is one of the country's most talented and visionary editors, and with experience at the coalface, so to speak, there couldn't be a better person for the job.'

Kate liked and respected Amber and was glad that she was 'back in the saddle', although not quite in the role she would have imagined for her. Two down, she thought, since Jasmine had secured a new job too, as De-Vine Beauty's director of PR for the United Kingdom and Europe. She said she was excited about the prospect of unlimited cellulite treatments.

'Do you think I should call to congratulate her?' Kate asked Chloe. 'I know she's probably bogged down with calls, but ... what do you think? It wouldn't be weird, would it?'

'No, not at all,' Chloe said.

'I wonder if she still even has the same mobile number. She might have changed it, what with all the press.'

'No harm in trying,' Chloe said. She picked up Kate's phone and handed it to her.

Kate expected to be met with a busy signal at best, or a dull out-of-service buzz at worst, but to her surprise, the phone rang. Seconds later, Amber was on the other end of the line.

'Kate Richmond?'

'Hi. Yes, hello. Sorry, Amber, I'm sure you're inundated with calls right now, but I wanted to congratulate you on your new job.'

'Thank you, that's sweet,' Amber said. 'So you've seen the papers?'

'I have, and it sounds … interesting.' Kate was annoyed with herself for hesitating, as it made her sound like a prude.

Amber laughed. 'Yes, it's certainly a departure from women's magazines, but I do believe you're right: it's going to be interesting. What about you? Has anyone snapped you up yet?'

'No,' Kate said, flattered by the use of the term *snapped.*

'That's surprising. Do you have anything in the pipeline?'

'Nothing long-term, just a couple of potential freelance jobs,' Kate said.

'I'm sorry, I should have been in touch with you earlier,' Amber said, 'but there's been so much to negotiate, and, of course, everything had to be hush-hush until it was official. Now that I have a small breather, however, I do want to see what I can do to help anyone. The market must be very bad indeed if you haven't found anything yet.'

'Thanks,' Kate said.

'So let me think. There are a couple of positions at the new publication; in fact, I spoke to Harry about the role of chief sub earlier today, but of course it's not going to be everyone's cup of tea.'

Or bra cup, Kate thought. She was happy that she could cross another name off *Be*'s unemployed list, imagining that Harry would be ecstatic with this new role, in which he would be surrounded by shelves lined with 'jugs'.

'There's nothing to fit your skill set here, unfortunately,' Amber continued, 'but perhaps we can find you something on one of Newday's other titles.'

It only now occurred to Kate that the website job had coincidentally been advertised by Newday's television arm. In a world in which mergers, acquisitions, and hostile takeovers were so commonplace, it wouldn't surprise her if a single media giant soon owned every remaining magazine and newspaper in the dwindling market. She told Amber about her application.

'Of course, there's the TV side of things; I didn't think of that. Who did you see?' Amber asked.

'No one,' Kate said. 'They didn't ask me in for an interview.'

'What? That's very strange,' Amber said. 'You're one of the best food editors out there. I wonder why. Did they give a reason?'

'No,' Kate said, basking in Amber's use of the word *best*. 'Maybe it's because I have no Web experience.'

'Well, I can look into it for you, if you'd like. In fact, I know someone on that side of things quite well from way back. I can't promise anything, but let me give him a call and see if we can get to the bottom of this.'

Kate gave Amber a few more details about the show, and then said goodbye, not expecting to hear from her again, and certainly not that day, but less than an hour later her phone rang.

'I've got bad news and good news,' Amber said. 'I've spoken to the show's producer, Nigel, who confirmed that the position has been filled internally, unfortunately, although they were extremely impressed with your ideas and thought your homemade tart was delicious. Nice touch, by the way.'

'Where did I fall short?' Kate asked.

'That's just the thing,' Amber said. 'You didn't. They were all set to call you in when they asked someone in the company for a reference, and I'm afraid it wasn't good. Well, to be honest, it was damning.'

'Who?' Kate asked.

'I don't think I'm at liberty to divulge. Oh, to hell with it, it was Roberta. I don't know if you've heard that she's working at *Glam* now.'

Kate was stunned that even now Roberta was casting her evil spells. It also seemed enormously unfair that, having put *Be* into an irreversible coma with her poisoned apple, she had secured a plum job at *Glam* while far worthier people were still out of work.

'Why does she hate me so much?' Kate asked.

'She hates everyone equally,' Amber said. 'But before you despair, here's the good news. They'd like to consider you for the role of host.'

'Host?' Kate asked incredulously. 'As in presenter?' *I'd rather eat nails.*

'I know it probably sounds daunting,' Amber said, 'but it's actually a very natural extension of what you've been doing. The only real problem is time. They've already narrowed things down to three strong candidates, so they're hesitant to start interviewing from scratch, but I told Nigel they'd be crazy not to give you a try.'

'Thank you,' Kate said. 'I'm grateful, very grateful, but I really don't think I'm television material.'

'Au contraire,' Amber said. 'You're perfect for TV. Now that I think of it, your energy and passion are a little expansive for the page, like Maria cooped up in the nunnery in *The Sound of Music*. But I understand it's a lot to digest. Would it help to talk about it in person? If you're free later today, I could meet you for a drink or an early supper.'

Kate considered the items on her agenda: research hotel kitchen hygiene and watch box set of Audrey Hepburn DVDs. 'Yes,' she said, 'that would be great, if you're sure you have the time.'

'You live in Chalk Farm, I recall, and I'm not far away, so we can meet somewhere near you if you'd like,' Amber said. 'Pick a spot, and make it a nice one because I'm going to expense it.'

* * *

Amber was already seated at a table in the small walled garden at the back of Odette's when Kate arrived at the restaurant. She had a large glass of red wine and a small bowl of green olives in front of her, and she looked as relaxed as Kate had ever seen her. She stood up when Kate reached the table, kissing her on both cheeks. *A first.* 'This is a lovely spot.'

'Thanks,' Kate said, as though she were the one responsible for picking out the pretty white cast-iron chairs and striped cushions on the banquette that ran along the red-brick wall, where Amber was seated.

'You look well,' Amber said. 'You've lost weight.'

'You do too,' Kate said. Amber looked like a different person. Her porcelain skin glowed like Royal Doulton. And rather than being pulled back in a tight bun, her glossy red hair swept her shoulders, glinting in the soft summer-evening sunlight. She had also put on a bit of weight – in her case a good thing – and looked as stylish as ever in jeans dressed up with a midnight blue and black lace camisole top and a vintage Chanel jacket with a fob watch around her neck. Kate now wished that she had stuck with jeans rather than upgrading to a dress with small polka dots, teamed with a denim jacket and espadrilles, which suddenly seemed too cutesy.

She sat down and ordered a gin and tonic, raising her glass to Amber when it was delivered. 'Congratulations again,' she said. 'I like the sound of your plans for the magazine, by the way – very different from the norm. Are you excited?'

'Honestly, I didn't leap at it,' Amber said, 'but when I realised how committed they were, it began to excite me. As you know, it's a good, solid company. What's more, they seem to give people the freedom to do what they're hired to do, unlike the Three Mouseketeers.'

'The Three Mouseketeers?' Kate laughed. She had never heard the Lowell brothers and Simon referred to in this way, but it was a fitting description.

'God, they're a lily-livered lot, and so patronising despite the fact that they know *nothing* about putting out a quality publication.' Amber's cheeks reddened and her features tightened. Kate realised that the difference in Amber's face earlier had been a lack of tension, which had always been lurking below the surface at *Be*. 'I have to say that as much as this experience has been like losing a child,' Amber continued, 'I also feel an overwhelming sense of relief it's over. It's wonderful to think I will never have to sit across a desk from Simon again and haggle with him over something or other.' As she tipped the last of her wine into her mouth, a waiter appeared at her side immediately.

He must have been watching her every move, Kate thought, *perhaps recognising her from the recent press images.*

'Shall we order?' Amber asked. 'I'm starving.'

The waiter speedily presented menus, and Amber surprised Kate by opting for the braised beef in ale with smoked mashed potatoes. 'It's great to be able to let go for a while,' Amber said as though reading Kate's mind. 'What about a bottle of wine?' She picked up the wine list and looked at it briefly before handing it to Kate. 'What am I doing? You're the expert.'

'Do you want to stick with red?' Kate asked.

'I thought fish and red was the ultimate sin,' Amber said, since Kate had ordered roasted monkfish. 'I remember there was that James Bond movie where Double O says he should have known his dining companions were suspect when they ordered red wine with their fish.'

'"From Russia with Love,"' Kate said, 'but that was sole, which is very delicate; monkfish can carry a light red.'

'Said like a true foodie,' Amber said. 'I *would* prefer it, if you're sure.'

The waiter returned with their bottle of Chilean Pinot Noir, and once their glasses were filled, Amber got down to business. 'So, as I said, time is against us and we have to act fast and smartly.' Kate was touched by the use of *us* and *we*.

'Nigel's in L.A. at the moment,' Amber continued, 'and gets back on Tuesday, so I've taken the liberty of setting up an interview for you at 10 a.m. on Wednesday. Okay?'

'Sure,' Kate said, 'but I'm still not convinced I'm cut out for television. I definitely don't look the part; everyone's so skinny.'

'You're looking decidedly skinny yourself right now,' Amber said, 'and Nigel thinks you're gorgeous. Mm, this wine is superb. I do adore Pinot Noir. There's something so rarefied and sensitive about it. If it were a dog, I think it would be a standard poodle.'

'That's a good analogy,' Kate said, also enjoying the silky wine, which had an earthy aroma of black truffle and layers of berries and spice. 'I love Pinot too, partly, I think, because it's so vulnerable.' She wished she could share both the wine and the poodle analogy with Daniel, for whom the cultivar was a pet passion. He had told her that Pinot Noir grapes were more high-risk than other cultivars because their skin was particularly delicate and therefore easily broken by rain, making them susceptible to fungi and bunch rot. He said that a wine farmer friend had once joked that the three easiest ways to lose money were fast cars, slow horses, and a hillside planted with Pinot Noir, which Kate now shared with Amber.

Amber laughed. 'Your boyfriend's in wine, isn't he?'

'Was,' Kate said. 'I mean, he's still in wine, but he *was* my boyfriend. It's over.'

'I'm sorry to hear that.'

'It's fine,' Kate said. She then promptly turned the conversation back to the job, not keen to delve into emotional territory with Amber. 'How does Nigel know what I look like?'

Amber pulled the July issue of *Be* out of her bag and flicked to the third spread of food, where she pointed to the photograph of Kate placing the whole barbecued fish on the table. It was a flattering picture thanks to the dusk light and the fact that her body was partially obscured by the large platter. Nigel would probably be disappointed when he saw her in the flesh, she thought.

The waiter arrived with their mains, and Amber closed the magazine. 'It really is a beautiful cover,' she said, looking at it dreamily before tucking it back into her bag. 'I know I had my misgivings, but it was a superb shoot all round.'

'I'm just sorry it wreaked such havoc,' Kate said. 'In fact, I've wanted to apologise to you ever since it all happened because I feel like I'm to blame. Everything would probably be just as it was if I hadn't been so darn stubborn and gone ahead with the shoot, giving Roberta cause to …' *Oops,* she thought, *there has never been an official mention of any connection between Roberta and the leaked photographs.*

'Don't be silly,' Amber said. 'For one thing, it was my decision to use the photograph on the cover, and for another, Roberta's response was totally out of proportion, so she and I share the blame. Anyway, even if this hadn't happened, the Mouseketeers would have found a way to shut us down within the year. Roberta just brought it forward by a few months.'

'I don't get why she's so vindictive,' Kate said.

'Roberta's had a chip on her shoulder for as long as I've known her,' Amber said. 'Not altogether without reason, to be honest, but whatever happened to her in the past doesn't begin to justify her recent actions. Do you know she got the model from the Mauritian shoot fired and, as a result, the girl attempted suicide?'

'I heard,' Kate said. 'I wonder how she's doing.'

'I've persuaded the agency to take her back on, but considering that Roberta was aware the girl was unstable and precariously positioned visa-wise, it's unforgiveable. It was also grossly unfair of her to give you such a bad review.'

'What was it in her past that made her the way she is, if you don't mind me asking?' Kate said.

'You could say it started with the stock market crash of '87,' Amber said. 'Black Monday; you've probably heard about it. At the time, Roberta was quite the New York princess. Her father was as rich as Croesus, and she had never wanted for anything – until the crash, that is, when he lost everything. And that was the easy part. Shortly thereafter, a client who blamed him for the loss of his own substantial fortune came into his office and shot him dead before killing himself.'

'God, that's horrific,' Kate said. 'How old was Roberta?'

'Twenty-one,' Amber said, 'but still totally dependent on her father. And for some reason, he had made his third wife, and Roberta's nemesis, the sole beneficiary of his life insurance. So the foundations of her existence were literally ripped from under her feet. Of course the loss of her father was devastating, but I think losing face hit her just as hard. When I met her, she was so angry ... with her father for dying, with his murderer, with her stepmother, and with those snooty friends who cut her off when she could no longer charge at Barneys. I think that apart from the promise of earning easy money, she got into adult modelling to give them the finger.'

Amber opened up about her own story and told Kate that she had moved to New York from London in order to do a master's degree in journalism. She had gone into adult modelling because it paid much better than waitressing and left her time to write and submit stories to all and sundry. 'That's how I met Roberta,' she said, 'and we became friends. Well, truth be told, it was more than that; we became an item for a while.'

The sun dipped behind the wall, and their waiter lit the lantern on their table. Amber savoured a few mouthfuls of her beef in silence with a contemplative look in her eyes, clearly travelling back to that time. Then, with a blink, she returned to the present. 'This is delicious,' she said. 'Refined comfort food – my idea of heaven. But you've barely touched yours. I hope I haven't made you lose your appetite.'

'Not at all.' Kate had been so riveted that she had simply forgotten to eat. 'It's interesting to see this other side of Roberta.'

After several more mouthfuls, Amber put down her knife and fork and, leaning back against the wall with her wine in hand, picked up where she had left off. Their relationship had ended after less than two years, she said, because for Roberta, she had always suspected, it had been more about experimentation and rebellion. By then, Roberta was gracing the pages and covers of leading international glossies and, helped along by her first marriage to an entertainment lawyer, was back on New York's A-list, moving in her old circles again. But having been spurned once before, she was fiercely protective of her regained status. 'I believe she developed her superiority complex as a defence mechanism,' Amber said, 'but perhaps because I shared her darkest hour, I was immune to this side of her. She actually got me my first writing assignment at *Harper's Bazaar* and I never looked back, so I've always been enormously indebted to her. Offering her a job at *Muse* was the least I could do after her last disastrous divorce from a musician who turned out to be an abusive drug addict and spent all her money.'

'Wow, what a story,' Kate said.

'Yes,' Amber said, 'Roberta's been through a lot, but, be that as it may, she's gone too far this time. I've told Newday that there's not room for both of us in the company.'

Kate was happy that Roberta would finally get her comeuppance, but she also felt that slight pang of pity she sometimes did for the villain who tumbled to her death at the end of a fairy tale.

'Now, back to the job,' Amber said. 'I do think you have an excellent shot at this. One of the final candidates is apparently seriously on the chunky side, so, based on appearances, you're one up on her. And Nigel thinks you've got a more diverse and approachable range than the recipe-book writer. Your biggest competition will probably be the *MasterChef* finalist.'

'*M-M-MasterChef* finalist?' Kate stammered. 'Amber, this really is crazy.'

'You've no reason to be so nervous. I've seen how you light up when you talk about food; I'm sure you'll be a natural. The problem is that the other candidates have all done their screen tests, so if the interview goes well, you'll have to do yours more or less immediately.'

'S-s-screen test?' The prospect of a screen test was like a pinprick to the helium balloon of excitement that had inflated in Kate's chest. She suddenly realised how ludicrous the whole idea was. She had absolutely no experience in front of the camera; she even felt self-conscious cooking in front of friends, shooing dinner-party guests into the living room until she was ready to serve. And what if things fell apart out there in front of the camera? She wouldn't be able to call on her mother to remedy the situation and tweak things as she had always done for magazine features. She would thus be exposed as the pseudo cook she was. It would be the *Cyrano de Bergerac* story gone wrong for Christian, involving his exposure early in the game.

'I wouldn't know where to begin with a screen test,' Kate said.

'Of course you would,' Amber said. 'Besides, you're halfway there. They already like your formula, so all you'll have to do is translate it to the screen.'

Their waiter asked if they would like to see the dessert menu, and Amber surprised Kate again when she said, 'Yes.' In the end, she opted for the cheese plate, and persuaded Kate to share it, along with a glass of Sauternes to wash it down.

'Cheers.' Amber held up her glass of honey-coloured liquid. 'Here's to the next big thing in lifestyle television.'

Kate touched her glass to Amber's lightly, far from convinced that the next best thing in lifestyle TV was in the room. Amber made it sound so easy, but Kate was terrified.

'And I'll tell you what else we should drink to,' Amber said. 'The fact that even in a recession, people can't live without food and sex, which means that as long as we both stick to what we're good at, we'll be fine.' Kate laughed with her, struck again by how much lighter and happier she seemed. It was ironic, she thought, how something that had seemed set to destroy Amber had resulted in a golden career opportunity. It was comparable to the way in which the strain of the fungus *Botrytis* known as noble rot improved rather than destroyed grapes' juices by depleting their water content to produce the intense sweetness of the wine she was drinking. Kate feared, however, that the rot in her own life was of the less noble variety known as grey rot. While this job prospect was a ray of hope, any viticulturist would tell you that a dash of sunshine couldn't save the day once the latter form of the disease had set in.

CHAPTER 16

Fashion Plates

Kate hadn't been to the Columbia Road Flower Market since her break-up with Daniel. This was his territory, so it had felt out of bounds somehow. But duty had called her here today, and it felt good to be back. She relished breathing in the sweet scents mingling in the air around her as she walked past stalls selling dewy bedding plants, pot plants, fruit trees, herbs, and cut flowers in a colour palette that defied any fashionista's notion that there were rules about what went together and what didn't. She had a sense of coming home.

She remembered the first time Daniel had manhandled her out of bed to bring her here. 'Why are we getting up in the middle of the night?' she had asked as he navigated her towards the shower.

'Trust me. You'll thank me later,' he had said. 'There are smoked salmon and cream cheese pumpernickel bagels involved, and that's not even the best part.' He had been right, and early morning visits to the market had become a regular Sunday ritual, involving a slow meander through the stalls, picking up flowers and herbs, followed by those bagels.

'Three for ten pound on the delphiniums. One for four pound, three for ten.'

'Sunflowers a fiver; a fiver for them sunflowers. They should be eigh', but I'll take five pound, only today.'

'Mix and match, pick and mix, any three bunches for a tenner, all that for a tenner.'

Kate loved the banter of the traders here but, being on an important mission today, she walked past the stalls at a brisk pace without stopping, snatching excerpts from the different sales pitches as though she were tuning into and out of channels on the radio.

'Only three pound the bunch of freesias, two for a fiver. So cheap you could put them on your mother-in-law's grave.'

Kate laughed out loud at that one, feeling confident that she might never have the displeasure of a mother-in-law.

'Best Dutch roses, only a fiver a bunch, two for eigh' pound. So you can buy them for the wife *and* the girlfriend.'

Seduced by the scent emanating from buckets of roses in every conceivable colour, Kate stopped in her tracks. 'Wha'll it be?' the seller asked. He had a shock of white hair and arms festooned with tattoos of dragons, bleeding hearts, and skulls.

'I don't have a wife, but I've got two girlfriends I'll be buying for, guv,' Kate said with a naughty giggle. Jasmine and Kirsten had offered to give up a portion of their precious Sunday to help her later, so a token of thanks seemed fitting.

While she watched the salesman wrap the flowers, a man stopped beside her.

'Where can I get a cwawfee?' the man asked in an American drawl.

'A cwawfee? Sorry, never 'eard of them,' the seller said. 'Fact, I don't think you'll find them flowers round 'ere.' He turned to the other salesman, who was a younger version of him, with a gold cross dangling from one earlobe. 'Wha' abou' you, Col; ever 'eard of cwawfees?' he asked. He winked at Kate, who gave him a knowing smile in return. She might also be inclined to have a bit of fun with tourists, who generally came here to smell the roses rather than to buy them, which wasn't going to help anyone to buy that room somewhere.

'No, can' say tha' I 'ave,' the younger version said.

'No, I mean a cw*aaaa*wfee,' the man said, clearly frustrated. He wrapped his right hand around an imaginary cup and brought it to his lips. 'The drink … not a tea.'

'Ah, sorry, guv, it's a coffee you're after,' the older man said, throwing his muscular arms up in the air before directing the man to Jones's Dairy around the corner.

Deciding that she could also do with a 'cwawfee', Kate looked at her watch: ten past six. Diana had said she would do her best to be in by six thirty, so she had time to pander to her sleep-deprived body.

As she took delivery of her big mug of strong filtered coffee at Jones's Dairy, Kate found herself reaching for one of the salmon and cream cheese bagels piled up on the counter too – a symbolic gesture for old times' sake, she thought, like lighting a candle for a deceased loved one in a church. She paid and went outside, where she sat on 'her and Daniel's' bench in the narrow cobbled street. Soft sunlight crept through the crack between the buildings, and she turned her face up to it like a sunflower, closing her eyes and imagining Daniel's arm resting on her shoulder as they contemplated another lazy Sunday together. Having never wanted routine, she suddenly wished for it with all her heart. She found it hard to finally drag herself away from the bench and its memories in order to begin preparations for the decidedly non-routine Sunday that lay ahead.

Tucked behind the flower stalls in a Victorian building, Earthy Kit was in darkness when Kate peered through its window. Imagining that Diana had been delayed or had even forgotten, her heart froze. To her relief, however, the door swung open when she pushed it and the sound of a hosepipe confirmed there was life inside. She followed the sound past shelves filled with chic gardening gear – trowels, twine, gloves, aprons kneelers – and walked onto the covered patio at the back, where she found the proprietor dressed in jeans and an aubergine-coloured gardening apron, talking to her organic flowers and herbs as she watered them.

'Hello, Kate,' Diana said, peering past her expectantly. 'Daniel's not with you?' She looked disappointed. 'I supposed he's on one of his trips.'

'Yes,' Kate lied. She hadn't informed Diana of the break-up, partly because the wine-loving septuagenarian had a soft spot for Daniel, so the information might have made her less accommodating. 'I'm sorry, I'm running late, so I am going to have to be rude and get the stuff and dash,' she said, paranoid that Daniel could arrive and expose her lie. Then she kicked herself because being branded a liar was a small price to pay for seeing Daniel face-to-face, even if she was sleep-deprived, make-up-free, and dressed in the bronze cargo pants that had never been the same since their soaking in Mauritius.

'Yes, of course,' Diana said. 'I have everything ready for you in the quantities you've asked for, but you'd better make sure that I haven't left anything out. It sounds like a lovely meal you have planned.'

Kate took her notebook out of her bag as she followed Diana back inside, where she ticked off the items on her list as Diana called them out: 'Borage flowers, elderflowers, courgette flowers, nasturtiums, pink roses, lavender … I think that's it. Oh, and I mustn't forget to give you the beakers and string and things; I've got them all packed somewhere.' Diana placed a finger on her temple pensively for an interminable amount of time before finally ducking below the counter and emerging with a bulging hessian bag. '*Eureka!*' she said. 'The dementia hasn't set in quite yet.'

Kate loaded up her shopping trolley and had to suppress a gasp when Diana gave her the bill. *Did I really need vintage beakers?* she asked herself. In answer, the phrases '*MasterChef* finalist' and 'recipe-book writer' popped into her head. She wanted this job desperately – needed it – and would spend whatever it took to make this a *Babette's Feast* of a food shoot, even at the risk of a bank balance resembling that of the film's protagonist, who had also used every last penny to create the ultimate meal.

Although now officially running late, Kate slowed her pace as she walked back to the car with her haul. If this were the penultimate scene in a chick flick, she thought, she might trip over a bucket of delphiniums and fall to the ground, only to look up to see Daniel there. Her body went momentarily limp at the idea of running into this sweet and loveable hero, although in this version of the movie, he would most likely just step over her.

As a result of her dawdling, Kate got home half an hour later than arranged with Jasmine. Her heart sank when she didn't see *Be*'s former beauty editor on her doorstep. She opened the front door, cursing herself for falling at the first hurdle, and was still saying, 'Idiot, idiot, idiot,' when she entered the kitchen to find Jasmine having a cup of tea with Chloe.

'Oh my God, you look shocking,' Jasmine said. 'You haven't slept a wink, have you?'

'I was prepping and cooking all night,' Kate said. At *Be*, this had been par for the course ahead of a shoot, but then she had never been anything more than a minor accessory to the food in the odd picture. *This could be just another sign that I'm not cut out for a TV role,* she thought. 'So sorry I'm late,' she said. 'Thank you for waiting; I so appreciate this. What are *you* doing here, Chlo?' Her housemate should have left for Camden Market by now.

'I thought you might need some help, so Luke's setting up the stall for me,' Chloe said.

Kate gave her a kiss on the cheek. 'You're an earth angel. Thank you.'

'Well, a little eyebrow shaping should work wonders,' Jasmine said. 'You've been neglecting them again, I see.' If the eyes were the windows to the soul, then the eyebrows were the window frames, or so Jasmine maintained. If they were properly shaped, she believed they could transform one's look and even one's apparent mood. 'But for starters, I want you to get upstairs and wash that revolting hair so that I can begin the salvage job.'

The restoration was well under way when Kirsten arrived. 'Sorry I'm late,' she said, 'but I almost forgot the most important thing.' She pulled a green cotton apron out of a paper bag. 'Ta-dah!'

'Perfect,' Kate said, relieved that Kirsten had remembered this detail, as her apron was now smattered with so many foodstuffs that it was a meal in itself. The new one was also a better match for the dress that Kirsten had helped Kate to pick out: a 1950s-housewife-inspired number with a cinched-in waist, covered with tiny, tightly packed pink roses.

'Much better,' Jasmine said, finally applying gloss to Kate's lips and standing back to admire her work. 'I'm a miracle worker.' She gave Kate a cosmetic bag. 'The blush, base, filler, concealer, highlighter, powder, lipstick, lip liner, eyeliner, mascara, and gloss are all here and yours to keep. You're a gorgeous girl, but a little more vigilance is required in your thirties.' She turned to Kirsten. 'Please make sure she reapplies the gloss regularly, because she has a habit of chewing her lips.'

Kate might have lost a job, but she seemed to have gained two real friends. She felt almost tearful but stopped short of crying since she knew that running mascara would not endear her to Jasmine.

* * *

Set in a quiet Maida Vale mews, Arabella's house stretched over four floors. It had an airy, white, open-plan living room on the ground floor flowing through glass concertina doors into a paved patio garden. This featured large square wooden planters sprouting a variety of green foliage and lavender, a row of manicured conifers along the back wall, and a long stone table with benches on either side, where the lunch would be served.

Following her interview, Kate had phoned Amber in a panic to tell her that she had been asked to do a screen test in a setting that reflected her vision for the show, but she had no idea what to do or where to do it. Amber had told her to take a deep breath and then said that a friend of hers had recently had her house redecorated, which might serve as a good backdrop. Kate had rushed over to view the space and, when she saw the garden with its profusion of lavender, had hit on the idea of working with the menu of edible flowers that she and her mother had so often discussed. Happily, the owner of the house, Arabella, had loved the idea and agreed to invite a few friends over for a late-afternoon al fresco lunch that Sunday.

Arabella now led Kate and Kirsten down to the basement kitchen. This was Kate's idea of heaven, with cupboards that stretched to the ceiling and opened to reveal swivelling storage racks and shelves, a Sub-Zero Pro fridge, a built-in espresso machine, a Boffi tap, and a central island with a teppanyaki plate embedded in it.

'Make yourselves at home,' Arabella said, pouring Perrier water into glasses with lemon and ice. 'There's wine in the fridge, but not much else, I'm afraid. This is the most food my kitchen has ever seen.' Her model-thin frame dressed in skinny white jeans and a teeny white T-shirt with a blue daisy on the front was testimony to this. 'Good luck,' she said. 'It's exciting.' She retreated upstairs, followed by Kirsten, who was laden with accessories to adorn the table.

Left alone, Kate was suddenly paralysed with fear. She stood in the middle of the kitchen and looked at the bags and boxes of ingredients, not sure where to start, until she glanced at the wall clock and was galvanised by the realisation that she had less than an hour before the cameras rolled.

'You do know this is just a test?' Nigel said when he and his team arrived to find Kate surrounded by an elaborate array of props, produce, and dishes in varying stages of readiness. These went from chopped herbs to ready-prepared pomegranate marinade and lavender chocolate mousses, which she would whip out after demonstrating their preparation, as she had seen done by the Barefoot Contessa. She had watched numerous cooking shows over the past few days in preparation for this screen test, which had only served to highlight how very different the process was from food preparation for print. She still had no idea how she was going to pull this off.

If she had already been nervous, she became a jabbering wreck as cameras and lights were assembled and everything suddenly looked very official. *Okay, let me come clean: I'm an impostor. I haven't a clue. You can all go home now,* she wanted to say.

Finally, Nigel ran through procedures in his clipped public-school accent. 'As I've said,' he finished off, 'we want to show viewers that entertaining is fun and easy, much as your features in *Be* did, so just relax and be yourself.'

Kate took a few measured Chloe-style breaths and began: 'Hello, I'm Kate Richmond. Today we're christening a newly landscaped patio garden with a ladies' lunch, so we've put together a menu befitting the occasion, incorporating a variety of edible flowers. Fashionable in Victorian times, these have recently made a kitchen comeback, finding their way into everything from cocktails to cakes, which isn't surprising, really, considering that they not only add a beautiful finishing touch but also have subtle, interesting flavours and aromas.'

She glanced at Nigel, who was scrutinising her through narrowed eyes, like someone trying to assess whether an item was real or fake in a shop owned by a questionable merchant.

'To kick things off, we're serving Pimm's, which is summer in a glass and just the thing for an al fresco lunch,' Kate continued. You're probably familiar with the fruity version, but we're serving ours with borage leaves and flowers, which taste of cucumber and add a pretty touch.' Kate scooped up some of the delicate blue flowers from one of the containers lined up on the counter. 'This version is also more authentic, as borage was a component of the original Pimm's cocktail, which was invented by a London oyster-bar owner called James Pimm in the mid 1800s. The fruit salad came later.'

Nigel gave an interested nod.

'On the food side, we're starting with an amuse-bouche of courgette flowers, which are among the few flowers tough enough to withstand deep-frying.' Kate picked up a prize specimen from the counter. 'There are female and male flowers, but the more delicate male ones on stalks will give you the deliciously light and crispy results you're after.'

Nigel was now frowning and making a twirling movement with his index finger. Kate interpreted this as a need to speed things up, which she did, tripping over her words in her haste. Finally Nigel put up his hand.

'Look, you clearly know your stuff, but your delivery is rather leaden,' he said, 'and too dense. We want the viewer to feel like you're sharing the experience with them, not lecturing them. Skip the long preamble and get down to the cooking. You can throw in the anecdotal stuff as space-fillers while you're prepping.'

Once Kirsten had reapplied Kate's lip gloss, she cleared her throat, chewed her lips, and began again. 'Hi. I'm Kate Richmond …'

And again.

And again.

On the fifth round, she was finally onto the first item on the menu. 'Since the chocolate mousse needs to set, you should get it out of the way first,' she said as she stirred chocolate and butter in a bowl over a pot of gently simmering water. 'When melting the chocolate, make sure that the bowl doesn't touch the water since excessive heat makes chocolate grainy. You therefore want to rely on the indirect heat from steam. Also, don't let any water get into the chocolate, as this will cause it to seize and make it unusable.' The smell of the melting chocolate was relaxing and by the time Kate moved on to beating the egg whites, she felt like she was getting into her stride. When she looked at Nigel, however, it appeared that this was far from the case. He was making a wild hand-puppet talking motion, and she realised that she hadn't said anything at all for several minutes. *What do I say about beating egg whites?* she wondered. 'Make sure the bowl is dry before you add the whites or they won't stiffen,' she said, slowing her speech to fill the space until she sounded like a stretched cassette tape. This was a lot more difficult than Nigella Lawson made it look, and it was like rocket science compared to Jamie Oliver's approach.

By the time Kate was spooning the mousse into miniature terracotta flowerpots, Nigel's expression was not dissimilar to that of her piano teacher after a year of giving lessons that hadn't yielded a tuneful moment.

'You need to loosen up, Kate,' he said. 'There will be time to work on technicalities later; we're simply here to find out whether or not you're comfortable in front of the camera and can truly engage with the audience.'

Which you clearly cannot, Kate thought.

'I'm sure you can do it. Just be yourself.'

It's a total disaster. You're not cut out for this. A TV chef, really. Pah!

'Here's an idea,' Nigel added as Kirsten dabbed some powder on Kate's sweaty brow. 'Rather than talking to the camera, talk to me, as you would to a friend sitting in the kitchen watching you cook. Actually picture that friend.'

Nigel morphed into Chloe, whose eyes glazed over the minute Kate mentioned that the mayonnaise was another thing that could be made in advance. *No, not Chloe; Daniel,* she decided.

Stop worrying. You know you can do this in your sleep, she heard Daniel say. *You were made for this.*

She relaxed a little as she continued: 'Take a medium mixing bowl and add two large egg yolks at room temperature.' Kate separated two eggs using her neat one-handed approach and then placed the yolks in the bowl.

Brilliant manoeuvring, Daniel said.

Thank you. Kate smiled at Nigel-become-Daniel, a very encouraging image indeed.

'Now add one teaspoon of Dijon mustard along with a tablespoon of lemon juice, some coarse sea salt, and a little white pepper, and whisk vigorously until the salt dissolves.' Kate did all of the above before adding, 'You might like to put a damp cloth under the bowl, as I have done, to stop it from moving. Now, while continuing to whisk, begin to add olive oil, drop by drop, making sure each addition is completely integrated before adding the next. You should choose a good-quality light olive oil with a nice flavour, as this will come through loud and clear in the mayonnaise, but I generally avoid extra virgin olive oil, which is a bit too strong.' She looked down at the mixture as the cameraman zoomed in to capture it emulsifying nicely. 'As you can see, it's beginning to thicken now, so you can start to add the oil at a faster rate, but always in a continuous stream. To save time, you can, of course, use an electric whisk or food processor, but I personally find it rather satisfying to actually feel the mixture swell and thicken.'

That sounded rather risqué, Daniel said.

Kate suppressed a giggle. She was beginning to enjoy herself. *Maybe I am up to the job, after all,* she thought until she looked down at the bowl. *Fuck, fuck, fuck, fuck, fuck, fuck, fuck.* Her mouth went dry as she stared for what felt like an hour at the curdled mixture before her.

Come on, how many times have you dealt with this kind of glitch? Daniel said. *What was that thing your mother told you to do the last time?*

Kate exhaled. 'There's no denying that mayonnaise is temperamental,' she said, 'and you might find it splits, as I've ably demonstrated here.' She tilted the bowl towards the camera. 'But I've learnt that there's a remedy for most things, and for me it's the same remedy for every problem – I phone my mother.' *Did Nigel just chuckle?* 'In this case, she'd tell me to break an egg yolk into a fresh bowl and to whisk in the split mayonnaise little by little.' To Kate's relief, the remedy worked. When she looked up, Nigel was beaming.

Done like a pro, Daniel said.

She set the bowl aside and reached for the thick and creamy finished batch of mayonnaise that she had made in the early hours of that morning, along with a small bowl of chopped nasturtium leaves. 'Nasturtiums pack an enormous amount of flavour, and their leaves are even more peppery,' she said, 'so add them to the mayonnaise gradually, tasting as you go, until it's spicy without being overpowering. Incidentally, the leaves also make a delicious alternative pesto sauce when blended with garlic, walnuts, and a little olive oil. And my mother, who has a thriving vegetable garden in Cornwall, pickles the buds in tarragon vinegar and uses them as a cheap substitute for capers – they're a bit tougher but a lot more aromatic.' On a roll at last, Kate found that the anecdotes, tips, and little extras continued to trip off her tongue as she steeped elderflowers in lemon syrup, poached lobster tails in white wine, and stirred rose water into the pomegranate marinade.

She was spooning goat's cheese into courgette flowers, grateful that she had recently practised the dish with her mother, when a pair of blue stilettos appeared at the top of the stairs. Arabella bent down to say that the first guests had arrived. At that point, Kate's habitual pre-dinner-party adrenaline kicked in and she focused solely on getting everything out, with the result being that she came across as more confident and natural than she had all day. Nigel appeared enraptured.

The trays of Pimm's cocktails were whisked away by Kirsten, followed by a platter of the crispy golden courgette flowers. Then, when everyone was seated, Arabella and Kirsten took the poached lobster salads upstairs, followed by Kate, who was carrying the toasted brioche arranged in two purpose-bought antique silver toast racks.

Six groomed and glossy women, all adhering to the floral dress code, were seated around the table under a large, square, cream-coloured umbrella. Among them, wearing pink-framed sunglasses and a wide-brimmed floppy white hat with an oversized rose attached, was Amber.

'I thought it would make you more nervous if you knew she was here,' Kirsten whispered.

'This is beautiful,' Amber said. She looked down at the rectangular plate in front of her, which bore a strip of nasturtium mayonnaise down its centre topped with slices of lobster and lemon segments, finished off with a light sprinkling of baby salad leaves and a nasturtium flower. 'I knew you'd pull it off.'

'Thanks.' Kate gave a mock curtsey, relieved that Amber hadn't witnessed the kitchen instalment.

'The table looks gorgeous too,' Arabella said, making a sweeping gesture with one arm to take it all in. Her other arm was draped over Amber's shoulder in a manner that suggested they were more than just casual friends.

It was the first time that Kate had seen her vision transformed into reality. She was happy to see that Kirsten had pulled it off with aplomb. Laboratory beakers and vessels were arranged in clusters down the middle of the white-clothed table, a single yellow courgette flower hanging over the edge of one, a cloud of tiny cream elderflowers bursting from another, and roses, lavender, borage, and nasturtiums pushed into others. Picking up the flowers' colours were white linen napkins embroidered with different coloured roses tied with gardening twine, bowls of sugar-coated almonds, and smoky green wine glasses.

The cameraman focused on the table for a while and then followed Kate back into the kitchen, where she spooned elderflower sorbet into pretty pink Moroccan tea glasses, before plating up the quails marinated in pomegranate and rose syrup with the herby quinoa salad. Finally, feeling exhausted but happy, she planted the last sprig of lavender into a chocolate-mousse-filled miniature terracotta pot. 'Well known for its calming qualities, lavender is also packed with phytonutrients and contains a polyphenol that aids digestion,' she said, 'making it the perfect end to a meal.' *Whether or not it marks the perfect end to a screen test is another question, of course,* she thought.

After clearing up, she joined the party at the table for a few glasses of wine and a generous serving of praise, before driving home in darkness. If the proof was in the pudding and the guests were the jury, then it had been a success, she thought, feeling a flicker of satisfaction. This immediately dissipated, however, as she reflected on her leaden starter and the mayonnaise debacle, which were mistakes that a *MasterChef* finalist, cookery book writer, and TV host would never have made. She was simply a food editor playing at being a TV chef, like a child dressing up in her mother's clothes. Of course Nigel would have seen right through her masquerade. So when her phone rang a block away from home and she saw the producer's name, she prepared to accept defeat as gracefully as possible. It was nice of him not to keep her hopes up.

'Sorry to call you after dark,' he said, 'but the schedules are being finalised tomorrow, which means we had to make a decision on this immediately. I've just been through all the tapes with the rest of the team and ...' Kate knew what was coming: *Despite some good moments, it's clear you lack experience. It was a good effort, but, truth be told, you just don't have what it takes for the screen. In fact, you ran a not-so-close fourth to the cookery book writer, who may be lumpy, but her delivery was smooth.*

'It was immediately clear to all of us that you're the one for the job,' Nigel said.

What? 'Sorry, could you please repeat that?' Kate said barely audibly.

'Obviously there are some issues you'll need to work on, like timing, but it was unanimous; we'd definitely like you to be the host of *Entertaining Matters*.'

'You mean ...'

'It's yours,' Nigel said.

Deafened by the sound of adrenalin rushing through her body and of Champagne corks going off in her head, Kate only later recalled Nigel's saying that they had liked the anecdotes, in particular her mother's tips and the references to her vegetable garden – 'There's such an emphasis on locally sourced, seasonal produce. It adds an interesting dimension.'

So her secret source had emerged from the shadows, Kate thought, marking a departure in her own story from that of the ill-fated Cyrano de Bergerac, whose brilliance was only revealed on his deathbed, when Roxane finally learnt that he, rather than Christian, was the poet of her dreams. Happily, a ménage à trois consisting of a TV presenter, a recipe writer, and an audience was a more acceptable scenario.

* * *

The flat was in darkness when Kate got home, which reminded her that Chloe was treating Luke to dinner as a thank you for manning her stall at Camden Market. Their relationship seemed to be gelling into something meaningful, making Kate wonder if Luke would permanently replace Matt as The One in Chloe's life. Kate too was beginning to believe in soulmates, but she thought that perhaps, rather than just one, everyone had several possible perfect fits like a piece in a jigsaw puzzle – four if you were a middle bit, three if you were a side piece, and two if you were a corner one. In Kate's case, one of her connectors had fit with Rupert and one with Fai, but Daniel was the one required to complete her picture. If she didn't find a way of slotting herself back with him, she feared she would end up rattling around in the box forever or, worse, suffer the fate of those who forced two ill-fitting connectors together and got stuck in a distorted marriage.

The kitchen's large railway clock read 9.15, which meant that her mother would be ensconced at an outdoor performance of *A Midsummer Night's Dream* with Megan and her daughters (Kate should have been with them, but she had cancelled her trip home because of the screen test). *Who else might I call?* Kate wondered, feeling the need to confirm that she wasn't having her own midsummer night's dream.

'Never underestimate the power of well-shaped eyebrows,' Jasmine said when Kate told her the news. 'No, really, sweetie, you so deserve this. Well done.' Kate heard splashing and giggles in the background. 'Sarah, sit down this minute. … Sorry, Kate, give me a moment. … How many times do I have to tell you … you'll crack your head open one day. … Kate, I'm giving the girls a bath; let me call you tomorrow when things are saner. I hope you're celebrating already. We must do that lunch soon.'

Kirsten was in Arabella's walk-in wardrobe when Kate called her. 'She wants some advice on what to wear for an awards dinner,' she told Kate. 'I've decided to add wardrobe consultancy to my portfolio. This freelancing isn't too bad, actually; I might just stick with it.'

'Spare a spot for some TV-host styling,' Kate said.

'I will. Fingers crossed.'

'No, I mean you *really* should.'

'What?'

'I got it. I know it's nuts, but …'

'Already?' Kirsten said. 'You got the job? Wow, yay, that's fantastic. I want all the details, but I'm in the thick of it right now, so I'll call you tomorrow. Well done.'

'Well done, *you*,' Kate said. 'I couldn't have done it without your help …' She realised that Kirsten had already clicked off.

'I guess it's just you and me,' she said to Mushy, who had followed her into the kitchen and was sitting expectantly next to his bowl. She emptied a tin of tuna into it as a celebratory treat and then opened the fridge in search of something to fill a rising void that wasn't in her stomach.

What is wrong with you? This is it, the big one, everything you've ever dreamt of on a platter; there should be no void.

Her eyes alighted on the bottle of pink Perrier-Jouët Champagne that she had turned down before her trip to Mauritius, the one that Daniel had sent to welcome her back and that had languished at the back of the fridge ever since for lack of any reason to celebrate. Now was the perfect time for it, Kate thought. In fact, if she didn't mark this new departure with bubbles, she might be beset with bad luck, like the *Titanic*, which had set out with no customary bottle of Champagne broken on its bow. She knew that sailors had long believed this omission to bode ill. Perhaps lost luggage, cyclones, a suicidal model, and a psychopathic fashion director wouldn't have plagued the trip to Mauritius if she had launched it appropriately.

Her hand hovered over the Champagne but at the last minute diverted to a bottle of Sauvignon Blanc, because drinking Champagne alone was rather tragic, she decided. Once she closed the fridge door, however, her eyes were drawn to a yellow fridge magnet that Daniel had given her, which gave pause for thought. It bore a quote by Champagne doyenne Madame Bollinger: 'I drink it when I'm happy and when I'm sad. Sometimes I drink it when I'm alone. When I have company, I consider it obligatory. I trifle with it if I'm not hungry and drink it when I am. Otherwise I never touch it – unless I'm thirsty.'

Sometimes I drink it when I'm alone. It was as though Daniel were speaking to her from their relationship's grave, telling her that there was absolutely no excuse not to celebrate this coup with bubbles. She retrieved the bottle of Champagne from the fridge, and placed it on a tray, to which she added a Champagne flute, a silver tastevin, and a lobster and nasturtium-mayonnaise sandwich. In the living room, after releasing the cork in a gleeful arc, she filled both her glass and the tastevin, and placed the latter on the floor for Mushy's consumption.

'Chin-chin,' she said to Mushy before taking a sip, wishing that Daniel were sharing the moment. For a nanosecond, she considered calling him to tell him the news and to suggest a drink, but her fear of further rejection froze her finger above the keypad. If she wanted a different result, she would have to try a different approach, she decided.

It occurred to her that, whereas she had always actively pursued her career by seducing potential employers with imaginative pitches, she had played a largely passive role in love. So, if she wanted to win Daniel back, perhaps it was time to put the same effort and passion into going after him. Since a casual phone call would lack the desired impact, she decided to hold the thought and to share the moment instead with Audrey Hepburn.

While simplistic and sexist, *Sabrina* never failed to entertain Kate with its romantic storyline, glamorous clothes, and Champagne lifestyle. On this viewing, she also found that the old movie had some intelligence to impart. Whereas in the past she had seen the protagonist's habit of wearing her heart on her sleeve as humiliating, she saw now that the Humphrey Bogart character would never have run after Sabrina in the end if he hadn't been sure that she loved him deeply.

As the final scene faded out to music and movie credits, Kate slugged the dregs directly from the bottle. Then, addressing Mushy, who was seemingly also drunk – lying on his back with his legs in the air, eyes closed, and mouth open – she said, 'If I'm going to get what I want in love, it's probably too late to simply wear my heart on my sleeve; I'm going to have to fly it from a flagpole.'

CHAPTER 17

Love Apples

Kate emptied a bag of fresh prawns into a large glass bowl, which conjured Mushy, like a rabbit from a top hat, onto the counter.

'Don't even think about it,' she warned, watching his eyes lustily follow one of the dull grey sea creatures from the bowl to the chopping board. 'I mean it, Mushy.' She picked up a small knife, thinking there was no harm done if he misinterpreted her intent. 'A lot is riding on this meal, and you don't want to fuck it up.' *If anything is going to be fucked, it had better be me,* she thought with an apprehensive giggle.

Wisely sensing Kate's nervous and unpredictable energy, Mushy slunk sulkily off the counter and settled close to the door, pointedly looking away although his ears were pricked up attentively. Kate snapped off the prawn's head, exaggerating the motion for his benefit, and he disappeared around the corner. She then peeled the prawn and made a shallow incision at either end of its back before taking one end of the intestine between her thumb and forefinger and pulling gently. The entrails came out cleanly, along with all remnants of the prawn's last meal on the ocean floor. Kate thought how convenient it would be if she could so easily remove all remnants of her own insatiable appetite in the Indian Ocean. But as she continued to work her way through the prawns, she realised that she no longer wished her Mauritian affairs away. Because, just as the prawn's intestine was the conduit to its tasty flesh, the events in Mauritius were an integral channel leading to where she was now. She was reminded of something Chloe had once said: it's the muck that gives rise to the lotus flower.

She dropped the last cleaned prawn into the colander and then looked down at the next step in the recipe.

> *Place the tomatoes in a bowl, and cover them with boiling water for one minute. Then immediately immerse in cold water. Peel them, cut them in half, and remove the seeds. Chop coarsely.*

The tomatoes acquired for the job were identical to those she had seen piled up in pyramids in Mauritius's markets – plum-sized, spherical, and the deepest red – which was because they *were* Mauritian tomatoes. Wanting the formula to be exactly right, Kate had called her favourite fruit and vegetable supplier and told him that it was imperative he find tomatoes grown on the Indian Ocean island. Steve had sounded sceptical but, to Kate's delight, had rung back the next day to say that he had been able to track some down. 'They'll cost you a bob or two,' he said. 'You'd be far better off getting some nice Marzano tomatoes – best in the world for less.' But much to his bewilderment, Kate had remained firm, because they weren't called *pommes d'amour* in Marzano, and a tomato by any other name was no substitute for what she had in mind tonight.

> *Next, pound the garlic with the sea salt using a pestle and mortar. Add the coriander stems, chilli, and ginger, and pound to a paste. Pour three tablespoons of olive oil into a thick-bottomed pan and heat slowly. Add the onion. Cook, stirring, until soft and golden (about five minutes). Add the chilli-ginger paste, along with the ground cumin and turmeric, and stir over heat for one minute.*

Kate didn't usually follow recipes so religiously, but on this occasion she didn't want to diverge from the words in front of her by so much as a milligram or a millilitre because she had imbued them with the powers of a magic spell that would render a prince blind to certain deviances, make him fall madly in love, and cause him to believe in happily-ever-after again. Admittedly, it was a lot to ask from a recipe, but Kate suddenly found herself ready to believe in all sorts of things.

She had spent sleepless nights deliberating over the perfect meal. At first, she had been certain there could be no better dish for the occasion than the salmon in Pinot Noir butter that had seduced Daniel in the pages of *Be* even before she and he had met in the flesh. But after further consideration, she deviated to the spicy West African–style poussins she had cooked on their third date, when the birds simmering in spicy peanut and chilli sauce had not been the only things steaming things up in the kitchen. Then she had asked herself, *Why cook baby chickens when pigeon is Daniel's favourite bird? Pigeons in pomegranate marinade, perhaps?*

No, no, no, came the quick response; it should absolutely be the ravioli Niçoise with sauce vierge that they had relished on a hotel terrace on the Côte d'Azur, when he had said those three little words that have more intrinsic value than the best Scrabble combination of *z*'s and *x*'s on a triple word score.

Since there were no words she would rather hear at the end of this meal, the decision seemed final until, while jotting down the ingredients for the dish (beef, Swiss chard, avocado, lemons, basil, tomatoes), she had thought, of course, it had to be pommes d'amour. And then she had landed contentedly on the recipe given to her by Paradise Bay's chef.

> *Add the chopped tomatoes, tomato paste, thyme, curry leaves, cayenne pepper, and salt to the pan. Cook over moderate heat, stirring from time to time until the tomato juice has evaporated (about ten minutes). Add half the chopped coriander, check the seasoning, and set aside.*

Kate turned off the flame and covered the pan before wiping the tomato-splattered mosaic behind the stove and piling her various utensils into the dishwasher. Her kitchen usually looked like the scene of a bar brawl at this stage in dinner-party proceedings, when she would invariably be running late. But with so much riding on this dinner, she had systematically cleaned as she cooked, and everything was prepped and on standby for the final touches. She cast an eye over the kitchen to make sure the stage was set for seduction in the first degree. She had already laid the table with the grass table mats from Mauritius, her grandmother's silver, her mother's crystal, and a jar filled with pale pink damask roses. That these particular blooms were symbolic of love was no coincidence, and neither were the flowering sprigs of basil tucked among them, since Kate had read that in Italy, in days gone by, women who wanted to get married used to place pots of the herb outside their front doors.

She dimmed the lights and lit the candles in the wire candelabra that hung above the table. *What else? Music.* She slipped Finola's debut album into the slot and pressed Play. As promised, Finola had sent the CD to Kate soon after its release and had emailed later to share her excitement about *Recipe for Love* hitting Australia's Top 10. The press had picked up on her appearance on *Be*'s cover, she said, which had certainly helped her publicity campaign. 'Big thank you.' Serge had also emailed to say that the food feature had elicited a positive response from magazines in South Africa. Solange was delighted with the coverage for the Sunshine Group, and, most gratifying of all, Fai had come in from the cold. He had phoned Kate to thank her for the heartfelt letter hand-delivered by Sanjay, along with copies of *Be*. He understood, he said; he had chosen to ignore the boyfriend, and it was true that people often weren't themselves in paradise. He had laughed. Although the fire was out, some warmth had returned to his voice. Kate was happy to find closure. She was also delighted to hear that her feature had drawn a large number of tourists to Fai's father's shop, for which he was very grateful. Even from the grave, *Be* was affecting people's lives. All was not lost.

'Cherry lips and a sweet sugar kiss; a bit of chilli and a cool lemon twist; you're my chocolat, my baby chocolat; my chocolat, my baby chocolat …' Kate was humming along to the chorus, hoping that she had got the mix of ingredients right for success tonight, when the doorbell rang.

The expression 'She felt like her heart would leap out of her chest' had never rung so true. Not even on the threshold of one of her most hotly anticipated first dates had Kate felt this level of nervous energy. But a first date was a bit like taking a gamble on an enticing, unexplored holiday destination; if it didn't match up to the fantasy, one could try somewhere else the next time. In this case, however, Kate was intimately familiar with the terrain, and there was nowhere else in the world she wanted to go – not only for a vacation, but to take up permanent residence. Daniel's own prickly discoveries in the area, however, could mean that his only interest was more in line with a brief revisit to confirm the wisdom of his discernment. As Kate readied herself at the door, she told herself that she must be prepared for the possibility that Daniel had only accepted her invitation because of her desperate measures to get him there.

He was wearing a blue and white shirt with a 1970s-influenced swirly print that she knew and loved. Her whole body swooned as she took him in, barely able to believe that he was really there in front of her. He was looking at her questioningly, which made Kate realise that she was standing there, staring at him with her mouth open. *You're no longer behind the wheelie bin,* she reminded herself. *Say something, stupid.*

'Hello, come in, come in,' she blurted out like an overly jovial innkeeper inviting guests in on a cold Christmas Eve.

He had a bottle of Dom Pérignon Champagne in one hand, which Kate hoped was a good sign. But his smile seemed strained and he made no attempt to kiss her hello. *Bad sign.*

They moved awkwardly through to the kitchen, where Daniel, seemingly deep in thought, unsheathed the Champagne, adeptly removed the cork, and, with his usual finesse, delicately transferred the bubbly nectar into the waiting crystal vessels.

'Here's to the new job,' he said as they clinked their glasses together. 'Congratulations.'

'Thanks,' Kate said, privately drinking to a renewal of their relationship rather than to her career-ship, all too aware that the former was a flimsy raft and she a refugee with a very slim chance of being thrown a rope by the promised land. Daniel was ill at ease, and clearly here under duress.

'This is the kind of thing you've always dreamt of,' he added. 'You must be thrilled.'

Correction, Kate wanted to say. *I've got what I always thought I wanted, but what I* actually *want more than anything else is leaning nonchalantly on my kitchen counter, drinking Champagne – physically close but perhaps romantically as far away as the moon.*

Being with Daniel was both totally familiar and not familiar at all. Kate imagined she felt much like people did after first discovering that, rather than flat, the earth was a magical sphere spinning on its axis and keeping everyone attached to its surface by virtue of the force of gravity. Feeling an equally strong tug drawing her to him, she wanted to touch a whole lot more than her glass to his.

'Ground control to Major Tom?' Daniel said, observing her quizzically. Kate had lost her train of thought for a moment, having drifted off into his eyes. 'How did it all happen?' he asked.

'Sorry,' she said, 'how did what happen?'

'You say there was a screen test?'

As they nibbled spiced nuts and sipped Champagne, Kate told Daniel about Amber's help in securing the interview after Roberta had tried to put the kibosh on it. She also told him that Roberta had been fired. Amber had given Newday a simple choice: 'Roberta or me!'

'So her evil deeds have finally come home to roost,' Daniel said.

'Yes, and weirdly, in spite of everything, I feel quite sorry for her.'

'Don't be,' Daniel said. 'I have a funny feeling that she'll land right back on her feet.' He popped a nut into his mouth and then offered Kate the bowl rather than feeding them to her, as he would have done in the past. 'Nice nuts. Spicy.'

'I've had better,' Kate said suggestively, hoping that the aphrodisiacal cayenne pepper she had added to the mix was taking effect, although there was no evidence to suggest this. While Daniel appeared to be relaxing, she didn't detect a hint of desire emanating from him. He didn't seem to have even noticed her newly svelte form dressed in skinny jeans and a diaphanous cream lace top bought especially for the occasion from Harvey Nichols (that first salary cheque could not come a moment too soon).

She told him about the lengths to which she had gone to pull off the perfect screen test, describing Nigel's frantic hand-puppet motions and the mayonnaise debacle, not yet confident enough to mention Daniel's part in her transformation mid shoot. Daniel laughed out loud. 'You're fierce when that adrenaline kicks in; I'm not surprised you nailed it.' Finally there was some warmth in his voice and in his smile.

As Kate began to cook, she realised she was feeling the happiest she had felt in weeks. She only wished Daniel was participating in the dance rather than merely watching it. She missed their touches in passing and the way he would pin her against the corner unit and refuse to let her save whatever was simmering until she had given him a kiss. But having him back in the kitchen in the flesh was a good start. And it looked like things were about to get a whole lot better when she turned from dipping a piece of halloumi cheese into flour and Daniel leant towards her. Holding her breath, she watched his hand move, as if in slow motion, to her cheek. As it touched her skin, heat like melted candle wax ran in rivers through her body.

'I love you,' Kate said.

'Flour,' Daniel said simultaneously as he swept her cheek and held up his finger with a dusting of white powder on its tip.

The words had just bubbled out of her, and they hovered in the ether waiting for an acknowledgement that never came. Kate hid her disappointment by turning to the stove, where she dropped the floured halloumi pieces into sizzling clarified butter and felt their pain, as if it were her heart being fried.

What do you expect? a voice inside her asked. *That, like Mushy, he's going to rub himself up against you while purring because you're feeding him? It will take time to regain his trust and prove that you're worth a second chance. Heart on a flagpole, remember.*

She placed flatbreads under the grill and, avoiding Daniel's eyes, watched them puff up before taking them out of the oven. She then put them on the table alongside the platter of fried halloumi sprinkled with shredded basil (because the scent of basil was said to promote desire) and a bowl of beetroot hummus, the latter chosen for its aphrodisiacal boron content.

'This is good,' Daniel said, after helping himself to some hummus.

'It is,' Kate said, not referring to the hummus. 'I'm glad you came. I wasn't sure you would.'

'How could I refuse?' Daniel said. 'That was a pretty compelling invitation. Not only can I now die a happy man with Vin de Constance on my lips, but no one has ever written a poem for me before.'

'I just wanted to get your attention,' Kate said, 'even at the risk of humiliation.' *Humiliation is certainly a given,* she thought, feeling a little edgy again.

When Kate had awoken feeling hazy after drinking the entire bottle of pink Champagne, her decision to fly her heart from a flagpole hadn't seemed so much of an epiphany in the sober light of day. *So if a mere phone call won't do, then what?* she had asked herself. Her bank balance dictated something cheap, which ruled out skywriting or a string quartet serenading Daniel outside his window, so it would have to be something simple but effective, she concluded. *A singing telegram? A special dinner? A peace offering?* She had finally decided on a combination of all three.

She remembered that Daniel had said that he would die happy if he could get his hands on a few more bottles of Vin de Constance, which wasn't available in the United Kingdom since its high alcohol content meant it didn't comply with the classification system. Recalling its added cachet as Jane Austen's cure for a disappointed heart, and that for Baudelaire its sweetness was surpassed only by a lover's kiss, Kate had decided that it was the only thing for the job. And so, with Jasmine's help, she had secured a couple of bottles remaining from De-Vine Beauty's special consignment. To this she had added Alessi's Anna G corkscrew, shaped like a woman whose arms rose above her head – begging forgiveness? – as the screw penetrated the cork. But then she thought she needed to articulate all the things the gift signified, so she had decided on the poem. Finally, to guarantee that Daniel didn't discard it without reading it, she had hired an actress friend of Chloe's to recite it to him before handing it over along with the gifts and an invitation to dinner.

'I think it was pretty good,' Daniel said. 'Excellent.' These words, while welcome on a report card, were not quite what Kate was hoping for here.

Daniel pulled a folded piece of paper out of his back pocket and pressed it flat on the table. As he did, their hands touched, and Kate gasped as her body went instantly lame with desire. To detract from her embarrassment, she picked up the page and, feeling strangely vulnerable and exposed, began to read:

'Were it as easy to unscrew what I've done
As removing the cork from a Cab Sauvignon
Or from that heavenly nectar, Vin de Constance,
Favoured by Napoleon and writers of romance.
Baudelaire thought it as sweet as a kiss,
But it could never surpass the ones that I miss
From my lover, best friend, the man I adore,
Who's the whole world to me and then a bit more.
Austen prescribed Constance for a broken heart,

But if in a thousand pieces, where does one start?
To put all the fragments together again
Is not a job for all the king's men.
So I can't let it go without one last fight,
For really, without you, there's just no delight.
My days all lack lustre, the nights are the same,
Without you beside me or calling my name.
So please, my love, dine with me one more time.
I'm eager to show you that I am still thine.
There are no obligations, but if I don't try,
It will be a regret that I'll have till I die.'

'Bravo,' Daniel said. 'It's even better hearing you read it.'

'Poetry isn't my forte.' Kate brought her hands up to her burning cheeks. 'But I do mean everything I said, and I'm glad it got you here.'

Daniel's brow wrinkled as he sighed and became pensive. 'I've missed you,' he said. 'I've wanted to call you so many times, but I couldn't; I was just too messed up. And angry.'

'I know,' Kate said. 'Understandably! And my believing that a poem, a corkscrew, and a bottle of sweet wine could begin to put things right is kind of ridiculous.' *It's a pathetic, immature stab at happily-ever-after.* 'I'm basically trying to sweep it all under the carpet like dust rather than something as precious as your love and your trust, which I've broken into smithereens. Why would you want to even try to pick up the pieces, let alone put them together again, when you have every reason to hate me?' She felt that her tension might give way to tears.

'I don't hate you,' Daniel said. 'I could never hate you. It's true, I was angry … cut up … by what you did. I didn't expect it, and I felt so stupid that I hadn't seen it coming and let it happen again. I really was in love with you, you know, and thought that you felt the same – that we were going somewhere.'

'We were,' Kate implored, feeling his use of the past tense like a stab in the heart with a jagged piece of broken glass.

'I suppose the most hurtful thing was that it seemed to mean something to you,' Daniel said. 'I couldn't have imagined loving anyone else. There just wasn't room. And the fact that you could …'

'I do love you,' Kate said, feeling the prickle of tears welling behind her eyes, 'more than I thought possible. I won't lie to you and say that my love affair in Mauritius meant nothing, but there's been some kind of, um, some kind of alchemical shift that's happened as a result of everything, bad and good, and I can honestly say that I want to be with you more than I've wanted anything in my life before. I love you so much, Daniel. Please find it in yourself to forgive me.' Kate closed her eyes; she felt paralysed. 'I'm begging you, please give me a second chance,' she whispered as tears began to flow.

Daniel leant across the table and wiped away a tear. This time his hand lingered on her cheek.

'To poem, corkscrew, and sweet wine, shouldn't you add tiramisu, profiteroles, and a kiss on the bonnet of my car?' he asked.

'Oh God, you know about that?' Kate wasn't sure whether she should cry harder, but Daniel's delicious smile was back.

'The security guard in my building asked me if I recognised the person captured on CCTV embracing my car. It was a cunning disguise, but I don't know many people who go around hugging and kissing cars.'

On the Sunday night before the screen test, when Daniel hadn't appeared on schedule to pick up his pizza – and his cassata – Kate had panicked, fearing that while her back was turned he had slipped away. So she had waited for a car to enter his underground parking garage and then ducked under the descending steel door to enter it. She had been so happy to find his racing-green Alfa Romeo Spider in its place that she put her arms around the bonnet and planted a kiss on it. She had then registered that, it being the last Sunday of the month, Daniel would be hosting his wine club upstairs, with something more appropriate than a pizza accompaniment.

'And the rest? The profiteroles?' Kate asked.

'Well, once your cover was blown, I realised I'd seen someone fitting that description emerging from Il Bordello. And for all his Sicilian stealth, Luigi couldn't deny it. He was worried about you – said it looked like you were living rough.' Daniel pushed a strand of tear-drenched hair behind Kate's ear, and she suddenly found it difficult to breathe. It seemed her heart had found its way into her throat and was blocking off her air supply. She couldn't take the suspense any longer.

'So can we ... can you ...?'

'You had me at Baudelaire,' Daniel said. Then, very slowly, he slid his hand behind her neck and pulled her towards him to drink her in as she became as liquid as a medium-bodied Pinot Noir.

> *Season the prawns with sea salt, and sprinkle with powdered turmeric. Heat the remaining olive oil in a very hot pan. Add the prawns. Cook without stirring for about two minutes on one side, and then turn over and cook for another two on the other side.*

Kate watched the prawns turn from dull grey to subtle pink, mirroring her emotional transformation from dark to rosy in response to Daniel's kiss, which continued to radiate warmth through her whole body. *This is it,* she thought, *la vie en rose*. Daniel crossed the room to the fridge, touching her hair as he passed and elevating her temperature even more. As she watched him reach for the bottle of white wine, she admired his strong, beautiful profile, which was lit up like a deity's by the fridge's yellow light. *I was blind, but now I see.*

> *Incorporate the prawns into the heated rougaille sauce, but don't allow them to cook further. Sprinkle with chopped coriander. Serve immediately with basmati rice and coconut chutney.*

'This is a Mauritian dish called rougaille,' Kate said as she placed a plate in front of Daniel, topped with the prawns in their aromatic sauce alongside a neat mound of jasmine rice and a dollop of coconut chutney. 'It's made with pommes d'amour – real ones from the island.'

'You really found Mauritian tomatoes?'

'I wasn't sure that any of the other ones would have the desired effect.'

'Which is?' Daniel asked.

'Hmm ... well, that kiss was a good start.'

'Then we'd better keep going; there's always such promise in a good opener.' Daniel pulled her onto his lap for a much longer and deeper kiss, and although he still hadn't said those three top-scoring words, Kate was sure she could taste them right on the tip of her tongue, where any oenophile worth her Châteauneuf-du-Pape knew that sweetness registered.

As they savoured their prawns and pommes d'amour, intense feelings simmering below the surface, Kate gave a thought to Fai as the catalyst for this alchemical transformation. Like the contradictory myths surrounding the exotic tomato, he had been at once poison to her relationship with Daniel and love potion, because, had she not bitten into the forbidden fruit, she wouldn't have lost paradise and, in so doing, recognised it for what it was. *Sometimes we have to get lost in order to find our way home,* she thought as the meal gave way to slow, romantic lovemaking, she straddling Daniel as he sat in his chair, their bodies and spirits melding together like two cultivars in a blend that worked on every level, from its nose to its toes.

Having worked up an appetite once more, they moved on to dessert: lemon and white chocolate soufflé. This was a risky choice given the fact that (*a*) it wasn't a dish one could prepare in advance, (*b*) Kate had never actually achieved the perfect soufflé or (*c*) even come close, and (*d*) the dessert's success could only be revealed in the cooking. But in life's multiple choices, she was suddenly prepared to tick a few more boxes and risk getting things wrong. She had, however, learnt that you can't have your soufflé and eat it. So she had chosen what she wanted to give up and what she wanted to keep, much as she had eliminated other dishes in order to create a delicious menu tonight.

This time round, Daniel joined her in the kitchen shuffle, squeezing and zesting lemons while she brought butter, flour, and milk to a gentle boil; chopping white chocolate and stirring it into the pot with lemon juice and zest as she separated eggs; and whisking the whites and sugar into sweet meringue while whisking sweet magic in Kate by virtue of his sheer presence.

Finally Kate spooned the frothy mixture into soufflé dishes and put them in the oven, aware that there was no guarantee they would rise, but happy to be in a position where she was willing to take her chances. *There are, after all, no happy endings, only happy beginnings,* she thought, and this was as good a beginning as she could hope for.

Entertaining Matters

A collection of recipes for meals best shared

Kate and Annie Richmond

INTRODUCTION

These recipes are all designed to entertain – whether a love interest, a friend over for a casual supper, or a large group for a sumptuous weekend lunch. None is overly complicated, and they all reflect an eclectic approach, mixing up cultural influences and culinary styles. The only rule is to combine flavours and colours that complement one another to seduce the palate, delight the eye, fuel conversation, and foster that feel-good factor.

Measurements

1 teaspoon = 5 millilitres
1 tablespoon = 15 millilitres
1/2 cup = 125 millilitres
1 cup = 250 millilitres
1 gram = 0.035274 ounces (16 ounces = 1 pound)
1 kilogram = 2.2 pounds

To convert grams to ounces, multiply the gram amount by 0.035274
To convert kilograms to pounds, multiply the kilogram amount by 2.2

Dinner Date

Stuffed chicken breasts with beetroot relish and parsnip crisps

Serves 6; divide quantities in half for 2 people.

6 chicken breasts, preferably organic, without skin or bones
60 grams butter
3 tablespoons olive oil
6 slices Fontina or Camembert cheese
toothpicks or cocktail sticks to seal

For the stuffing:
2 tablespoons peanut oil
1 onion, finely chopped
1 clove garlic, peeled and crushed
1 tablespoon grated root ginger
1 teaspoon powdered cumin
6 fresh coriander stalks, chopped
2 teaspoons palm or brown sugar
salt and pepper to taste

To serve:
beetroot relish
parsnip crisps
wilted spinach

Preheat oven to 200 degrees C/400 degrees F.

To make the stuffing, heat peanut oil in a pan and add the onion, garlic, ginger, and cumin. Fry to soften, and continue cooking until all the liquid has evaporated. Add the chopped coriander stalks and sugar, and season to taste with salt and pepper. Stir for another 2 minutes before removing from stovetop. Set aside to cool.

Cut pockets into the chicken breasts, and insert one slice of cheese into each pocket. Add a little mixture, and then seal closed with one or two toothpicks. Heat the butter and olive oil in an ovenproof pan large enough to hold the six chicken breasts. Season the chicken and place it in the pan. Turn the chicken breasts carefully so that both sides are brown (no longer than 1–2 minutes on each side).

Put the pan into the oven or transfer chicken and juices into a similar-size oven dish. Cook for 15 minutes, remove from oven, and transfer to serving plates. If cheese has oozed out during cooking, stir it into the pan juices before spooning a small amount over each breast.

Serve with beetroot relish, parsnip crisps, and wilted spinach.

Cook's note:
If time allows, stuff the chicken breasts a day ahead, wrap in cling film, and leave overnight in the refrigerator. (Cooling the chicken prevents it from drying out during cooking and also helps to keep the cheese from melting too quickly.)

For neater parcels, prepare the chicken as follows: Place breasts between two sheets of cling film. Use a meat mallet to flatten as thin as possible, without making holes in the chicken, which would allow the stuffing to escape. Remove the top layer of cling film and divide the spice mixture between the six breasts, spreading over the centre of each. Top each with a piece of cheese. Fold one side over the mixture, fold over each adjacent side, and then fold over the last side. Secure closed with toothpicks or a cocktail stick. Wrap each breast in the bottom layer of cling film, and refrigerate overnight. Cook as above.

Beetroot relish

Earthy and sweet, beetroot's deep pink hue alone gives it the edge for a romantic meal, but it might bring a little more to the table thanks to its high level of the libido-boosting trace mineral boron.

3 young medium beetroots, peeled
30 grams butter
2 tablespoons orange marmalade
1 large orange, juiced
1/2 lemon, juiced, plus extra to taste
a pinch salt

Cut the beetroot into fine julienne (use a mandolin or the julienne grater on a food processor). Melt thc buttcr and marmalade with the orange juice in a pan, and bring to the boil. Add the julienned beetroot, and turn down the heat. Simmer for about 10 minutes. Add the lemon juice and a pinch of salt. Cook further to reduce the liquid until it becomes a syrupy glaze. Taste for seasoning and texture (it should be slightly chewy). Add salt and lemon juice as required. If not cooked to your liking, add a little water and further reduce.

Parsnip crisps

1 parsnip for every 2 people
vegetable oil for deep-frying
sea salt

Shave the parsnips lengthwise using a mandolin or vegetable peeler. Place 7–8 centimetres of oil in a heavy-based, medium-sized saucepan. Heat to around 180 degrees C/350 degrees F (if you don't have a thermometer, the oil should be ready when a breadcrumb dropped into it turns brown in 25–30 seconds). Add the parsnip shavings, making sure that they don't overlap. Deep-fry, in batches if necessary, until crisp and golden brown (do not allow to turn dark brown or they will taste burnt). Remove with a slotted spoon, drain on a paper towel and keep warm. Sprinkle with sea salt before serving.

Chilli and chocolate almond cakes

The combination of chilli and chocolate is not an original idea. Centuries ago, the Aztecs enjoyed a cold drink combining ground cocoa beans and chilli that the emperor Montezuma drank for its aphrodisiacal powers before visiting his harem. He was definitely onto something, as chillies have been proven to release energising endorphins and to quicken the heart rate, while the chemical phenylethylamine in chocolate creates a sense of excitement and euphoria. These quick and easy chocolate cakes are therefore just the thing to spice up a romantic soirée.

Serves 4–6.

100 grams butter, cubed
80 grams dark chocolate, broken into squares
1 tablespoon honey
80 grams icing sugar, plus more for dusting
4 tablespoons all-purpose flour
1/4 teaspoon cayenne pepper
1/4 teaspoon chilli powder
60 grams ground almonds
1 egg yolk
3 egg whites

To serve:
ginger ice cream, or crème fraiche and a few pieces preserved stem ginger
4–6 sprigs mint

Preheat oven to 180 degrees C/350 degrees F. Grease six muffin moulds, or prepare four ramekins as follows: cut rounds of baking parchment to fit the bases of the ramekins, butter the ramekins' bases and sides, and place one round of parchment paper into each.

Place the butter, chocolate, and honey in a bowl over a saucepan of simmering water (making sure the bowl doesn't touch the water to prevent the chocolate from burning). Stir every now and then until melted. Set the mixture aside to cool.

Once the chocolate mixture is cool, sift the icing sugar, flour, and spices onto it. Add the ground almonds, and stir gently until well combined – it will be a moist paste. Stir in the egg yolk until well combined.

In a separate bowl, manually whisk the egg whites until frothy but not stiff (the whites should still have small bubbles and not be very smooth). Gently fold the whites into the chocolate mixture until incorporated. Spoon the mixture into four prepared ramekins or six muffin moulds, and bake for 15 minutes or until firm and springy on top (ramekins might need a few more minutes). Remove from the oven, and set the cakes aside until cool enough to handle.

To remove the cakes from the ramekins, use a small, sharp, thin-bladed knife to run around the sides of the cakes. Pick up each ramekin and turn onto the palm of your hand, and then turn it the right way up on individual serving plates. Serve with a dusting of icing sugar, a scoop of ginger ice cream, and a sprig of mint. Alternatively, substitute the ice cream with a dollop of crème fraiche and a few pieces of preserved stem ginger.

Cook's note:
The ramekins produce nice-looking flat-sided cakes, whereas the muffin moulds are quicker to prepare and make more. Opt for a silicone muffin tray, which makes removing the delicate cakes easier. The recipe can also be made without the spices.

Ginger and vanilla ice cream

Being a digestive, ginger is the perfect end to a meal, while homemade ice cream always impresses and is a cinch to whip up with an ice-cream maker. It's possible to make ice cream without a machine, but the results can be icy, so if you don't have one, opt for a good-quality, shop-bought alternative.

Serves 4–6.

1 1/2 cups full-cream milk
1 1/2 cups cream
1 vanilla bean
6 egg yolks
3/4 cup caster sugar
6–8 pieces preserved ginger* in syrup, drained and chopped
** Preserved ginger is available in good supermarkets and in Chinese and Asian grocery stores.*

Place the milk and cream in a saucepan. Split the vanilla bean and drop it into the liquid. Place the saucepan over medium-low heat and bring the liquid slowly to just under the boil. Remove from stovetop.

Remove the vanilla pod, and scrape the seeds into the milk and cream mixture. In a heatproof bowl, beat the egg yolks and sugar until pale in colour. Add the warm milk and cream to the egg mixture, and beat until well mixed. Return the mixture to a clean saucepan, and stir over a medium-low heat, being careful not to boil, until the custard has thickened and coats the back of a spoon (around 10 minutes). Cool the mixture by standing the saucepan in a large bowl of ice blocks. Add the chopped ginger.

When mixture is cool, churn in an ice-cream machine, following the manufacturer's instructions. Scoop into a suitable container, and freeze for a minimum of 2 hours before serving.

Seafood Barbecue

While a gas barbecue is acceptable, charcoal adds a lovely smoky flavour to fish or meat and is definitely preferable. Build a decent fire by piling up charcoal in the middle of the barbecue, along with a couple of firelighters broken into pieces. Light these, and then wait until the flames have died and the coals are glowing red before you start cooking (30–40 minutes). Spread out the coals, and test their readiness by holding your hand 15 centimetres above them; if you can keep it there for 2 seconds, you're good to go. A decent fire should last an hour to an hour and a half, but if at any time it's too cool to cook, add coals and wait 12–15 minutes. To prevent sticking, make sure the barbecue grill's bars are clean, and brush them with a little oil. You'll need tongs, a long-handled fork, a brush for basting, a spray bottle or water pistol to douse the fire, and a hinged barbecue grid.

Watermelon Martinis

Makes 2 cocktails (multiply quantities to make more).

For the simple syrup:
1 cup white sugar
1 cup water

For the cocktail:
1 cup watermelon juice or 2 cups seedless watermelon cubes
1/4 cup vodka
1/4 cup watermelon schnapps
juice of 1 lime
1 cup ice cubes

Make the simple syrup ahead of time by combining the sugar with water in a saucepan and bringing to a boil. Stir until sugar has dissolved. Allow to cool.

Puree watermelon cubes in a blender until smooth. Pour through a sieve, pressing on the mixture with a spoon to extract all the liquid.

Pour 1 cup of the juice over ice in a cocktail shaker. Add vodka, watermelon schnapps, 1 tablespoon of simple syrup, and lime juice. Cover and shake until the outside of the shaker has frosted. Strain into Martini glasses.

As an alternative to using a cocktail shaker, you can whizz up all the ingredients with ice cubes in a blender and then serve as above. This approach is ideal for parties, as you can make larger quantities at a time, plus the thicker icy texture means it goes further.

Oysters with chicory leaves

Chicory leaves beautifully complement the fresh, subtle, sea-salty flavour of oysters. They also add visual impact and are a good idea for cocktail parties since they enable your guests to pick up the oysters with the chicory leaves, leaving the shells on the platter.

Serves 6–8 as an amuse-bouche.

18 oysters
18 chicory leaves
Tabasco sauce
lemon wedges
black pepper

Rinse closed oysters under running water to remove any dirt from the cracks. Holding the oyster with a thick cloth, use an oyster shucker or strong, short-bladed knife to ease the shell open a crack by inserting and twisting. Run the knife around the underside of the top shell to cut the muscle attaching it to the bottom shell. Pull the top shell off, and then slide the knife under the oyster to detach it from the bottom shell.

Drain juices, slip a chicory leaf under each oyster, and serve on the half shell atop crushed ice, with Tabasco sauce, lemon wedges, and black pepper on the side.

Cook's note:
As an alternative to Tabasco and lemon wedges, serve the oysters with a classic mignonette sauce made by mixing together 1/4 cup red or white wine vinegar, 1 tablespoon finely chopped shallots or red onion, 1/2 teaspoon freshly ground black pepper, and salt to taste. Chill for at least 1 hour before drizzling over shucked oysters.

Turmeric bread

Unless you're in the wilderness, baking bread over a fire is more hassle than it's worth, so make this subtly spiced loaf ahead of time and concentrate on barbecuing the important stuff.

5 1/2 cups stoneground white bread flour
1 teaspoon turmeric
2 tablespoons sugar
2 teaspoons salt
1 (10-gram) sachet dried yeast
1/4 cup vegetable oil (or a combination of sunflower and olive oil)
450 millilitres lukewarm water
2 egg yolks
egg wash: 1 egg mixed with 1 tablespoon milk

Preheat oven to 180 degrees C/350 degrees F.

Sift the flour, turmeric, sugar, salt, and yeast into the bowl of an electric mixer. Separately, mix together the oil, water, and egg yolks. Pour the liquid mixture into the flour mixture, and knead well with the dough hook of the electric mixer. Cover with cling film, and put in a warm place for one hour to rise.

Punch down, and knead again for 3 or 4 minutes. Divide in two and shape into balls. Place on a large oiled baking tray, and press down to create flat rounds. Put in a warm place to rise again for an hour.

Brush on the egg wash very lightly so as not to lose any air. Bake for 25–30 minutes. When ready, the bread will sound hollow when rapped with your knuckles.

Lobster with coriander butter and chilli-papaya salsa

The best type of lobster for barbecuing is the marine rock lobster, or crayfish, as it's known in Australia, New Zealand, and South Africa (not to be confused with freshwater crawfish). These have smaller claws than those associated with the United States and Maine, and most of the flesh is on the lobsters' bodies, making it easier to cook them over coals. If using Maine-style lobsters, crack the claws (leaving the shell on) before barbecuing to ensure that they cook through.

1 lobster or crayfish per person, or just lobster tails

For the coriander butter:
150 grams butter at room temperature
1/2 cup fresh coriander, chopped
2 teaspoons ground coriander
1 teaspoon lime zest
1 teaspoon freshly ground black pepper
1 teaspoon salt

For the salsa:
1 teaspoon brown sugar
1 tablespoon fish sauce
1 1/2 tablespoons lemon or lime juice
1 clove garlic, crushed
1 teaspoon fresh ginger, minced or grated
1 1/2 teaspoons lemongrass, finely chopped
1–2 red chillies, finely chopped
3 spring onions, white parts only, thinly sliced
1 medium-large papaya, deseeded, peeled, and chopped into small pieces
bunch fresh coriander, chopped

Make the coriander butter ahead of time by placing all the ingredients in a food processor and blending to form a smooth paste. Spoon the mixture along the middle of an oblong piece of wax paper, and roll up to form a log. Chill in the fridge for at least 2 hours.

Next, prepare the salsa. Place the sugar in a large bowl with the fish sauce and lemon or lime juice, and stir to dissolve. Add all other salsa ingredients, in the order in which they appear. Mix and transfer to a serving bowl.

If using whole lobsters, cut them in half lengthways as follows: Hold the lobster with the underside facing you. Using a very sharp knife or kitchen shears, cut it in half through the middle and right through the head, giving two perfect halves. Remove the intestinal tract and any green matter in the head with a fork. If using lobster tails, hold the tail with the underside facing you and, with kitchen scissors, cut away the membrane. To prevent the tail from curling while cooking, hold it on both ends and then bend it backwards to crack the shell – this will keep it flat.

Brush flesh with a little olive oil, and then place the crayfish on a barbecue grid, shell side down. Cook for around 5 minutes on this side, and then turn over and cook for 4–5 minutes or until the flesh is an opaque colour. (Cooking the lobsters shell side down first allows the juices to collect in the shell and keeps the lobsters moist.)

Transfer to a serving platter or to individual plates. Place a slice of the coriander butter on each lobster half while hot. Serve with papaya salsa on the side.

Whole barbecued linefish, served with salsa verde

While barbecuing fish in foil with herbs and wine is popular, this can result in a watery stew. It is far better to grill the fish directly over the coals, which will produce crispy skin, firm flesh, and a smoky flavour.

Serves 4 comfortably or makes 6 small portions. Barbecue two fish for larger crowds.

1 whole firm-textured (1 1/2–2 kilogram) linefish (snapper, rock cod, and barracuda are good), cleaned, gutted, and scaled

For the marinade:
2 teaspoons paprika
1 teaspoon turmeric
1 teaspoon chilli flakes or chopped fresh red chillies
2 cloves garlic, crushed using a pestle and mortar with 1 teaspoon sea salt
1 1/2 teaspoons lemon zest
2 tablespoons olive oil
1 tablespoon honey
freshly ground black pepper

For the cavity:
1 handful each of dill, basil, and Italian parsley
1 red onion, sliced
1 lemon, sliced

To serve:
lemon wedges
salsa verde

In a small bowl, mix together marinade ingredients to form a paste. Cut two or three slits 1 centimetre deep into the thickest part of the fish on both sides, and rub the marinade over the fish. Cover and refrigerate for 1–2 hours.

Before barbecuing, fill the fish's belly cavity with the fresh herbs, onion, and lemon slices. Place in a well-oiled hinged barbecue grill or fish basket for easy turning. Cook for 7–10 minutes on each side, depending on the fish's size (as a rule, a whole fish needs to be cooked for 15–20 minutes per kilogram). While there's nothing worse than undercooked fish, it's imperative not to overcook it, as it becomes dry very quickly. Test it by inserting a fork into one of the slits. If it's opaque all the way through and flakes easily, it's ready. If any part is transparent, cook it for another couple of minutes on each side.

Carefully remove the fish from the hinged grid, easing the skin away from the grid with a knife to prevent it from sticking and coming away. Place on a platter with lemon wedges and fresh herbs for garnish, and serve with salsa verde. To divide up the fish at the table, cut the top side of the fish down the middle with a knife or serving spoon, and then transfer each side with a fork and spoon to individual plates. Remove the bone by pulling it up from the tail side and snapping it off, or turn fish over and divide the bottom half in two.

Salsa verde

2 cloves garlic, crushed in a pestle and mortar with 1/2 teaspoon sea salt
1/2 cup capers, finely chopped
1/2 cup green olives, finely chopped
1/4 cup pickled gherkins, finely chopped
6 anchovy fillets, finely chopped
1 cup Italian parsley, finely chopped
1/2 cup basil leaves, finely chopped
1/2 cup mint leaves, finely chopped
1 tablespoon Dijon mustard
3–4 tablespoons red wine vinegar or lemon juice
up to 1 cup extra virgin olive oil
black pepper to taste

Combine all the chopped dry ingredients in a bowl. Mix in the mustard and 3 tablespoons vinegar or lemon juice, and then gradually add the olive oil until it's the desired consistency. Season with pepper and add more vinegar or lemon juice as desired, ensuring that the flavour is not too sharp. Place in a serving dish.

Cook's note:
Chopping everything manually creates a nice crunchy-textured salsa, but to save time you can also blend everything in a food processor, which produces an equally tasty, smooth sauce that can be drizzled over the fish.

Grilled octopus with baby tomatoes and herbs

Octopus can be rubbery, so it's essential to get a good-quality, tenderised specimen from your fishmonger. Alternatively, a good way to tenderise it yourself is to store it in the freezer for two months before cooking. For delectably juicy barbecued tentacles – charred on the outside, tender in the centre – the octopus should be boiled ahead of being grilled.

Serves 6.

1 whole octopus (1–1 1/2 kilograms)
1 small red onion, sliced
2 bay leaves
1 tablespoon whole black peppercorns
3 tablespoons red wine vinegar
olive oil
sea salt and freshly ground black pepper to taste

To serve:
1 package baby tomatoes, halved
1/2 cup parsley, roughly chopped
1 red onion, finely chopped
red wine vinegar
olive oil

Ahead of the barbecue, wash the octopus under cold running water to remove any sand, paying special attention to its suckers, and then cut off its head (or ask your fishmonger to do this for you). Place the octopus in a large pot and cover with cold water. Add sliced red onion, bay leaves, peppercorns, and vinegar. Bring to the boil. Reduce heat and simmer for 50–90 minutes or until a skewer slides easily into the thickest part of a tentacle. Cut up into individual tentacles and set aside to barbecue.

When the barbecue is at its optimum temperature, brush each tentacle generously with olive oil, and then place on grid over the fire. Grill for 3–4 minutes on each side. Cut tentacles into pieces of around 3 1/2 centimetres in length, and season with salt and pepper. Toss with baby tomatoes, parsley, and chopped onion, plus a splash or two of red wine vinegar and olive oil.

Cook's note:
As an alternative to serving the octopus as described above, cut the tentacles into larger chunks, sprinkle with chopped parsley, and serve with chilli mayonnaise (see recipe for mayonnaise under Floral Feast).

Minty North African roasted aubergine salad

Serves 6 as a side dish.

6 medium-sized narrow aubergines, not globe-shaped
salt for sweating
olive oil for roasting (enough to coat aubergines)
1 tablespoon *ras al hanout* or other North African spice mix

For the dressing:
4 tablespoons extra virgin olive oil
2 tablespoons lemon juice
2 teaspoons honey
salt and pepper to taste

To serve:
bunch fresh mint (around 1/2 cup), chopped

Preheat oven to 180 degrees C/350 degrees F. Remove aubergine stems, but do not peel. Cut into four wedges lengthways. Sprinkle wedges with salt. Leave to sweat for 30 minutes, and then rinse in a colander and pat dry.

Place wedges, cut side up, on an oiled baking tray. Brush flesh generously with olive oil to coat, and sprinkle over ras al hanout spice mix or alternative. Roast for 20 minutes, and then shake pan and turn wedges in the oil, or brush with extra oil, to ensure that they are well coated and don't dry out. Roast for another 15 minutes, by which time they should be brown and soft. Test with a fork. If not soft enough, continue roasting for an additional 5–10 minutes. Remove from oven and arrange, cut side up, on a serving platter.

In a small bowl, combine dressing ingredients and mix well. Pour over aubergines while still warm, and allow to cool to room temperature. Sprinkle over chopped mint before serving.

Cook's note:
You should be able to find ras al hanout in good supermarkets and Middle Eastern stores. Otherwise, whip up this quick version yourself. In a dry frying pan, toast 1 teaspoon each whole black peppercorns, whole cloves, coriander seeds, and cumin seeds to release their aroma. Pound to a powder using a pestle and mortar or spice grinder, and then combine with 1 teaspoon each ground ginger, cinnamon, paprika, and turmeric, plus 1/4 teaspoon ground nutmeg. Store in a sealed container.

New potato and watercress salad

Serves 6 as an accompaniment.

800 grams new potatoes, skin on
2 1/2 teaspoons black mustard seeds
5 tablespoons extra virgin olive oil
2 tablespoons white wine vinegar
1 package watercress, broken up into pieces
sea salt

Boil the potatoes in salted water for approximately 12 minutes or until soft when pierced with a fork. Drain and cut in half lengthways.

Crush the mustard seeds, using a pestle and mortar, and then place in a bowl that's large enough to take the potatoes. Add the olive oil, vinegar, and salt. Whisk to combine well. Add the warm potatoes to the bowl and mix, taking care not to break them or tear their skin.

Once cooled to room temperature, transfer to a serving dish, add the watercress, and toss gently.

Cook's note:
You can substitute the watercress with chopped parsley or baby rocket leaves. For a quick alternative, although not as interesting, replace the mustard seeds with a tablespoon of grainy Dijon mustard.

Vanilla bavarois with fresh tropical fruits

A barbecue simply demands a fresh, fruity finale, and this bavarois is a deliciously creamy accompaniment to nature's colourful bounty.

Serves 6–8.

2 cups whipping cream
15–20 grams gelatine powder
3 tablespoons cold water
2 cups full cream milk
1 vanilla pod
8 egg yolks
125 grams caster sugar
pinch salt
4 tablespoons caster sugar (for later use)
almond oil or flavourless vegetable oil for greasing

To serve:
a mix of fresh tropical fruit such as pineapple, mango, guavas, and lychees (tinned lychees are fine if fresh are not available)
pulp of 4 or 5 passion fruits (or a tin of passion-fruit pulp)

To ensure it sets, make the dessert a day ahead.

Chill the cream in the fridge.

Mix the gelatine with 3 tablespoons cold water, and then set aside.

Heat the milk and vanilla pod in a double boiler or heavy-based saucepan over medium heat. Meanwhile, in a large heat-resistant bowl, whisk together the egg yolks and caster sugar until thick and smooth. Remove the vanilla pod from the hot milk, and then pour onto the egg and sugar mixture. Stir until well mixed, and then strain back into the double boiler or saucepan.

Stir over a medium heat until the custard coats the back of the spoon. Do not boil at any stage. Remove from the stove and immediately stir in the soaked gelatine until it is completely dissolved.

Stand the saucepan in a basin of cold water and ice blocks. When the custard has cooled, pour it into a glass bowl and put it into the fridge until completely cold. When the custard is just beginning to set, remove it from the fridge.

Whip the chilled cream with the remaining 4 tablespoons sugar until it reaches soft-peak stage. Fold the whipped cream into the custard. Oil a fluted dessert mould or heat-resistant glass bowl with almond oil or flavourless vegetable oil. Pour in the custard and set in the fridge overnight.

Shortly before serving, briefly dip the dessert mould or bowl into hot water. Turn onto a platter, and surround with the chopped tropical fruit. Finally, spoon the passion fruit over the bavarois and fruits.

Cook's note:
This is also delicious served with mixed berries (strawberries, raspberries, blackberries, blueberries).

Midweek Meal

Caramelised onion, potato, spinach, and goat's cheese frittata

Quick, easy, tasty, comforting – this is the perfect recipe for a relaxed post-work supper or a light lunch.

Serves 4.

cooking spray
1 tablespoon butter
1 tablespoon olive oil
1 large red onion, peeled and thinly sliced
1 1/2–2 cups just-cooked waxy potatoes, peeled and cubed
2 cups baby spinach
6 large eggs
4 large egg whites
1/2 cup full-cream milk
2 tablespoons fresh basil, finely chopped
1 cup soft goat's cheese or feta, crumbled, or 1/2 cup provolone or cheddar, grated
1/2 cup Kalamata olives, pitted and halved (optional)
salt and freshly ground black pepper to taste

Preheat oven to 180 degrees C/350 degrees F. Spray the sides of a thick-bottomed stainless steel pan (that has straight sides and an ovenproof handle) with cooking spray.

Heat butter with olive oil in the pan. Add onion and fry over high heat for 1 minute. Turn down the heat to low and cook slowly for 15 minutes or until caramelised. Remove pan from heat, add potato and spinach, and gently mix together.

Combine the eggs and egg whites with the milk, and beat until light and frothy. Add chopped basil to the egg mixture, and season with salt and pepper. Pour the egg mixture into the pan. Sprinkle over cheese and olives, if using. Cook on the stovetop for 1–2 minute to set on the bottom, and then place in preheated oven.

Bake for 20 minutes or until centre is set. Remove from the oven. Place under a preheated grill for 3–4 minutes or until golden brown and puffed up. Cut into wedges and serve immediately with a green salad.

Cook's note:

For speed and convenience, peel and cube your potatoes before boiling. Place in a pot, cover with cold water, add 1 teaspoon salt and bring to the boil then reduce heat to medium and simmer uncovered for around 10 minutes. Test potatoes with the tip of a knife to ensure they're firm (undercooked is better than overcooked). Drain immediately. As a brunch alternative, leave out the olives, replace basil with dill and serve with smoked salmon.

Green salad with chive dressing

Since the frittata is loaded with flavour, keep the salad simple. A mix of greens is perfect, with a chive dressing adding a nice bite. Chives are easy to grow in a pot on the windowsill and lovely to have on hand for flavouring and garnishing dishes, along with their pretty purple edible flowers.

Serves 4–6 as an accompaniment.

2–3 cups or a package of mixed baby salad leaves (lamb's lettuce, frisée, rocket, red chard, etc.)
a handful chive flowers (optional)

For the dressing:
1 teaspoon Dijon mustard
1/2 teaspoon honey
coarse sea salt
freshly ground black pepper
1 tablespoon white wine vinegar
3 tablespoons extra virgin olive oil
1 tablespoon chives, thinly sliced

Wash greens and combine in a salad bowl. In a separate bowl, whisk together the mustard, honey, salt, pepper, and vinegar. Slowly add the olive oil, whisking constantly so the dressing emulsifies and thickens, and then stir in the chives. Allow to sit for at least 10 minutes so that the flavours develop.

Whisk again before dressing the salad. Add around 2 tablespoons of the dressing to the greens, and toss gently but well so that the leaves are thoroughly coated. Add more if required, but avoid overdressing (you don't want heavy, soggy leaves). Transfer to a salad bowl or individual plates, and sprinkle over chive flowers, if using.

Long, Lazy Weekend Lunch

Chilled pea soup

With its fresh taste, vibrant green colour, and pretty floral garnish, this easy soup is summer in a bowl – the perfect thing to kick off a sunny lunch.

Serves 6 as a starter.

cooking spray
2 teaspoons butter
1 cup leeks, white part only, cleaned and chopped
3 cups vegetable stock
1 kilogram frozen peas
1/2 cup mint leaves, de-stemmed
1/2 teaspoon salt
1/2 teaspoon black pepper

To serve:
sour cream or yoghurt
lemon zest
pea tendrils or chopped chives
handful fresh pansies, violets, and/or violas (optional)

Spray a large pot with cooking oil. Add butter and leeks, and cook over medium heat until leeks are soft (7–10 minutes). Add stock, and bring to the boil. Add peas and, once stock has returned to the boil, cook for 3–5 minutes. Take pot off stovetop, and add mint, salt, and pepper. Blend with stick blender. Strain and set aside to cool.

Once cool, put in a covered container and place in the fridge to chill for at least 2 hours. To serve, pour into bowls, add a dollop of sour cream, and top with lemon zest and pea tendrils or chives. If available, finish off with a sprinkling of pansies and violas. Serve with croutons or crusty bread.

Roast loin of lamb with juniper berries and port jus

The key component of gin, juniper berries have a citrusy, peppery taste, which also beautifully complements meat dishes, taking this roast up a notch, and giving it a bit of pizzazz.

Serves 6–8.

1 loin of lamb, divided into two (this will give you two slim rolls)
2 tablespoons olive oil
2 tablespoons lemon juice
3 teaspoons (or more to taste) crushed garlic
salt and pepper
2 onions
1 cup white wine
stock, if required

For the stuffing:
2 tablespoons olive oil
2 tablespoons butter
1 large onion, finely chopped
100 grams walnuts, finely chopped
2 tablespoons raisins
1 tablespoon fresh rosemary leaves, finely chopped
salt and pepper
6 tablespoons fresh breadcrumbs or enough to bind the mixture
10 juniper berries, dried or fresh

For the jus:
1 cup white wine
60 millilitres port
6 anchovy fillets
1–2 tablespoons redcurrant jelly
1–2 tablespoons cold butter

Buy and prepare lamb 2 days ahead. If your butcher is amenable, ask him or her to roll the lamb for you, using your stuffing.

For the stuffing:
Heat the oil and butter in a frying pan, and fry the onion until soft and golden. Remove from heat. Mix in the walnuts, raisins, chopped rosemary, and breadcrumbs. Add salt and pepper to taste. The mixture should be fairly firm; if not firm enough, add more breadcrumbs, making sure the stuffing isn't dry, as it will firm up more when cooking.

Divide the stuffing in half and spread on each loin before rolling and tying using kitchen string (or get your butcher to do this for you). Press juniper berries all the way along the seam of the rolled lamb, pushing them in about 2 1/2 centimetres.

For the lamb:
Put the two rolled loins into a refrigerator-friendly container with a lid, and rub with olive oil, lemon juice, crushed garlic, salt, and pepper. Refrigerate, covered, for 2 days, turning in the juices twice a day. Remove lamb from the fridge 2 hours before roasting. Preheat oven to 180 degrees C/350 degrees F. Thickly slice the onions, and place in a lidded roasting pan. Put the lamb on top of the onions with the juices, and add white wine. Cover with lid and roast for 2 1/2 hours, checking on the liquid every half hour and adding stock if the liquid has evaporated. Remove cover and roast for an additional half hour. Transfer the lamb to a serving platter/board. Cover loosely with foil and allow to rest while you make the jus.

For the jus:
If there is a lot of fat, remove it from the roasting juices using a fat-separating jug or large kitchen spoon. Place the roasting tin over medium heat on the stovetop. Add white wine. Boil the mixture while scraping all the browned bits off the base and sides of the tin. Add port and then mash in the anchovy fillets and redcurrant jelly. Whisk in the cold butter, and then strain into a jug. Slice the lamb thickly. Serve with vegetables and port jus.

Roast potatoes

These roast potatoes are rather decadent as they're fried before roasting, which also adds an extra step and pan to the process, but the results are unfailingly deliciously crispy.

Serves 6 as a side dish.

1 kilogram medium-sized starchy potatoes (Maris Piper and Desiree are good), peeled
1 teaspoon salt for boiling
1 tablespoon all-purpose flour
sunflower or groundnut oil for frying
sea salt to serve

Preheat oven to 180 degrees C/350 degrees F.

Cut potatoes into quarters or halves, depending on their size and then rinse well in a colander under cold running water to remove surface starch. Place in a saucepan, cover with cold water and add salt. Bring to the boil and cook on high for a further 4–5 minutes (they should be soft on the outside but still feel firm in the middle when pierced with a skewer). Drain in a colander and then dry out in the saucepan over a low heat. Place lid on the saucepan and shake gently to roughen up the edges a bit – the secret to a crispy crust. Sprinkle with flour and shake again to ensure all potatoes have a dusting. Place on a plate to cool for 15 minutes. Heat 1/2–1 centimetre oil in a deep, flat-sided frying pan. Add potatoes and fry over a medium heat for 10 minutes, ensuring they're browned all over. Using a slotted spoon, place potatoes in a roasting tin in a single layer and roast for 25 minutes or until golden brown and crispy, turning over halfway through. Sprinkle with sea salt and serve immediately.

Oven-glazed baby carrots

Serves 6 as a side dish.

700–800 grams baby carrots, trimmed, with 1/2 centimetre of leaves left on
juice of 1 orange
2 tablespoons honey
1 tablespoon olive oil
sea salt
1 tablespoon butter
chopped parsley to garnish

Preheat oven to 180 degrees C/350 degrees F. Place carrots in a roasting tin. Add orange juice, drizzle over the honey, and then mix. Pour over olive oil, season with salt, add a few dollops of butter, and roast for 20–25 minutes or until sticky and slightly blackened. Sprinkle over chopped parsley. Serve immediately.

Green beans with walnut oil

Serves 6 as a side dish.

800 grams green beans, washed and trimmed
1 1/2 tablespoons walnut oil
sea salt and coarsely ground black pepper

Bring a saucepan of salted water to the boil, and add the green beans. Cook uncovered (this helps to maintain the beans' colour) for 5 minutes or until tender with a bit of crunch. Drain in a colander and then return to the pan and dry out over low heat. Add walnut oil, salt and pepper, and toss through. Serve immediately.

Vanilla and cardamom panna cotta with rose-flavoured rhubarb compote

Pretty in pink, rhubarb's colour alone makes it a good dessert option, added to which its tartness offsets the richness of creamy panna cotta. Dead easy to make, this dessert looks deceptively sophisticated on the plate, making it an impressive lunch or dinner-party finale.

Serves 6.

almond oil or flavourless vegetable oil for greasing
400 millilitres double cream
350 millilitres single cream or full-fat milk
1 vanilla pod
4 green cardamom pods, slightly crushed
75 grams caster sugar
4 sheets leaf gelatine

To serve:
rhubarb compote
handful pesticide-free rose petals or sprigs of mint

Grease 6 (125-millilitre) metal dariole moulds with oil, and set aside. Put the double cream and single cream or milk in a medium-sized pot. Split the vanilla pod lengthways, scrape the seeds into the pan, and then add the pod, along with the cardamom pods. Add the sugar. Heat until simmering. Remove from stovetop and infuse for 30 minutes.

Meanwhile, soak the gelatine in a bowl of cold water for 5 minutes. Squeeze out excess liquid with your hands. Strain the cream mixture to remove vanilla and cardamom pods, and reheat. Remove from heat just before boiling. Add the gelatine, stirring until dissolved.

Divide the mixture between the six greased moulds (not all the way to the top). Cover with cling film, and place in fridge to chill and set for 4–6 hours – but no longer or else they won't be lovely and wobbly. Just before serving, dip the moulds into hot water for a couple of seconds and then turn the panna cottas onto plates (if they don't come out immediately, tap the mould with a spoon, hold the plate and mould tightly together, and shake). Place a large spoonful of rhubarb compote on each plate, and garnish with a sprinkling of rose petals or a sprig of mint.

Rose-flavoured rhubarb compote

600 grams rhubarb, washed and trimmed (do not peel)
85 grams caster sugar
1 teaspoon rose water mixed with 3 tablespoons water

Cut the rhubarb stalks into 4- to 5-centimetre pieces, and place them in a sauté pan or a medium-sized saucepan. Sprinkle over the sugar and then add rose water mixed with water. Stir to combine. Cover and simmer over a medium-low heat for around 7 minutes. Shake the pan from time to time to prevent sticking, but resist the temptation to stir, since this will cause the rhubarb to break up (it becomes soft very quickly). Taste and cook for a couple more minutes if not tender enough. Remove from the heat and allow to cool before serving with panna cotta or ice cream.

Sunday Brunch

French toast à la bananas Foster

French toast, or *pain perdu* (lost bread), was invented in France as a means of using up leftover bread, and was traditionally eaten on feast days such as Easter. Now enjoyed around the world throughout the year, it is still best made with slightly stale bread, since fresh bread will fall apart. This variation of the classic, topped with boozy bananas Foster, is a sublime brunch option for the sweet tooth.

Serves 4–6.

For the French toast:
4 large eggs
2 tablespoons caster sugar
1 cup full-cream milk
1/2 cup heavy cream
1 teaspoon ground cinnamon
1 teaspoon vanilla essence
4 tablespoons butter, plus extra if necessary
2 tablespoons vegetable oil
8 thick (2 centimetre) slices 1- or 2-day-old white bread (Portuguese loaf is good) or brioche

For the bananas Foster:
70 grams butter
2/3 cup brown sugar
1/2 teaspoon ground cinnamon
6 small bananas, cut in half lengthways and then halved across
1/4 cup plus 1 tablespoon dark rum
1 tablespoon lemon juice

To serve:
1 cup crème fraiche or thick Greek yoghurt

1 1/2 teaspoons finely grated orange zest
sprigs of mint or spearmint

Preheat oven to 80 degrees C/150 degrees F. In a small bowl, combine the crème fraiche or yoghurt with the orange zest, and set aside.

To prepare the French toast, whisk together eggs and sugar until well blended. Add the milk, cream, cinnamon, and vanilla essence, and whisk to combine. Lay the bread or brioche slices in a rectangular dish large enough to hold all the slices in a single layer. Pour the egg mixture over the bread slices, and set aside while you make the banana sauce.

To make the bananas Foster, heat the butter, sugar, and cinnamon in a frying pan over a low heat, stirring until the sugar dissolves. Do not be tempted to speed things up by raising the temperature, as this will cause the sugar to caramelise too quickly and potentially burn. Once the sugar is dissolved and the mixture has a caramel-like consistency, turn heat up slightly and add the banana pieces. Cook until they begin to soften and turn brown (approximately 1 minute each side). Add 1/4 cup of the rum and heat for around 1 minute, and then set alight with a match or, if using gas, tilt the pan so that the rum ignites. When the flame dies, carefully stir in remaining rum and lemon juice, and then set aside until ready to serve.

To cook the French toast, first turn the bread or brioche slices over carefully with an egg lifter to make sure all the milk is absorbed. Melt some of the butter with some of the oil in a large frying pan. Lift the soaked bread slices carefully with an egg lifter and place in the pan. Fry in batches for around 2 minutes each side or until golden brown, adding more butter as required. Keep the French toast warm on a baking tray in the oven while you heat the remaining butter and oil, and repeat the process with the rest of the bread.

Remove French toast from oven. Place 1 or 2 slices per person onto plates. Warm the bananas Foster, and spoon over the French toast slices. Top with a dollop of orange-zest-infused crème fraiche or yoghurt, and finish off with a sprig of mint.

Floral Feast

Fashionable in Victorian times, edible flowers have recently made a kitchen comeback and are finding their way into everything from cocktails to cakes. Apart from adding subtle flavour and aroma to dishes, many have therapeutic properties too, while their pretty colours make them a perfect garnish – just the thing for a girly lunch. Given the current popularity of edible flowers, you'll find them everywhere from farmers' markets to supermarkets, and online.

Pimm's with borage flowers

While accompanied by a fruit salad of ingredients these days, the original Pimm's cocktail – created in the mid 1800s by a London oyster-bar owner called James Pimm – was simply served with lemon slices and borage leaves. Rich in vitamins, minerals, and antioxidants, borage leaves taste of cucumber, while the small blue flowers have honeyed undertones, making both a healthy, tasty, and pretty addition to this quintessentially British summer drink.

Makes 12–15 drinks.

1 bottle Pimm's Cup No. 1
1 cup borage flowers
2 litres fizzy lemonade or 7Up, chilled
1 English cucumber, very thinly sliced lengthways using a vegetable peeler
2–3 lemons, thinly sliced
a handful young borage leaves or 1 bunch mint, separated into sprigs

Make borage-flower ice cubes a day ahead. Half fill two ice trays with water, drop a borage flower into each compartment, and freeze. Once frozen, top up each cube with water and then refreeze; the flowers will now be in the middle of each cube.

Fill highball glasses with ice cubes, including one or two with borage flowers. Add 50 millilitres Pimm's, and top up with fizzy lemonade or 7Up (approximately 150 millilitres per glass). Garnish with a twist of cucumber, a slice of lemon, borage leaves or mint sprigs, and a couple of borage flowers. Serve immediately with a swizzle stick.

For a large party, Pimm's can be made in a jug by pouring 1 part Pimm's Cup No. 1 to 3 parts fizzy lemonade over ice, and then adding the accessories. For a bit more colour, add a punnet of strawberries, hulled and halved.

Courgette flowers filled with goat's cheese and herbs

Among the tougher edible flowers, courgette flowers stand up to deep-frying, turning deliciously crispy in minutes. For the best results, use the more delicate male flowers on stalks rather than the female ones attached to the marrow.

Serves 6–10 as finger food; serves 6 as a starter.

18 male courgette flowers, stems trimmed to about 5 centimetres

For the stuffing:
125 grams soft goat's cheese or ricotta, well drained and liquid squeezed out
2 tablespoons Parmesan cheese, finely grated
1 teaspoon lemon zest, finely grated
1 tablespoon dill, chopped
1 tablespoon Italian flat-leaf parsley, chopped
1 tablespoon tarragon, chopped
1 tablespoon olive oil
salt and freshly ground black pepper to taste
vegetable or sunflower oil for frying

For the batter:
150 grams all-purpose flour
1/4 teaspoon salt
1/4 cup white wine
1 cup ice-cold sparkling water or soda water

To serve:
sea salt
2–3 lemons, cut into wedges

Carefully open each flower and remove the stamen. Check for bugs and dirt, and remove any found with a damp cloth (keep contact with water to a minimum, as this will make the flowers limp and difficult to crisp in oil).

In a small bowl, mix together the soft cheese, Parmesan, lemon zest, herbs, and olive oil. Season with salt and pepper. Gently place one rounded teaspoonful of the mixture into each flower; push down with your fingers, press the petals together, and twist slightly to ensure the filling doesn't fall out. Set flowers aside as you prepare the batter.

To make the batter, sift the flour and salt into a large bowl, and combine. Mix in the wine, and then gradually whisk in the sparkling water or soda water until you have a smooth batter that is the consistency of thick cream. Add more water if too thick, more flour if too thin.

Pour 4–5 centimetres of oil into a deep-frying pan or saucepan. Heat to around 180 degrees C/350 degrees F (if you don't have a thermometer, the oil should be ready when a breadcrumb dropped into it turns brown in 25–30 seconds). Holding its stem, dip a flower into the batter and allow the excess to drain off for a couple of seconds so that the coating doesn't mask the petals' beautiful yellow colour. Drop into the hot oil, and then repeat with remaining flowers, making sure that flowers don't touch one another. Cook flowers in batches for 3–4 minutes each, turning once or twice, until golden and crispy all over. Remove with a slotted spoon. Place on a plate covered in several layers of kitchen paper to soak up the oil.

Transfer flowers to a platter. Sprinkle with coarse sea salt, add lemon wedges, and serve immediately as a snack. Alternatively, place stuffed flowers on top of small individual dressed green salads as a starter (3 flowers per portion). See Midweek Meal.

Cook's note:
The herbs in this recipe are suggestions; use other combinations as desired. In Italy, where fried courgette flowers are popular, another classic recipe involves stuffing the flowers with cheese and anchovy fillets.

Poached lobster salad with nasturtium mayonnaise

Low-maintenance and easy to grow in a window box, peppery nasturtiums probably pack the most flavour punch of all edible flowers and are high in vitamins. The leaves are edible too and even more peppery, so use sparingly and choose only the young ones, which have a more subtle flavour. It's also advisable to pick both leaves and flowers early in the morning, as they become more pungent in the heat of the day.

Serves 6.

6 lobsters or lobster tails
3 litres cold water
2 tablespoons sea salt
1 cup white wine
2 white onions, chopped
3 sticks celery, chopped

For the salad:
A handful each of baby rocket, watercress, and baby chard (or other mix)
1 fennel bulb, sliced very thin
1 tablespoon extra virgin olive oil
2 lemons, supremed*
sea salt and freshly ground black pepper

To serve:
nasturtium mayonnaise
6–12 nasturtium blossoms
toasted brioche

Place the water, 2 tablespoons of sea salt, wine, onions, and celery in a very large pot, and bring to the boil. If using whole lobsters, drop them head first into the boiling water, return to the boil, and cook for 10–15 minutes; otherwise, simply place tails in the boiling liquid. Take lobsters out. Plunge into cold water to stop cooking immediately. Once cool, remove the tails from the heads by twisting and then pulling. Remove the large claws (if using Maine lobsters). Cut each tail down its back using a heavy knife or kitchen shears. Pull the shell apart slightly and peel it off, keeping the tail in one piece. Remove the intestinal tract. Cut tail in half and then into nice big chunks. If using Maine-style lobster, crack the claws using a lobster cracker or heavy knife, and remove the meat in one clean piece. Set aside in fridge.

Just before serving, mix the salad leaves with the sliced fennel in a bowl and toss with extra virgin olive oil to coat leaves.

Spoon and spread a strip of the nasturtium mayonnaise down the centre of individual rectangular plates, and then arrange pieces of lobster along each strip at intervals. Add several lemon segments and a sprinkling of salad leaves to each plate. Garnish with one or two nasturtium flowers. Alternatively, place mounds of salad leaves on individual round plates, sprinkle over lemon segments, and arrange lobster slices on top or to the side. Add a swirl of mayonnaise to the plate with a squeeze bottle, or include it in a small bowl beside the salad. Finish things off with a nasturtium flower or two. Serve with toasted brioche or crusty white bread.

Cook's note:
* Supreming means removing the segments from citrus fruits without any membrane or pith attached. To achieve this, slice off the top and bottom of the fruit, make deep cuts in the skin from top to bottom at several intervals, and then peel. Next, insert a knife between the membrane and the fruit on either side of each segment and remove it, leaving the membrane behind.

Nasturtium mayonnaise

2 large egg yolks at room temperature
1 teaspoon Dijon mustard
1 tablespoon lemon juice
1/4 teaspoon coarse sea salt
sprinkling white pepper
1–1 1/4 cups good-quality mild olive oil
2 teaspoons white wine vinegar
1–2 teaspoons nasturtium leaves, finely chopped

Place the egg yolks, mustard, lemon juice, salt, and pepper in a medium-sized bowl. Mix with a wire balloon whisk until the salt dissolves and the sauce begins to thicken. Place the olive oil in a jug and begin to add it drop by drop, whisking constantly. Allow the mixture to emulsify after each addition before adding more. As it thickens, add more oil at a time. When the mixture starts to get really thick, add the oil in a slow stream.

For speedier results, make the mayonnaise in a food processor, running it on a low setting as you add the oil in a continuous stream. In either case, when all the oil has been added and the mayonnaise is a nice, thick consistency, fold in the vinegar, followed by the chopped nasturtium leaves. As these have a strong peppery flavour, taste the mayonnaise after adding 1 teaspoon and then add more as desired. Add salt, pepper, and lemon juice, as required.

Cook's note:
For a milder mayonnaise, replace the olive oil with sunflower oil or use half of each, adding the sunflower oil first. You can substitute the nasturtium leaves with herbs such as parsley, basil, dill, or chives (use 2–3 tablespoons of these, as they're not as strong as nasturtium leaves); alternatively, add 1–2 chopped red chillies for a tasty accompaniment to grilled octopus or prawns. If the mayonnaise is too thick, add a little water at the end. If it splits, break an egg yolk into a fresh bowl and whisk in the split mayonnaise little by little.

Elderflower and lemon sorbet

A common weed, the aromatic elderflower grows fairly prolifically in early summer, so forage for it in hedgerows, fields, and empty lots, steering clear of congested and polluted areas.

Serves 6.

250 grams sugar
350 millilitres water
6 or more elderflower heads, plus more for garnish, leaves and any insects removed
juice of 3 medium lemons
1 egg white

Place the sugar and the water in a saucepan. Heat gently, stirring, until all the sugar has dissolved. Bring the mixture to the boil, and then turn down heat and simmer for 5 minutes. Add the elderflowers (minus 1 or 2 for garnish), and stir to cover. Remove from heat, and allow the flowers to steep in the syrup for 1–2 hours. Strain the liquid into a bowl and add the lemon juice.

In a separate bowl, whisk the egg white until not quite stiff, and then stir into the elderflower mixture. Immediately pour the mixture into the freezer bowl of an ice-cream machine with the paddle turning, and follow manufacturer's instructions. The egg white might separate out initially, but it will gradually combine with the syrup. Transfer sorbet to a plastic container and freeze for at least 2 hours. Serve as a palate cleanser in Moroccan tea glasses or similar, sprinkled with elderflowers, or in bowls with fresh berries for dessert.

Quail marinated in rose water and pomegranate syrup, served with almond and pomegranate quinoa salad

Used in cooking since ancient times, roses bring a subtle taste and fragrance to dishes. They also have digestive properties and make a beautiful garnish. Often used to flavour chicken dishes in the Middle East, they work equally well with more flavourful quails, which are native to Iran.

Serves 6.

6–8 quails, butterflied

For the marinade:
1 small to medium onion
2 cloves garlic, crushed using a pestle and mortar with 2 teaspoons sea salt
6 tablespoons olive oil
1 1/2 teaspoons ground cumin
1 1/2 teaspoons ground coriander
3 tablespoons pomegranate syrup*
1 1/2 tablespoons rose water*
2 tablespoons chopped fresh coriander
* *You'll find pomegranate syrup and rose water at Middle Eastern grocery stores and delis. There are also a number of online sources.*

To serve:
fresh organically grown rose petals
almond and pomegranate quinoa salad

To butterfly the quails, use kitchen scissors to snip along either side of the backbone of each, from top to bottom, and then remove the bone along with the neck. Open them out, and press down to flatten. You might like to ask your butcher to do this for you.

Grate the onion into a medium-sized bowl. Add remaining marinade ingredients, and stir to combine. Pour the marinade into a flat dish that's big enough to take all the quails. Place quails in the marinade, rub the marinade all over them, and let them sit for 1–2 hours.

Place quails under a preheated grill, breasts down, and grill for 7 minutes. Turn over and grill for 7–10 minutes or until browned and cooked through. Serve alongside a mound of herby almond and pomegranate quinoa salad sprinkled with fresh rose petals.

Almond and pomegranate quinoa salad

1 1/2 cups quinoa
2 1/2 cups water, plus more if required
1 cup Italian parsley, roughly chopped
1 cup coriander leaves, roughly chopped
1/4–1/2 cup mint leaves (mint can be overpowering, so limit quantity)
8 spring onions, thinly sliced
150 grams sliced almonds, toasted in a dry pan
seeds of 1 pomegranate, divided
zest of 1 lemon
juice of 1–2 lemons
extra virgin olive oil
sea salt and freshly ground black pepper

Soak the quinoa in water for 10 minutes, and then rinse thoroughly. Bring 2 1/2 cups water (or amount stated on packet instructions) to the boil. Add the quinoa to the pot along with a pinch of sea salt. Bring back to the boil, turn heat down, and simmer, covered, for around 12 minutes – check after 7 minutes, as the water can be absorbed very quickly. Add more water if required, but be sparing, as you want light, chewy grains rather than porridge. Allow to cool, and then add herbs, spring onions, almonds, 3/4 of the pomegranate seeds, and the lemon zest. Finally, mix in lemon juice and olive oil to taste. Season with salt and pepper, and place in a serving dish or on individual plates. Sprinkle over remaining pomegranate seeds.

Cook's note:
The easiest, least messy way to remove the seeds from a pomegranate is to top and tail it, and then make deep cuts down its side following the segment-demarcation lines. Submerge the whole fruit in a bowl of water, pull the segments apart, and remove the seeds. Skim off any pith that has floated to the surface. Drain in a sieve to leave just the seeds.

Lavender chocolate mousse

Given its antidepressant phenylalanine content, chocolate makes a happy ending to any meal. This effect is only enhanced by calming lavender, which is packed with phytonutrients and aids digestion. Delicious, uplifting, relaxing, digestive – what more could you ask from dessert?

Serves 6–8, depending on size of pots/cups.

200 grams dark chocolate (with at least 70 per cent cocoa solids), broken into pieces
2 tablespoons butter
1 tablespoon brandy
3 large eggs, separated
375 millilitres cream
2 tablespoons caster sugar
1/4 teaspoon pure culinary lavender extract or essence (optional)

To serve:
fresh organically grown lavender

Place a heatproof glass bowl over a pot of gently simmering water. Make sure that the bowl does not touch the water (direct heat will burn the chocolate and make it grainy). Add the chocolate, butter, and brandy to the bowl, and allow to melt, stirring gently every now and then. When the mixture is smooth and glossy, remove from the heat and allow to cool.

Stir in the egg yolks one at a time until well combined. Beat the egg whites to soft-peak stage and set aside. Whip the cream with the caster sugar, and then add the lavender essence, if using. Fold half the egg whites into the chocolate mixture to loosen. Stir in the whipped cream, and then fold in the remaining egg whites.

Divide the mixture between miniature terracotta flowerpots (with wax paper taped over the drainage hole underneath each pot) or coffee cups. Chill in the fridge until set (at least 3 hours).

If using flowerpots, remove tape and wax paper from underneath pots, plant a sprig of lavender in each pot, and then place on drip tray and serve. If using cups, lay a sprig of lavender over the top of each, and place an almond biscotti in each of the saucers. Works equally well without the lavender essence or lavender.

Cook's note:

To make your own lavender extract, place 1/2 cup dried organic lavender flowers and 2 cups vodka in a large sterilised jar (with a sterilised lid). Place jar in a dark cupboard and leave for 3–4 weeks, giving it a shake a few times a week. Strain the liquid through a sieve, pressing down on the flowers. Strain once again through a muslin-lined strainer. Place in small sterilised bottles and store in a dark cupboard.

Seductive Supper (aphrodisiacs included)

Meze

Meze make a great starter for a casual supper – and the more people, the 'mezier'. For a couple or small group, all you need is one or two dips, some fried halloumi cheese, marinated olives, and a good supply of warm flatbread.

Beetroot hummus

This contemporary spin on the Middle Eastern dip is delicious, easy to make, and pretty in pink. Add in beetroot's aphrodisiacal boron content, and it's the perfect fuel for romance.

Serves 6.

300–350 grams medium-sized fresh or canned beetroot
400 gram can chickpeas, rinsed and drained
2 garlic cloves, crushed
3 tablespoons tahini
2–3 tablespoons lemon juice
sea salt
2–3 tablespoons olive oil

To serve:
flatbreads

If using fresh beetroot, wash and top and tail them (do not peel), and then place in a pot of boiling salted water, ensuring that the water covers them. Return to the boil, reduce heat to a vigorous simmer, and cook for 45 minutes or until a knife slides easily into and out of the beetroot. Place under cold running water, and then rub off the skin with a paper towel. Chop and set aside to cool.

Place cooled beetroot in the bowl of a food processor. Add chickpeas, garlic, tahini, lemon juice, and salt, and then whizz to a paste. While the machine is still running, add the olive oil in a steady stream until the dip is smooth and creamy. Taste and add more salt and lemon juice, as required. Serve with warm flatbreads.

Fried halloumi cheese

Of Cypriot origin, halloumi is made from sheep's and goat's milk and has a high melting point, which means it holds its shape when heated. If romance is on the menu, sprinkle the fried cheese with chopped basil, which is a key ingredient in Caribbean voodoo love spells, and was in the past used to attract husbands in Italy.

Serves 6.

1 standard (225-gram) block halloumi cheese
flour
2 tablespoons clarified butter or olive oil
fresh basil, shredded, to serve

After removing the cheese from its packaging, pat it dry with kitchen paper. Cut into thick slices (about 1 centimetre each). Pour flour onto a plate, and press each piece into it to cover both sides. Heat the oil or clarified butter over medium heat in a large non-stick frying pan. Place the pieces of cheese in the pan. Fry for about 1 minute on each side or until golden and crispy. Serve warm on a platter scattered generously with shredded basil.

Cook's note:
Available at good supermarkets, clarified butter is basically butter from which milk solids have been removed, allowing it to be heated to a higher temperature without burning. If using olive oil, use a light oil rather than cold-pressed extra virgin olive oil, as the latter has a low smoke point and, when overheated, gives off toxic gases and is depleted of its nutrients (as a rule, extra virgin olive oil should only be used cold).

Prawn rougaille

Spicy, tasty, and simple to prepare, this mild Mauritian curry is not merely the colour of love; it also contains aphrodisiacal pommes d'amour (love apples), as tomatoes are known on the island.

Serves 4–6.

1 1/2 kilograms queen prawns (or 8 per person), peeled and cleaned with tails intact
1 1/2 kilograms ripe vine tomatoes (*pommes d'amour*)
3 cloves garlic
1 teaspoon coarse sea salt
1 bunch coriander, leaves stripped off stems, plus 1 tablespoon stems, chopped
2 red or green chillies, deseeded and chopped
2 tablespoons grated ginger
4 tablespoons olive oil, divided
2 medium onions, peeled and thinly sliced
1 teaspoon ground cumin
1 teaspoon ground turmeric
3 tablespoons tomato paste
2 sprigs thyme
12 fresh curry leaves
a pinch cayenne pepper
salt to taste
a pinch turmeric for dusting

To serve:
chopped coriander
basmati rice
coconut chutney

Place the tomatoes in a bowl, and cover them with boiling water for 1 minute. Then immediately immerse in cold water. Peel them, cut them in half, and remove the seeds. Chop coarsely. Next, pound garlic with sea salt using a pestle and mortar (the sea salt dissolves the garlic). Add the coriander stems, chillies, and ginger, and pound to a paste.

Pour 3 tablespoons of the olive oil into a thick-bottomed pan, and heat slowly. Add the onion. Cook, stirring, until softened and golden (about 5 minutes). Add the chilli-ginger paste, along with the ground cumin and turmeric, and stir over heat for 1 minute. Add the chopped tomatoes, tomato paste, thyme, curry leaves, cayenne pepper, and salt to the pan. Cook over moderate heat, stirring from time to time until the juice from the tomatoes has evaporated (10 minutes or more, depending on how juicy the tomatoes are). Add half the finely chopped fresh coriander, check seasoning, and set aside.

Season the prawns with sea salt, and sprinkle with a little powdered turmeric. Heat the remaining olive oil in a very hot pan. Add the prawns. Cook without stirring for about two minutes on one side, and then turn over and cook for another two on the other side. Immediately incorporate the prawns into the heated rougaille sauce, but don't allow to cook further. Sprinkle with chopped fresh coriander. Serve with basmati rice and fresh coconut chutney.

Coconut chutney

This fresh chutney offers a sweet-and-sour contrast to the curry and adds a dash more heat, which hits the palate like a surprising afterthought.

150 grams desiccated coconut, or the flesh of 1 fresh coconut, grated
2 bunches (around 2 cups) mint leaves, stripped from stems
2 cloves garlic, chopped
4–5 fresh green chillies (with seeds), chopped
2 tablespoons tamarind paste, without seeds
1/2 teaspoon salt

If using desiccated coconut, place it in a heatproof bowl, pour over 250 millilitres boiling water, and leave for 10 minutes.

In a food processor, blend the garlic, chillies, mint, and tamarind paste together. Add the coconut and salt, and blend for a couple of minutes. Add water a tablespoon at a time to achieve a fine, wet paste. Add more salt to taste. Place in a serving dish and chill for at least 1 hour before serving.

This is best on the same day, but it can be stored in an airtight container for up to 2 days.

Cook's note:
The tamarind paste makes this a not entirely attractive brown colour, but the zingy taste is what it's all about. If not happy with the colour, sprinkle over some shredded mint before serving.

Lemon and white chocolate soufflé

Soufflé is a risky choice since you can only prepare it at the last minute, but if you pull it off, it's guaranteed to impress. If you ensure that your egg whites are stiff but still soft enough to fold into the custard without losing air, you're halfway there. Add a little love and tenderness, and your soufflé – among other things, one hopes! – will almost certainly rise to the occasion.

Serves 6.

For the ramekins:
2 tablespoons butter at room temperature
caster sugar to coat ramekins

For the soufflés:
50 grams butter
1/4 cup all-purpose flour
a pinch of salt
3/4 cup whole milk
250 grams white chocolate, chopped
2 tablespoons lemon juice
zest of 1 lemon
5 large eggs (at room temperature), separated
1/4 cup caster sugar

To serve:
icing sugar for dusting
fresh cherries or strawberries
dessert wine

Brush the insides of six ramekins with butter, keeping your strokes vertical, which will help the soufflés rise. Dust ramekins with sugar, turning to coat the insides, and then shake off any excess. Refrigerate until needed.

Preheat oven to 180 degrees C/350 degrees F, and place a baking sheet on the middle shelf. Melt the butter in a saucepan over medium heat. Add the flour and salt, and stir with a metal balloon whisk for 2 minutes or until smooth and the flour has cooked a little (without browning). Add the milk, and stir briskly with whisk until the mixture is smooth and free of lumps. Remove from the stovetop, and immediately add the chopped white chocolate, stirring until melted.

Stir in the lemon juice and zest. Add the egg yolks one at a time, and keep stirring briskly until they are amalgamated. In a separate bowl, using an electric mixer, whisk the egg whites until soft peaks form. Gradually add the caster sugar, whisking constantly until the mixture is stiff and glossy.

Stir 2 tablespoons of the meringue into the white chocolate mixture to loosen it, and then fold in the rest using a large metal spoon, taking care to retain as much air as possible. Divide the mixture between the ramekins, filling to come level with the top, and smooth with a spatula. Run your finger around the inside rim of the ramekins to ensure the soufflé doesn't catch and, as a result, rise unevenly.

Place on the heated baking sheet, and bake for 20–25 minutes or until well risen and golden (you want them to be firm on the top but creamy in the middle). Remove soufflés from oven, dust with icing sugar, and serve immediately with berries and a glass of chilled dessert wine.

RECIPE INDEX

A

Almond and pomegranate quinoa salad..................................285

B

Beetroot hummus..........................288
Beetroot relish...............................240

C

Caramelised onion, potato, spinach, and goats cheese frittata......261
Chilled pea soup............................264
Chilli and chocolate almond cakes 242
Coconut chutney...........................293
Courgette flowers filled with goat's cheese and herbs.................277

D

Dinner Date.................................238

E

Elderflower and lemon sorbet........282

F

Floral Feast...................................275
French toast à la bananas Foster.....273
Fried halloumi cheese....................290

G

Ginger and vanilla ice cream..........244
Green beans with walnut oil..........269
Green salad with chive dressing.....263
Grilled octopus..............................254

I

Introduction.................................237

L

Lavender chocolate mousse............286
Lemon and white chocolate soufflé294
Lobster with coriander butter and chilli-papaya salsa...............249
Long, Lazy Weekend Lunch..........264

M

Measurements...............................237
Meze..288
Midweek Meal..............................261
Minty North African roasted-aubergine salad...........................256

N

Nasturtium mayonnaise................281
New potato and watercress salad....258

O

Oven-glazed baby carrots...............268
Oysters with chicory leaves............247

P

Parsnip crisps..................................241
Pimm's with borage flowers 276
Poached lobster salad......................279
Prawn rougaille 291

Q

Quail marinated in rose water and
pomegranate syrup.............283

R

Roast loin of lamb with juniper berries
and port jus.........................265
Roast potatoes 267
Rose-flavoured rhubarb compote...272

S

Salsa verde......................................253
Seafood Barbecue 245
Seductive Supper............................288
Stuffed chicken breasts 238
Sunday Brunch................................273

T

Turmeric bread...............................248

V

Vanilla and cardamom panna cotta270
Vanilla bavarois with tropical fruits259

W

Watermelon Martinis 246
Whole barbecued linefish 251

ACKNOWLEDGEMENTS

I would like to thank a number of people who have directly or indirectly made a valuable contribution to this book. First of all, thank you to my mother, Meg van Maasdyk, one of the best cooks I know, who not only inspired my love of cooking and entertaining but also provided many of the recipes here, tested others, and checked every one with her trained foodie eye. Thanks also to my sister Penelope van Maasdyk, a beautiful writer and blogger, who meticulously and sensitively edited a recent draft of the novel, bringing her own wit and wisdom to the page. Journalist friend Sue de Groot and lecturers at New York's Gotham Writers Workshop (Susan Breen, Greg Lichtenberg, and Katherine Taylor), along with fellow students, provided valuable input into earlier drafts and encouraged me to keep going, and I am also very grateful to editors at Lulu Press for smoothing the rough edges and helping me to get the final cut to print.

On the food and wine front, I'm grateful to sommelier Kevin Denecke and wine writer Ingrid Casson for their premier cru advice on wine tasting, and to many talented chefs with whom I've worked on food stories in the past, particularly for South Africa's *Style* magazine, who inspired some of the recipes and dishes mentioned. These include Jacqui Rey, whose recipes for barbecued lobster with coriander butter, salsa verde, and bavarois inspired those in Kate's barbecue; Suzie Holtzhausen, whose recipe for stuffed chicken breasts is adapted in Dinner Date, and whose salmon and Pinot Noir butter not only seduces Daniel in the novel, but earned Suzie and me an invitation to lunch with an impressed winemaker; and Aristotle Ragavelas, whose recipe for turmeric bread appears in Seafood Barbecue. Culinary wizards Andrea Burgener, Karen Short, Craig Cormack and

Annette Kesler have also been an inspiration, along with foodie friends Jenny Lincoln, Victoria Runge, and Walter Kahn.

Credit is also due to the many recipe books that have flavoured my cooking over the years by chefs such as Delia Smith, Jamie Oliver, Nigella Lawson, Gordon Ramsay, Martha Stewart, and Donna Hay. Specifically, the chilli and chocolate almond cakes and ginger ice cream in Dinner Date were inspired by recipes in Bill Granger's recipe books *Holiday* (Murdoch Books, 2007) and *Sydney Food* (Murdoch Books, 2000), respectively; and the new potato and watercress salad in Seafood Barbecue, by Fran Warde's *Eat Drink Live* (Ryland, Peters, & Small, 2005). The salad in Midweek Meal, the rhubarb compote in Long, Lazy Weekend Lunch, and the fried courgette flowers and mayonnaise in Floral Feast were inspired by *The Cook and the Gardener* by Amanda Hesser (W. W. Norton & Company, 1999), while the elderflower sorbet, also in Floral Feast, is based on a recipe by Christopher Lloyd in *Gardener Cook* (Frances Lincoln, 1997) – both excellent guides to growing and cooking seasonal produce. The coconut chutney that accompanies the prawn rougaille in Seductive Supper is adapted from a recipe in Sandy Daswani's book *A Feast of Mauritius* (Paperback, 2008), which was a useful reference in respect of Mauritian cuisine, while the *Larousse Gastronomique* culinary encyclopaedia (Mandarin Paperbacks, 1990) was a valuable resource on cooking techniques in general. Further inspiration came from lifestyle magazines such as *Gourmet*, *Marie Claire*, *Red*, *InStyle*, *House & Garden*, and *Wallpaper*, as well as food programmes and websites, including *BBC Food, Food Network, and MasterChef.*

Since all recipes are adaptations or simply inspired by these cooks and publications, however, no one mentioned can be held responsible for imperfect results. All of the above chefs and recipe-book writers are highly recommended and well worth investing in – or sampling in their restaurants.

The soundtrack to the novel was provided by extracts from songs including '*Quelqu'un M'a Dit*' by Carla Bruni, among other tracks on the CD *Paris* by Putumayo World Music; 'Tomorrow' from the musical *Annie*; '*Le Diable dans la Maison*' by La Compagnie Creole; and 'I Want to Know

What Love Is' and 'Cold As Ice' by Foreigner. Special thanks are also due to singer-songwriter and friend Fiona Campbell-Webster, who lent my character Finola both her rich voice and the chorus from her catchy original composition 'Recipe for Love'.

Finally, thank you to my wonderful husband, Glenn, for his unstinting support, both material and psychological, on the long and sometimes fraught journey to completion.

ABOUT THE AUTHOR

Author Photograph ©Loredana Mantello

Melissa van Maasdyk has worked as a writer, sub-editor and editor on various magazines, including *Elle Decoration* in the UK, *Marie Claire* in South Africa, and *Time Out* in Bahrain, where she also wrote a travel guide to the kingdom. Food writing has featured prominently in her career, nurturing her passion for cooking, and adding flavour to *Love Apples*, which is her first novel. Melissa currently lives in Abu Dhabi with her husband.